Gold Albatross

Gold Albatross

By

Tate Volino

ISBN 978-0-557-52795-3

To my favorite foursome:
SV, RV, and CV

1

B ryan Minton smiled. Driving up the palm lined road leading to the Stone Ridge Golf and Country Club he started to feel the pangs of excitement that he always got before a round of golf, no matter how often he played. For late spring in Florida the temperature was relatively mild and several checks of the weather had indicated that the skies should be clear all day. Looking up through the open sunroof he thought about maybe even playing an extra nine holes, if his swing was working.

A sudden jolt of the car sent him back to reality as he caromed over a large speed bump and bottomed out on the other side.

"Damn those things!" he griped, while shaking his head. Had he been driving at the posted limit of fourteen miles per hour the impact would not have been so drastic. He wondered why so many communities and country clubs now posted odd numbers for their speed limits: 14 m.p.h., 19 m.p.h., 24 m.p.h. Some traffic study must have found it to be a good idea, as though a strange number was going to encourage people to follow the limit more closely. Everyone, including the residents, did at least twice that speed. At least until they hit a speed bump.

Driving more attentively now, he rounded the next bend in the road and saw the guard station up ahead. The tires began to rumble as the smooth pavement turned to brick pavers. He drifted into the left lane earmarked for guests and visitors.

As he pulled up next to the guard building the sliding glass door opened and an officious looking man in his sixties emerged with a clipboard.

"Good morning,sir," he said, leering down into the car as though he wanted to issue Bryan a ticket for breaking the speed limit.

"Here for golf today," Bryan said.

"Do you have a tee time?"

"Yep, 9:48 under the name of Minton." Although he played here every few months or so, he was certainly not enough of a regular to be known by sight.

"Got you right here," the guard said while placing a checkmark on his list. He wandered to the back of the car and noted the license plate number. "You're all set."

"Thanks, has anyone else checked in under that time?"

"It doesn't look like it on the list, but I just started my shift a few minutes ago so they might have."

"Thanks again."

The guard tapped the remote control clipped to his belt and the gate opened. Minton checked the right lane and then sped on towards the clubhouse. Entering the parking lot he drove down the first two rows before finding a spot. He popped the trunk and got out, still scanning the lot for a black Mercedes with the license plate: 4SALE. The car belonged to his playing partner today, C. Thomas Manson. Manson was always late so Bryan would have been more surprised if the car actually was in the lot. Bryan grabbed his clubs and shoes from the trunk and headed toward the clubhouse. He placed his golf bag in the rack at the drop off and then entered the door to the pro shop.

"Good morning, sir," said the pro working the counter.

"How's it going?" asked Bryan, his frustration starting to simmer. "Has anyone else checked in for the Minton tee time?"

"No, not yet."

"And I don't suppose anyone has called in either?"

"No calls either."

"Great. Well I'm here for the 9:48 spot but I'm not sure where my partner is. Let me see if I can track him down." Bryan headed back outside, snapped open his cell phone, and called his friend.

"Hello," said the familiar voice that answered.

"Were you planning on playing golf with me today?" Bryan asked.

"Hey, Bry'! Sorry, I meant to call you but I wanted to keep my line open in case my morning appointment tried to call back. They didn't show on time."

"You really need to get your priorities straight: golf and then work," Bryan lectured.

"You know the risks of golfing with me. I think these people may be pretty serious so I don't want to let them go. Again, I'm sorry but I'm starting to get the pipeline pretty steady and I can't afford to start coasting now. Maybe in a few years I'll be able to pick and choose my deals, but right now volume is volume."

"Alright, Tommy, I'll let you get back to business and get off the phone. But you owe me one now, I'll probably get stuck playing with some old relic today."

"You're right; I'll make it up to you though. These prospects are a couple of early retirees, I'll see if they have a daughter."

"Matchmaking too? What's your commission for that?"

2

"Hey, I earn my keep."

"I'm going to go hit some balls, see ya'."

Bryan closed the phone and headed back into the pro shop. Although he wasn't excited about playing with pot luck partners, he didn't want to skip playing on a day like this. "It looks like I'm going to be a single today," Bryan told the pro.

"No problem, we'll be able to work you in with another group," he replied. "If you want to go warm up we'll call you shortly."

After lacing up his shoes, Bryan drove down to the driving range, grabbed a few clubs from his bag, and headed up to the practice tees. As he stretched out and took practice swings he looked up and down the line at other players trying to evaluate who he might be playing with today. Bryan wasn't a scratch golfer, but when he played courses like Stone Ridge he didn't want to be stuck for hours with a bunch of hackers. As expected, there were a few decent looking players and a few dirt farmers sending divots further than the ball. Although he was aggravated that Tommy was a no-show, Bryan knew better than to let it spoil his round. He started hitting a few irons and gradually worked his way up to swinging the driver. After working through about three dozen range balls he decided to see how the greens were feeling. He grabbed his cart and drove around to the practice green.

Reading the break of the greens at this point in the morning was easy. Even on the footprint covered practice green putts left tracks in the dew that looked like tracer bullets. By mid-morning, however, the cheat sheet would evaporate and players would be on their own. Bryan was working on some short putts when the starter pulled up.

"Mr. Minton?" he asked.

"That's me," Bryan responded.

"You're just a single, right?"

"I'm solo now."

"No problem we're going to get you out with that gentleman over there who's loading up. You can take two carts or partner up on one, whatever you like."

"Thanks, I'll just stick with the one I've got." Bryan preferred riding on his own rather than with unknown partners.

"His name is James Garris, he's a member here. You fellas will be a twosome today and you'll be going off number one in about five minutes. There are going to be a few foursomes ahead of you and a few behind so just try to pace yourselves."

"Will do, thanks."

"Hit 'em straight!"

Minton walked over to his cart, dried off his putter, and headed over to introduce himself to Mr. Garris.

"Hi, Mr. Garris?"

"Yes."

"I'm Bryan Minton, looks like we'll be playing together today."

"Nice to meet you Bryan, please call me Jim."

Bryan was always a bit uncomfortable calling people who were near the age of his parents by their first names, at least until he knew them better. Tommy, on the other hand, called everyone by their first name, including Bryan's parents. He had always been that way, even when he was very young. Bryan could remember the look on older people's faces when Tommy would just refer to them as Harold, or Martha, or Barbara, or whatever and not even think twice. Sometimes it was funny, but sometimes it came off as just being rude. At least on the golf course when someone told you to call them by their first name they were typically being sincere.

"We're going to be up on the tee in a few minutes. Did you need to warm up or anything?" Bryan asked.

"No I'll just get going during the first few holes. I might have to hit one or two extra tee shots as long as you don't mind."

"Not a bit," Bryan replied in a friendly manner. He didn't mind as long as Garris wasn't someone who turned the golf course into their own personal driving range.

"It sure looks like we picked a nice day to be out on the golf course," Garris said, looking up at the sky.

"I think so too. If you want to head on up I'll follow you."

When they arrived at the first tee, Garris got out of his cart and started doing some casual stretching. "So have you played here before, Bryan?"

"Yeah, I get out every few months through my dad's membership over at Oak Run."

"What tees do you play?" he asked.

"I'll go off the whites or the blues, whatever you play," Bryan answered.

"As long as you don't mind why don't we go with the whites. I used to be able to handle the blues but my health hasn't been the best the last few months."

"No problem at all, it'll probably save me a few balls today. If you're ready why don't you go ahead and lead us off."

"Thanks." Garris teed up his ball and took a few practice swings. He quickly addressed the ball and slapped a solid drive

4

down the left center of the fairway. As he watched it come to a gradual stop he grabbed his tee and motioned to Bryan that the box was his. "At least I didn't embarrass myself on the first one."

"No, that was a good shot," replied Bryan. As he teed up his ball he felt a bit more pressure to hit a nice drive, especially since Garris hadn't even had any practice at the range. Bryan went through his routine and then hit a slight draw that easily flew thirty or forty yards past Garris's shot but rolled through the fairway and into the rough.

"Even with modern technology I just can't keep up with you younger guys anymore," Garris said as he tapped his tee on the face of his oversized, titanium driver.

"Sure, but distance doesn't do much if it gets you into the rough or a hazard."

"Still most people these days are going to be more impressed with the long drive rather than the straight one."

"Well, I'd have to agree with you there," said Bryan, feeling somewhat glad that he hadn't come up short of Garris's ball.

As they walked off the tee and got into their carts Bryan sized up his partner for the day. Garris didn't appear that old, but physically he looked a bit worn out. He had the appearance of someone who had been in good shape most of his life, but had finally let himself go a bit. Based on Garris's comment about switching to the white tees from the blues, Bryan guessed that Garris had perhaps undergone some kind of surgery recently. Nonetheless, Garris seemed to move reasonably well and still had a good golf swing. Hopefully it would hold up through eighteen holes.

After making their way up the fairway Garris was first to play and landed his approach shot safely on the front edge of the green. Feeling a slight bit of pressure again, Bryan surveyed his ball in the rough. He had a decent lie so he decided to be reasonably aggressive and go at the pin, despite needing to carry a sizeable bunker. He caught a bit of a flyer and the ball sailed to the back of the green. Luckily, it impacted softly and stayed on the putting surface. Once on the green, both players hit solid lag putts and knocked in the short remainders for par.

"Nice start there, Bryan."

"Thanks, you too. It's always nice to get the first hole out of the way without too much damage," Bryan replied. He didn't sense that Garris was trying to be competitive, but all players had some urge to win on the course, even if they said they were just playing for fun. Occasionally he would come across players whose only goal was to

5

get a money game going. He would usually indulge them if the stakes were just a few bucks, but beyond that he normally wasn't interested. It was too easy to start losing money, especially if you didn't really know your opponent's golf game.

Over the next few holes they were in different directions between the tee and the green so they had a limited amount of interaction, other than the usual compliments. Bryan was glad that the groups ahead were moving quickly so there wasn't a lot of dead time waiting around to hit. Garris seemed like a nice guy, but since they had started playing he hadn't shown much interest in conversation, which was fine with Bryan.

As they climbed a short set of railroad tie steps to the ninth tee, Bryan glanced at his watch and realized that they would finish the front side in less than two hours. "We're moving along pretty nicely today," he noted.

"Yep, not too bad at all. The club has been pretty good about getting on the slowpokes and keeping up the pace of play. It is important to enjoy yourself on a golf course but no need to waste time."

"I agree," Bryan replied, pleased with Garris's attitude.

"It looks like we have a decent gap behind us though. How about stopping for some lunch?"

Somewhat surprised at the invitation, Bryan answered, "Sure."

After finishing number nine they parked their carts near the restaurant located at the back end of the clubhouse. "Let's just order inside and we can sit out here on the patio to eat. That way we can see when the next group starts coming up behind us," suggested Garris.

"Sounds good," replied Bryan, fishing his wallet out of a pocket on his golf bag.

"You don't need that. Lunch is on me today."

"Thanks, but I don't want to impose."

"Don't worry about it. I have to meet my food and beverage limit anyway and I'm not anywhere close this month."

"Well, alright then," Bryan said. He knew that the club did have a spending requirement for members so Garris was probably telling the truth.

The inside of the restaurant was dimly lit and covered in dark wood paneling. The furnishings were upholstered with dark, burgundy leather. Obviously the intention was to portray wealth and opulence, but to Bryan it came off as old and dreary. After being outside soaking up the sun on a nice day it was like wandering into a cave. As always, there were a few tables of older ladies playing cards. They had likely gone out early and played only nine holes.

Bryan and Jim both ordered sandwiches and picked at the pretzels on the bar while they waited. Garris surveyed the tables and waived casually at someone across the room. He rapped his fingers on the bar and glanced at his watch. Clearly he wasn't one to spend a lot of social time in the club. Bryan was glad that Garris had suggested eating on the patio as he too had no interest in hanging around inside. When the food arrived they grabbed the baskets and quickly headed out.

After getting settled at one of the wrought iron tables Bryan asked, "Have you been a member here long?"

"About eight or nine years now I guess. We joined a few years after we retired down here. With all of the building the last few years there are a lot more choices now, but I've been pleased with the club for the most part. They keep it in pretty good shape and the fees haven't increased a whole lot."

"Does your wife play too?"

"No, she passed away five years ago."

"Sorry."

"That's alright," Garris replied, casually waiving his hand. "She would dabble in the game but never really wanted to take it up seriously. She primarily enjoyed the social side of things, which worked out well. Once you retire it can be tough spending too much time together. You need to have some activities that you do apart. So what about you? Do you have a wife?"

"No, I haven't really even gotten close yet. More and more of my friends are disappearing into marriage and kids so sooner or later I guess I'll give into the peer pressure."

"Don't be in a hurry, but keep your eyes open and she'll show up one of these days."

"I wish it were that easy. At this point dating and all of that seems like work. Even my parents are starting to fix me up with girls."

"I can empathize," said Garris, grinning and nodding.

"Really? You're out there playing the field?" replied Bryan, somewhat surprised.

"Yeah, but in my case it has to do more with life expectancy. Once you get to my age most women start outliving their husbands. You end up with a higher proportion of single ladies at places like this so the odds are stacked in your favor, or maybe against you, depending on how you look at it. I have lots of people set me up with lady friends here. Unfortunately, many of them have gotten lonely and once you go out to a few dinners and movies they start wanting to do everything together. Then they want you to meet their families and they want to meet yours. At this stage I'm just not interested in getting that involved. That's one reason I try to avoid the card players inside."

"Yeah, I kind of noticed that."

As they talked about golf and finished their lunches Bryan began to feel like he had a bit more in common with his playing partner, despite the age gap. Seeing the group behind them approach the clubhouse they grabbed their drinks and drove down to the number ten tee.

After the first few holes on the back side they caught up to the group ahead and play bogged down a bit. Bryan didn't mind as much at this point, however, as he was more at ease chatting with Garris.

On the fifteenth tee Garris began explaining to Bryan some of the renovations they had done in the past few years. "This is one of my least favorite holes out here. It used to be a decent par four but two years ago they tightened up the fairway and lengthened it about thirty yards. Unfortunately they left the green the way it was so now it is too small for the hole. When it gets a bit dry it's almost impossible for the average players out here to hold the green. You have to try to hit it a bit short and run it up, but with the bunkers in front that's like threading a needle. If you send it through the green there's an upslope so coming back down is a very tricky shot. The green doesn't need to be any wider, just a bit longer front to back."

"That's pretty much the way with most changes these days," nodded Bryan.

"Everyone is trying to keep up with technology and the distance gains of the better players. I think in reality though, the majority of regular players have only had modest gains, if any. I may have gained a few yards with new equipment, but age has offset most of it. When I play a hole like this I know *I* certainly haven't picked up thirty yards.

For the most part they've done a good job keeping the course in solid shape, which to me is the primary factor when it comes to playability. The course is about twenty-five years old, but they did a major renovation ten years ago. There were apparently a lot of arguments amongst the members about the cost and downtime. Luckily the true golfers won out over the cheapskates and they ended up doing an excellent job. That was just before we moved in and the course was probably one of the best I'd ever played at that point. It definitely sold me on becoming a member and moving out here."

"So do you live on the course?" asked Bryan.

"No, that was a compromise I had to make with my wife. I was hoping to find a place on the right hand side of one of the par fours. Since most players are slicers I would never need to buy golf balls ever again, just walk out in the yard and have an Easter egg hunt. My wife, however, didn't want people always wandering by and looking in and she also didn't want me sneaking out on to the course all the time. She was probably right about that. We ended up in a place in West Chase, one of the developments off of the main road as you come into the club. There also weren't a lot of choices on the course at that time. Being an older style course there was more of a focus on golf rather than just where to put the houses. In most of the newer developments around here they put up the houses and then squeeze the golf course in wherever it will fit."

"It's funny that you mention that. I've always felt that that was one of the stronger points of this course," replied Bryan.

"Unfortunately that has continued to change, especially on these last few holes. The land that borders sixteen, seventeen, and eighteen was part of a parcel that was originally slated to be another eighteen holes. To do it they would have had to annex an additional plot that had both tax and environmental issues. It was going to be expensive and time consuming so they let it go. The developer eventually broke it up into pieces and sold it to residential builders. There are some beautiful homes out here now, but I think it still takes away from the golf."

"I hear you, but it's a tough call. With weather like we have here it's hard to stop the flow of people who want to live here too. It's a big part of the economy as well. The guy who was supposed to be playing with me today is a realtor and he certainly wants to keep the growth going. He'd love to play on golf courses without houses too, but it would be a lot tougher for him to make a living."

"I know. It's just that common mentality that once you move here to paradise you want to put up the big golden gate and keep everyone else out. The upshot is that the new homes have also brought some younger blood that will help keep the club going in the future. That's another problem that you have here in Florida: clubs where the membership just gets too old. Heck, just look at me," Garris said as he smiled at Bryan and then swung away with his driver.

Walking off the fifteenth green Garris stopped and turned back toward the fairway. "See, what did I tell you? Two decent golfers and the best we could manage was a pair of bogies. I bet if we played that hole three or four times in a row we'd only get one par between us."

"You're probably right. But I don't know of too many courses that I can say I like all eighteen."

"That's true, but all I'm asking for here is a little more green to work with."

On the sixteenth, a slight dog-leg to the right, Bryan tried to take a little too much off the corner and clipped one of the trees. "Ahhh, couldn't just keep myself out of trouble for a few more holes."

"I think it came down there so you should be alright," replied Garris, doing his best to spot the errant tee shot.

Garris had easily found the fairway so when they reached to corner he wandered over to help Bryan find his ball. The base of the tall pines was surrounded by thickets of palmetto scrub, which appeared to have swallowed yet another ball. After picking around for a few minutes Bryan walked out and assessed his options. "I don't see any stakes so I guess I'm going to have to play it as a lost ball and head back to the tee."

"Unfortunately, they don't have it marked so you're right. It's nice to see that you actually know the rule, since most people would try to play it as a ball lost in a hazard, even in a match or tournament. I don't think we have a lot riding on our game today, however, so just drop one and save yourself the ride."

"Alright, for the sake of time I'll accept your ruling. But I'm still sitting three here. I agree with you though, it's amazing how many good golfers really don't know the rules on calls like that. Or they do and just want to stretch their interpretation a little too far," nodded Minton.

"It goes back to character I suppose," said Garris approvingly.

On the seventeenth tee Bryan tried to forget the last tee shot and just swung away. This time he hit a much better shot as his slight draw rolled down the backside of a ridge in the fairway of the reachable par five.

"That's more like it," said Garris as he shook his head with envy.

"I need to try and get one back here on the par five. If fifteen is there to take a stroke away from you, this hole is here to get one back."

When they arrived in the fairway at Bryan's ball Garris had already hit his second shot to a safe distance. "Alright, I layed up like an old man should. Let's see what you've got," said Garris extending his arm toward the green.

"Just trying to get it close and make sure I've got a good chance for birdie," Bryan responded as he lined up the shot. With about two hundred and forty yards to the middle of the green Bryan knew he could easily get it there with a solid three wood. Unfortunately he now felt pressure to impress Garris. He made his practice swing and then took a deep breath as he addressed the ball. He swung away but immediately cringed after impact as he knew he'd caught the shot thin. The ball shot off like a low line drive, but at least the direction was good. "Shoot! I couldn't get it clean."

"I don't know what you're grumbling about, that's going to come out pretty nice," Garris said as Bryan's ball hit well short of the green but skidded ahead.

"It felt lousy though."

"Better to be lucky than good sometimes. That's going right at the pin," Garris noted as the ball began a decelerating roll on the green.

"Wow. That is...in the hole!" Bryan blurted as he dropped his club and jumped in the air. "It went in didn't it?" he asked, turning to Garris.

"I'm pretty sure it did," nodded Garris, still somewhat in disbelief himself. He walked over to Bryan and extended a hand. "Congratulations. A double eagle. That's rarer than a hole-in-one."

"Thanks. I just can't believe it went in," Bryan said, shaking Garris's hand while still looking at the green in joy.

"Come on, let's go make sure," Garris said, motioning to their carts.

When they arrived at the green both men walked over to the hole and looked down. "Sure enough, there it is," observed Garris.

"Unreal," said Bryan as he snared his ball that was nestled against the flagstick at the bottom of the cup. Coming back to reality he apologetically patted Garris on the shoulder and said, "Sorry, you've still got your shot to play. I just didn't want to give that ball a chance to come back out of the hole."

"Don't give it a thought. That's a once in a lifetime shot there. I've had two holes-in-one and I've seen a couple others happen, but that's the first double eagle I've ever seen. And I'm not really that worried about my round," he added.

Garris drove back down the fairway and was able to get up and in for an easy par on the hole. They headed up to the eighteenth tee where Bryan was still all smiles.

"Well I'm glad you were here as my witness. I know Tommy wouldn't believe me if I'd been playing alone."

"Mark down that two on your scorecard and I'll be happy to witness it. Now let's finish up with a good hole. I'd have to say you have the honors on this one."

Bryan finished with a bogey, but it didn't bother him in the least at that point. He and Garris again shook hands as they walked off the green towards their carts.

"Great playing with you today Bryan, I really enjoyed it. Let me sign as your double eagle witness and you can frame that card for your wall."

"Thanks. I enjoyed it as well," replied Bryan as he grabbed his scorecard from under the clip on the cart's steering wheel and handed it to Garris.

Garris printed and signed his name next to the box for number seventeen and handed it back. He also handed Bryan his scorecard and said, "Here, write down your phone number. I'll take you out again sometime as my guest."

Bryan felt at little strange about the request at first but figured that Garris was just being nice so he obliged. Moreover, he was never one to turn down a free round of golf. Glancing at his watch Bryan said, "I know it's tradition for someone who gets a hole-in-one to buy a round of drinks, so I imagine a double eagle is the same. Unfortunately, I need to hit the road. I've got a couple of errands I need to run this afternoon."

"Not a problem. I'm not a big drinker anyway. Again, great shots out there today."

They shook hands one last time and then Bryan headed off to the parking lot to unload his clubs. Once he had dropped off his cart and returned to his car he turned his cell phone back on to check for messages. Sure enough, he had one voicemail from Tommy. He had just called to let Bryan know that his deal was going to go to contract. To make up for missing golf and celebrate the deal he told Bryan that drinks were on him. Bryan obviously also had a reason to celebrate so he called back and set up a time to meet later that night.

2

U nlike this morning, Bryan actually saw Tommy's car as he pulled into the lot outside the South Town Grill. There was an empty spot next to Tommy so he turned in and parked his grimy Toyota next to the gleaming, black Mercedes.

Being a Saturday night the Grill was packed. The flirtatious hostess asked Bryan if he needed a table but he let her know that he was here to meet someone. Tommy was sitting sideways at the bar talking with the bartender while also watching one of overhead TVs. Bryan walked up and slapped him solidly on the shoulder.

"Hey Bry'! Good to see you man."

"You too buddy."

"Have you forgiven me yet?"

"The pain is wearing off gradually," Bryan responded as he rolled his eyes.

"Well, as I said, I'm buying tonight so order up and then we'll get something to eat."

"I'm just a charity case today I guess; free lunch and free dinner."

"Free lunch?" said Tommy, cocking his head. "Did you find yourself a sugar mama out at the Ridge today?"

"I doubt some guy in his sixties qualifies as a sugar mama."

"Oooo. A sugar daddy then. I didn't know you were branching out. You can't give up on the ladies yet."

"Gee, thanks. Why do you say stuff like that?"

"Because I know how easy it is to get you aggravated, which is a lot of fun for me," Tommy said with a laugh. "Alright, let's get you a drink. Maybe something fruity with a tiny umbrella in it?"

"Okay, are you done?" asked Bryan.

"See! You need to thicken your skin," Tommy said as he pinched Bryan in the gut. "What do you want?"

"Just a beer is fine. Something in a bottle."

"Very manly," replied Tommy. He ordered a beer and handed it to Bryan when it arrived. He dropped a twenty on the bar and then got up and led Bryan over to one of the high tables in the bar area where they could order food.

"So tell me about the round," queried Tommy as he saddled up to the table.

"Oh, pretty much my normal game. But there was that two on the par five seventeenth."

"What?"

"Just your everyday double eagle."

"That's awesome."

"I can't say it was the prettiest shot, but it went in the hole."

"Now I'm really sorry I didn't play with you today. I would have loved to have seen that."

"It was pretty cool. One of those things that makes all of the other misery of golf worthwhile. I'm certainly glad that Jim was there as a witness. Not that I would lie about it, but it obviously makes it more official."

"So who is this Jim? One of the old codger members out there?"

"Well he certainly isn't young, but he wasn't bad. Probably a single digit handicapper once, now low teens. I didn't mind playing with him at all. He kept a good pace, didn't talk too much, and wasn't stodgy like a lot of the members."

The waitress arrived and leaned on their table. "I see you have some drinks, how about something to eat?"

"Let me get a cheeseburger, medium well, with some bacon," said Bryan.

"That's all you're going to cost me?" said Tommy. "Come on, get a steak or something."

"Hey, that bacon costs extra."

"Alright, you're letting me off the hook easy," replied Tommy, turning to the waitress.

"I'll go with the grilled chicken sandwich tonight, please."

"Anything else, guys?"

"Nope," said Tommy as Bryan shook his head.

"I'll put it right in," she said.

"So how is the course these days?" asked Tommy.

"Solid all the way around. They're keeping it up pretty well. Greens immaculate as always."

"Yeah, the other day I saw a listing that sold pretty quickly out there. I was impressed by how much they were getting per square foot. The course helps maintain the values of the whole development. Some of the other older courses around here are seeing their prestige fade. Of course that's no surprise when most of the membership is off the actuarial tables."

"Come on. My folks aren't that old."

"They qualify as junior members don't they?"

"You're probably right," nodded Bryan. "So how did your deal go today?"

"Not too bad. I think it was already a done deal but they still wanted to get over any final doubts. I feel bad for the lady. Her husband is a bit of a head case. He wanted to evaluate all the details of the house today. In the kitchen he tried moving dishes from the sink to the dishwasher to make sure it didn't take too much effort. Unfortunately there were no actual dishes. It was like a bad June Cleaver pantomime skit. He opened and closed every door and window and flicked every light switch. The grand finale was when he wanted to test the toilet. No, he didn't just flush it; he wanted to have a seat. Even better, he didn't want to sit with his pants on. Said he spends enough time there that he had to be comfortable. We decided to give him some personal time and started going over the paperwork. By that point his wife was completely mortified so there was no turning back. He came back and of course started nit picking about the documents. She just glared at him and told him to start signing and initialing. I'm hoping the inspection comes back relatively clean otherwise I know I'll be doing a lot of negotiation with this guy."

"I guess if you're making that kind of a commitment you want to know what you're getting. I wonder what *she* had to go through to pass his test?"

"She's a decent looking lady so I think he had to be happy that she'd take him. They have grown kids so they must have been together a long time. I'm sure they've gotten used to each others eccentricities and found ways to overlook them."

"I suppose that's how my dad's been able to deal with my mom all these years," said Bryan.

"Your mom is a whole different category, man. Your dad deserves a medal. So how are the folks doing?"

"The usual. Mom's hitting the social scene and building her political empire. Dad just goes fishing and golfing. It seems to work fine for both of them."

"I see your mom's picture in the social pages and local magazines pretty regularly. I don't see your dad too often though."

"He's a pretty good sport. He puts in his time but lets her have all of the limelight she wants."

"So what have you got for me, Bryan? Any news?" asked Tommy.

"You don't want to hear about the rest of my round today? It would probably be more exciting than my personal life. Besides, I didn't think I had to keep looking. I thought that's what I had you for."

"I'm always keeping my eyes open for you. But you need to do your part. You didn't put in a whole lot of effort when I sent Karen your way."

"Oh, come on. Don't even bring that up again. She was a hand-me-down! I know you like to do your part for the environment, but stick to recycling bottles and cans, not your ex-girlfriends."

"She was too uptight for me, but I thought it might be a good fit for you," shrugged Manson.

"Enough!" Minton said, raising his hand. "Since I've got nothing to discuss tell me how wonderful things are for you."

"Well, since you asked, things are moving along pretty well with Tina. At this point it seems like we are still on the same page - moving forward, but at a measured pace. Take tonight for instance. She had something going with a girlfriend and I get to hang out with you. Neither of us feel like we have to spend all of our time together."

"What about the other stuff? You haven't come across any quirks or flaws yet?"

"Not really, but that's what worries me. I'm just waiting for something to come out of left field. But now that we've been together a while we've been in a lot of different situations and nothing serious has reared its head. Plus I've gotten to know her family now so I can tell what kind of stock she comes from."

"Her dad is still giving you a passing grade?"

"Definitely. I love the fact that he's never played the tough guy, over-protective dad angle. I'm sure he did that when she was a teenager, but now he realizes she's an adult and is happy to see her in a relationship."

"Relationship?" asked Bryan.

"I'm not afraid to say it. I'm not anywhere near ring shopping, but we're pretty serious."

"I'm happy for you. I hope it keeps working."

Their waitress arrived with a smile and two plates. "Burger for you and chicken for you. Can I get you anything else?"

"A couple more beers would be great. Thanks," said Tommy.

"Sure thing," she replied.

"So tell me about that scramble you played in last week with the realtors," Bryan said, while rearranging his burger and sorting the food on his plate.

"We had fun," replied Tommy through a mouth full of chicken. "Being a scramble you can only expect so much. If you go there wanting to win you better bring a couple of ringers or plan on cheating your butt off. As expected, the group with the ringers won the low gross and the group with the cheaters won low net."

"Well, you're a solid player. Who else did you have with you?"

"We had a guy from the downtown office named, Bob Smith. He's a good all around player and has a single digit handicap. He's a member at Royal Siesta but that's about the only course he ever plays. He knows it backward and forward and can go toe to toe with anyone on his home turf. But he's a bit out of his element when you get him somewhere else. Based on the way he actually played, the handicap he listed probably hurt us. I knew the greens were different than what he's used to but he should have been able to adjust after a few holes. And complaining about it as we walked off every green didn't help our cause."

"Sounds like my dad," said Bryan. "No other course can ever have greens as good as Oak Run. Who else?"

"Do you remember, Steve Stanton? He played with us about a year ago."

"Yeah, he wasn't too bad."

"No, he earned his keep for the team. Made a few long putts and got us out of a few tough spots. The real killer was our fourth, Ron Pierce. He's relatively new and nobody had played with him before. He estimated his handicap as an eighteen, but he was clearly well into the twenties. I think he didn't want to scare us with too big of a number and was hoping the scramble format would hide some of his flaws. Not a chance. By the second nine he had completely broken down and was spraying balls everywhere. Unfortunately it was an event where they required that you use at least two of everyone's drives."

"Oh, man, that's always brutal when you've got a hack," said Bryan, shaking his head.

"Tell me about it. So we're down to three holes and still need to use one of Ron's drives. Steve knew that thirteen and fourteen were tough driving holes so as we walked up to the tee on twelve we decided to have an intervention. It's a short par three, but the edge of the lake comes into play. Therefore, we told Ron to bring his putter up to the tee."

"No way!" said Bryan, cracking up.

"Had to do it," said Tommy laughing. "You don't want to emasculate a guy like that, but you also don't want to post a huge number in a scramble. The way he was hitting at that point who knows what his regular shot would have led to. We told him to just put his ball behind the tee markers and tap it to the other side. From there we would have three of us taking shots with eight or nine irons."

"So what did he say?"

"He was completely stunned. He stood there waiting for the punch line, but there wasn't one. It just wasn't computing in his head what we were asking him to do. So Bob pipes up and says, 'Just tap it across the tee line with you putter. Come on. Let's go!' So he does it and backs off without a word. We didn't even ask if he wanted to have a go at the second shot. Bob and I hit shots to about ten to fifteen feet and then Steve gets up and sticks it to about four feet. Easy putt for par."

"Oh, that's so harsh. He won't be living that down any time soon."

"Steve and I weren't going to make a big deal about it, but Bob is a talker. He went back to work on Monday and had to tell anyone who plays golf about the round. He of course highlighted the drive with a putter strategy. By that afternoon I had a couple people call me and ask about it. I know it's embarrassing for him, but maybe it will inspire him to take a few lessons and tighten up his game."

"I know I'll think twice before agreeing to play in a scramble on your team," said Bryan.

"You? Mr. Double Eagle. You'll be my ringer from now on!"

"I doubt there's many more where that on came from," shrugged Bryan.

"See, there you go again with the low confidence. You need to believe in yourself more."

"You realize, Tommy, that not everyone can have such a high level of self esteem as you, right?" replied Bryan, folding his arms after sensing he was in for another lecture.

"It's not just self image, it's attitude. There are lots of people that have a lousy self image but if they have some attitude it can get them a long way. There's a difference between the two."

"Enlighten me."

"Alright. Check out this guy at the table over by the end of the bar, the one sitting with the gorgeous blond."

"Wow! Look at her. I hadn't seen her earlier," said Bryan, looking over his shoulder.

"Okay, I said check 'em out, not stare at them."

"Sorry."

"So he easily has ten or fifteen years on her. I don't see any rings so I doubt they're married. He's ok looking, but she could certainly do better. So why is she having dinner with him?"

"Because he's in town visiting his little sister?"

"No, wise guy. He's got the right attitude. At his age I'm sure he's been married and divorced at least once. But rather than just finding someone at his level he's aiming higher. The attitude gets you over the fear and then once you succeed the improved self confidence will follow."

"I bet he's got money, too," observed Bryan.

"He probably does, less of it after the divorce of course, but that's not the only factor. He could be broke, but if he dresses right and carries himself a certain way he'll still get that girl. Again, that's the attitude."

"Alright, I'll get a fashion make-over and act like a jerk."

"If you always have a closed mind you're not going to get ahead. Not that I'm interested, but you're a good looking guy. You're, what? Five foot ten, fighting weight about a buck eighty?"

"One seventy-five."

"Close enough. You've got your messy, sandy blond hair and blue eyes working for you. You should be on a lot more dates."

"Thanks. I'm glad to know I'm not repulsive."

"Think about it in terms of your golf game. You're a solid player, but if you're with a group deciding whether to play the blue tees or the white tees you always lean toward the whites. That's your comfort zone. You need to step up to the blues, Bryan. Once you realize you can play at that level your comfort zone moves up. That guy over there – he's playing the tips my man."

"You're right, but it's easier said than done."

"What tees did you play today?"

"Whites," sighed Bryan.

"See! Your double eagle may have been a fluke, but you should still build off of it. Maybe you'll never have another one, but the fact that you've done it once means that you can do it again. Attitude."

"I agree on the golf side, however, I'm not sure I'm buying it in terms of women. Sure she's great looking, but is that going to make him happy? Maybe he's faking it because he thinks that's what everyone else wants," argued Bryan, gesturing over his shoulder.

"You'd have to ask him that question. But I'd sure take his fake happiness over your real malaise!" Tommy replied.

"You make it sound like I'm depressed."

"No, I know that's not the case. I just think you can be happier than you are right now. It seems like you're waiting for things to happen instead of making them happen."

"I'm not in any hurry," said Bryan.

"Maybe you should be; the clock is ticking. You're not twenty anymore."

"Now you're starting to sound like my mom."

"Alright, enough serious talk, unless you want to tell me about work," said Manson sarcastically.

"Definitely not. That *will* get me depressed."

"Ok, I'll leave that for another session. Do you want another drink?"

"No, I'm set."

"Let's grab the waitress and settle up."

"Are you ditching me early tonight?" Bryan asked.

"Nah, I've just got an open house all day tomorrow so I need to be rested up. Talking to a bunch of prospects hour after hour really wears you out. Plus we need to get there early to make sure everything is staged properly and do any last minute housekeeping."

"If nothing else, you're certainly committed to your job."

"I can't say that I love it, but it's a pretty good gig. Always meeting new people and the more I put into it the more I seem to get out of it."

"Here she comes," Bryan said as he motioned to the waitress.

Tommy paid the bill and they finished off the last of their drinks before heading out to the parking lot together.

"Alright big guy, thanks again for dinner," said Bryan, shaking hands with Tommy.

"Good to see you buddy and congrats on that double eagle."

"Thanks. Let's get out in the next week or two if you can make some time."

"Sounds good," said Manson getting into his Mercedes.

"Nice and shiny as always. How many coats of wax are you putting on that thing?"

"Gotta keep it looking good. Like I told you, Bry' – attitude."

"I'll work on it."

3

E ven though his alarm clock made the exact same sound each morning, it seemed to change in Bryan's mind. On Monday it was an annoying, painful buzz, but by Friday it had transformed into a more soothing, friendly hum. On Monday it seemed to be saying: "You need a paycheck to pay your bills so drag your bones out of that bed!" Friday's voice was more along the lines of: "Come on, you can do it. Only one more day to go." Nearing his fifth anniversary with the company, Bryan had grown to hate his job.

As he went through his morning routine Bryan did his best to not think about the day ahead. Fortunately, Bryan liked his current apartment. He had a third floor unit overlooking a lake and park area. In the morning he would normally make his breakfast, eat it on the balcony, and then spend some quality time reading the paper. He spent so much time out there that he recently ran his cable and installed a small flat screen TV. Today, however, he left the TV off, preferring to get some fresh air and enjoy the relative quiet. As the sun's glare off the lake began to increase, he checked his watch and realized his respite was over; time to go to work.

When Bryan arrived at the office complex he pulled in and found his normal parking space available. Although there were no assigned parking spots, most employees seemed to have marked their territory over time. On his way up to the building Bryan noticed one of his co-workers coming across the lot.

"Morning, Bryan."

"Hey, Jason. How's it going?"

"Good, and you?"

Bryan just smirked and pointed at the building.

"Ah, there's the positive attitude that keeps our team running strong," Jason remarked.

"You seem pretty juiced up for a Monday. Good weekend?" asked Bryan.

"Not too bad. Went downtown on Friday, hit the beach and bars on Saturday, and recovered on Sunday. My brother was down for the weekend and we always have a good time."

"Sounds like fun."

"How about you?"

"Played golf on Saturday and watched a few games on Sunday."

"How did you play?"

"Well, not to brag, but I had a double eagle."

"Whoa! Aren't you just a player."

"It felt pretty good. I'm still looking for my first hole-in-one, but this was almost as good. Are you playing much?"

"Just every once in a while. I really want to play more but it's tough. I probably need to get some lessons; I'm too inconsistent across eighteen holes."

"It's definitely a game that takes a lot of work," said Bryan, opening the door to the main lobby.

"Thanks," Jason said going in first. "Do you have any suggestions for where I could get some good advice?"

"You should probably just start at one of the local ranges. They all typically have a few teachers available for hourly lessons. That way you can try out one pro and if you don't hit it off with them you can try another. It's also not too much of an investment. If you go to some of the clubs the teachers will try to get you on a 'program'. It's like going to a chiropractor; they want to keep you coming back. If you really want to get serious maybe that's the way to go, but you should start out small and work your way up.

"I don't have a lot of extra money right now so maybe I'll check out the range guys."

"Give it a shot. There is a great place out by me. Next time I'm there I'll grab some information for you."

After crossing the lobby they stopped at the large wooden door that led to their department. They each swiped their ID cards and headed inside. This section of the building covered several thousand square feet and consisted of a mix of cubicles and offices. Bryan did appreciate the fact that the office was well lit and well furnished. Chambers Data Systems had moved into this facility three years ago after bringing in several private investors to help fund the company's growth. The cash infusion led to a fixed asset spending spree so most of the furniture and equipment was still relatively new and in good shape. Bryan and Jason marched down the main aisle to their area near the end.

"Any lunch plans today, Bryan?"

"Nada."

"Want to go out for something?"

"Sounds good to me."

"Alright, start thinking about where you want to go so we don't stand around trying to decide in the parking lot."

"I'm Mr. Decisive," said Bryan, sounding unsure.

"Uh huh, right. I'll see you at the staff meeting," replied Jason, heading to his desk.

Bryan turned and entered his cubicle. Finding everything just the way he'd left it, he flopped down in his chair and latched his laptop to its docking station. As he waited for it to boot up he leaned back and made a few graceful spins.

One rotation was all it took to survey his domain. His work space was exactly nine feet by nine feet. One day when he was particularly bored he took out a ruler and hand measured all of the dimensions of his office. Although it didn't have a door, his eighty-one square feet of paradise did afford him a reasonable level of privacy. He didn't have to cover the hand set and could talk at a normal level when chatting with friends or taking care of personal business on the phone. He was always careful nonetheless. The walls here were eight feet tall so he could also stand up and walk around without seeing everyone else. Bryan had friends who worked in offices with much lower partitions and they would actually sit on the floor to get a little private time.

Some co-workers were highly focused on working their way up to offices, but at this point in his career Bryan was comfortable toiling away in a cube. He knew that on any given day there could be a corporate shift and his department could be eliminated or outsourced. In the span of a few hours his section of the cube farm could be flattened by a few guys with screw guns. There would be a much greater sense of loss if he got booted from a real office. Bryan felt that he was on even terms with his employer since he could pack his belongings in two boxes and be on his way in less than an hour.

Although it was only a few minutes, starting up his computer seemed to take forever. While waiting for it to go through the myriad of different security and systems layers, Bryan began getting organized for the week ahead. He sorted through several stacks on his desk and jotted down a few notes so that he would be able to provide status updates at the morning staff meeting. Most of his projects were on track; however, one was starting to languish. He had hoped to catch up over the weekend, but he just wasn't able to get himself into the work mode.

The desktop finally appeared on his screen and Bryan fired up his e-mail. It was only 8:45 but he already had a dozen new messages waiting for him. He deleted a few unimportant ones and quickly worked on a few others. At 8:55 a reminder popped up on his computer and like a robot Bryan grabbed his notes and headed for the conference room.

Entering the room Bryan took a seat next to Jason.

"Got your homework ready?" asked Bryan.

"As ready as I'll ever be. It's not like much has changed since last week. Why is it that we have to do this every Monday?"

"Tradition."

"Here comes the man with all the answers," said Jason, gesturing toward the glass door. "Did you decide on lunch yet?"

"I've been busy."

Their boss, Joe Kelly, came in and walked briskly to the head of the table. He sighed and acted as though he'd already been working for hours, even though he'd probably arrived only a few minutes ahead of his charges.

"Alright everyone. Lots to cover today. Let's get started," he said officiously. Kelly always liked to make it seem that it was the employees that caused the meetings to run long, whereas in reality it was his inability to properly run a meeting. He started with some corporate updates and then gave a detailed analysis of everything he was working on. He then went around the table to each employee on his team. Unfortunately many of Bryan's teammates felt that they needed to use this forum to justify their jobs. They would talk at length about what they supposedly did and, in turn, the other employees, even those that didn't want to, would try to keep up. It was a vicious circle. There was excessive repetition from week to week, but Kelly never took it upon himself to stop the madness. As it got closer to Bryan's turn he started taking some deep breaths in preparation.

"Minton. You're up. What have you got for us?"

"Pretty much steady progress across the board since last week, Joe. Most of the projects have already been touched on by my respective team members so I'll keep it brief. "

After Bryan had droned on for a minute or two Kelly interrupted him. "Sounds good, Bryan. How about the Mid-American project? Seems like we're lacking momentum there."

Bryan had hoped to casually sneak that into the middle of his rundown, but now it was front and center. "Unfortunately, as you know, we are running into some hurdles there. I tried to catch up over the weekend, but it's hard to generate accurate reports with so much incomplete data." This was only half true since his laptop hadn't left its case over the weekend.

"It seems like that's where we've been for a while, Bryan. I was really hoping the four of you could manage it and that you could handle being the lead," said Kelly, shaking his head in mock disbelief.

Bryan usually stayed under control, however, comments like that made it tough. Gritting his teeth, Bryan responded, "It'll be our top priority this week. We are going to escalate it to the heads of their reconcilement and research departments."

"Yeah, that's a good start but I really need to get a better grip on our timeline. I want you to put together an outline for me with some concrete action steps."

"Concrete action steps?" thought Bryan, looking down at the table. "How about some concrete shoes and a boat ride? Spend time doing another report for Joe? Yep, that'll help get the project done faster." After taking a quick breath Bryan said, "We'll get right on it, Joe."

"Thanks, Bryan. I know you'll get it back on track. Alright, let's move on to Watkins. Jason, maybe you'll have some better news for us," said Kelly, getting in one more jab at Bryan.

With his torment over, Bryan began doodling on his notepad and mentally removed himself from the meeting. He started replaying Saturday's round hole by hole in his head. First he counted the number of fairways he'd hit, then the number of greens, and then the number of putts. Of course there was only one number from Saturday that held any real importance for Bryan: a two on the seventeenth. His spirits started to rise as he replayed his double eagle over and over in his mind. He was amazed at the euphoria it induced, like some new drug he'd suddenly discovered. He hoped that its effectiveness would last for a while. Bryan knew he would need it if he was going to last much longer at Chambers.

After working his way around the conference table, Kelly finished his own agenda items and finally concluded the meeting.

On the way out Jason elbowed Bryan and inquired, "How's that lunch plan coming?"

"About as well as Mid-American. Hopefully I'll have some concrete action steps for you before noon."

Bryan trudged back to his desk and got to work. Rather than delegating tasks on the Mid-American project he decided to tackle it directly. He started making calls and got one voicemail after another. Everyone was of course in a meeting. He followed up his messages with e-mails. At least the ball was rolling.

Bryan decided that he might as well get the monkey off his back and knock out the report to Kelly. He knew that he really didn't have to come up with anything *concrete* since his boss truly loved fluff. Catch phrases and consultant speak were the only effective way to communicate with him. Original ideas? Creative thinking? Real problem solving? That would only lead to derision and comments like: "not a team player" on his annual review. Over time, as Bryan began to understand what made his boss tick, he developed better ways to deal with him.

Bryan kept a separate file on his hard drive full of corporate memos and prior reports. Rather than paraphrasing, he would often just cut and paste passages, changing names if necessary. Many of his co-workers did the same thing and they would even swap information. Bryan quickly outlined his report to Kelly and then started sprinkling it with some fanciful extras. After proof reading one last time, he attached it to an e-mail and sent it on its way. With that off of his list he decided to start working on some of his other projects. These he didn't mind quite as much since it sometimes felt as if he was doing productive work. A short time later, when he felt like he was just hitting his stride, an e-mail flagged as important popped up from Jason. Time for lunch. He locked up his workstation, sent his phone to voicemail, and headed around the corner.

"Ready?" asked Bryan.

"I'm ready. So do I even need to ask?"

"About what?"

"About where we are going to lunch."

"Oh yeah, I'm thinking we should hit Mi Casa."

"Mexican on Monday for you, Bryan? That's pretty bold stuff."

"You're not dealing with the same old Bryan anymore. This is the new Bryan. My buddy Tommy told me I needed to change my attitude."

"He's right," chuckled Jason.

"Thanks. You guys are really making me feel good about myself."

"I'm not being mean. You just spend a lot of time stewing about stuff around here but not doing anything about it. You don't have to tell Joe where to stick his reports, but you know that if you let him he'll just keep walking all over you."

"Regardless, I'm still clinging to my dream of telling him what to do with the reports. Let's go. Maybe I will pick up some lottery tickets while we're out and then I'll have a chance to make my dream come true."

***

Bryan used to bring his lunch to work but now he ate out most days. He knew that he could save a lot of money by brown bagging; however, his mid-day escape from the office was priceless. Mi Casa was a favorite among Chambers employees; although many of them saved it for Friday when they were more in the fiesta kind of mood.

Despite the fact that this was supposed to be a reprieve from the office, they seemed to have no choice but to talk about work.

"So did you make any headway yet?" asked Jason, thumbing through the menu.

"Nah, just sent out feelers to everyone over there. They're all in meetings or just not answering their phones."

"I hate that. We waste so much time just going in circles and playing phone tag. Remember a few months ago when I was working with those morons out in Texas? I think they had a spy in our office who was tipping them off because they always returned my calls when I was away from the desk. It was probably Joe. He wanted to create a problem that he would then have to deal with; a little job security."

"And even with e-mail they can still dodge you. That's what Mid-American has been doing. I'll send a request and they'll only get me half of the information. Then by the time I get the rest of the info the first part needs to be updated. If these clowns don't get everything to us in the next few days I'm just going to tell them that Joe is going to call their CFO and let him know that the data they need to report to the state insurance commissioner won't be on time. Most of our clients fear dealing with Joe more than I do so I guess he's good for something."

"Luckily most of my stuff is running pretty smooth right now. I just know that any day now though I'll call one of my companies and all my contacts will have been axed in a restructuring. Then I'll have to start from scratch with people that have no clue what they're doing.

"Sad but true," agreed Bryan.

"I think we at least have some decent job security for now at Chambers. With all of the growth that we've been seeing we just keep adding people."

"That's what worries me. Eventually the pendulum will swing too far and they will start printing pink slips faster than they are printing job offer letters right now."

Although they had barely looked at the menu, it didn't matter since they knew the lunch specials by heart. When the waiter arrived they ordered immediately.

"I'll take the taco platter con carne," said Jason.

"And I'll do the same but con pollo," said Bryan.

"Gracias," said the waiter with a bow.

"I just hope the good times last long enough for us to cash in on an IPO of the company's stock," said Jason.

"Yeah, but we'll only get some crumbs. At our level they'll give us a few shares and some options. You're talking maybe a new car at best. A lot of the guys at the executive level will be set for life. The investors will be looking to cash out, pocket a big profit, and head on to the next project. Plus, once we are public management will have all kinds of new hoops to jump through. And you know that all of the work will flow right down to the cube dwellers. No, I'm not in any hurry to see us get a ticker."

"Thanks for shattering my dreams, Bryan. I'll be sure not to bring up the Easter Bunny or Santa Claus with you."

"Just living in the real world, Jason."

"You're probably right. It would be nice to score a big payday early in my career, but I know I've got a lot of years to go no matter what. I'd like to at least work my way up a bit here at Chambers for a few years to build the resume and then maybe hop somewhere else if the money's right."

"Work your way up? Are you gunning to take Joe's job?"

"Maybe. Somebody like Joe should be fired, but he's such a company man that they'll move him up instead. There are lots of other team manager spots that I could post for besides our group. What about you, Bryan? Are you going to be a worker bee for the rest of your life?"

"I don't know about that. But I certainly have no interest in management right now. It's always presented as an 'opportunity', but I don't think it's all it's cracked up to be. I mean, come on, who really wants to manage a bunch of idiots like us?"

"I think it would be a good challenge. If you ever hope to make it to senior management you've got to put in your time in middle management."

"I hope to move on to greener pastures before that even becomes and option."

"Doing what?" asked Jason.

"I don't know at the moment, but hopefully something other than just being a cog in the corporate machine. Maybe I'll go back to school in a few years; open some new doors. It would be nice to have a job that I actually like. I love golf; maybe I can find a golf related gig. Unfortunately, I don't think there's a lot of money to be made unless you're a tour pro."

"Start practicing more."

"No, I think that ship has sailed. These days you need to start young. Top players on the rise just keep getting younger and younger. Being a caddie is about as close as I could hope to get."

"So why don't you get out there and go for it?"

"I wouldn't even know where to begin. Right now I suppose I'll just bide my time and collect a paycheck here. I don't like it but I know it could be worse. I've got friends who are putting in a lot more hours each week and are not earning as much as me."

"So what are they paying you, Bryan?"

"I doubt it's much different than what you're getting. Still, I'm not telling you. And I don't want to know what you're making either. It might be too much of a slap in the face."

"Alright, enough work talk. Here comes our food. Let's not spoil a good lunch at the Casa."

***

By Thursday Bryan's mood was starting to improve. He had connected with everyone on the Mid American project and all of his teammates at Chambers were now moving forward on their tasks. He put everything else on the back burner and was focused on getting it completed in the next week or two. But at this point Bryan's objective wasn't to impress Kelly so much as it was to spite him. Kelly would certainly delight in re-assigning the project to someone else at a staff meeting. Bryan was determined to not let that happen.

In the middle of the afternoon Bryan needed to take a break and stretch his legs so he decided to spend a few minutes visiting his neighbors. He headed around the corner and down the hall. Halfway to his intended destination Bryan was snagged by one of his teammates.

"Oh, hey Bryan. Glad I caught you. Got a second?"

Bryan froze, knowing he was trapped. "Hey, Christie. Sure, what have you got?"

"I'm making good progress but I have a couple of issues that I want to run by you."

Issues were ok. He just didn't want to hear the word *problems.* Christie Sherman was relatively new at Chambers, having just graduated from an MBA program last year. As with many of the newbies, she was full of energy and positive attitude. She hadn't been in the corporate world long enough to have these traits ground and beaten out of her. All those years of college had provided her with plenty of analytical skills, but not much in the way of common sense. She could create and examine data all day long, but filtering it and ultimately making a decision based on it always seemed to be just beyond her reach. Bryan assumed that that was what her current *issues* involved. He headed into her cubicle and stood next to her chair, hoping that his afternoon wasn't going to take a wrong turn.

"Let me show you some of the spreads I've been working on," she said as she pushed her chair forward and angled her monitor upward.

As she clicked through several tabs and detailed what she'd already accomplished, Bryan did his best to remain attentive. He nodded his head and periodically uttered "ums" and "uh-huhs". He just wanted to cut to the chase. Bryan was relieved as it became clear that she was heading in the right direction with her assignment. He grabbed a note pad from her desk and jotted down a few items that he needed to help her with.

"Ok, let's call Taylor and get some of the forecast factors that you can use." He leaned over, clicked on her speakerphone, and punched in a few numbers. "Hey Taylor. It's Bryan. I'm over with Christie right now. Can you send her some of the assumptions that you've been using in the forecasts recently?"

"Will do. I'll e-mail them in a few minutes."

"Thanks," said Bryan, clicking off. "So once you have those you should be able to tighten up your projection results. Then you can run it against the year-to-date and trailing twelve month info to come up with your recommendations."

"Do you have any thoughts on that?" she asked sheepishly.

"Sure, but we need some new ideas and I bet you can add something to the equation. You've already put one and one together, now you just need to come up with the answer. Give it a go. If you're still running dry tomorrow afternoon give me a call."

"Alright, I'll see what I can do."

"Good deal. Anything else?"

"No, I think that's it. Thanks, Bryan."

Bryan headed back to the hallway and continued on his original journey. He was going to pay a visit to Alex Barrett, who was one of his closest associates at Chambers. Alex had started at the same time as Bryan and they went through the same training class. They were the same age and Bryan liked working with Alex since he was very sharp. He could have moved up a lot faster by now but he didn't seem to be overly driven. He was probably restrained by his highly cynical attitude, another common trait that the two of them shared. As with Bryan, he would probably be working somewhere else in a few years. Around the next corner and down a few doorways he stopped and tapped on the rough fabric wall. "Anybody home?"

"Oh, hey Bryan."

"Got a minute?"

"Sure, what's up?"

"Nothing actually. Just taking an office road trip. Seeing what's going on. Everything going okay on your numbers?"

"Oh yeah. I'm in good shape now that I finally have all of the turnover figures. I've been punching out the last part of one other project, but I should have all of our stuff done in the next day or two. Is everyone else on track?"

"I think so. I just went over some things with Christie and she's up to speed."

"She's definitely coming along. I was a little worried about her early on. I guess she just needed a little experience. Plus, Joe likes her so she has an advantage there."

"She has to be careful there though. If he decides to try and escalate their working relationship to something else and she rebuffs him, she could run into problems."

"Nah, then she just sues and collects a nice bonus."

"You think she'd do that?" asked Bryan.

"You never know. Right now I wouldn't think so, but if she's miserable and feels like her career is in peril then it could quickly become an option. She seems more focused on her career than anything else so that's probably what she'd fight to defend."

"Do you think Joe has other intentions beyond just shepherding her along as one of his favored pupils?"

"He's such a screwball that he's probably into her in the professional sexual way. Like the metro sexual who wants to dress

31

and live a certain way, but doesn't actually live the whole lifestyle. He wouldn't want to take her out to dinner; he would take her to see motivational speakers. If he took her on a corporate retreat his goal would be to make sure that they both attended all of the sessions together. Sleeping with her would probably be a secondary goal for him," Alex said.

"What do you think of her?"

"She's cute, but seems like she'd be a bit too high maintenance for me. Besides, I know better than to even think about an office romance; just too many things that can go wrong there. Maybe I could consider someone in an entirely different department, but definitely no one in our division."

"The sales and marketing groups have some good candidates," said Bryan.

"Oh yeah. Some of the ones in sales are making serious money too. I'd love to find a girl that could pay her own way and maybe even support me too."

"Of course you have to remember Barbara and Richard Adams? If you ever need a reason not to fish from the company dock, they're it."

"That was crazy. They seem like a happy couple making tons of money and he goes and blows it all. I still can't believe he was telling her that he was working late when really he was having an online affair using his company computer. What an idiot! Even better was when they fired him and didn't tell her. I wish I could have been there when she found out from a co-worker via the rumor mill. 'Oh, Barbara, sorry to hear about Richard' - 'What's wrong with Richard?' - 'About him getting fired.' - 'Richard got fired?' Oops. That's embarrassing," Alex said.

"She lasted about a month after that if I recall."

"At least she was gone by the time the IT guys leaked the profile information of his cyber-lover. Overweight, unemployed lady in Orlando. Likes drinking, smoking, watching TV, and spending lots of time on the Internet. Sounds like it was really worth ruining his life. If he was going to do that he should have just spent a little cash and found himself a professional," joked Alex.

"I know they got a divorce but I didn't hear anything more after that."

"I'm sure she left town and he probably went to shack up in Orlando."

After chatting a bit more Bryan glanced at his watch and decided to get back to business. He took the long way back so he could walk past one of the exterior glass walls and see how it looked outside. The sun was shining and the palms were swaying in the sea breeze. The full force of summer hadn't arrived yet, so the evenings were still rather nice. Bryan thought about heading out to the driving range near his apartment rather than going to the gym today.

When he arrived back at his desk he sat down and wiggled his mouse to undo his screen saver. As he leaned back he noticed that the voicemail light on his phone was lit. Once again he hoped it wasn't something that was going to spoil the little bit of workday that he had left. He picked up the receiver and hit the voicemail button.

"Hi Bryan. It's Jim Garris from over at Stone Ridge. I just wanted to let you know that I've been telling everybody over here at the club about your shot. Nobody seems to know of another double eagle out here so it's truly a historic shot. Anyway, I'm sure you're busy over there, but I did want to extend a formal invite to come over and play sometime when you have a chance. I figured that if I didn't call you this week, I'd put it off and never get around to it. I know I've got a few years on you, but I enjoyed our round. Please don't feel obligated in any way, but if you are up for it let me know."

Bryan scribbled down Garris's phone number on the edge of a report by the phone as the voicemail disconnected. He sat back in his chair and looked at the number on the paper. When he wrote down his number the other day he certainly hadn't expected Garris to call him. Bryan thought Garris was a nice guy, but was afraid he was a bit lonely and maybe looking to latch on to a new friend. Kind of like the old ladies in the clubhouse out at Stone Ridge. He figured he better get some protocol advice so he grabbed the phone and dialed Tommy's number.

"Tommy, it's Bryan," Minton said, surprised that he reached Tommy and not his voicemail. "Do you have a second?"

"Sure, just cleaning up some paperwork. What's up?"

"I just got a call from that Garris guy I played with on Saturday. He invited me to come back out and play a round with him some time. I never thought he'd call. I don't want to be rude, but I'm not sure I want to accept."

"Boy that is a tough call. You said he was a pretty good guy though, right? And a pretty decent golfer too."

"Oh yeah. Definitely," said Bryan.

"Well as long as he's not going to take you into the woods out there and whack you over the head with a wedge I think you should be okay playing. Are you calling me to chaperone?"

"No, he just caught me a little off guard."

"I think you can play with him. But when you call him back don't seem too eager. Play a little hard to get; you don't want him to think you're easy.

"Come on, Tommy."

"I'm being serious! As tough as that may seem to believe. If he was inviting you over to his house for dinner I'd be a little bit creeped out. But he just asked you out for a round. That's what golf is all about. So before you go and get all booked up, when are we going to get out?"

"Well this weekend is spoken for. I've got to put in some hours for work. I've got a big monkey I have to get off my back. What about next weekend?"

"Let me grab the calendar. Next weekend is looking pretty good right now. Saturday or Sunday?" Tommy asked.

"Saturday should be good. Maybe around nine?"

"That works."

"Alright, I'll call around and find us a tee time next week. Thanks for the advice buddy. I'm getting ready to head out of here so I'll call Garris tomorrow. Whatever I may be, I'm not easy."

"Talk to you later, Bry'."

***

After stopping at his apartment to change and pick up his clubs, Bryan drove down to the Buckets and Brews driving range. It was hands down the best in town. He liked the fact that they had mats and natural grass to hit from. Bryan preferred to play off the grass, but if it had rained and was too wet he could still hit off the fake turf. The range covered a good size piece of property so even big hitters could hit full drivers. Even though Bryan wasn't fanatical about practicing, the B and B, as it was known, made it more enjoyable and productive.

Besides the Buckets, the Brews were also a highlight. The current owners had completely remodeled the restaurant and opened a microbrewery as well. Because of the golf related theme they apparently had no choice but to give their beers clichéd names like Long Ball Lager, Dog Leg Draught, and Albatross Ale.

Customers didn't mind the hokey names since they brewed some excellent beer.

Bryan just wanted to hit balls for fun tonight so he fed a few dollar bills into the machine and it instantly filled the bucket he'd placed below. It was a mild evening with a slight breeze and the sun was getting low. The range faced north so Bryan was able to hit with the bright orange sunset at his back. There was still enough daylight to see his shots, but soon the powerful stadium lights would kick on and gradually reach full brightness. To avoid disturbing the neighbors, only the hitting area was lit. At night longer shots would take off in clear view and then slowly fade into the darkness at the end of the range.

Bryan hit his short irons to get warmed up and then worked his way through his bag. Eventually he grabbed his driver to let loose on the remaining balls. He opened his stance and started out by hitting steadily rising power fades. After a dozen or so he shifted his feet and started pounding draws, gaining added distance with each one. He was always amazed at the level of control and consistency he could achieve on the range. If he could ever find a way to translate it to his on-course game he'd be able to play at a truly different level.

With just a few balls left lying next to the overturned, green wire bucket and his back feeling fully stretched, it was time for his grand finale. He took a few extra long practice swings making a progressively louder whipping noise with each one. The first two shots finished short of the range's most distant target at three hundred yards. He dug in his feet a little harder and went full bore. Including roll, he was able to hit each of the last five balls past the marker. Bryan met lots of people who'd say they could hit three hundred yards, but in reality most of them couldn't do it without a little help from the cart path. Bryan realized that Tommy was right; he needed to play more rounds from the blues.

Bryan wiped down his clubs and packed up his bag. He stowed it in his trunk and headed into the restaurant for some dinner. Bryan was a frequent visitor to the B and B, but didn't know most of the staff other than by sight. The owner, Barry Gilbert, however, took it upon himself to know anyone that was at least an occasional customer. Gilbert was one of those guys that had almost made it to the PGA Tour. He'd spent a number of years as a club pro before sharpening up his skills and making a run at it. He had managed to Monday qualify a few times and played in lots of second and third tier tours, but after a few years the pressure and a drinking problem got the best of him. He crashed and burned, eventually giving up golf and booze. Somewhere along the way he took golf back up, but had managed to leave the drinking in his past. Opening a bar seemed like it would be a bad idea, but Barry said it had strengthened his resolve. He proclaimed that the booze wasn't the problem; it was the drinker. After chatting with another patron at the bar he made his way down to say hello to Bryan.

"Hey young man. Good to see you back in," said Gilbert, extending his hand.

"Evening, Barry. Good to see you too," replied Bryan, shaking back.

"Did they get your order yet?"

"Yep, I'm all set."

"So how's your game?"

"Not too bad. I had a double eagle last Saturday."

"Really? Good for you. I've had five aces, but no double eagles. Where was it?"

"Over on the seventeenth at Stone Ridge. I thinned it a bit but it stayed on line and ran all the way to the bottom of the cup."

Just then the server returned with Bryan's beer. Barry turned to her and said, "The next one for this fella is on the house. An Albatross Ale of course."

"That's not necessary, Barry," Bryan said, feeling a bit like a celebrity.

"My pleasure."

"Oh, before I forget do you have any cards for the teachers out here?"

"Sure, are you looking for some lessons?"

"I'm okay for now but I have a friend that I want to send over."

"I'll go get you a brochure with their rates and contact information. I certainly appreciate it, Bryan."

"My pleasure," said Bryan, raising his glass.

"Cheers," responded Gilbert, lifting his empty hand in a mock toast.

Bryan leisurely enjoyed his dinner and his free beer before settling up and heading home. He was in good spirits and felt even better knowing that tomorrow he'd wake up to his Friday alarm clock.

4

B ryan gave in and sacrificed most of his weekend to the Mid-
American project. He estimated that the project was now
about eighty-percent complete. After going through his
normal Monday morning routine, Bryan gathered his materials and
strode confidently down to the conference room. Jason was already
there so Bryan took the seat next to him.

"Are you ready to step back in the ring, Bryan?" asked Jason
with a smile.

"You better believe it. Eye of the Tiger, baby," replied Bryan,
making a few fake punches.

"Did you work all weekend?"

"Yeah, pretty much. And you?"

"You don't want to know."

"That good, huh?"

"Oh yeah, that good," nodded Jason with a sly grin.

"You're right. I don't want to know. Hey, I brought you a present
this morning. Here's a brochure that lists the teachers, times, and
rates out at the range by my house," said Bryan handing the flyer to
Jason.

"Thanks. Do you know any of them?" asked Jason opening it up.

"I haven't taken any lessons, but I've seen most of them out
there at some point or another and they seem qualified. Most of
them will bring out the video camera and a launch monitor so they
can also critique your equipment and suggest any changes. They
don't sell clubs so it should be reasonably unbiased advice. The
technology they have these days is just amazing. We can thank
NASA and the Department of Defense for the modern day golf
game."

"I guess I just need to get out there and do it now."

"Even if you only improve a little bit, my guess is that you'll
start to enjoy the game even more. Then you'll want to improve
further and at some point you'll become addicted. That's pretty
much how the cycle goes."

"Maybe I should stop before I head down the slippery slope."

"Nah, just do it. Everyone's doing it," prodded Bryan.

"Peer pressure, eh? Are you getting a kickback on the lesson
fees?"

"No, just a free beer."

"Ah, so your recommendations are tainted!"

"Actually, the beer was for my double eagle so my conscience is clear."

Bryan saw Jason's eyes dart to the door and he realized Kelly had arrived. They both sat up quickly and turned toward the end of the table attentively like two boys that had been caught misbehaving. As usual Kelly kicked off the meeting with a full rehash of last week's agenda. Once that was over, he started working the table and made his way down to Bryan. This week Bryan was almost looking forward to his turn. He had spoken to Kelly at the end of last week and intentionally sandbagged about his progress. Better to under promise and over deliver.

"I'll go ahead and steal your thunder this morning, Joe," Bryan said with a touch of sarcasm. "We've made stellar progress on Mid-American in the past week and I fully anticipate completion this week. Our team really worked hard and worked together to overcome the hurdles that had been in our way."

"Wow. That's great news. I didn't realize things were moving so quickly," said Kelly, clearly caught off guard. "I guess that fire I lit under you last week did the trick," he continued, trying to take some of the credit.

"As we discussed last week, the team was certainly capable and ready for a quick turnaround. It was really more a matter of me lighting a fire over at Mid-American," countered Bryan, pushing back but trying not to cross the line.

"So do you think the forecasts and quantitative review will be done as well?" asked Kelly, looking for a weak spot.

"I would say so. Right, Christie?"

"Uh, yes. We're fine," she said, clearly avoiding eye contact with Bryan.

"Great work, Christie. You're proving yourself once again," said Kelly with enthusiasm.

Jason kicked Bryan under the table. He too was well aware of Kelly's favoritism toward Christie. Bryan had to hide a smile as he continued on with his report. After he was done he looked over at Christie but got no reaction. He wasn't overly worried about the project getting derailed, but he wasn't getting a positive vibe from Christie this morning. He didn't want Kelly to think anything was less than perfect so after the meeting finished he let her head out without stopping her.

As they left the conference room Jason put his arm around Bryan's shoulders and said, "I hope you didn't leap before you looked my friend."

Bryan shook his head and replied, "I saw her work last week so I did look. We'll be fine. I hope."

When Bryan got back to his desk he immediately picked up the phone and called Christie. "Hey Christie, it's Bryan."

"Hi Bryan."

"So how is it going? Really?"

"Okay. I just seem to have some writer's block."

"I thought we agreed that you'd give me a call if you were spinning your wheels."

"I know, but it was getting late on Friday and I didn't want to ruin your weekend."

"Well I appreciate the thought but I worked all weekend anyway. It was pretty much pre-ruined."

"I'm sorry."

"Don't worry about it. Let's just get it knocked out. I'll be over in a few minutes."

Bryan checked his e-mail, grabbed a few file folders, and then headed across the office. As he poked his head around her doorway he found her on the phone with her back to him.

"You really did that?" he overheard her saying inquisitively.

Bryan casually cleared his throat.

She turned with a start. "Oh, hey Bryan." Turning back to the phone she said, "I'll talk to you later." She hung up seeming somewhat disappointed.

"Sorry, didn't mean to interrupt," said Bryan, crossing over the threshold into her cubicle.

"Just a friend catching up on the weekend. Were you standing there long?" she said, sounding a bit worried.

"No, just got here. I don't know what she did. Not sure I want to know. It might make me an accomplice."

"I don't think it's a crime. Well, it might be. She's quite a party girl," Christie replied, following Bryan's humorous exit from the uncomfortable moment.

"Maybe she ran into Jason this weekend."

"Jason?"

"Nevermind. Let's get going. Go ahead and pull up your reports. I'll grab a chair from the conference room."

They spent the next couple of hours fixing a few items in the work she'd already done and putting together a summary. Bryan knew he could have done it a lot faster if he'd just done it himself, but he really wanted her to gain some confidence. It wouldn't benefit either of them if he just took the path of least resistance.

"I think that should do it," Bryan said as they proof read a printout.

"That went well. Thanks for sharing some of your prior reports for inspiration. And thanks for spending so much time today. I know you have plenty of other things to be doing on a Monday."

"That's what teamwork is all about," Bryan said as he started gathering up his things. "I'm thinking that we try to get everything wrapped up on Wednesday. Perhaps have the four of us meet briefly in the morning and then I'll meet with Joe in the afternoon. Are you open Wednesday?"

"Let me check," she said, clicking up her calendar. "Yeah, I'm open."

"Good deal. I'll send out an invite after lunch. Anything else we're forgetting?"

"Not that I can think of."

"Alright then. You did a great job. I appreciate it," Bryan said as he headed out.

***

Bryan spent most of Tuesday putting together all of the pieces of the project and interconnecting them where necessary. It was their habit to mark information that required linking with different colors or font sizes in the documents. That way it would stand out in the final phase and hopefully not be missed. Despite the system, occasionally something would still slip through and Kelly would have a fit. He was now, however, a bit more careful before launching into a tirade on these types of things. Last year a new employee missed a number of minor items in a report and Kelly could have addressed it one-on-one. Instead, he waited and let loose at a staff meeting, clearly looking to make an example. When Kelly finished the employee calmly apologized and then let Joe know that he was color blind. Kelly was so mortified that he didn't even bark at the team members who were snickering uncontrollably. It was a classic moment that Kelly would like to forget, but one that everyone on the team would remember for as long as they worked at Chambers. As for the new guy, he apparently had lots of other issues besides being color blind and didn't last much longer at the company.

Wednesday morning's meeting was basically a rubber stamping session. Everyone had reviewed the finished product so they did one final run through to check for any errors or omissions. Bryan did very little the rest of the morning, trying to avoid stress before his meeting with Kelly. He was very confident in their product, but he still dreaded presenting to Kelly. No matter what it was he always felt like he was on trial.

At 2:30 Bryan began getting ready and started getting anxious. He tried to stay calm and mentally prepare himself to deal with his boss. He knew Jason was right about showing more backbone so he resolved to not let Kelly bring him down. At 2:55 he made sure he had everything and headed down to Kelly's office.

Bryan tapped on the glass door and waited to be acknowledged. Kelly looked up and waived him in. "Afternoon, Bryan. Have a seat."

"Thanks, Joe."

"Let me get this stuff off my desk and we'll get started."

Bryan laid out several stacks on the front edge of Kelly's desk. "I'm ready when you are."

They spent the first twenty minutes going through the boiler plate items with little difficulty. As they began to work on the more technical areas Kelly started jotting notes down on a pad on his desk. Bryan tried to casually read the items upside down but had trouble deciphering Kelly's handwriting. As Bryan wrapped up he let out a deep breath of relief. Kelly dropped his pen on the desk and leaned back with his hands behind his head.

"Well, Minton, I have to say that for the most part I'm comfortable with what you've done here. There are a couple of areas that may need a bit of polish, but I'm pleased with the conclusions and forecasts. It seems like Christie is starting to come into her own. I'm considering giving her some lead roles on upcoming projects."

Bryan took his time before responding. He was debating which route he should take. He didn't have any ill will toward Christie, but it wasn't right to base her advancement on work that was only partly hers. "She's improving, but I think she still has some ground to cover."

"Hmm. Is it really the learning curve or are you just nervous that she's coming along too quickly?"

"No, Joe. Not at all. I want to see her flying on her own as much as anyone. That way I won't have to help her as much as I did on the report that you like so much."

"So this is your work and not hers?"

41

"Joe, I'm not here to bring her down. I'm here to do my job and finish this project. It was a joint effort, but I was leading the way. Okay?"

"Why are you getting so defensive, Bryan?" asked Kelly, now leaning forward on his desk.

"I'm not getting defensive. Like I said, I'm just trying to do my job," replied Bryan, not giving any ground.

"I made a simple comment and you seemed to get pretty fired up. I know you've been working hard, but you can't be so sensitive. Bryan, sometimes I think you just need to toughen up a bit."

Toughen up, thought Bryan, flashing back to his conversation with Tommy. What was this – a conspiracy? He realized that Kelly had been caught off guard about Christie and was now trying to turn the tables on Bryan. In the past Bryan would have let it go, but not today. "I am being tough, Joe. So let's stop this game and finish up. Whatever's on your little punch list here *we'll* knock it out and get ready to ship this off," Bryan said firmly, as he grabbed Kelly's list off the desk to both of their surprises. He scanned it quickly. "I don't see anything substantial here; this can all be done in an hour or so. We can get this done before the end of the day and have it ready to print hardcopies in the morning."

Kelly leaned back again, clasped his hands, and sat thinking for a moment. Bryan had no idea what was going to come out of his mouth next. If he had to take a guess "You're fired!" might be high on the list of possibilities. Kelly nodded and finally responded, "Alright, that sounds good. Get to it Bryan."

"Will do, Joe," Bryan responded with confidence. He gathered up his work and tore the top sheet off of Kelly's notepad before carelessly tossing it back on the desk. As he turned and headed for the door Kelly stopped him.

"Bryan."

"Yeah," Bryan said hesitantly.

"Good job."

"Thanks," Bryan replied and quickly went out the door. He didn't want to give Kelly a chance to change his mind. As he walked around the corner a wide grin spread across his face. He knew that the meeting probably wasn't going to change his boss much, but Bryan's confidence has skyrocketed. For the first time in a long while the pendulum of power had swung back in his direction.

***

When he returned to his desk he sat down and kicked his feet up on his desk. He took just a moment for this celebration before regrouping and putting the final touches on the project. Because he was in such a good mood it took even less time than he thought. A few emails and quick phone calls and he was done.

As he prepared a final copy to run in the morning Bryan glanced at his desk calendar and realized he hadn't made a tee time for Saturday. He slid open his top desk drawer and pulled out a local golfing guide. The first course he tried had a charity event while the next one had just aerated the greens. The next two he tried were both full until noontime; he was starting to get frustrated. Warrington Country Club wasn't his favorite layout, but it was usually in pretty good shape. Like many of the older private courses, it had been forced to shift to a semi-private format. The members of course resented the change, but they had no choice since the dwindling membership couldn't support the course year round. Bryan called and they had several times available, but they wouldn't set a time for just a twosome. They would be paired with another twosome at 9:15. He knew Tommy wouldn't be happy about it, but he was starting to run out of options and patience. Rather than call Tommy, Bryan typed up an e-mail and sent it off.

Bryan also realized that he hadn't called Garris. He felt a little guilty, although he had been busy. He was considering just letting it slide, however, his conscience won out and he decided to make the call. He found the note with Garris's number and dialed it. To his relief he got an answering machine. He left a message thanking Garris for the invite and apologized for taking a few days to call back. Bryan said that he was busy this weekend, but maybe one of the next two would work.

Once Mid-American was officially on its way Bryan decided he deserved to coast into the weekend. He knew that there might be some modifications, but they wouldn't respond for at least a week. Knowing the people over there it might even be longer. He killed some time catching up with friends on the phone, surfing the web, and taking some extra long lunches. By Friday afternoon he was nice and relaxed and ready to play some golf.

***

After being stood up by Tommy last time, Bryan debated calling him before leaving for the course. He figured that Tommy knew better

43

than to do it twice in a row so he didn't bother. Unfortunately when he pulled into the lot he once again couldn't find Tommy's car. He unloaded his clubs and changed shoes while keeping an eye on the driveway. Bryan started getting aggravated as he walked up to the clubhouse; he didn't want to check in and pay until he knew Tommy was going to show. Standing on the stairs, he fished his phone from his pocket. As he flipped it open he noticed a black Mercedes rounding the corner. He left his clubs on the steps and walked back down to the lot to meet Tommy.

"Were you getting worried?" Tommy asked as he emerged from his car with a yawn and a stretch.

"No, not at all. Why would you think that?" Bryan replied.

"I wasn't going to leave you hanging. Plus it's too nice of a day to miss golf."

The two of them walked up to the clubhouse and went in through the back entrance to check in at the pro shop. They waded their way through the forest of pastel logo merchantdise to the main desk. Years ago polyester shirts were for golfers who had just come from the bowling alley. Now it had found a new life as a *performance* fabric. Colors that would have gotten you beat up in the past were now widely accepted. Pink was in full bloom and lime green was growing like a weed. Being the more fashionable one, Tommy had spruced up his golf wardrobe in recent years. Bryan, however, was sticking with neutral colors and solids. He was a firm believer that the only people that should be wearing a white belt were beginner karate students. Moreover, if you did want to dress like a pimp you better have the game to back it up.

Bryan stepped up to the desk first. "Good morning, Minton at 9:15."

"Do you have a member number?" asked the guy at the desk.

"Ahh, no. Just a public player," said Bryan holding out his credit card.

"Oh, okay," said the assistant pro with a touch of derision.

"Thanks," Bryan said half-heartedly as he signed his ticket. He walked over and looked at some of the demo clubs sitting in an oversized golf bag. He nodded at the starter who was grabbing a cup of coffee while holding his clipboard under his arm.

"Same for me," said Tommy, tossing his credit card on the counter nonchalantly while intentionally looking out the window. "So what are memberships running out here these days?"

"Well sir, there are several levels available. To go through the particulars we typically schedule appointments with a membership representative. Would you like to set up a meeting?"

"Nah, I was just curious. I heard the prices were coming down quite a bit. But what kind of number are we talking?" pressed Tommy.

"We typically don't just quote the prices. The membership representatives prefer to review that with the prospective members."

"You're not going to add a lot of new members by keeping it a secret. I can't believe you have to go to a meeting just to get a price."

"Well sir, the meetings aren't only for pricing. They are also looking to qualify potential candidates. If your interest is only price I'm sure they can send you out a term sheet and information package."

"That's okay. I'm good. Thanks, chief," Tommy said before walking away without ever making eye contact.

Bryan gave an apologetic smile and followed him out.

As they walked down to the staging area Bryan scolded Tommy, "You know that you're the reason they're mean to outsiders."

"No, no, no. Don't give me that. He started it."

"*He started it*? Real mature, Tommy."

"He did. He knew you weren't a member and he gave you that attitude for no reason."

"You still didn't need to be so confrontational. Just relax and let's have some fun today."

"Hey, fun is my middle name."

"No, Thomas is your middle name."

"Yeah, you're right about that. Anyway, I'll try to behave."

Bryan and Tommy both spent a few minutes on the range before wandering over to the practice green. Tommy rolled a few long ones across the surface to get a feel for the speed and then took a few short ones around the hole. Each one of his putts from five feet and in clanged the bottom of the miniature pin in the practice hole. He picked up his balls and headed over to the cart while Bryan continued to putt diligently. Tommy didn't spend a lot of time practicing his putts since he didn't have to; he had always been an above average putter. It seemed to be one facet of the game where his confidence really helped him excel. He was aggressive off the tee and with his irons, but in those areas he could be shaky from time to time. On the greens he was one of those guys you never wanted to bet against if he was standing over a four footer.

Eventually Tommy called over to Bryan, "Come on, let's go over to the tee before they give us grief for being late."

"I'm coming," replied Bryan, gathering his balls and putter cover.

They drove back around to the first tee where they saw an older couple chatting with the starter.

"Oh, man," groaned Tommy. "Why do they have to pair us up? There's plenty of room on the course for twosomes."

"They're nuts about their foursomes. You know the drill. Even if there are a few holes open they don't want us flying around and running up behind other groups."

"Yeah, God forbid anybody tries to do anything to speed up the pace of play."

"I hear ya'. Maybe they're only going for nine."

Tommy accelerated the cart and then stopped hard as he approached the tee, drawing stares from the group already there.

Bryan turned to him with a scowl, "I thought you said you were going to behave?"

"I am behaving; just doing a pre-round safety check on the cart. Need to make sure the handling is up to snuff and know that the brakes aren't going to let us down in a pinch."

"Sure."

Byran got out and walked over to the starter. "We're the 9:15 group."

"Do you have your tickets?" the starter asked as he consulted the tee time sheet on his clipboard.

Bryan groped around in his pockets and produced a crumpled up receipt. Tommy walked up and was searching his pockets in vain. The starter and Bryan were both staring at him wanting desperately to hear the sound of paper.

Tommy shrugged, "I don't know where it is. I just had it."

The starter cocked his head, "I need the ticket."

"Jeez. You were in there when I was checking in fifteen minutes ago. Do you really think I didn't pay?"

"Sorry, we need a ticket for everyone," said the starter, not even slightly phased by Tommy's plea.

Tommy shook his head and muttered as he walked back and searched the cart. Unzipping the pockets on his bag he finally was able to locate the evidence. He walked back and handed the paper to the starter.

"Crisis averted," he announced.

"Thank you, sir. We've got to stick to our policies," the starter said as he finally checked off the names on his tee sheet. He turned to the couple standing beside him. "This is Dorothy and Richard Simon. You'll be playing with them today."

Bryan stepped forward and shook hands. "Hi, Mr. and Mrs. Simon, I'm Bryan and this is Tommy."

"Nice to meet you," replied Mrs. Simon sweetly. "You can call me Dot and he goes by Dick."

"Dick and Dot. That's easy enough," said Tommy as he shook their hands. "We're going to be playing the blue tees today. How about you guys?"

"I'll be hitting from the ladies' tees obviously and Dick plays white usually."

"I'll go ahead and play the blue with these fellas today," Mr. Simon piped in.

"Sounds good," said Tommy as he shot Bryan a questioning glance and went to the cart to get his driver. As much as he believed that Bryan should play from tougher tees, he felt just as strongly that players needed to move up if age or the course dictated it. He'd seen plenty of guys make the macho move like Mr. Simon not wanting the youngsters to show him up in front of the wife. He would probably hang with them for a few holes, but as the round wore on the strategy would normally backfire. His game would suffer unnecessarily and he'd look even more feeble. The better bet would be to suck it up and play the tees he was used to. In turn, he'd be hitting approaches with the clubs he knew and he'd be draining a lot more pars. Then the pressure would shift to Tommy and Bryan to try and keep up with his scoring.

Everyone hit solid tee shots and they were on their way. As they drove down the path from the tee Bryan made one more appeal to Tommy. "Alright, Manson. I came out to enjoy my round today. That's going to be tough if I have to babysit you for eighteen holes."

"Babysitter, eh? Well after that egg and sausage biscuit I had for breakfast I may be in need of a diaper change in a few holes."

"Tommy, I mean it. Just ignore these people and play golf."

"Again, how am I supposed to react when the guy is that anal about receipt collection?"

"Just find your ticket and give it to him. Like it's any different at other courses?" pleaded Bryan.

"That guy was on a little power trip. He probably never had any authority in his career and now he takes it upon himself to be defender of the course. He has his pen as his sword and his clipboard as his shield and he'll use every policy at his disposal to protect the club from invaders."

"Pretty dramatic. Just drive. My ball's over there."

"Okay, so are we playing match or stroke today?"

"Why don't we go match. Five bucks a side and five overall."

"Alright. Do I get any strokes?" Tommy asked, already knowing the answer.

"Do you ever?"

"Well after your performance at Stone Ridge I'm not sure what I'm going up against."

"It was one shot. Not even a very good one at that."

"Sure sandbagger."

Despite having different swings and different games, Tommy and Bryan normally posted similar scores. For years they had been able to play straight up in their games.

Both of them hit the green but had long birdie putts. They each lagged them to a few feet and marked to let the Simons putt. Mrs. Simon rolled her putt to a few inches and then knocked it away before picking it up. Mr. Simon had a ten-footer but managed to only get it to about four feet. As he walked up he turned to his wife and said, "That one's inside the leather." He scooped the ball with the back of his putter and joined his wife on the side of the green.

"These are both *inside the leather*. Good-good?" Tommy said facetiously as he bent down to replace his ball. Tommy would concede a six inch put but not much beyond that. He knew shorter putts were his strength and he was always willing to make opponents sweat it out. He stepped up, took a practice swing, and then drained it easily. At this point Bryan wasn't too concerned about their match so he walked up and easily made his as well.

Things went pretty smoothly over the first several holes with everyone hitting decent shots and moving along at a good pace. From Bryan's perspective, he didn't have an issue with their playing partners taking long gimmes or rolling the ball over in the fairway. They were just out for fun and it certainly aided the pace play. Bryan and Tommy had each won a hole and split the other three so they remained all square.

On the fifth green Bryan looked over and saw Tommy striking the classic putting pose: one leg crossed behind the other, one hand on the hip, and the other hand resting his bodyweight on the top of the putter. He was looking at the houses across the way; no doubt evaluating the homes and what they might list for. Holding the pin, Bryan looked back to see the Simons finish out. Mr. Simon had an eight-footer that just made it to the hole and curled in the side. He walked up to the hole to retrieve his ball and Bryan was suddenly struck with a pang of anxiety. *Oh no*, he thought to himself as he quickly replaced the flag and headed off the green.

When they reached the green on the next hole Bryan was immediately on high alert. He tried his best to focus on his game, but missed a makable birdie putt. He was more intent on tending the flag for the Simons' putts. When Dot made hers Bryan quickly fetched the ball from the hole and gave it to her. Dick missed his to the side and it rolled a foot or so past.

"You're going to give him that one aren't you, Mrs. Simon?"

"Oh, of course," she said.

"Here you go," Bryan said as he picked up the ball and handed it to Dick.

He followed the same routine on number seven and planned to do so for the rest of the round if necessary. As he walked up to the eighth green Bryan realized that his approach had rolled off the green and into short rough. After seeing how the ball was sitting he decided to head back over to the cart to grab a wedge. He turned to head back up and saw that the pin was pulled and the others were putting. Mr. Simon lagged his putt to a couple of feet and he heard Tommy tell him it was okay to finish while Tommy lined up his own putt. Instead of picking it up, he addressed the ball and made it. At that point Bryan suddenly felt like he was watching the scene in slow motion and couldn't move fast enough to intervene. Sure enough, instead of bending over to pick the ball up, Mr. Simon jammed the head of his putter into the hole and wrenched it out. Bryan could even see a few blades of grass fly up from the edge of the cup as though a small explosion had gone off. Certainly small in comparison to the one he knew he was about to see. As the scene in Bryan's view suddenly returned to full speed, Tommy leapt up from his crouched position and yelled, "What are you doing?"

The jolt startled Mr. Simon so much that Bryan was afraid he might have a heart attack. At least the course had a set of defibrillator paddles if someone needed to revive him.

Regaining his composure, Dick sheepishly said, "Excuse me. Did I step on your line?"

"No, you just desecrated the hole with your putter."

"I was just getting my ball out. It didn't hurt anything."

"That's not the point. Jamming your putter down into the cup greatly increases the chances that you might damage it. You shouldn't damage the course if you can avoid it; that's just basic etiquette. If you're putting to a cup with torn edges it can mean the difference between making it or missing it," Tommy said, clearly ready for a sermon.

"Well, I'm always careful not to hit the edges. Besides, there are a lot more serious breaches of etiquette than that." Dick responded as he glared at Tommy.

"Okay, if you say so. I'm not sure where that grass came from that I saw fly up."

Mrs. Simon sensed the growing tension and stepped in, "Now Dick, let's not get all excited about nothing. Just say you're sorry and let's finish up."

"I'm not apologizing! I'll pick up the ball however I damn well please," Dick retorted, clearly not interested in taking advice from a non-member.

Bryan arrived at the green and also tried to intervene. "Tommy it's time to putt," he said while waving his fingers across his throat signaling Tommy to cease fire.

Tommy shook his head and bent down to line his putt up again. "I hope he wasn't a proctologist," Tommy muttered loud enough for the Simons to hear.

Dick scowled over his shoulder as Mrs. Simon led him away by the elbow.

Tommy casually walked up to his putt and sank it as though nothing has just happened.

"You couldn't just let it go could you?" Bryan asked as the walked off the green.

"What do you think? Someone's got to put an end to the madness. Why can't he just get one of those big suction cups for the end of his putter grip?"

"I know Tommy. It's just sacrilege. You must get Christmas cards from all of the superintendents in town," Bryan said, throwing up his hands. "I was hoping to make it through the round without your drama but now we're screwed. I can't believe I let the hole go unsupervised. I should have just putted instead of going for my wedge."

"What? You knew?" said Tommy, stopping Bryan with the shaft of his putter.

"Yeah, I saw him do it a few holes back when you weren't looking," Bryan replied as he shoved Tommy's putter out of his way and continued to the cart.

"That makes you an accomplice,' Tommy said, standing in place with his hands on his hips.

"Let's go and get on with this round that's going to be chocked full of good feelings."

As they arrived at the ninth tee they could already sense the cold shoulder. The Simons were sitting in their cart slightly ahead of the tee box. Mrs. Simon turned and let them know that Dick had already hit his drive. Bryan and Tommy teed off and they drove off without a word. Bryan tried to break the ice by complimenting Mrs. Simon's drive, but it was pretty transparent and didn't change the mood.

On the green the tension started to build as Mr. Simon lined up his putt. He came up a little short and Mrs. Simon quickly knocked it back to him before he could sink the remainder. He gave her a look that seemed to indicate that he had wanted to finish it and retrieve it as he saw fit. She flashed a look back that indicated the game was over. She seemed like a nice lady, but now she was laying down the law.

As Bryan finished the hole, Mrs. Simon walked up to him. "We're only playing nine holes today so this is it for us. It was nice to meet you," she said to Bryan while giving Tommy just a friendly nod.

"I hope he didn't drive you off," Bryan said, motioning to Tommy.

"Oh, no. Not at all. Take care."

Mr. Simon gave a half-hearted goodbye from the edge of the green and they headed off.

"That went well," Bryan said sarcastically to Tommy.

"Hey, look at the bright side, now we have the back side to ourselves and I can focus on taking your money," replied Tommy, still unfazed.

"Tommy, that was just embarrassing. This isn't my favorite course, but I don't mind playing here occasionally. I'm not sure if I'll be able to show my face here anymore."

"Do you think they'll put our pictures up in the locker room on the black-balled board?"

"Mine? No. Yours? Definitely. As far as my money is concerned you were one down on the front nine so you're already in the hole."

"I'll be changing that soon enough," said Tommy confidently.

"I don't think so."

Normally Bryan's game suffered if he was mad. Tommy knew this well and expected the incident with the Simons to grate on Bryan, at least for the next few holes. However, instead of dwelling on it he quickly put it out of his mind. He found himself mentally replaying the round with Garris and quickly found a calm that solidified his swing. After halving the tenth hole, Bryan won the eleventh with a par and then carded back-to-back birdies to take the next two holes.

By the fourteenth hole Tommy knew he was in trouble and needed to make something happen. Bryan had out driven him on the reachable par five and he was first to play in the fairway. Tommy knew he could reach the green, but it was guarded on the front right side by sizable lake. He stood next to his ball debating clubs as Bryan watched for the decision. When Tommy pulled the headcover off of his three wood Bryan crossed his arms and looked to the hole. Tommy took a few swings and then stepped back to line it up again. He took his stance and paused just a little longer than usual before swinging away.

A split second after impact Bryan heard Tommy grunt, "Go! Go!" Bryan stood motionless as he waited for the ball to enter his field of vision up against the bright, blue sky. It was a towering shot, but it was ballooning and drifting right. His gaze shifted down to the dark surface of the lake and he managed a slight smile as he saw a small, white plume erupt well short of land.

"Hmm. I think I'll lay up here," Bryan said as he walked to the back of the cart.

"Chicken," Tommy said, still shaking his head from his shot.

"A smart chicken though," replied Bryan as he casually addressed his ball and hit it in the dead center of the fairway about one hundred yards short of the green.

Bryan knocked his next shot on and won with an easy two-putt par. As they walked off the green he brought Tommy up to speed. "That puts you four down with four to go on the overall. Three down on the back side so you're just hanging by your fingernails there. You feeling like you've got a big comeback in you today?"

"No. I think that would be a bad bet. I think the smart chicken would take his punches and live to fight another day."

"What about Mr. Step-up-to-the-blues?" chided Bryan.

"Today I'm Mr. Hang-on-to-the-green," Tommy said as he padded his pocket.

Tommy only managed to halve one of the remaining holes so Bryan's domination of the day was complete. As they unloaded their clubs in the parking lot Tommy fished his wallet out of his bag to settle up. "So where did that come from?" he asked as he pushed some bills towards Bryan.

"What? You can't handle the new me? You're the one who was lobbying for it so you're the one who's going to have to deal with it."

"You must have misinterpreted what I was saying. I didn't mean you should pummel *me* on the golf course."

"Sorry, my bad. To avoid confusion in the future maybe you should just keep your mouth shut."

"See, now that's just being rude; that's not being assertive."

"Okay. So are you up for some lunch today?"

"I probably need to get going. I have to get cleaned up and meet Tina this afternoon," said Tommy, looking at his watch. "But I've got enough time for a quick beer here at the clubhouse."

"In there? The Simons have probably gathered the members and they'll be waiting for us with pitchforks."

"Come on. I'll fight them off. And I promise not to offend anyone else. I've already hit my quota for the day."

5

B ack at work during the week, Bryan found himself wallowing through his normal tasks with the hours moving by at a painfully slow pace. Although he didn't want to admit it, he somewhat missed having a big project to work on. It livened up his job and certainly made time go by faster.

On Wednesday afternoon Bryan's phone rang. On the caller ID display Bryan saw that it was an outside number that he didn't recognize.

"Hello, this is Bryan."

"Bryan, it's Jim Garris from over at Stone Ridge."

"Oh, hi Mr. Garris. How are you doing?"

"It's just Jim, remember?"

"I know. Sorry, Jim."

"So what do you have going on Saturday?"

"Nothing at the moment."

"Do you want to come over for a round with me and a few buddies?"

Bryan hadn't considered playing with Garris's friends, but figured they couldn't be too bad. "Sure, what time were you thinking?"

"We've got a tee time at 8:05 and a spot for you. Does that work?"

"Definitely. I'm not barging in on your regular group am I?"

"Nope. Most of the winter league games are over and our ranks thin out a lot this time of year as the snowbirds head north. Don't worry, you're not stepping on any toes."

"Alright, count me in," said Bryan.

"We'll see you then," replied Garris, before hanging up.

***

On Saturday morning Bryan was excited to be playing Stone Ridge again, but was a bit nervous about the circumstances. He felt comfortable about playing with Garris, however, he felt like he was going to have to impress Jim's friends. He assumed that Garris had told them about the double eagle so they would probably have high expectations for his game.

Today Bryan was a bit more attentive to the speed bumps as he headed up the entry road. As he approached the guard house today he marveled at how well fortified it looked. There were enormous white pillars at each corner of the small, stone-clad building. Behind was a towering wall that anchored the wrought iron gates on either side. The gates themselves were probably eight feet high with an ornate Stone Ridge crest in the middle. Across the top was a row of twisted spikes that did little more than prevent birds from landing. Entrances like this certainly added to sales appeal and gave the residents a feeling of security, but in reality all they did was inconvenience friends and drive up the homeowners' dues.

As Bryan pulled up he was greeted by a different guard today. "Good morning young man, what can we do for you today?" he asked cheerfully.

"Here for golf today. Joining Mr. Garris."

"And your name?" he asked, consulting the all powerful clipboard of knowledge.

"Bryan Minton."

"Super, got you right here. Do you know the way to the clubhouse?"

"Yep, been here before."

"Excellent. You have a good day out there."

"Will do," Bryan said as he rolled up his window and headed through.

Bryan left his clubs at the bag drop and parked. He checked in at the pro shop and they let him know that Garris was out on the range. Bryan went out the back door and found his clubs already loaded on a cart with Garris's; he grabbed a few and headed up the slight slope to the practice ground.

"Good morning, Bryan," Garris said as Bryan approached.

"Hey, Jim. Thanks for having me out," replied Bryan, shaking hands.

"Go ahead and hit some. We've got enough time so don't rush. We're going to be playing with Bill Robalo. He just went in for some coffee. Unfortunately our fourth had to drop out; had to take his wife to physical therapy."

"Sounds good," Bryan said as he started taking some practice swings.

Bryan worked his way through about forty or fifty balls and was very pleased with what he saw. Jim had just finished wiping down his clubs so the two of them walked to the putting green together.

They each started with some short ones, working around the practice holes in a circle.

"So it looks like you've had that putter a while," Garris said, motioning to Bryan's club.

"Yeah, it comes and goes but overall I've been pretty happy with it. I've probably had it for at least fifteen years. I think I've only re-gripped it once. There are so many new shapes and styles coming out all the time, but putting is so mental that you just need to be confident when you look down."

"You are certainly wise beyond your years. We've got guys out here that change putters more often than I change socks. A lot of them stick with the same woods and irons, but they just think that if they keep trying they'll find that magical putter that will automatically put the ball in the hole every time. Most guys give them away or sell them at a yard sale, but there are a few collectors. A guy down the street from me has a museum in his garage. We all give him grief about it, but at some point they'll probably be worth a lot of money."

"My dad has churned through his fair share over the years. He's tried to send a few of them my way but I always tell him that if they didn't work for him they probably won't work for me either," replied Bryan, still rolling putts.

"Here comes Bill. Hey Bill, this is Bryan."

"Ahh, this is the guy with the double eagle," Bill said, extending his hand to Bryan.

"That's me," Bryan acknowledged, shaking hands and feeling a bit embarrassed already.

"He looks like an F.B.L.B., Jim," Bill said, examining Bryan.

"F.B.L.B.? Do I even want to know? " asked Bryan.

"Flat-bellied, limber-back," laughed Bill. "The kind of guys we were a long, long time ago."

"You guys ready to go?" asked Garris.

"I am now," Bill said, holding up his coffee.

"All set," said Bryan.

They headed up to the first tee and checked in with the starter. Being with two regular members, no one was worried about Bryan's ticket today. The morning air was still comfortable, but by this point in the year the humidity was quickly starting to rise. Soon the regular summer afternoon rains would arrive and each morning the moisture would be baking off the ground. Early mornings such as this would become particularly oppressive. In the summer Bryan liked to play later in the day when the air temperature was higher but the ground level humidity dropped and the breeze kicked up.

Wandering over, Garris asked Bryan, "So do you want to play for a few bucks today? No obligation, I just thought I'd ask before we teed off."

"Sure. As long as the stakes aren't too high."

"Don't worry about that. We keep it very modest. Besides, Bill here is as cheap as they come," Garris said smiling, clearly trying to goad Bill a little. "He's never bought a golf ball in his life. He's a professional ball hawker; carries a fifty-foot retriever with him."

"Hey, it's twenty-five feet for your information. And you never seem to complain about it when I'm dredging one of your wayward shots out of the drink for you."

"Anyway, no matter how well you play you're never going to take much of his money. Since we're a threesome today we'll play two on one, switching every six holes. If the single wins the hole he gets two points and if the pair wins they each get one point. Most points wins the pot. Everybody in for ten bucks?"

"Good for me," said Bryan.

"Jim, if I have to pay you can I settle up in golf balls?" joked Bill.

"I've got plenty of balls, Bill. Only cash will be accepted."

"So how many strokes is this guy giving us?" Bill asked, pointing his driver at Bryan. "I know about your double eagle, but what's your handicap?"

"I try to enter most of my scores over at Oak Run and the system has me right at a seven now," said Bryan proudly.

Bill whistled, "Boy, that's not too bad. Right now I'm at a thirteen and Jim's at a twelve so we'll play straight up. Five or six strokes can be pretty tough to make up so what about you playing the blues and we play the whites? It's about four hundred yards difference, but most of that is on just a few holes."

"Sounds like a decent trade, I'll play the blues," Bryan said with a smile, thinking about what Tommy had said at dinner.

"Alright, we'll go me and Bryan first six, then me and Bill, then Bill and Bryan," said Garris.

The fairway had cleared so Bryan sauntered back to the blue tee while Garris and Robalo edged off to the side. Bryan had loosened up on the range but noticed he was tensing up as he pierced the damp grass with his tee. He took a few extra practice swings to try and relax. He took a deep breath and addressed his ball. His back swing was solid and smooth but things went wrong as he headed down. As soon as he made contact he knew that he'd over-steered and the ball headed right. Bryan watched as his push crested and then fell with a thud in a bunker well right of the fairway.

"What was that?" he asked no one in particular.

"You're okay. Don't worry about it," said Garris as he walked to his set of markers. He teed his ball without hesitation and then slapped it nicely down the middle of the fairway.

Bill was up next. He took a few practice swings and Bryan wondered what kind of shot to expect. He clearly didn't have the golf swing that Garris did, but he had huge forearms that lead Bryan to believe he could put the ball wherever he wanted. He stood over his ball, paused, and then unleashed his unorthodox swing on the ball. Sure enough, he hit a controlled, rising fade that carried past Garris and found the right center of the fairway.

Bryan headed to the cart and tossed his driver into his bag. "Sorry about that, partner," he said to Garris as they drove off.

"Shake it off. We're just out here for fun."

When they got to the bunker Bryan saw that he actually had a decent lie. He walked into the sand and sized up his options. The prudent play would have been to punch out and try and hit his third shot close. But since he had Garris in the fairway he decided to have a go at the green. Just like on the tee his swing started fine but then quickly went awry. He tried to pull up at impact and skulled it right off the lip. It flopped over the top and died a quick death in the rough beyond the bunker. It was a shot he'd seen lots of other golfers hit and it was one of the most painful sights in golf. Although his back was to Garris, he could sense that Jim had winced in the cart while watching.

"That's a tough shot to pull off, especially on the first hole," Jim said, trying to rationalize Bryan's poor choice.

Bryan's shot had barely covered twenty yards so he had the indignity of having to hit again. His ball was sitting down in the thick, damp rough so his chances of getting to the green were even worse than on his last shot. A voice of reason kicked in and he grabbed a wedge. Bryan simply lined up and hacked it back into the fairway, finally getting past Garris's drive.

"That was a good call," Garris said approvingly.

Garris had played this hole hundreds of time over the years and knew exactly what club to take without even measuring the distance. He stepped up, took an easy practice swing, and then hit a good looking shot right into the middle of the green.

"Good ball," admired Bryan.

Bryan's next shot looked good in the air, but landed sadly five yards short of the green. He wondered where he'd left the swing that he had on the range just a short time ago.

It was finally Bill's turn and he struck his approach to about ten feet.

"Oh great," said Bryan, sensing that they had already lost the first hole.

"Don't get worked up, Bryan. You haven't seen him putt before. I can assure you he's gone through a lot of putters in his career."

When they arrived at the green Bryan took a couple of clubs while the others walked up with just putters in hand. Bryan had left himself a tricky little chip. He hit what he thought would be a good shot, but it landed a few feet in front of the hole and then rolled fifteen feet past. He now had a tough downhill putt coming back; thus far his course management was really lacking.

Garris was first to putt. He had a chance for a birdie but it was about twenty-five feet over a slight crest and then down the hill. He looked it over and then lagged it beautifully to less than a foot.

"Jeez, how do you hit that putt on the first hole?" groaned Bill.

Garris tapped in and smiled at Bryan.

At this point Bryan just wanted the hole to be over. He eased his ball down the hill and then backhanded the short comeback for a seven.

Bill's birdie was only ten feet or so, but it had both the downhill and a strong right to left break in it. Garris's easy two-putt had made it a lot more difficult. Bill was clearly nervous and stabbed the shot short and low of the hole. When it came to rest he still had a couple of feet left; definitely not a gim'me. After lining it up he stood over it way too long before missing the cup by three or four inches. He knocked that one in and grumbled under his breath. He placed the ball back at the spot of his second putt and proceeded to miss again on the other side of hole.

"Don't wear yourself out, Bill," said Garris. "We've got seventeen more to go."

Bill walked to his cart still talking to himself.

"So you pretty much got a case study of Bill in one hole there Bryan," Garris said as he jotted down their scores on the card clipped to the cart's steering wheel.

"He can't putt can he?"

"Nope. His hands and his head are both a mess. The guy is great tee to green; if he could putt he'd be a single digit handicapper. Those big old Popeye arms work fine with a driver, but he has no touch on the green. On the mental side he's dug himself into a hole over the years."

"I feel bad for him."

"I used to, but he needs to accept that it's just part of golf. It can happen even to the best players. The physical part he can't do much about so he needs to deal with that and do the best he can. Pick a putter, pick a stroke, and go with it."

"Having you grind him down probably doesn't help either. That was a great putt back there, partner."

"Thanks."

The rest of the first six holes went pretty much the same way. Bryan settled down a little and won one hole, but he still wasn't on his game. Bill also managed to win a hole, but Garris was clearly leading the pack.

On the second six holes Garris switched to carrying Bill instead of Bryan. Jim's game was very steady and even when it looked like they might be out of a hole he just stuck to his gameplan.

Despite not playing particularly well, Bryan was enjoying his round. It was always good to play a course with someone who knew it well. Bryan and Garris talked about the game and the course and not much else, which seemed to be fine with both of them. Garris did offer a few well timed words of encouragement when Bryan seemed to need it most. He could tell Bryan's game was off and he did a good job of keeping Bryan on an even keel. It would have been embarrassing for Bryan if he'd lost his cool, especially playing as a guest with one of Jim's friends.

Bill seemed like a good guy but Bryan didn't get to talk to him too much since he was riding on his own. The two of them were standing together on the green at number fifteen waiting for Garris to come up when Bill gave him some insight into Jim's game. "I think we're going to have to adjust Jim's handicap faster if he keeps playing like this."

"Has he been sandbagging?" asked Bryan jokingly.

"Not intentionally. For a while he wasn't doing well and his scores were really rising. Now he's regained some strength and stamina and he's playing more like the five or six handicapper he was. It takes a while for his scores to catch up though," explained Bill.

"Was it something serious?"

"Definitely cancer, but I'm not sure of the type or the extent. He doesn't talk about it much. He doesn't want people worrying about him and he certainly never wants any pity. Physically he appears a lot better now, but with cancer you can't always tell from the outside."

"Wow, that's a shame."

"Don't tell him I told you. I just figured you should know."

"Thanks, Bill."

Bryan's game did warm up down the final stretch, but as expected it was too little too late. Garris continued his dominance and hit some clutch shots. He won four of the last holes. On seventeen Bryan only managed to back up his double eagle with a par, which wasn't even good enough to beat Garris's birdie.

By the time they'd reached the eighteenth green the game was already over. Bryan and Garris were standing to the side as Bill sized up a forty foot birdie opportunity. Just off the green was one of the massive new homes complete with a two-story pool cage area. Several boys were playing in the pool; splashing, screaming, and yelling.

"See here's the problem with these houses," Garris said to Bryan in a hushed voice. "You've got that monstrosity right on top of the green. They have us looking right into their house and we have them raising all that racket right next to the eighteenth green."

"I agree wholeheartedly," said Bryan. "But golf course homes continue to sell. Just ask my friend Tommy. I wouldn't want golfers in my backyard either."

Bill lagged his putt well short of the hole; definite three-putt range.

Bryan really wanted to finish with a par, but his putt slid a foot or two past after just missing the right edge of the cup. He quickly tapped in for bogey and picked up his ball.

Garris went through his normal routine: getting a read, taking a practice swing, and then lining up. The putt had a fair amount of break but was probably one Garris had seen before out here. He set his feet and drew the putter back. Just as he started his stroke one of the boys in the pool yelled "cannonball!" and landed with a tremendous splash. Amazingly, Garris didn't even flinch. He completed his motion and sent the ball rolling smoothly at the hole - dead center for par.

"Wow that was clutch," said Bryan.

"I think he must be deaf," Bill said quietly as he lined up his chance to tie Jim with a par.

"I heard *that*, Bill. By the way you need this to halve the hole with me."

Bill fidgeted over his ball and proceeded to miss by a wide margin.

Garris replaced the pin and shook hands with Bryan.

"That was a solid round, Jim."

"Thanks. Next time I know you'll make me work a bit harder for it."

"That was a great putt there, Jim," Bill said shaking hands. He pulled a large slab of bills from his pocket and unsnapped the clip. "Here's my ten dollar contribution. I could have just given it to you on the first tee and saved all of the pain in between. Your game is getting better than your handicap so I'm getting a few strokes next time."

"Alright. Or maybe I'll just let you play the ladies' tees."

"You're a funny old man aren't ya'?" joked Bill.

After walking back to the carts Bryan found his wallet and pulled out a ten to give to Garris. "Here you go, Jim."

"Oh, that's okay, Bryan. You can keep it. I just take Bill's money for the fun of it."

"Oh, no. I insist. No point in betting if you don't settle up. I think that is rule number one in the Unofficial Rules of Golf."

"Alright. I can appreciate that. I'm starving. Are you up for a free lunch?"

Glancing at his watch, Bryan replied, "Sure, I'm pretty hungry too."

"Bill, are you staying for lunch?" Garris called.

"No, not today. I'm heading out to meet the wife," Bill said as he walked back around his cart. Putting his hand on Bryan's shoulder he said, "Bryan, thanks again for playing with us geezers, it was fun."

"Thanks for having me. I enjoy the course and I had a good time."

"You guys have a good lunch. Jim, I'll talk to you this week."

"See you, Bill," waved Garris.

Garris drove back to the clubhouse where they dropped Bryan's clubs on the rack and turned the cart over to an attendant who took Jim's bag to storage. After a stop in the locker room to get cleaned up, Jim took Bryan through to one of the members' dining areas.

"This is nice. I haven't been in here before," Bryan said, taking in the atmosphere.

"They have a couple of separate rooms off the main one that they use. Although it's technically not men only in this one I don't think I've ever seen a female member in here. It's pretty much understood that this is ours and they have one across the way."

"You have to be politically correct even at a private club these days."

"Luckily no one here seems to care about that. You're not going to see a group of ladies come in here to make some kind of statement. People here are grown up enough to accept that sometimes men just want to hang out with men and sometimes women just want to be around other women. The club has plenty of inclusive events to keep everyone happy."

Their waiter arrived with some drinks and quickly took their lunch order before leaving them to their discussion.

"So is the membership reasonably content here now? It seems like a lot of the clubs in town are starting to have some infighting for various reasons."

"Various *reasons*, but all the same root cause: money."

"Yeah, I suppose you're right."

"I think I told you about some of the disputes a while back, but right now things are on pretty solid ground. I'm sure something will come along and spoil it soon enough. You mentioned that your father is a member over at Oak Run. How are they doing?"

"Not too bad. The rift that they always seem to have is between the serious golfers and the social players. Guys like my dad like to keep the course playing tough while the infidels want to have it more forgiving."

"That's pretty common," agreed Garris. "There are some guys here who say they want it tough but don't have the game to justify it. For them it's just an ego thing. They want to brag about how tough their home course is. So besides our fine fairways where else do you like to play, Bryan?"

"Oh, pretty much anywhere that will have me. I play all around, especially in the summer when it's cheap and everywhere is wide open. One course that I like to play is Lakeside Links. It has a lot of character and you can walk the course. It seems like true golf when you play out there. I just wish they would keep it in better shape. The group that owns it is clearly trying to take as much out of it as they can without spending anything. The place has a lot of potential; it's a great location and there's plenty of room to update most of the holes without completely changing the course."

"I've played there a few times. It is fun to play, but you're right about the conditions; most of the guys here won't play it."

"So what about you, Jim? Ever think about defecting to another club?"

"Nah. Not at this point. They'll bury me here."

"I'm not sure that's legal."

"No, but I've already chosen cremation; they can just sift me into one of the bunkers. I used to be surprised by some people's final wishes, but not anymore."

"If you're going to primarily play one course this is a nice place to do it," Bryan said.

"When I was working, especially later in my career, I traveled a fair amount and had a chance to play a lot of the big name courses. Many of our clients had corporate memberships to high end private courses so I checked off plenty of those too."

"So what was the most memorable?"

"It's got to be Augusta. It was in pristine condition, all of the flowers in bloom, and we had absolutely perfect weather. I think I was more nervous about the forecast than playing the actual round. I was so afraid that we'd get rained out or something and I'd miss my chance. It was both a great course to play and a great experience."

"So do you still have that connection to get back out? Maybe bring a guest with you?" prodded Bryan.

"Unfortunately no. That was a one time deal. That's the kind of place where if you're too eager or ask too much you won't ever get invited. You have to carefully let it be known that you're a decent golfer and that you'd be willing to play if the opportunity presented itself."

"Any others that really stick out?"

"I played Pebble a few times; you've got to play there at least once. Pine Valley was memorable and we made a couple of trips to Scotland, definitely worth it if you have a few weeks and some extra money to spend."

"It'll probably be a while before that happens then," shrugged Bryan.

"Ahh, you're young. I'm sure you've got a long career ahead of you and you'll get to places that you think are out of reach now. So what do you do?"

"I'm a desk monkey. I pretty much move paper from one side of my desk to the other."

"Sounds exciting. Do they pay you in bananas?"

"Might as well. I'm an analyst over at Chambers Data Systems."

"Analyst, eh? What do you analyze?"

"Great question. A lot of times I'm not sure; it seems like we're just analyzing someone else's analysis. After a while you lose track of what was being analyzed in the first place. I'm sure you think I'm just being facetious, but sadly enough I'm not. To answer your question about what we look at, it's usually processes and systems data, hence the company name. Chambers works with many types of companies, however, our group deals mainly with insurance companies and financial service entities."

"Do you do a lot of number crunching?" asked Garris.

"Sometimes. We certainly generate lots of reports. The two segments we often work with are smaller companies that don't have their own resources and bigger companies that want an independent set of eyes to review things. They're looking for ways to save money and also mitigate risk."

"I get the sense that you aren't fulfilling your life's ambitions there right now."

"Definitely not. It's a job, but I'm not sure how much longer I'll last there. We'll see. So what did you do for a career, Jim?"

"Early on I tried a lot of different things. I worked in retail, ran a restaurant, and spent a short time working for the government."

"CIA?"

"No, desk monkey. My dad was a career civil service and government man and he wanted me to follow in his footsteps. If you think corporate America is bad you should spend some time working for the government; it'll really put things in perspective for you. Eventually I landed a job with a small petroleum company. I started off just doing office work but gradually worked my way into sales, which could be a lot more lucrative. Along the way I met my wife and started our family so that job basically turned into my career. Our company grew by buying a few other companies then an even bigger fish came along and swallowed us up. Overall, I enjoyed it and I did pretty well financially so I don't have too many regrets about it."

"And it sounds like you got some nice fringes in terms of golf too," added Bryan.

"Yeah, can't complain there. I was lucky in that during most of my career it was accepted and even encouraged that you did business on the golf course. It seems to me that that's not always the case anymore."

"I know some of our executives get in their share of rounds, but it's kept pretty quiet. They've just taken all of the fun out of it," lamented Bryan.

"I first started playing golf because of my job. I saw how many of our senior people belonged to clubs and played with clients so I just assumed that it was something I would have to do. So I picked up some used clubs and started taking lessons.

I'll never forget a round I played with my boss at his club. He invited me and one of the sales guys out on the weekend. I had already been playing for about a year and was really starting to get the hang of the game. I didn't want to make a fool of myself so I sandbagged a little and told them I only played once in a while. That was, in fact, the truth since I practiced a lot but only made it on a course every month or two. Apparently I overdid it since I stomped on my co-worker and actually gave my boss a run for his money. I was having so much fun playing on such a nice course that I just shot the lights out. I had been playing on some of the local cow pastures so it was like I was playing a different game. I had an eighty-four, which was my best score ever by five strokes. My boss shot an eighty-two and the other guy didn't break a hundred even with some liberal scoring. On top of that I carried myself well on the course, which impressed my boss more than my score. From there on I was the one that got invited back and taken out on client rounds."

"Did you ever want to play golf when you were younger?" Bryan asked.

"Not really. I followed it a little bit, but it was nothing like today. It was still mainly a country club sport. Also, my dad didn't play until he retired so I didn't have anyone leading me into the game."

"My dad used to take me out to the range and sometimes we'd play an executive course, but he never forced the game on me. I began to take it more seriously during high school when I started playing more competitively with friends. I've always enjoyed it. I just wish I had the time to work on my game a little more in order to drop my scores another notch."

"Yeah, and once you do that you'll want to do it again. That's pretty much all of us; that's golf, Bryan."

"True. So you mentioned your family, how many kids do you have? If you don't mind me asking."

"Two daughters. One about your age and the other a bit older. We had, Nancy, the older one, not too long after we got married and weren't sure if we'd have any more. But as time went by and we were doing better financially we decided to give it another shot."

"Were you hoping for a boy?"

"I'd be lying if I said no, but I didn't love the girls any less because of it. Overall they were both good kids; however, they are very different. Unfortunately my relationship with them hasn't been as good as it should have been. They were always closer to their mother, which is certainly natural, and I haven't seen them nearly as often since she died. They've always had some issues between them as well; a big part of which is probably the age difference. When Nancy was young things were a little tighter so she didn't get a lot of the things that Lisa did. We tried not to spoil Lisa, but that's just how things happen. Nancy's always had a chip on her shoulder and is very independent. Lisa's much easier going and willing to rely on others, especially her parents. She doesn't always make the best choices though, and we've often butted heads about her level of responsibility.

After my wife died I pretty much told Lisa it was time for her to start flying on her own. At the time she was living with some deadbeat, another one of her poor choices, and we had been fighting with her about that for a while. So sure enough she goes and gets pregnant. I did my best to reach out to her and offer to help but spite is a pretty strong emotion. I know it's tough love but maybe it's what she finally needed to make her grow up. So now I have a grandson that I only see occasionally. We're still working on it, but it takes time."

"Wow. That's too bad."

"I'm sorry. That was probably a lot more than you wanted to know about my family."

"Oh, please. We all have drama somewhere in the family."

"So do you have any brothers or sisters, Bryan?"

"Just one sister. We've always gotten along pretty well. In most cases I don't think you have as much sibling rivalry with a brother and sister as you do with two boys or two girls."

"What about your folks? Do you get along with them still? If you don't mind *me* asking."

"For the most part. My dad is pretty mellow so we've always been friends. My mom is a bit tougher to deal with. She's quite obsessed with her image and sometimes it's too much. She was always into the social scene and then somewhere along the line she started wandering into politics."

"Is your mom Carol Minton, the one on the City Council?"

"Yes, can we count on your vote in the fall?" joked Bryan.

"I hadn't made the name connection."

"I don't advertise it normally. You never know who she may have upset with one of her votes. You can't keep everyone happy; although politicians certainly try. She likes her current post, but definitely has aspirations to climb higher."

"There are some other things that I would have liked to do, but I never had a desire to enter the public eye. Especially in this day and age; every single thing you do can be scrutinized instantly by the rest of the world."

"My mom is all about appearances. Even when it's just us around it seems like she is on; doesn't want to slip up."

"So who else do you play golf with? Do you have a regular group?"

"No, it's pretty much whoever I can cobble together. So many of my friends have gotten married and a lot of them are having kids so it keeps getting tougher to get guys to play on a regular basis."

"Hey, there are worse reasons. You get to be my age and they start dying."

"Valid point. Nonetheless, if I ever get married and have kids I plan to still get some rounds in. There are a couple of guys that I know from my old job that I still play with fairly often. Then there's Tommy. He's the guy that was supposed to be out here the day that we first played. He's a realtor so he has to work on the weekends a lot, but he's still good for a game most of the time."

"Where do you know him from?"

"We go way back. We grew up in the same neighborhood and although he's a few years older than me we were pretty good friends. Also, people regularly would mistake us for brothers since our last names were similar. Over the years we went our separate ways, but bumped into each other a few times. He had taken up golf along the way so we got together to play and that's what renewed our friendship. He's a good guy, but like any friend you've got to be able to put up with his quirks. His attitude about things can be quite different from mine and he's always harping on me for being too uptight."

"You don't seem that uptight to me. Of course I'm old so that might not make me your best defense."

"Well sometimes he's right, but I was probably born with some of it, so that can be tough to change."

"I saw that with my kids. There were a lot of characteristics that they showed early on that have continued to this day. You change what you can and deal with the rest."

"In Tommy's case that's probably his name."

"What's wrong with his name?" asked Garris, raising an eyebrow.

"C. Thomas Manson."

"Let me guess; the C is for Charles?"

"Yup."

"Ouch."

"He was named about a year too soon. Charles was the first name of his grandfather on his mom's side. They wanted to honor his name and in 1968 there wasn't anything particularly wrong with it when you added it to Manson. So after the murder spree they thought about changing it, however, Grandpa Charles wasn't too keen on that idea. To keep the family peace they left it alone, but everyone started calling him Tommy; except for his proud grandpa of course. Since it is his legal name it still haunts him occasionally. Even when he was a little kid he would notice the strange reactions of other kids' parents when they'd see it on something at school. I think some people were genuinely concerned that he might try to recruit their kids to join The Family. Luckily my parents only knew him as Tommy so I was allowed to play with him."

"They say that kids can be so cruel; most of the time it's just the parents. Did he ever consider changing it when he got older?"

"Sure, but by that time he had made it through the worst of the teasing years. At this point the crimes have faded in a lot of people's minds so it's more ironic than horrifying to close a real estate deal with Charles Manson."

Bryan and Garris finished their lunches and talked for another hour. He thanked Garris several more times for the round and lunch and they agreed to play again soon. Bryan liked the idea of having someone different to play with; however, he was concerned that he might not be playing with Garris for long. Bryan had a suspicion that Jim might be headed in the same direction as many of his golf buddies at Stone Ridge.

6

As summer set in, Bryan's outlook continued to brighten. Work was a little better, he was playing a lot more golf, and the longer days always seemed to cheer him up. Still, Bryan couldn't let go of all of his worries. Things at Chambers almost seemed too quiet, which usually meant it was time for some kind of shake-up. Coming up on the calendar were two big events: the midyear company meeting and the annual Fourth of July picnic. Usually these were both good indicators of where things were headed for the company.

In the days leading up to the meeting, rumors would invariably start shooting around among the employees. Most of them this year revolved around if and when the company might go public. Although the majority of employees knew that the likelihood of an announcement in this forum was highly unlikely, the dreams of new wealth and prosperity kept the hopes alive.

Bryan, who had no such fantasies of easy money, spent his time preparing in other ways. This year he was helping Greg Larson, a friend from another department, organize the Chambers Derby. The Derby was a variation of BS Bingo, where employees would have a bingo card filled with words or phrases that they thought the executives would use most frequently during the meeting. Employees had tried bingo, but no one had ever had the guts—or the complete lack of concern for their job—to stand up in the meeting and yell "Bingo!" So the last few years they set up a pool and let players choose their top three "horses" to win, place, or show. Because a lot of players submitted similar entries, Greg applied his skills to set up a spreadsheet and create odds. Greg had been a math major and enjoyed handling the numbers for their backroom wagering. Bryan had a reputation as a trustworthy guy, so he was responsible for the money. From the pool of players they chose three judges. These three were like boxing judges that tried to decide who landed the most punches. With a week to go before the meeting, Greg stopped by to see Bryan and review the field.

"So, Bryan, are you getting excited?" asked Greg, leaning against a file cabinet in Bryan's cubicle.

"I'm just giddy. How are the horses looking?"

"The odds-on favorite so far has to be *robust*. People must have actually been reading some of our corporate memos this year and noticed how it's been used to death. Just about everyone has it as one of their picks, so the odds are driving its value way down. Some of the other top picks are *paradigm, leverage, stakeholder,* and *forward looking*. It's interesting how *leverage* has really morphed from having a negative taint to being used in a positive light. When you were talking about debt, too much leverage was a bad thing. Now you can leverage everything in the company: leverage our brand, leverage our client base, leverage our skill sets. Hey, Bryan, we really need to work on leveraging your file cabinet here to help the company succeed. We should also look into leveraging the water cooler to better hydrate our employees."

"It takes all my effort just to leverage my butt out of bed each day to come to work. I harbor a robust hatred toward this place, and I'm looking forward to a new paradigm that doesn't involve me."

"I'll give you three out of four. We were looking for *forward looking*, not *looking forward*."

"My bad."

"Based on a lot of the entries, there seems to be a tilt toward bets on IPO-speak."

"Not you too," groaned Bryan.

"What?" asked Greg innocently.

"You're part of the IPO conspiracy now?"

"No. I'm just saying that I'm listening to my people, and that's what I'm hearing. Even an old-school phrase like *synergy* is getting dusted off by a lot of people; I think that bodes well for some type of M&A activity in the air."

"I like *synergy*. It's kind of a cool word; unfortunately in most cases where it gets used, it never actually happens. It's never really one plus one equals three; it's more like one plus one equals two, then you fire one and get one to equal the work of two."

"As a math major, I can appreciate that analysis," Greg said, nodding at Bryan's logic.

"I'm glad we've moved on from some of my other favorites. I guess the good thing is that if something gets used excessively, it also dies faster. It seemed like a while back *empower* was omnipresent, and now it's six feet under. *Win-win* and *think outside the box* held on for a while, but now they're just punch lines: 'You lost your job and your wife? Hey, sounds like a win-win to me!' or 'Wow! Your first original idea in five years, way to think outside the box, Einstein.' I'm certainly looking forward to *robust* resting in

71

peace someday. You can still use it to describe a good barbeque sauce, but that's it."

"So anyway, you don't think anything is going on with the company?" asked Greg, his suddenly serious tone indicating that it was a pressing issue on his mind.

"No, I *do* think something's coming; I'm just not sure what, and I'm not sure if I should care. I've been worrying about all the rumors going around, but I've realized that they're certainly not going to ask my opinion, so why bother fretting about it anymore? I also can't understand why everyone thinks that an IPO will be the road to riches rather than the road to the unemployment office. Everybody seems to have been brainwashed that going public suddenly puts the company in the big leagues; it's just so sexy."

"You are a wet blanket, aren't you?" poked Greg.

"No, I just think I'm the only guy who didn't drink the Kool-Aid."

"Alright, at the start of next week I'll do a final run of the numbers, and we'll be ready to go for the big show. Well, I guess I'd better go do some actual work now. I'll let you get back to business."

"I've got a couple of things going but not too much. I'm just trying to pace myself right now. If my workflow gets too thin, God only knows what Joe will assign me."

"Is he still slapping you around?"

"Not too much lately. We had a little scrape a while back, and it seemed to take away some of his bark. He's still a pain, however now it's more of a dull, throbbing one rather than a sharp, stinging one."

"That a boy, Bryan. Stickin' it to the man."

"Back to work."

***

With Chambers' growth over the years, it became more and more difficult to have companywide meetings. One of the attractions of the office park where they were currently located was the large on-site conference center. When Chambers held a meeting there, it was like the employees were back in grade school: they would all file out of their classrooms and head for the auditorium. On meeting day the company tried to get as many employees to the meeting as possible, however a skeleton staff was left behind to man the phones and make sure nobody stole the furniture.

The meeting was held on a Friday morning and would normally run until lunch time. Bryan was sitting at his desk and passing the minutes by surfing the web when he received the companywide e-mail notifying workers that it was time to go to the meeting. A wave of rustling and murmuring swept across the floor as dozens of employees got up from their desks and began marching out in unison like a band of industrious ants. Bryan hurried along one of the side hallways, trying to locate Greg among the throng. As he made his way toward the large glass doors that exited to the courtyard, he spotted Greg loitering beside a large potted plant.

"There you are," Greg said as Bryan approached.

"The electro shock zapped my chair, and I just got up and started walking. You better fall in with the herd before they send the dogs," Bryan replied with a mock paranoid look.

As they headed out the door together Greg said, "I checked with the judges, and none of them got stuck with stay-behind duty. They also headed over a few minutes early to make sure they could get some good spots up front."

When they reached the conference center, they merged into lines that had spilled out into the corridor before slowly filing into the meeting hall. The room was set up like a college auditorium with rows of interconnected blue chairs rising gradually up an incline from the stage area at the front. Each seat had an aluminum-trimmed, faux oak desktop that folded and collapsed into the armrest.

Bryan and Greg found spots about halfway up, sat down, and waited for the room to fill. Several executives and HR personnel were milling about on the stage, checking connections on equipment and organizing their materials. Bryan hoped that they had brought some extra bulbs for the projectors because it was a well-known fact that one would always die at a critical point during the presentation.

"I know those are the guys who run the show around here, but I feel rather powerful sitting up here looking down on them," Greg said, unfurling his hand toward the scene below.

"Yeah. Dance for me, you overpaid puppet masters. Dance!"

"So how long do you think we'll be this time?" Greg asked.

"Hopefully we'll be out of here in under two hours. We'll see how much grandstanding each of the group heads wants to do. None of them want to be outdone, so they'll all have some serious PowerPoint firepower. I expect a full array of waterfall charts, Venn diagrams, and bullet points of things that shouldn't be bulleted. And because most of them will just read the slides to us verbatim, any of our horses that appear will certainly get verbalized," Bryan said as he flipped up his desktop and set down the notepad he'd brought. He chuckled as he noticed a small mark of graffiti carved into the wood. He nudged Greg and pointed to the script "C" inside a circle, which was the Chambers logo; however, this one also had a slash mark across it. "Apparently someone wasn't enjoying their training session."

"Come on. Not that I don't agree with them, but why does somebody have to do that? Did they stick their gum underneath too? I can be pretty juvenile at times, but I'm certainly beyond doing that kind of stuff anymore," Greg said.

"I think it's something at the genetic level. Some people are just always going to be inclined to leave their mark no matter what. I'm sure when our founding fathers were sitting around working on the Declaration of Independence, a few of them were carving comments in the tables. Look at ancient cave drawings and petro glyphs. We try to preserve them now at any cost, but back in the day it was probably just some Neanderthal punk trying to spite the tribe."

"Maybe so. Alright, let's get this show on the road," Greg said, looking around impatiently.

The room filled quickly, and after a few minutes one of the company's executive vice presidents came out to emcee the meeting. He made some comments before introducing the company's founder, Phil Chambers. Chambers was now Chairman of the Board, which meant that these days his main responsibilities were ceremonial tasks. As usual he gave an upbeat speech about how much the company had achieved since the early days. The year Bryan had started with Chambers, Phil's speech had lasted nearly half an hour. This year it was down to a quaint ten minutes, further indicating how his role had been marginalized. Phil happily turned over the podium to Wayne Marsh, President and CEO.

Wayne was the hired gun brought in by the investor group a few years back to take the company to the level that they didn't think Phil could achieve. Bryan had only met Marsh indirectly on a couple of occasions, but he seemed to be a decent guy. With the company still growing, he hadn't been forced to make any large-scale layoffs yet. This certainly helped to maintain his popularity with the company's workforce. Marsh's presentation was more in-depth than Chambers', it was still very high level in scope. Bryan and Greg exchanged nods several times during the comments as Marsh ticked off words that were in the Derby.

Marsh was followed by individual group heads that dove more into the minutia of what the company was actually doing these days. Most of these speakers were indeed eager to show off their PowerPoint skills. At this level the speakers weren't quite as polished, and many of them showed their nerves: fumbling with remotes, stumbling over their words, and bumbling their facts. When Joe Kelly's supervisor took the stage, Bryan listened for a moment before realizing he wasn't going to learn anything new. He gazed around the room and noted the various activities of the crowd. Many employees were dutifully playing along, but others were spending their time texting messages or communicating the old-fashioned way by passing notes.

After an hour or so of steady tedium, Marsh retook the stage for his closing comments. His upbeat demeanor certainly seemed genuine, and he went deep into the well for buzzwords to talk about where the company was headed. He wrapped up, and everyone reactively rose and filed back out to their hovels.

"Wow! That was enlightening as always," Greg said sarcastically as they slowly headed out.

"What? You don't feel that you were cross-pollinated with new ideas and information?" Bryan asked with equal skepticism.

"Ahh, no. But on a more important note, are we getting together with the judges this afternoon?"

"Yeah, I told Martin that we'd meet around 2:00. I don't want to do it via e-mail; Big Brother could get suspicious. What do you think was the winner?"

"Not sure, may depend on the odds. Although no one picked it the clear winner was *Chambers-centric*. All of the executives clearly got the memo telling them to give it plenty of air time."

"I know. Obviously we'll be seeing lots more of that to come in the near future."

"I'm dreading it already."

"So did you pick up any clues on the company's strategic planning?" Bryan asked, already knowing the answer.

"No, you were right. But I didn't feel like they were trying to hide anything that might be bad news either so that's good."

"Well we still have the company picnic coming up so maybe someone in the know will get liquored up and spill the beans."

"Alright, I'll see you at two," Bryan said, as they headed off in different directions.

***

Bryan got a quick sandwich and then headed back to his office. He tried to get back into a work groove, but at this point the day was pretty much shot. Luckily one of the judges, Nicki Cole, stopped by early and was in a chatty mood so Bryan had an excuse to blow off his tasks. As two o'clock finally rolled around everyone had arrived and they got down to business.

"Alright, let's tally up the totals. Nicki, what do you have for your top five?" asked Greg.

"As expected, *leverage* was the clear winner with nine," said Nicki, tapping her notepad with her pen. "It was a little unfair since Ron Holden used it in four consecutive bullet points."

"Oh, that was so brutal," Greg said, interrupting her. "If you're going to read your presentation you should at least practice it once or twice. It seemed like that was the first time he'd ever seen it. He must have had some of his underlings throw it together for him. Sorry, Nicki."

"That's ok, you're right. After that I had a two-way tie at five between *result driven* and *robust*. I had *big picture* with three and *key concept* and *value added* with two each."

"Excellent. How about you, Martin?"

"I would have to agree. I had the same numbers."

"And last but not least, Josh?"

"It looks like I was right in line except that I only had *leverage* eight times. However, it is very possible that I dozed off for a few minutes and missed one."

"Thanks for the honesty, Josh. We'll go ahead with nine as our official number. Alright, let's see who the lucky one is. Do you have the spreadsheet up, Bryan?"

"Sure do."

Greg stepped over to Bryan's computer and grabbed the mouse. "Looks like Doug Jenkins is going to be the man this year. He's one of the few that had *results driven* so he benefited from the odds. He also had *leverage* and *value added*."

"Shall I ring him up?" asked Bryan.

"Yeah, get him on the speaker phone," said Greg.

"Thank you for calling Chambers Data Systems, this is Doug."

"Wow, you are a company man aren't you?" said Bryan. "You knew it was me from the caller ID."

"Just because it says your name on the phone doesn't mean it's you calling. Besides, I can tell you're on speakerphone; maybe old man Chambers stopped by your office for a post meeting debrief. I learned my lesson at my last job. One of my coworkers called and I carelessly said: 'What the hell do you want?' There was a very uncomfortable silence before he notified me that he was on speaker with our boss and one of the auditors. I felt like such an idiot."

"What did you do?"

"Apologized profusely and then answered their questions."

"Did that lead to your departure from the company?"

"No. I called our boss later and apologized again, but he said not to worry about it. Nonetheless, I avoided him the best that I could for the next few days. Anyway, I don't imagine you are calling me about work. Did I win?"

"You did indeed," chimed Greg.

"Sweet."

"Stop over and see Bryan to collect your winnings and don't gloat too much; we want to keep it quiet."

"No problem. Thanks guys."

The rest of the group congratulated him as well before hanging up.

Turning to Greg, Josh asked: "So what's up next? Are we going to do some betting on the company picnic?"

"Sure, should we go with most inappropriately dressed or over consumption of alcohol?" said Greg, scratching his chin.

"Maybe we combine the two of them," Josh added.

"You would think people would learn but they never seem to," said Nicki, shaking her head.

"Jenna Hambrick?" guessed Bryan, raising his eyebrows.

"See! What was she thinking wearing a G-string to a company function?" replied Nicki.

"Yes, but she covered it so discreetly with the fishnet mini skirt," deadpanned Greg.

"She was just looking to get a raise," said Martin.

"She should probably focus on her work then," said Nicki. "I'm no prude, but that was the wrong venue to be getting cheeky. And if you're going to put it on display at least have the decency to go and get a spray-on tan. I mean, come on, it was shining like the full moon on a dark night."

"Boy, you sound like the incident scarred you for life," said Bryan, looking concerned.

"It did!" Nicki said, throwing up her hands. "I think I suffer from post-Jenna traumatic syndrome, and I'm not alone. I bet you think the male workers spent a lot of time talking about it afterward, well trust me, it pales in comparison to the analysis that the women made."

"Oh, we know. If one of the cats strays from the rules of the pack the rest of you pounce," Greg said.

"It's just the law of the jungle my man," shrugged Nicki.

"Anyway, I don't think we'll do any betting on the picnic. I think we'll just make it a spectator sport and hope for some new special memories. I guess that wraps up the Derby for this year so I better get back to my day job. See you guys later," Greg said as he bowed out.

The rest of the group hung around for a while longer until Bryan eventually sent them on their way. Doug stopped by to pick up his winnings and Bryan finished up a few loose ends before calling it a day.

***

Each year Chambers held its company picnic on the Saturday following the Fourth of July. Despite attendance officially being classified as voluntary, over the years it had come to be common perception that showing up was indeed considered mandatory. The company didn't hold a lot of pep rallies, but when they did they wanted all hands on deck.

The picnic was once again being held at Harborside Park. The facility had plenty of room for activities and it adjoined the jetties at the south end of Sand Dollar Beach. The location was ideal for a picnic in July since there was usually a steady breeze to offset the heat and humidity.

Bryan arrived a little too early and had to spend his first half an hour making small talk with co-workers that he didn't know personally. Bryan was relieved when he finally saw Alex Barrett arrive; followed shortly thereafter by several other friends from the office. They were able to spend a few minutes of quality time commenting on the female attendees before Christie showed up and they had to change their fraternity talk to coed appropriate topics. Their group had taken up its position at a table near the side of the covered pavilion, which afforded them a good view of the proceedings and also had close access to one of the bars.

"It's hard to believe that it's already picnic time again. I can't believe a year has passed since the last time we were out here," Alex said.

"So you must be the guy who's actually having fun if time is flying by," replied Bryan.

"No, that's just a cliché. Time is flying by but it's not due to the fun factor at work. But the picnics have usually been a good time. Today we've got beautiful weather, delicious food, and the drinks are flowing. On top of all of that I get to spend it with some good friends," Alex said, raising his bottle.

"Aww. That's so sweet," Christie said in earnest.

"Boy, after that I think our next round of beers needs to be Löwenbräu," added Greg with less sincerity.

"It looks like we have a pretty good showing today. It also looks like the budget didn't have too many restrictions; I like that," Bryan said.

"I'm definitely getting a good vibe. Check out the band: not just one steel drummer today, they've got two," Alex stated observantly.

"And how about the raffle prizes they're giving away: sixty-inch TV, a couple of new Macs, and a bunch of nice trips. They were all seven-dayers too, none of that three day, two night junk," noted Jason.

"Well it looks like the official festivities are getting ready to begin," Greg said, motioning to the stage where the band was set up.

Bryan looked the other way and zoned out for a moment. He stared out at the beach and took in the sights. Even though he didn't spend a lot of time at the beach these days he always liked having the sense of knowing that it was there. Other than the drudgery of his job, Bryan liked living here and could never see himself living anywhere that was landlocked without the beach being a short drive away. Bryan was quite certain that this was the place for him; he just needed to find something different to do to occupy his time and earn a paycheck. He nodded his head and smiled before turning back and rejoining the Chambers celebration.

On stage were several of the company's executives who had presented at the recent meeting. Today, however, they were clad in untucked Hawaiian shirts and baggy khaki shorts. After some welcoming comments and some uncomfortable staged banter amongst themselves it was show time.

"Oh no," muttered Jason.

"Oh yes!" chimed Greg. "It's time for some Jimmy Buffet karaoke."

"C'mon. Is there some kind of law in Florida that requires Jimmy Buffet to be a staple at beach-related activities? It's bad enough having to hear Margaritaville a minimum of five times at the picnic each year, but now they've decided to take it to the next level," said Bryan, throwing up his hands in disgust.

"Actually it is a law. It's in the same section with the rules requiring all DJs to play the *Electric Slide*, the *Macarena*, and *YMCA* at weddings," said Greg.

"Oh, I love Jimmy Buffet," Christie said, bobbing her head as the music started.

"Okay, Christie, that's fine. But this is not Jimmy Buffet. This is some freakish abomination of Buffet. Don't tell me you want a *Cheeseburger in Paradise* cooked up by a bunch of talentless, middle aged dudes," Jason countered.

"No, no, you're right, Jason. This is a train wreck, but you still have to watch," admitted Christie. Meanwhile the head of marketing started butchering lyrics while choking down his laughter. Only the rest of the guys on stage were laughing with him; everyone else in attendance was laughing at him.

Despite their sarcasm, the group all got a hearty laugh out of the performance. The crooners knocked out a three song set of Buffet before moving on to a few of the standards, including *YMCA*. By that point it had become a participation sport with members of the audience joining in. A Gloria Estefan tune even led to a spontaneous outbreak of conga lining. Bryan was having a good time, but he still decided to exercise his better judgment and leave the dancing to more inebriated co-workers.

The picnic stayed lively for a few hours longer, but gradually started to wind down. Bryan didn't want to stay too long and get stuck with the brown-nosers who felt they had to remain until the end or the revelers who'd already had too much to drink and were pushing their limits further. On his way out Bryan checked the door prizes and discovered that he had won one of the gift cards. It wasn't as valuable as the giant TV, but at least he knew it would fit in his apartment. All in all Bryan had to give the picnic high marks and hoped that it signified a positive direction for Chambers.

7

T he afterglow of the picnic didn't last long as Bryan got back to business the following week. Near the top of his to-do list was putting in a call to Garris. He was waiting for Monday afternoon to roll around figuring that Jim might be out playing in the morning. Garris had called Bryan the previous week and left a message to give him a ring. Bryan had left two messages at Jim's home, but hadn't heard back. He was initially worried that maybe he was outlasting his welcome at Stone Ridge, but realized that probably wasn't the case. Over the past several months he had become comfortable being a regular guest.

As soon as he got back to his desk after lunch, Bryan retrieved Jim's number and gave him a call.

"Hello?" answered an unfamiliar female voice.

"Ahhh," stammered Bryan, caught off guard by the response and checking the number on his phone's display, "Who's this?"

"Who is this?" the voice shot back.

"Oh, this is Bryan. Is Jim there?"

"Oh, the golf guy. He said you might be calling."

"Yeah, the golf guy," Bryan said, realizing this must be on of Jim's daughters. "So is this Nancy?"

"Yes, it is. So what did he tell you about me?"

"Nothing really, just that you were on of his daughters," replied Bryan, feeling very uncomfortable. "Is Jim there?" he said, trying to get back on track.

"No, he's not here."

"Okay, can I leave a message?"

"Sure I'll tell him you called but I'm not sure when he'll be able to call you back."

"Did he go somewhere?"

"He's in the hospital."

"Oh, sorry to hear that," Bryan said. "What hospital is he in?"

"He's not well."

"Well, I'd at least like to send him a card or something."

"He's at Foster Memorial. I'll let him know that you called."

"Thanks.

Click.

Bryan usually tried to keep an open mind and not pass judgment on people too quickly, but it was hard not to make a real fast appraisal of Nancy. Maybe she was under pressure due to her father's situation, but that shouldn't preclude at least a little bit of courtesy. The call had only reinforced the negative image that Bryan had based on the conversation he'd had with Garris about her. It seemed as though she didn't want Bryan to go see her father, but her actions had assured that he would do the opposite.

Bryan leaned back and considered his course of action for a moment. He felt that he should get in touch with Garris but he also didn't want to cause added family distress at an already difficult time. He clicked open his web browser and pulled up the local phone directory. He typed in William Robalo and quickly found the number he was looking for.

"Hello?"

"Hi, Bill? It's Bryan Minton calling."

"Oh, hey, Bryan. How are you doing?

"Good, thanks. I'm sorry to bother you; I hope you don't mind me calling you at home."

"No bother at all. Besides I'm retired, you can't really reach me at the office anymore. So what's on your mind? Are you calling about Jim?"

"Yes, I was returning his call and just spoke with his daughter."

"She's a peach, isn't she?"

"She wasn't real friendly. She clearly didn't want me to bother Jim, but I wanted to at least send him a card or something. I thought I'd get your opinion, what do you think?"

"Don't send him a card; guys our age aren't real big on cards anymore, Bryan. You should go out and see him. I think it would really do him some good. Don't let Nancy scare you, she's always been a pit bull."

"That's pretty much what I thought, but I didn't want to interfere. She told me he was at Foster but didn't give me a room number."

"Hang on, I have it written down here. He's in West – 309. I was over to see him yesterday and he seemed to be feeling okay. Non-family members can visit from nine in the morning until seven at night."

"Thanks, Bill. So what's his prognosis?" asked Bryan tentatively.

"Well that's tough to say. He was starting to feel weak a few days ago and then it got to the point that he called his doctor and they admitted him to the hospital. They did some updated tests and started him on some new medication. It sounds like they are going to keep him at least a few more days to see how things go. As usual he wouldn't give me too many details and the doctors aren't really allowed to disclose any information to me. I'm pretty sure that whatever he had has either recurred or spread or both. Like I told you before, he just doesn't want to feel like he's burdening anyone with his problems and he doesn't want anyone pitying him. So when you get out there don't be all sappy. Just talk to him like you're standing on a tee box waiting for the fairway to clear."

"Will do. I really appreciate your advice, Bill. I'll probably head over tomorrow after work."

"Sounds good, Bryan. Feel free to call if I can help out in any way."

"Thanks, take care."

Bryan was glad that he'd made the call and now felt a lot better about visiting Garris.

***

Bryan pulled into the main entrance of the Foster Memorial campus and followed the signs to the parking garage. After going in circles until he found a spot a few floors up, Bryan grabbed his presents from the passenger seat and headed for the elevators. On the ground floor he consulted a map of the complex and located the route to the West building.

The entrance led to a large atrium that was several stories high and wrapped in green glass and aluminum tubing. The room was filled with the blended white noise of multiple conversations echoing off the glass walls and marble floors.

Bryan walked across to the horseshoe shaped main desk to check in. "Excuse me. I'm here to visit Mr. Garris in room 309," he said to the attendant.

"Are you an immediate relative?" she asked reflexively without looking up from her computer monitor.

"No, just a friend."

"Please sign in on the sheet, please write neatly, be sure to fill in the patient's name and room number, visiting hours end promptly at seven o'clock," she replied, allowing Bryan a slight glance of acknowledgement.

"Thanks," Bryan said as he completed the sign in log. "How do I get there?"

"What was the number?

"309."

"Take this hall on the right to the elevators, up to three, follow the signs."

Bryan followed her instructions and rode up to the third floor. When he stepped out on three he immediately wanted to get back in the elevator. The hall was well lit but pale and sterile; compared to this his cube farm at Chambers seemed downright vibrant. In terms of his search for future careers, Bryan knew for sure he could cross off his list anything that involved a hospital.

The small laminated signs indicated that Garris's room was down to the left. Making his way down the hall, Bryan was glad to at least hear a few sounds of life. But as he passed the first several rooms he realized it was just the patients' televisions that he heard. Bryan had assumed that there would be more security, but for the most part there probably weren't that many criminals who went around stealing sick people. As he reached 309, Bryan gathered himself and knocked quietly on the door that was slightly ajar.

"Come in," a voice within responded.

Bryan let himself in and found Jim sitting up in bed watching TV.

"Well look what the cat dragged in," Garris said with a smile. "How are you doing Bryan?"

"Me? I'm fine. You're the one who's in the hospital," Bryan replied, already relieved that Garris seemed far better than he expected. "How are you doing?"

"They're doing their best to kill me in here, but I hope to escape before they get their chance. Come on in and have a seat," Jim said, motioning to a chair near the bed.

Bryan headed across the room and sat down in the heavily padded lounge chair. It gave a loud sigh as Bryan sank into the cushions.

"I hope you don't mind that I stopped by," said Bryan apologetically.

"Oh please. I was hoping you would."

"Good. I was a little worried after I talked to Nancy."

"Like I told you before, she's one of a kind," Garris said with a smile of understanding. "I'm glad she didn't frighten you away."

"I called Bill and he said it would be fine."

"He's had a few hospital stays himself so he knows how tough it can be in here. It's amazing just how slow time can pass when you're stuck in a bed in a strange place."

"I figured you didn't have a lot to do so I picked up a few things for you at the bookstore," Bryan said, reaching into the bag he'd brought. "I of course picked up the requisite copies of *Golf Digest* and *Golf Magazine*. I also saw that this month's issue of *Popular Science* had a cover story about futuristic oil exploration; I thought you might want to keep up with what's going on in the industry in case you need to go back to work. And here's a puzzle book. I don't know if you like puzzles, but this one has a few of just about everything."

"Thanks, Bryan, I appreciate that," Garris said as he surveyed the items that Bryan had set on the bed. "It's funny that you brought the puzzle book. I don't do any on a regular basis, but since I've been in here I've been trying to do the ones in the newspaper they bring me each day. I think there's a real surge in puzzle activity in hospitals and doctors' offices. Oh, and of course on airplanes, too."

"Then the book will come in handy next time you fly. You know how tough it is to find a virgin puzzle in the airline magazines; somebody has always half completed it in pen."

"Not sure I'll be flying any time soon, but I'm sure there will be plenty of doctor visits with time to kill."

"I tried to find a good golf book, but nothing really stood out. I didn't think you'd be too interested in an instruction book and most of the golf novels were so clichéd. There's always either a dead body in the sand trap or a cheesy pro sleeping with the members' wives. You'd think somebody could write a good story about golf."

"I'm sure there likely is someone, but if he's smart he's probably out playing instead of inside writing."

"I brought some golf jokes too," said Bryan, fishing a folded piece of paper from his pocket. "A buddy at the office forwarded these the other day so I printed them out. These are the names of some different types of shots or players you might encounter. They're pretty good, but some are a little more tasteless than others. A Princess Grace tee shot – should have taken a driver, a Princess Diana tee shot – should *not* have taken a driver."

"Oh that is tasteless, but funny," Garris said with a chuckle.

"An Adolf Hitler – two shots in the bunker; a Saddam Hussein – from one bunker straight into another; a Cuban putt – needed one more revolution. Some celebrity shots: an O.J. Simpson – got away with it; and of course some politicians: a Jeb Bush – too far to the right, out of play; a Nancy Pelosi – too far left, clueless on how to get home from there. I like this one: the Unabomber – explosive, but spends a lot of time in the woods. There's a bunch more here that I'll let you read."

"Good stuff. I'll definitely have to start using some of those. That's the first good laugh I've had in a while."

"So you look pretty good, Jim. I was a little worried coming over; I didn't know what to expect."

"Things aren't great, but I'm not going down yet. I think I've only got a few more days in here and then they'll let me go home. One of the medications can have some pretty harsh side effects so they want me here in case something goes wrong. So far, so good; I haven't grown any horns or started turning different colors."

"Is there anything else I can help with?" offered Bryan.

"No, I'm in pretty good hands here. I've been pleased with the care here and I've got some good doctors. Unless you are buddies with Dr. Frankenstein and can get me a whole new body."

"What about when you go home? Anything you want me to get?"

"Thanks, but I don't think I need anything. My strength is coming back a bit and Nancy is planning to hang around for a few weeks if need be. I was kind of surprised that she told her boss she would be gone as long as need be. She brought her computer so she can still work remotely, which is good. I know that she feels the need to fill her mother's role, but she has her own life now so I don't want to interfere."

"Come on, Jim. It's great to be independent, but everybody needs some help once in a while. Anyway, if I can help I want you to ask. No strings attached."

"Alright, I'll let you come over and clean my bathroom if it'll make you feel better."

"That's not really my strength, but I'll find you a good cleaning person if need be. So what else have you been doing to keep busy in here?"

"Oh the usual: strolls up and down the halls, visits to the lab for pin cushion training, and today I was actually allowed to head down to the cafeteria to feed myself for the first time in a few days. The food wasn't anything special, but if felt great to get out and see some other people."

"Have you been catching up on your soap operas during the day?" Bryan asked, motioning to the TV that was on but muted.

"No, but that's another reason to stay out of the hospital: TV during the day just stinks. The talk and shock shows are just unbearable. They all have to keep stepping it up a notch to try to get viewers. At first you want to watch it like a car accident, but it's just so bad that you can't. It seems like the people are either too ignorant or too bored so they have to concoct problems to make their lives more interesting. I just never had an interest in that kind of stuff. In fact, that was one thing that I always loved about my wife: no unnecessary drama."

"You're a lucky man then," said Bryan.

"Now with two daughters I can't say that there was no drama at all, but she was pretty good at avoiding the really childish stuff. Back when I was working I'd hear co-workers talking about their personal lives and I'd have to just shake my head. You probably already know this Bryan, but if you want to help your career be sure to avoid those people."

"Oh, I try. Like every company though we've got our share of crazies. They are pretty well known so you just have to be sure not to engage them; you never ask how their weekend went or how their family is doing."

"So how is that job of yours going? Are you keeping the economy moving by shuffling paper?"

"It's been okay lately. Not getting much better, but certainly no worse. We just had our big company picnic this weekend."

"How was that?" asked Jim.

"I'll have to admit that I actually had fun. It was probably the best one they've put on since I've been with the company. Seeing people in a different light can help improve your image of them at the office. It was good to see the executives that are always so serious at work be able to relax a bit and show some self deprecating humor."

"Anyone show up in drag?"

"Oh, God, no. I'm glad they didn't go that far! Why do you ask?"

"We had a themed company meeting, you were supposed to wear a fun outfit in company colors, and a few guys decided to dress up in drag. The day before a couple of them chickened out and decided to skip the dresses and just stick to the color theme. Well apparently one guy, Don Parker, didn't get the retreat message. He showed up in full glory: his wife did his makeup, he was wearing a fancy dress and heels, and was even carrying a purse, in company colors mind you. When he arrived outside the meeting room he saw that the other guys had shown up straight. In turn, he went nuts and tried to take off, but of course he couldn't get too far in heels. So the other guys picked him up and carried him into the meeting. The doors flew open and there's this guy in a dress screaming obscenities, getting lugged into the event. The room went completely silent and everyone just stared for a moment. The company president was nearby so he walked over to Don and just stared at him. Everyone thought that he's going to fire him on the spot. Then the President put his arm around Parker and said: 'Don heard that we were trying to promote more women into management so he's decided to step up to the plate and set the example. He's quite a company man – I mean company woman. In fact I'm going to have him sit up at the head table with me.' And he led Don to his seat. Everyone just lost it. It was the best ice-breaker I've ever seen in a meeting," Garris said, chuckling heartily as he reminisced.

"Wow, the power of cross dressing."

"Once he settled down he took it in stride and even hammed it up a bit. Boy, I'd forgotten how funny that was," Garris said, still laughing.

"I don't see anyone doing that at Chambers. I don't think it would be so much the embarrassment factor as much as the fear of offending someone"

"I imagine it's a minefield these days. Good thing I'm no longer in the workforce; I'd probably be offending people left and right," Garris said, shaking his head. "So there's certainly not much to watch on Tuesdays," he added as he flipped through a few channels with the remote.

"Yeah, no golf until Thursday."

"I think the scariest part of my stay here was when I got to this room and the cable wasn't working properly. There were a few channels missing, including the Golf Channel. They had already moved in all of my stuff so I couldn't switch rooms. The nurse here told me not to worry about it since there were plenty of other channels to choose from. Well that of course wasn't going to do. I think the Geneva Convention allows that even prisoners should be allowed access to the Golf Channel, so I asked real nicely to have them send up a serviceman. He couldn't figure out what the problem was so he just unbolted the thing and switched it with the one in the next room; problem solved."

"Wow, that was a close call."

Bryan and Jim watched TV and talked for a while until Bryan noticed that it was already approaching 7:00. They said their goodbyes and Jim insisted that he'd be giving Bryan a call soon to have him out to Stone Ridge again. Bryan thanked him for the offer and said he'd be there, but as he left he thought to himself that a round with Garris anytime soon would be pretty unlikely.

***

Bryan was very busy at work the next two weeks. It seemed that activity in general was increasing at the company. Bryan was deep in thought in front of his computer on Thursday afternoon when he was startled by his ringing phone.

"Hello? This is Bryan."

"Bryan, it's Jim. Got a minute?"

"Sure. How are you feeling?"

"Not too bad. I'm starting to get some strength back and I even got back out on the course this week. I did a couple of nines, but felt like I could have done eighteen if it weren't so darn hot out."

"Wow, that's great news," Bryan said, highly surprised.

"So I know it's short notice, but I wanted to see if you were up for some golf on Saturday."

"Yeah, I think so. I don't think I need to work this weekend so I should be available. What did you have in mind?"

"They're having a fun scramble event with an 8:00 shotgun start. Nothing serious, just knocking the ball around. I've already got two other guys lined up for a group. So are you up for it?"

"Definitely. Count me in."

"Great, I'll see you out there."

"Bye, Jim," Bryan said, hanging up the phone. He sat back in his chair and puzzled over the fact that Garris was already back to playing golf. Maybe things weren't as bad as they seemed in the hospital. Maybe Nancy had been over-reacting to the situation. Regardless, he now had a good reason not to work this weekend.

***

On Friday Bryan found that he really had to grind his way through the afternoon. At around 3:00 he caught himself checking golf scores online and then started thinking about playing at Stone Ridge. With a scramble format he could play the course a little different than usual so he began making mental notes about his options on certain holes. By 5:00 he was shot, but he was content with the status of his projects so he shut down his computer and wrapped up for the weekend.

As part of his afternoon wanderings Bryan had done a mental inventory of his golf accessories and realized that he probably needed some extra golf balls. One of the large golf chains had a store that wasn't too far out of his way and he knew that they were open until six. Pulling into the parking lot he tried to promise himself that he was only there for balls; no impulse shopping allowed no matter how shiny it was or how many yards it promised to add to his shots. However, when he walked through the door he knew he was already in trouble. Bryan was greeted by a towering display for the newest version of the driver he was currently playing. The rack looked like a giant golf club altar and Bryan had no choice but to stop and worship. Bryan stepped up, found one in eight and a half degrees, and lined up the club. He decided against taking a full swing, but gave it a few waggles; he liked the look and the feel already.

"Nice club, huh?" came a voice from over his shoulder. "We just got those in the other day. Unbelievable distance and forgiveness."

"Yeah, it looks nice," Bryan said, turning to the salesman.

"We have some demo models in back if you want to take some swings."

"No, I'm okay. I have the last version of it and it's been serving me pretty well," Bryan replied as he replaced the club on the rack.

"Are you sure? They've added some new technology to this model," the salesman inquired hopefully.

"Thanks, but I'm not ready to upgrade yet. Of course that could change during the span of one round."

"Alright, well let me know if I can help you with anything," he offered before skulking off disappointed.

Since he didn't have any plans for a Friday night Bryan decided to loiter a bit longer and see what else might be new. He wandered around and eventually made his way to the putting area. He worked his way around the edge of the mat hitting a few balls across the well worn, ultra thin carpet. Some putters were worth a couple of shots while others Bryan just looked at and immediately returned to the rack. Some designs seemed to be strange just for the sake of being strange, not for getting the ball in the hole.

Once again Bryan sensed a presence behind him.

"You've got a nice stroke there. Looking for a new flatstick?" asked a different voice.

"Oh, thanks," said Bryan, draining one last putt before setting the club down and turning for another sales pitch. "I'm just checking out the good, the bad, and the really ugly. Right when I thought I'd seen every crazy putter head imaginable they go and push the envelope further."

"Most woods and irons are relatively similar in appearance so golfers seek out their identities via the putter. We barely do any decorative or logo grips on regular clubs, but we do them on putters all the time. The putter could be lousy but if it looks good to your eye it's going to put the ball in the hole. Golfers are an odd group of people so that's why you see the companies trying to cover all of the bases. Even companies that focus mainly on classic designs have added crazy looking putters. Look at Ping for instance; they were at least honest when they named that goofy branding iron over there the Craz-E."

"I guess I'm a pretty boring golfer then. I've used the same putter for a long time and it's an Anser design so it's probably the most common look out there."

"Hey, if it's not broke, don't fix it. But even if you are happy with it you should still get the lie and grip checked. Over time they can both change slightly and that can eventually start to hurt you. If you want to bring it in we'll be glad to give it a look."

"Thanks, maybe I'll do that," said Bryan, pleased with the salesman's approach. "Really all I need today is some new ammunition."

"All of the balls are over there by the counter. Seems like you're the kind of guy who knows what he wants, but let me know if you have any questions."

"Thanks."

Bryan headed over and picked up two dozen balls. He set his boxes on the counter and looked at the sundry items near the register as he fished his wallet from his pocket. A small metallic box of divot repair tools caught his eye. He picked one up and rolled it in his fingers. He was immediately surprised by how light it seemed, despite clearly being made out of metal.

"Titanium," said the cashier, noticing Bryan's interest in the tool.

"Interesting. I really like the feel of that and it's a cool design too. Normally I wouldn't carry a divot tool like this because I don't want the weight knocking around in my pocket. This one wouldn't be a bother at all."

"They've proven to be a very popular item and we've sold a bunch of them." he said.

"How much are they?"

"Twenty-one bucks."

"Really?"

"Like I said, titanium," shrugged the cashier.

"Hmm," Bryan mused as he tossed the tool gently in his hand. "Yeah, I think I need on of these. I was being good, but you guys are sneaky putting this stuff by the check out."

"Marketing 101."

Bryan paid for his stuff and walked out to his car. As soon as he got in he reached into his bag and pulled out his new acquisition. He was quite smitten with it, certainly no buyer's remorse.

***

Walking down to his car on Saturday morning, Bryan was pleasantly surprised to find that the humidity was unseasonably low and a steady breeze was rustling the leaves. There were long strands of cirrus clouds up above, but no other clouds from horizon to horizon. Summertime in Florida was usually hit or miss in terms of golf weather so Bryan was glad that he would be able to focus on his game rather than worrying about dodging a morning storm.

At Stone Ridge Bryan found Jim by the cart line and they headed out to the range together. Bryan immediately started to take note of Jim's mannerisms to see if anything seemed different. His stroke didn't seem too bad, but he only hit a couple of balls with each club and took long breaks in between to watch Bryan hit and chat.

"So, Bryan, we've got a couple of decent guys to play with today. Both are solid all around players, but very different personalities. Roger takes it a little too seriously while Gerry doesn't take it seriously enough, especially for Roger. Part of my job today is keeping the peace and keeping them both leaning toward the center of the golf spectrum. Even though we're just out for fun, and maybe a couple of sleeves of golf balls, if we start dropping some birdies Roger will go into strategy mode and start over thinking each of our shots. I'm used to it, but hopefully it won't get to the point that it bothers you."

"Oh, no problem, I know the type. You can be playing the most rinky dink event and it'll still bring out the competitive monster in some guys."

"Let me know when you're ready and we'll head over and I'll introduce you," said Garris, motioning across the practice area.

Bryan addressed the ball he'd just teed up, took one last glance down the range, and let loose on a prodigious drive. "And with that I think I'm ready to go," he said.

"If you do that on the first tee you'll send Roger into immediate overload."

"Alright, I'll lay off of it a little to start with."

They drove over to the paved staging area where about two dozen golf carts were already lined up. Jim pulled into the line and stopped next to two players who were rifling through their golf bags.

"Ah, here's the big double eagle hitter. Hope you brought some more of that magic with you today," said one of the men, looking up.

Bryan still loved the thrill of re-living his glory shot, but it was now somewhat watered down by the preconceived expectations of his playing partners. "That's me. I see that Jim has been talking me up undeservedly again."

"I told you that I let everyone know about that shot. Sure there was some luck getting it in the hole, but is also took at least a modest dose of skill to reach a par five in two shots," Garris piped in.

"This is Roger and that's Gerry."

"Nice to meet you," Bryan said stepping out of the cart and shaking their hands.

"Don't worry about him," Gerry said, motioning to Roger, "we're not expecting anything from you, beyond a bunch of natural birdies of course."

"Thanks, I'll see what I can do," Bryan replied as he started organizing his equipment and bag for the round.

Bryan noted that Jim was in good spirits, cracking jokes and chatting with friends while they waited. A few minutes later the club starter arrived with a bull horn and quickly reviewed the format and rules for the day. He thanked everyone for coming out and then gave his blessing to head out onto the course. The line of carts began snaking out along the cart paths; breaking off into smaller segments as groups reached their appointed starting holes. Jim navigated their cart to the side of the fifth tee and pulled to the right to let the rest of the groups through. The foursome mounted the tee box together and, as Jim had expected, Roger began laying out his plans.

"So how are you feeling, Jim? Do you want to lead us off today?" asked Roger.

"Sure, I'll light one up and take all of the pressure off you guys," Jim replied, rolling his eyes at Bryan.

Jim hit a solid, albeit short, drive down the middle that did take the pressure off since they knew that they had a ball in play. After Gerry and Roger hit mediocre shots, Bryan teed up and hit a great drive way down in the fairway. He was rewarded with a complimentary nod from Jim and a fist bump from Roger.

Bryan's drive led to an easy birdie on their first hole. They also picked up a birdie on the following hole, the relatively short par three sixth. On the next hole Bryan finally hit a high approach shot that landed with a thud as it hit and left a deep ball mark on the green. Now he'd be able to put his fancy new repair tool to the test. On the green Bryan snatched the tool from his pocket like a gunslinger on the draw. With a few pokes and twists he leveled the turf and gave it a gentle tamp down with his putter head. Satisfied with his landscaping, Bryan stood up and saw Jim walking his way.

"Hey, Jim. Check this out," Bryan said, as he held out the small titanium lever toward Garris.

"Where'd you get that thing?" Garris queried as he looked at Bryan's hand.

"I got it at the golf store last night. Here hold it."

"Wow, it's light. Is it metal?

"Yeah, titanium. Pretty cool, huh?"

"Yes, I like it."

"It works well too," said Bryan with excitement.

"Hmm," Garris murmured, still pondering the item. He then surprised Bryan by thumping the toe of his putter into the green, intentionally denting the putting surface.

"What are you doing?"

"Gotta take it for a test run," Garris said as he bent down and undid his damage. Noticing Bryan's reaction, he added, "Don't worry, I'm a member. We get to do stuff like that if we want to. Besides, I've fixed thousands of other people's marks out here over the years. I can indulge in the occasional transgression. That thing does a nice job; see I've already atoned. I think I may have to get one of those things."

"As soon as I picked it up I was sold. Alright, enough playing, give it back now," Bryan said, seeing that Garris was just as enamored with it as he was.

Bryan and Roger hit the green on eighteen, but they both had long, tricky puts. Roger was taking his time evaluating the two options so Bryan and Jim stood patiently on the edge of the green.

"How are you feeling, Jim? You seem to be playing reasonably well so far," said Bryan casually, even though he was very curious to know Jim's status.

"Doing okay. Some extra strength pain pills make it a bit more bearable."

"Well, I'm glad you were able to make it back out on the course. Just make sure you're not overdoing it, especially out in the heat."

"I know my limits. Regardless, it's going to take a lot to keep me from playing golf right now. Are you having fun so far?"

"Absolutely. I love playing out here; I always appreciate your invites."

"Do you have anything planned for next Saturday?"

"Not that I know of. Why is there another tournament on the schedule?"

"No, I was thinking that we'd just play a round together. I may have some surgery coming up and I want to get my rounds in while I can."

"I should be open unless something comes up at work this week."

"I'll get us a tee time for early in the morning and will give you a call this week."

"Sounds good. Hey look, Jim. There's your young friends 'the canonballers' over there," said Bryan, motioning to the boys playing in the yard along side the house on eighteen.

"At least they're not in the pool screaming today. If they start yelling while Roger is putting it could get ugly. Alright it looks like Rog' is finally ready. Let's go knock this thing in and card another birdie."

* * *

The three Jacobs boys were doing their best to keep busy and stay out of trouble on a summer Saturday morning. They had set up their baseball field on the side of the house and were trying to get in some innings before it got too hot and they had to take their games to the pool. Even though their father had told them many times not to line up their small diamond toward the back of their property, they still went ahead and did it quite often as it made for the best layout. Although there was a steady stream of golfers wandering through their outfield, the eighteenth hole at Stone Ridge, the boys did their best not to let it bother them. The layout also brought their house into range on foul balls.

Ricky Jacobs was at the plate waiting while his brother, Trent, grabbed another ball from the bucket next to the pitcher's mound. They always tried to keep the yard games under control, but being competitive siblings things usually escalated as the game went on.

"I'm waiting," Ricky said impatiently as Trent rolled the ball in his hand.

"Let's take him down, Trent," brother Cameron added from the outfield.

Trent went through his wind up and put a little extra on a fast ball. Ricky swung a little late and sent a line drive barreling toward the house. "Uh-oh," he muttered.

"Dad's going to kill you," said Trent shaking his head.

"It wasn't my fault, you were pitching too hard."

"Let's go," Trent said, grabbing the bucket of balls and waving Cameron in.

* * *

The following Saturday Bryan arrived at Stone Ridge looking forward to his round, but with a bit of apprehension. Joe had assigned him two new projects during the week and Bryan knew that he needed to put in some weekend hours to get them on track. He had plenty of time to play on Saturday, but the thought of working all day Sunday was still weighing on his mind.

Bryan found Jim piddling around in the pro shop and they checked in together.

"Just the two of us today?" asked Bryan.

"Yeah, I talked to Bill, but his back is still bothering him and he doesn't want to aggravate it any further."

"Did you play during the week, Jim?"

"I did nine on Thursday, but that was all," Jim replied as they headed out to the cart. "We've got a few minutes to warm up if you want to hit a few."

"Sounds good, just a couple to get loosened up."

Once again, Garris hit only a few casual shots on the range while Bryan worked through several of his clubs. They putted for a few minutes and then headed out.

On the par three third hole Bryan hit a high, floating tee ball that peaked slowly, but then slammed into the green like a meteorite. When they arrived at the green Jim jokingly reminded Bryan to fix the damage. "Why don't you use that new tool of yours to clean up that mess? We try to keep a nice course here you know."

"Oh, that reminds me, I got you something," Bryan said as he jogged back to the cart. He returned to the green and headed over to Garris. "Don't just talk about keeping the course in shape, do it! Here you go," he said, handing a new titanium tool to Garris.

"Thanks, Bryan. You didn't have to get me one of these. What do I owe you?"

"I could tell that you liked it as much as I did so I stopped by the store the other night and picked one up. That's a gift from me so you don't owe me anything."

"Well, thanks. But what do they cost? I know Bill's going to have to have one."

"They're twenty-one bucks and the only place I've ever seen them is the store over on Venture Boulevard."

"Excellent."

Bryan could tell his gift was a hit as Garris took every chance he had to fix every mark he could find.

During the round Bryan could tell that Garris was not on his game. He wasn't playing poorly, but he certainly wasn't as sharp as he'd been in prior rounds over the past few months. In particular, Bryan noted that Jim was hitting a lot of shots with lower trajectory than normal. Bryan didn't ask what irons he was hitting because he knew that Garris was taking extra club to make up for distance. He was also aware of Garris spending more time taking in his surroundings. Normally Garris was very focused on his game and blocked out things going on around them.

Bryan, meanwhile, was playing quite well until midway through the back nine when he started thinking about work. He posted a string of bogeys before finally hitting the green on number eighteen. Bryan had a thirty foot putt for birdie but didn't spend much time analyzing it. He took a quick read, addressed the ball, and then drained it.

"Those are the ones that keep you coming back out the next time," Garris said, giving Bryan a polite golf clap.

"I suppose. That one was all luck though," Bryan said, holding up his hands in exasperation.

Garris then two putted for a bogey. Bryan met Garris at the hole and replaced the flag before shaking hands.

"Good round, Jim."

"Thanks, not my best, but it was fun. You had a solid round today, just gave a few too many back on the second nine. So Bryan, I know you said the tool was a gift, but I have to insist on paying today. Here's the dollar," Garris said, handing Bryan a folded one dollar bill, "and here's the twenty," he added, handing Bryan a small, clear plastic case with a twenty dollar gold coin inside.

"Jim, you don't owe me anything."

"Listen, Bryan. I was sort of joking about paying you, but I have made the decision that I want you to have this coin. It's called a Double Eagle and it seemed like fate when we played our first round and you hit that shot on seventeen. You probably know that I'm not real superstitious, but I got chills when that shot went in. It just seemed like a sign to me. My father gave this coin to me and I need to find a new home for it. I'm very confident that I'm giving it to the right person."

"Well, thanks, Jim," stammered Bryan, who was not really sure what to say. He was glad that Jim continued.

"I want you to know that this is yours. Period. It's a valuable coin, but it has more sentimental value for me. For some reason, or maybe lots of reasons, I just didn't feel it should go to one of my daughters. I'm sure they'd just end up fighting over it anyway. Besides, from a financial standpoint both of them and my grandson will be very well taken care of eventually. I also want you to know that although the coin has sentimental value to *me*, it shouldn't for you. I want you to know full well that I want you to do whatever you choose to with it."

"You're sure? I just...you know," said Bryan, making one last requisite turn down attempt, despite Jim's insistence.

"Bryan," Garris started again, putting his hand on Bryan's shoulder, "I'm an old man heading toward the sunset, don't argue with me. I try not to be too preachy, but I do want to give you some advice. Go out and make your mark now. It's only when you get old that you realize just how fast life passes you by. I've had a great life so far and don't have many regrets. But I've met a lot of people over the years that clearly wish they'd made some different choices. Back in my working days we had an acronym for them: CSWs. It stands for: could've, should've, would've. Those were the guys that were always looking back instead of looking ahead. They were constantly making excuses or blaming bad luck for things that didn't go their way. That fact is, Bryan, the harder - and smarter – you work, the luckier you get."

"Well, thank you, Jim," Bryan said with sincerity, shaking Jim's hand once more.

"Alright, let's get out of here. Thanks for playing today. We'll have to do it again soon," Garris said, patting Bryan on the shoulder.

"You bet."

8

After working all day on Sunday, Bryan got no respite on Monday as Joe spent most of the morning meeting distributing even more assignments. Following the meeting Joe asked Bryan to stop by his office. Bryan was glad that he had put in the hours on the weekend because now he was confident that he could handle whatever Joe was planning to throw his way. He dutifully followed Joe down the hall and took a seat when they arrived at Joe's office.

"Bryan, how's everything going?" Kelly began.

"Going good, Joe. What's up?" replied Bryan, not in the mood to waste time on small talk

"Well, I know we've got a lot going on right now around here, but I wanted to see if you had any conflicts next week."

"Conflicts?"

"We're going to be sending some folks up to the affiliate office in Atlanta for a few days and I wanted to make sure you would be available. The purpose is to share some information and do peer reviews. You'd go up on Monday and be back on Thursday. What do you think?"

Bryan was surprised as he'd almost never traveled for the company; however, he thought a road trip might be an interesting diversion. "It should be just fine with my schedule, but missing four days would delay the projects I'm working on right now. That's your call, Joe."

"This is an important assignment and I want to give you the chance to go. I know you'll get right back up to speed on the other projects when you get back."

"I can handle it."

"Good, I'm glad to know I can count on you, Bryan. They'll be setting up a meeting on Wednesday with the rest of the team members to coordinate everyone's role. Let me know if you need anything else."

"Thanks, Joe," Bryan said, getting up to leave. On his way back to his cubicle Bryan was at first excited about the opportunity to go to Atlanta; however, it quickly gave way to an uneasy feeling. He still didn't trust Joe and started wondering if his boss was truly recognizing him or possibly just testing him again, secretly hoping for failure. When he got to his desk he sat down and gathered himself. He decided that worrying about Joe's intentions was something the "old Bryan" would do. The "new Bryan" was going to work hard and get the job done and done right. He knew that if he did that there wouldn't be anything to worry about.

* * *

Bryan's worries were indeed unfounded, as the trip ended up being much less exciting than Bryan had anticipated. It was basically several days of discussing processes and systems and providing samples of recent projects. Many of the sessions were with other groups from within the company so he assumed that the purpose was primarily information exchange and cross training. However, various executives and managers came and went during the meetings and there were a number of other individuals that also made appearances and took notes. It was this latter group that Bryan was most curious about. He figured that there were three likely alternatives: consultants, investment bankers, or representatives from potential acquirers. With all of the recent rumors, it wouldn't be a surprise if this had been some form of a due diligence event.

When Bryan got back to the office he met with Joe to debrief on the meetings and it seemed clear to Bryan that his boss wasn't in the loop if something was happening. Joe seemed desperate for details. He wanted to know any names that Bryan could remember, where people may have been from, and even what they looked like. Bryan did his best to fill in the blanks, but he really didn't have anything concrete to share.

By Friday afternoon Bryan was back in production mode starting the daunting task of catching up on his regular work. Reviewing his work lists he already regretted having taken the trip. Bryan knew that he had a full weekend of work and would probably even have to come into the office. He was hoping to at least get enough work done to be able to squeeze in a few hours for a round of golf. His dad had invited him out for a game and they hadn't played for a while so Bryan was feeling a bit guilty.

Bryan was lost in thought when his phone rang. He glanced over and saw Tommy's number on the ID screen. He really wanted to let it go to voicemail, but decided that he should reserve that option for annoying co-workers rather than friends.

"Chambers Data Systems, this is Bryan."

"Yeah, yeah, I know where you work," mocked Tommy.

"What's going on with you, Tommy?"

"The usual, working hard on a Friday afternoon just like you my friend."

"You're not working. I hear a lot of people talking in the background. I think I hear a beer and grouper sandwich there too."

"You can hear the grouper? I never knew they were that loud of a fish. A couple of us are just adding an 's' to the lunch *hour* to make it lunch *hours.*"

"And you just wanted to call to rub it in? Are you going to email some pictures from your cell phone in order to add to my agony?"

"No, no, I actually had an important question for you. Your old buddy over at Stone Ridge, his name was Jim, or James, Garris, right?"

"Yeah, Jim Garris."

"Did you know he died on Monday?"

"What?"

"I've got to believe it's the same guy."

"Oh, man. I knew that he was sick, but I can't believe he died. We played two weeks ago," said Bryan, very much in a state of shock. "How do you know that he died?"

"My assistant was reading the obituaries and she mentioned one out in Stone Ridge. I asked her the name and she said it was James Garris."

"She reads the obits? Before or after the comics?"

"No, I have her do it. Besides if people aren't going to read them why even put them in the paper?"

"You have her read them?" asked Bryan curiously.

"Yeah, for leads."

"Leads?"

"Oh, Bryan. You cube dwellers are so naïve as to the workings of the real world. Let me go slowly. People live in those square things with a triangle on top, also called houses. People eventually move to the big house in the sky. Then their families usually sell the terrestrial houses. And who helps them do that? Tommy. Still with me?"

"No, you lost me at the house thing. I guess it makes more sense than chasing the ambulances, this way you don't bump into the lawyers. So once you've located the deceased's property do you go and case the place out?"

"Depending on where it is I usually start with a fly-by view."

"Fly-by?" interrupted Bryan, "I didn't know you could fly. I didn't even think you could fly a paper airplane."

"Actually we're a little more high tech, you can see a lot of places on Google and many of them have street views now. It gives you the chance to see what the curb appeal might be without even having to get in the car. Unfortunately most of the gated places aren't available yet so we try to pick up whatever we can from the bird's eye shot and other public records."

"I guess that's one thing good about a gated community. So essentially you're an electronic vulture."

"Hey, if it weren't for the vultures we'd be knee deep in roadkill."

"Well thanks for letting me know. I appreciate the secondary benefit of your macabre marketing."

"I'm here to serve. I just sent you the link to the obituary section of the newspaper's website."

"Thanks, Tommy. I'll check it out."

"Do you have big plans for the weekend?"

"I've got to do some work and I'm going to try to get a round in with my dad."

"Have fun. Give me a call when you're open and we'll get out and play again."

"Sounds good, have a good weekend."

"You too."

Bryan hung up and immediately turned to his computer and checked his email. He clicked the link that Tommy had sent and scanned the obituary page. He quickly found the one for Garris and read through the information. It was mostly boilerplate listing Jim's family, his work history, and his affiliations. As Bryan scrolled to the bottom he noticed that a remembrance service was scheduled for the following Saturday at Groveland Memorial Park at 8:00 a.m. Funerals were right up there on Bryan's list along with hospital visits, but he felt obliged to attend and pay his final respects to Garris.

* * *

Bryan woke up early on Saturday, but was in no hurry to be the first one at the cemetery. He had the same nagging uncertainty that he had felt when he visited Jim in the hospital. He hoped that Bill would be there since he was the only real acquaintance that he had via Jim.

Bryan had driven by Groveland many times, but had never entered the grounds before. He turned into the main entrance and squinted as the morning sun reflected off of the large gold letters that arched over the gateway. It was immaculately maintained and seemed very tranquil. Despite the fact that the property fronted on a busy road, the encompassing iron fence seemed to provide a formidable barrier to the outside world, which in turn made the facility a true resting place for its permanent occupants. The main road curled gradually through the park and Bryan proceeded slowly toward several small, gray buildings located in the middle of the property. Something felt odd to Bryan as he wound along the road, and then it dawned on him: there were no signs. No signs for speed, for directions, or for warnings. The lack of signs clearly made the assumption that visitors didn't need them. They knew they shouldn't speed, they knew where to go, and they knew not to be reckless amongst the dead. When he approached the buildings Bryan parked at the back of a line of cars that had formed there.

Bryan got out of his car and walked along the sidewalk that encircled the main building. In the distance he saw a group of roughly two dozen people gathered around a freshly dug grave. Bryan approached the ceremony cautiously and stood at the back of the group. He glanced at his watch and noticed it was already 8:20. A minister stood up near the casket and launched into a generic remembrance of someone he clearly didn't know personally. As the man spoke Bryan scanned the assembled mourners. He spotted Bill Robalo seated near the front and recognized several other Stone Ridge members he'd met over the past few months. His attention quickly swung to the two younger women sitting directly in front of the casket. They were obviously Jim's daughters, Nancy and Lisa. Next to the younger of the two was a small boy fidgeting around in his chair, clearly not interested in observing the formalities of the somber occasion. Nancy appeared very much as Bryan had expected: she was rather plain with shoulder length, brown hair framing a serious face. Even though she was at a funeral today, Bryan assumed that this was probably the same expression that she wore on most days. Lisa, however, was very different in appearance. She had long, flowing jet black hair and a very cute face. She was wearing sunglasses so Bryan couldn't see her eyes. Bryan started feeling a little guilty when his vision panned downward and he realized how good she looked in the small, black dress that she was wearing. He had to force himself to look elsewhere when his gaze arrived at her tan, well-toned legs.

The proceedings carried on for another ten minutes culminating with a song performed by a woman who worked at Groveland. When she finished she thanked everyone for coming and then began giving orders to two other employees who were standing by.

Bryan stayed where he was as the rest of the mourners began to file past. He made eye contact with Bill as he approached.

"Good morning, Bill."

"Hello, Bryan, good to see you again. Bryan, this is my wife, Sandy."

"Nice to meet you," Bryan said, extending his hand.

"Nice to meet you as well," she replied, shaking Bryan's hand lightly. "Bill told me you're a good golfer."

"Depends on the day."

Bill continued, "It was nice of you to come out to say goodbye to Jim. It was a nice, simple service today, just the way Jim would have liked it."

"Even with everything that happened recently, I'm still shocked that he's gone."

"It was his time and he knew it. He wasn't going to fight it anymore and be miserable. He mentioned to me the other day that he was glad to get his last few rounds in, including playing with you."

"I wish we could have had a few more."

"That's why you have to get in as many as you can while you're able. Take care, Bryan, I'm sure I'll see you around the club."

"You too. Bye."

Bryan waited a little longer until only a few people remained, including Jim's daughters. Bryan knew that there was no reason why he couldn't leave, but he still felt that he should offer his sympathies in person to Jim's children. He casually wandered over to where Nancy was talking to an older woman and made his way into her field of vision. When they finished Nancy received a tearful hug from the woman and then turned to acknowledge Bryan.

"Hi, I'm Bryan Minton."

"Ah, so you're Bryan."

"We spoke on the phone recently."

"Yes, I remember. I saw you arrive late this morning and assumed that you were the golfer."

"Oh, sorry about that," Bryan stammered, blindsided by Nancy's candor. "I just wanted to come over and offer my condolences. I'm very sorry for your loss. I only met your father recently, but he was a great guy and I really enjoyed getting to know him through golf."

"Well, thank you. I appreciate your thoughts," replied Nancy, thawing only slightly.

"I'm sure it's a difficult time and I just wanted to let you know that if there's anything I can do to help please let me know."

"Actually there is. We need to speak with you about some golf stuff. I found a number at my father's house for Chambers Data Systems. Is that still best way to reach you during the day?"

"Yes, that's where I work," Bryan responded, trying to keep his focus on Nancy as Lisa arrived next to her.

"Oh, this is my sister, Lisa. Lisa, this is Bryan, the golf guy."

"Hi, Bryan Minton, I'm sorry about your dad."

"Thank you," Lisa said, giving a polite smile.

"Well we've got some things to attend to here. We appreciate you coming and we'll be in touch," Nancy said, clearly letting Bryan know that the conversation was over.

"Whatever I can do to help please let me know," Bryan offered, ignoring Nancy and making direct eye contact with Lisa. Bryan turned and started back to his car. After a few paces he stopped and looked back one last time at the bronze colored casket glowing in the morning sun. He smiled and gave a nod signaling his final goodbye to Garris.

* * *

On Monday afternoon Bryan's phone rang and he immediately recognized Garris's phone number.

"Hello, this is Bryan."

"Bryan, this is Nancy Garris."

"How are you doing?"

"Good, thanks. As I mentioned the other day we need to go over some issues and I was wondering if you would be available to come by the house tomorrow evening."

"Sure. Like I said I'm willing to help out."

"Is 7:00 okay for you?"

"That's just fine. I'll be there."

"Thank you, Bryan."

* * *

Pulling up to the gate at Stone Ridge felt very odd on Tuesday night. Bryan had only been here at earlier times in the day and the scene seemed very different with the sun getting low in the west. Instead of telling the guard that he was here for golf he stated that he was here to visit the Garris family.

Bryan turned off the main road and followed a winding route that let to the West Chase section of the community. While checking the address at the office during the day, Bryan realized that he'd never been to Jim's home. It seemed strange to him that when he did finally see it Garris wouldn't be there.

Bryan followed the numbers on West Chase Court until he found 208. To his surprise he had to park on the street as the driveway was already full. Walking up to the house he examined two of the cars: a Mercedes, similar to Tommy's, and a BMW M5. He wondered if the girls were already spending their inheritance on some serious automotive hardware.

Jim's house was a typical Florida style home: stucco on concrete block with a barrel tile roof. It was a maintenance free community so the yard and landscaping were well manicured. From outside it appeared to have a decent amount of square footage; this was just the kind of real estate listing that Tommy would love. He continued to the front door and rang the bell.

Nancy answered, "Good evening, Bryan. Come in."

He walked in and followed her to a large, central living room where two men in suits were seated.

"That explains the cars," he mumbled to himself.

"Bryan, this is my father's attorney, Charles Padget."

"Evening, Bryan. Nice to meet you," he said, standing to shake Bryan's hand.

"And this is my attorney, Mitch Boyle."

"Bryan," he said also offering his hand.

"Please have a seat, Bryan," Nancy said, taking a spot next to Boyle on one of the couches. "I appreciate you coming by tonight. As I mentioned we have some issues to deal with that involve you. My father recently made some changes to his estate planning documents and my sister and I intend to challenge the modifications."

Almost on cue, Lisa entered from a sliding glass door that led to a porch where she'd been playing with her son. She left him with some toy trucks and joined the meeting.

"Hi, Lisa," Bryan said, standing quickly to greet her.

"Hello," she said, taking a seat on the couch with Padget across the table from her sister.

"I was just getting Bryan up to speed on the purpose of our meeting tonight," Nancy said to Lisa. Turning back to Bryan, she continued, "The changes that we are contesting involve you so we need to determine what your position will be."

Bryan was feeling a bit paranoid with the presence of not just one, but two lawyers. He was also not happy about the fact that Nancy hadn't bothered to mention legal issues when she invited him to the house. "Well, you've certainly caught me a bit off guard, Nancy. As for my *position*, I don't know yet. Did Jim leave me something? What is it?"

Padget answered, "We think you already have it, Bryan. Did Mr. Garris recently give you a gold coin?"

"Oh yeah, that. When we played our final round together out here at Stone Ridge he gave it to me at the end on number eighteen. He said it was valuable, but that it was also a sentimental item. I've just been real busy at work since then and honestly hadn't thought about it."

"Do you still have it?" Padget asked.

"Sure, it's in my golf bag where I left it."

"You have it in your golf bag!" interjected Nancy, clearly perturbed.

Bryan, still not grasping the importance of the coin, continued, "Yeah, why is there something wrong with that? I'm sorry if it's some important family heirloom, but Jim was extremely clear that *he* wanted me to have it."

Padget, remaining calm and motioning to Nancy to relax, said, "We have reason to believe that the coin may be highly valuable. None of us have ever seen it; we only have a description and photos that were included in his legal documents. It will obviously need to be authenticated."

"How valuable are we talking?" asked Bryan, whose heart had suddenly started to beat more rapidly.

"The last coin of its kind sold for nearly eight million dollars in 2002. If the coin is real and is still preserved in its original case it would easily be valued at over ten million today and likely far more than that."

"Whoa," said Bryan, realizing his pulse was now thumping. Despite his state of shock, the wheels in his head started spinning and he suddenly understood that Garris had been interviewing him over the past few months. You don't give a coin like that to someone who happens to drop a lucky shot during a pick-up round. He had a rush of quick flashbacks to particular things that Garris had said and questions that he had asked. Jim had definitely been trying to confirm that he was making the right decision. Snapping back to reality he looked directly at Padget and asked, "Obviously they're mad about the coin, but do I need to sign something to verify that it's mine now?"

Nancy, who was clearly fuming, blurted out, "It doesn't belong to you and we want it back! Why would he give it to someone he barely knows? I don't know what you were doing to my father, but clearly you were manipulating him and trying to take advantage of him. He was in no state to be making decisions such as this; it's simply incomprehensible."

Padget calmly cut her off once again as Boyle also asked her to settle down. "Bryan, Lisa and Nancy want to discuss the matter with you first. That's the real purpose of this meeting. Perhaps we can work something out; if not then they intend to contest the documents. This is just a preliminary discussion to see if we need to go any further, in which case you may want to retain legal representation."

"We're starting to run out of couches for lawyers," Bryan said facetiously. "Sorry, guys," he added as Boyle gave him a displeased look. "Anyway, I'm shocked. I don't want to upset the family any further at an already difficult time, but Jim clearly wanted to do this. His body may have been shot; however, there was nothing wrong with his mind. If anything, his thinking was becoming clearer toward the end. He told me that his daughters would be well taken care of financially without the coin. To answer your question, Nancy, I wasn't manipulating him; I was playing golf with him. And as to why he'd do it: a three-wood I hit into number seventeen at Stone Ridge for a double eagle the first time we played. This coin is apparently known as a Double Eagle."

"That's great to know, Bryan, but it's not yours," Nancy said, clearly unmoved.

"At this point it is his, Nancy. The documents were properly executed and Jim gave it to him," Padget added, looking to put her in her place.

Bryan's attention was distracted for a moment by the boy on the porch who had pushed a chair up against the pool safety fence and was starting his ascent. "Lisa, you may want to check on your son. It looks like he's interested in going for a swim."

"Oh, thank you, Bryan," she said, jumping up quickly and running to the door, "he knows how to find trouble." She exited to the porch and remained there with her son.

"So what do you want from me? To just give it back, despite that being the direct opposite of Jim's wishes?"

"They would like for you to return the coin and in exchange they would be willing to offer you a cash payment," Boyle said calmly.

"Well, how much are we talking?" Bryan shrugged. "Again, I'm still stunned that we're even having this conversation."

"See! I knew it. He just wants the money," Nancy barked.

"No. I'm just curious what we're talking about. Wasn't that the purpose of your little surprise meeting here tonight?" Bryan rebutted, as he began to get angry with Nancy.

Boyle continued, "They are prepared to offer you fifty thousand dollars from each of Lisa and Nancy's shares of the estate for a total of one hundred thousand dollars. In turn, you return the coin and give up all future claims to the coin and the estate."

"Well, a hundred grand certainly seems like a lot of money, but we're talking about a ten million dollar coin, right? I may be a bit new to this, but that doesn't really seem like that good of a trade. Let me ask you this, Mr. Padget, did Jim know the value?"

"Yes, I'm quite certain that he knew the current estimated value. He was aware that there would potentially be significant tax consequences and set aside additional funds for that purpose," Padget replied.

"So he knew what he was doing?"

"In my *opinion*, yes."

"And you were directly involved in handling these new documents, right?"

"Yes, I was."

"And you think he was competent?"

"Very. Again, in my opinion."

"His opinion, however, is moot, Bryan. His dealings with my father are confidential so it doesn't matter what he thinks. If this goes to court you're not going to win and Charles knows that. We'd all just as soon avoid that if possible so we're prepared to offer you two hundred thousand."

"Wow, the offer is going up quickly. As I'm sure you planned, I was caught a bit off guard with all of this so I'm going to need to think about it. It's not about the money; it's about what Jim wanted."

"Yeah, right," Nancy scoffed.

"You're really not advancing your cause here, Nancy," snapped Bryan, getting angrier by the minute. Turning back to Padget once again, "What's the next step?"

"Mitch and I have discussed it and they would be willing to give you a couple of days to consider things. Say, maybe next Monday?"

Boyle nodded his approval.

"If you accept their offer we'll draw up some documents for everyone to sign and then conduct the transaction. If not, then they we'll file the paperwork to challenge Jim's modifications. When that's filed we'll have a hearing with a judge to review the facts and likely determine the status of the coin until the outcome has been decided."

"Alright, that sounds reasonable. So unless there's anything else to cover I'd say meeting adjourned," Bryan said, standing up decisively. He shook hands with Padget and Boyle and gave Nancy an indignant glare as she sat on the couch still seething. He gave Lisa, who was still outside, a wave goodbye and she returned the gesture with a smile. Bryan sensed that this was entirely Nancy's idea. Lisa was indifferent and almost seemed apologetic.

Boyle indicated that he wanted to speak further with Nancy so Bryan and Padget walked out together. When they got to Padget's car Bryan asked him, "So what do you think I should do?"

"You seem like a good guy, Bryan, but unfortunately I can't advise you on your decision. If you are going to fight them you're definitely going to need to get yourself a lawyer. I can provide a list of some names from around town to help you find representation."

"I know you can't advise me, but what was the point of doing the new documents if they can just turn around and claim they don't count? Just off the record, what are their chances?"

"Well, off the record, Jim's wishes were quite clear. I warned Jim that it would be contestable, but he was adamant. You could see the reason for some of his decisions on display in there tonight. Even if he'd considered giving it to Lisa, Nancy would have immediately challenged that. I know from your perspective it seems like the decision would be open and shut, but based on the circumstances there's a lot of things that could be brought into question. The documents were modified in very close proximity to his death so they will try to show that Jim was under duress and will do their best to smear you. Nancy was already getting a head start tonight. It can be easy to turn the tables in court and make you prove that Jim was willing. As we talked about inside, I can vouch that he signed freely but that's about it, and even that won't hold much weight. I don't know Mitch that well, but I do know that he's smart and very fee focused. Depending on what he agreed to with Nancy, he may prefer a win in court over a quick settlement. Trust me, he won't pull any punches to win if that's the case. Just look at his car here," Padget said, motioning to the BMW.

"Hey, it doesn't look like you're doing too badly yourself," Bryan replied, pointing to Padget's Mercedes.

"I can't complain, but his still cost about twice what mine did. Hey, if you end up with the coin you can get one of each," Padget said as he got into his car. "Good luck to you, Bryan. I wish I could help you more but my duty is still to Jim. I've probably already said too much and I need to be careful."

"I fully understand," offered Bryan. "I'm not sure what I'll do, but I will call you about an attorney referral if necessary. Have a good one."

On the way out Bryan chose a different route that took him past the clubhouse at Stone Ridge. He stopped and looked at the building and grounds draped in the early twilight. The scene was quiet and still as the employees and members were all gone for the evening. He reflected on everything that had happened, particularly his first chance meeting with Garris. Bryan started to weigh his options and knew his choice would be a difficult one. Jim had obviously wanted him to have the coin, but would he have wanted Bryan to fight his daughters in court? Nancy had done a pretty lousy job of hiding her hand with her quick offer to raise the amount. Bryan figured that they would consider an even higher amount, so maybe he should just take the money and avoid the hassle.

Bryan tried his best to focus on the trip home, but his mind was swimming. When he got back to his apartment he bounded up the stairs and headed straight for the closet where he stored his golf clubs. He zipped open the side pocket and felt around, scared to death that the coin somehow wouldn't be there. He located the case and took it into the living room where he sat down and marveled at it. Bryan couldn't believe such a tiny piece of metal could possibly be worth so much money. It was indeed a beautiful coin and the gold seemed to glow as he studied its detail.

After powering up his laptop, Bryan searched for 1933 Double Eagle coins and started filtering through the numerous articles that he found. He began with the historical aspects of the coin. The twenty dollar piece was often known as the "Saint-Gaudens Double Eagle" after its designer, Augustus Saint-Gaudens. Saint-Gaudens was an American sculptor who designed the coin at the request of his friend, Theodore Roosevelt. The coins were originally minted in 1907, shortly after the death of Saint-Gaudens. They were produced in different quantities on and off through 1933, however, it was primarily the coins made in the final five years of production that took on significant importance. After 1929 most of the coins produced were held as part of the U.S. gold reserves. In 1933 President Franklin Roosevelt signed a gold recall order and the reserve coins were melted. A large number of the 1933 Double Eagles were produced, but the coins were never released and, other than two samples held by the government, all were thought to have been destroyed.

The 1933 Double Eagle coin only had a single eagle on the reverse side. However, ten dollar coins in the 1800's were known as "eagles", so the twenty dollar coins became known as double eagles. The face of the Saint-Gaudens featured a relief of Liberty walking in front of rays of sunlight. Liberty was depicted holding a torch and an olive branch and was circled by forty-six stars, the number of states in the Union in 1907. This same obverse design was brought back in 1986 and used on American Eagle gold bullion coins.

The coin that sold in 2002 was believed to have been part of a set that was stolen by a U.S. Mint employee. That coin had a long and storied past, including barely escaping the World Trade Center attacks on 9/11, but a settlement led to its eventual authorization and sale. The remainder of those coins were all tracked down by the government and destroyed.

As Bryan read through the information he was simply astonished that he was holding a 1933 Double Eagle in his hand. Based on what he was reading he couldn't even begin to fathom how Jim's father could have come into possession of such a spectacularly rare coin. But first things first, Bryan needed to make sure it officially came into *his* possession.

Although Bryan had a week to decide, he felt like he needed to make up his mind right away. He still thought some second opinions were warranted so he popped open his cell phone and called Tommy.

After a few rings Tommy answered, "Hey, Bryan, what brings you out this time of night?"

"I've got a bit of a situation on my hands. Am I interrupting anything?"

"Actually we are watching Tina's show tonight. She likes for us to watch it together."

"I see. I'm interrupting the emasculation of Tommy Manson."

"So what's your situation, Bry'?"

"It's pretty big so it might take some time and I don't want to interrupt your situation over there. What are you doing tomorrow night?"

"Should be clear."

"How about hitting some balls at the Buckets and Brews? Maybe 6:00?"

"Book it."

"I'll let you get back to your show. See ya'."

It was at moments like this that Bryan felt no remorse for not having a girlfriend.

***

On Wednesday night when Bryan arrived at the B and B he was amazed to see Tommy already mid way through his first bucket on the range.

"Sorry I couldn't wait for you, Bryan. Had to get down to business," Tommy said, stopping to shake hands with Bryan. "I already got you set up," he added, motioning to a fresh bucket of balls awaiting Bryan at the rack next to Tommy.

"Mighty thoughtful of you there, partner," Bryan said as he set up his clubs and warmed up.

"I felt a little guilty about blowing you off last night, especially if you've got a problem. So who is she?"

"Oh she's a beautiful lady with hair of gold," Bryan said with a smile as he hit his first shot. "And there's another one with black hair too."

"Oh my, you've gotten yourself into a little geometry problem. You've got a love triangle and you're doing the right thing by coming to me to help make it into a square, right?"

"Not quite, but I see your imagination is in full swing."

"So lay it on me, Bry'."

"Well it has to do with Jim Garris. He, ahh, kind of left me something."

"Really? What did you get?"

"He gave me a gold coin just before he died and as it turns out it is potentially quite valuable."

"Nice. So what are we talking about here?"

"Guess."

"I don't know. Ten grand?"

"Higher."

"Twenty grand?"

"And here I always believed that you were the one that could think big. You're still not even in the ballpark."

"Really? Hundred grand?" Tommy puzzled as he stopped hitting balls and stared at Bryan who kept hitting away.

"You're finally getting to the Little League field, but I'm talking about the big league ballpark."

"Come on, Bryan. A million?"

"I'm going to need a new bucket of balls soon if you keep dragging your feet like this Manson."

"Yeah right, Bryan. There aren't many single coins worth more than that," Tommy scoffed as he started hitting balls again.

"No, not many. But there are a few and this could be one of them."

"I'm waiting, Minton," Tommy said, addressing his next shot.

"Somewhere in the neighborhood of ten million."

"Jeez!" Tommy blurted as he topped his shot which kicked up a grass and dirt rooster tail as it zipped down the range.

"Could be more though," Bryan said slyly as he casually trued his eight iron right at the one hundred and fifty yard flag.

"Alright, enough games, Bryan," Tommy said, standing with his hands on his hips. "Stop swinging and give me the full story."

"A couple of weeks ago when I played my last round with Jim he gave me a twenty dollar gold coin when we finished on number eighteen. It's a 1933 Double Eagle. He said that it was valuable, but I was thinking maybe in the same range as you were. He told me it was from his father and he made it very clear that he wanted me to have it. After that I was busy at work and honestly hadn't thought about it. Then when I went to the funeral his daughter tells me that she needs to talk about some things. So last night I go over to Jim's house and get ambushed by two lawyers."

"Really?"

"Yeah, Jim's lawyer seems like a decent guy, but he had to give me the scenario. They seem to believe that the coin is the real deal and that it would be worth upwards of ten million dollars. I checked it out when I got home last night and that's probably accurate figure, again, if it's real. So that being the case the one daughter, Nancy, doesn't seem real keen on letting it go to an interloper like me. Adding to the mix is the other daughter, Lisa. She's the black haired one that I mentioned. As it turns out she's pretty hot. She also doesn't seem to care too much about fighting for the coin. The bottom line from the meeting is that they want to give me some cash

- two hundred grand was the number we left on - and have me go away without the coin."

"Two hundred grand for a ten million dollar coin? I don't think so."

"Well it is still a lot of money, but I think they started with a low-ball figure just to see what I'd do. My guess is that we could get it up a few hundred grand more. It seems like a lousy deal, but I definitely got the feeling from Jim's guy that he thinks they have a pretty good shot of winning if it goes to court, which means I'd get nothing. So that makes me think maybe I just take the sure thing and run. It would save time, headaches, and certainly legal costs."

"Do you have enough money to fight?"

"I don't know. I have about fifty thousand in savings, but that could go quick. Then I'd really be kicking myself if I lost. The other issue is that Jim was insistent that I get the coin. I keep playing our conversation over in my head and it's almost like he was imploring me not to give into any pressure. There are a lot of variables to consider."

"Good points, but here's how I see it. Even if you get five hundred thousand that's not set-for-life kind of money these days. Now ten million, that's you-make-the-rules kind of money. Plus Garris wanted you to have it, not them. I'd fight that money grubbing little girl, Bryan."

"That's already how I'm leaning, but this is obviously not something to make a snap decision on."

"So who else have you told about it?"

"You're the first. And I'm counting on you not to mention it to anyone, even Tina. You need to keep it quiet, okay?"

"No worries, Bryan. Speaking of locked up, what did you do with the thing?"

"I took it over to the bank today at lunchtime and put it in my safe deposit box. I have some wheat pennies and buffalo nickels in there so putting the Double Eagle in there made them seem pretty insignificant. I think the only other person I'm going to tell is my dad. If things get ugly I may have to borrow some money from him so I better get him in the loop early."

"I may not be able to finance you, but let me know if I can help in any way."

"Thanks, Tommy."

"So are you ready to play for dinner?"

"Sure, what have you got?"

"Let's do call your shot."

"Alright, lead us off."

"I'm going with a draw five iron," Tommy said as he rolled his ball into position on the ground. He closed his clubface and shifted his stance to the right before initiating his swing. On impact the heel of the club caught and the ball line-drived to the right of his target line.

"That would be a block," Bryan said, as he grabbed his own five iron.

"Let's see what you can do."

Bryan lined up and overcompensated his normal draw setup to make sure his shot would be traveling from right to left. Bryan's ball shot off to the right like Tommy's, but quickly began changing course. It swung left and then landed with rapid top spin.

"That's a hook, not a draw," griped Tommy.

"Doesn't matter, my hole," replied Bryan. "My pick. Let's go straight to the three hundred yard drive." Bryan grabbed his driver and took some big looping swings, letting the lag in his wrists build with each one. He teed up and set the ball slightly toward the toe of the club to encourage a high draw and, in turn, maximum distance. Bryan made a relaxed turn and then unleashed a shot that followed the exact flight path he'd envisioned. The ball landed just short of the three hundred yard marker before bouncing and rolling easily past it.

"Nothing to it," Tommy announced as he went through his routine. Tommy also hit a strong drive, but his ballooned slightly and faded right, sapping just enough distance to come up short.

"That's a quick two for me," Bryan said confidently. "Maybe you should pick something that you know you can handle so you can at least halve one with me."

"There's that new Bryan showing up again, awful cocky he is."

Tommy managed to win a few rounds, but Bryan had no problem winning overall. His confidence with the clubs remained high and he'd been playing more than Tommy lately. On their way inside for dinner Tommy challenged Bryan to a putting contest double-or-nothing, but Bryan knew better than to put his free dinner on the line. They had a good meal and stayed late even though Bryan knew he had a long day of work ahead of him. His mind was focused on things besides work right now.

***

Bryan had to drag himself through the rest of his work week even more so than usual. He had hoped his job would distract him somewhat from the decision at hand, but it kept resurfacing at the forefront of his mind and he would go over all of the variables again and again. He also tried not to think about the ultimate outcome if he did win, but again that was almost impossible. The value of the coin was such that it meant he would finally be able to fulfill his dream of telling his boss goodbye. It was tough to keep a smile off of his face as he would think of different ways he would do it. Perhaps a solemn one-on-one, maybe a public swan song at the Monday meeting, or better yet, maybe just not coming in at all.

On Saturday morning Bryan was mentally exhausted; however, he was looking forward to playing a round at Oak Run with his father. The burden of carrying such an incredible secret was weighing on Bryan and he was eager to share it with someone besides Tommy.

Oak Run had a lot of similarities to Stone Ridge in terms of the course, club, and membership. Oak Run, however, was much more of a stand alone facility. It was not directly tied into an overall planned community and was not defended with an entry gate. The residential development surrounding the course consisted of a variety of different styles of homes that had been built over the years. The golf course itself had drawn higher end homes, but over time the mix around Oak Run had become quite eclectic. Bryan always enjoyed the winding route that he took to the club and noted the different homes and how they'd evolved over time.

The colonial style clubhouse at Oak Run was a tribute to the old South with massive white columns and brick lined verandas. It was surrounded by mature, towering oaks and manicured lawns. Regardless of whether or not people liked the architectural style, it certainly achieved its objective of portraying elegance and exclusivity.

After parking and dropping off his clubs, Bryan made his way up the wide and low flight of steps to the front entrance. Inside, the main hall had a soaring ceiling and faux columns and arches that gave it a cathedral feel. Along its length were alcoves filled with an abundance of tables and hutches. These were covered with flower vases, books that nobody had ever read, and an assortment of club trophies. The walls featured plaques honoring club champions over the years with small, engraved brass rectangles. There was also a row of photos exalting the glory of past club dignitaries. Most clubs that wanted to survive were at least trying to diversify their membership in terms of age, sex, and race, but the photos attested to the homogenous history of the club up until this point.

Exiting the rear doors to the back veranda Bryan thought for a moment he might find Rhett Butler lecturing Miss Scarlet. Instead he found his dad reading the paper and having his morning coffee.

"There's my boy," Jeff Minton said as Bryan emerged from the clubhouse. He stood up and gave Bryan a hug.

"Hey Dad."

"Have a seat. Do you want anything?"

"No, I already had breakfast, but thanks," Bryan replied as he sat down on the heavy wrought iron chair.

"So what have you been up to?"

"Oh, the usual, working pretty hard lately."

"Is that boss of yours back to giving you grief?"

"Not so much. He's left me alone for now and has been picking on the other kids. I'm sure he'll get bored and come back to me at some point."

"Well if he does, don't lie down and let him walk all over you."

"I know, Dad. I can take care of myself," Bryan said, embarrassed by his dad making him feel like a kid.

"Just watching out for my son."

"I do have something important I want to talk to you about today," Bryan said as he looked around over his shoulders and moved closer to his dad.

"Uh-oh, this must be big," his dad said, noting Bryan's body language. "Did you knock someone up? Because if you did, your mother's going to be ecstatic. You'll have to marry her of course, but that'll just be for show."

"Dad. Come on. Unfortunately, the chances of that happening even by accident are pretty slim right now."

"Well you know I'm rooting for you, Son."

"Great, I appreciate it. Anyway, remember how I told you that Jim Garris over at Stone Ridge died. Well at the end of the last round we played he gave me a coin. He said it was valuable and that he really wanted me to have it. It's a twenty dollar gold piece called a Double Eagle. When I made that double eagle on number seventeen the first time we played together he thought it was kind of an omen. Now it seems that just calling it 'valuable' may have been a bit of an understatement."

"Really?"

"It's dated 1933, which basically means its one of the most valuable coins in the world. That's of course if it's real, which no one is sure of yet. The last one that sold went for around eight million dollars and in all likelihood this one would be worth over ten million."

"Really?" his dad said again, clearly somewhat skeptical about what his son was telling him.

"So here's the problem. He has two daughters and one of them is certainly less than enthused about her father's decision. I was summoned to a meeting over at his house the other night and they told me that they want me to give it back. They offered me two hundred grand to settle now or else go to court."

"You're serious? You're not just making this up?"

"I almost wish I was. I've been pretty freaked out the last few days. All of a sudden I'm on a roller coaster ride and it's just getting started. I'm not kidding, Dad." Bryan added, noting his father's questioning look.

"Alright, so what are you going to do?"

"Right now I'm leaning toward fighting them. Jim was very clear about his wishes to me and he changed his legal documents as well. He apparently left plenty of other money to the daughters so it's not like he'll be leaving them destitute. The real decision revolves around the fact that if I fight them and lose I'll get nothing besides some legal bills. Garris's attorney gave me the impression that I'd have an uphill battle in court so taking the easy money and walking may not be a bad idea. That's the situation. What do you think?"

"I can see your conundrum. I'm still trying to digest all of this. It's like you won the lottery and now you have to play again. I think you have to look at it this way, Bryan. You're still young so even if you lose you've got plenty of time to make your fortune, if that's what you want. But if you win, it would be a life changer and you'd have a lot of years to enjoy it. So many of the wealthy guys around here worked liked dogs and only got to savor the fruits of their labor when they were already old.

What you also need to consider though is not just winning or losing, but going one step beyond that. All that money would come with a lot of responsibility, issues, and problems. You hear all the time about people who come into a big windfall and it brings nothing but trouble. If you're not prepared for that then you may want to take the lesser amount. I of course believe in you and think you could be responsible, but you need to weigh it yourself."

"I know. I've tried not to think too much about the money aspect, but it's almost impossible. I could quit my job, buy a house –

a nice house no less, a new car, and anything in the golf realm would be within my reach."

"And just think about all of the gifts you could lavish on your family," added his dad.

"Sure, I'll be able to afford to put you out to pasture when the time comes. Or maybe I'll save my money and just drop you off on the porch of some shabby, state-run facility. Erika and I will stop by every once in a while to read you a story or something."

"Thanks, glad to know I have such loving children."

"Well, before I get ahead of myself I'm going to need to go to battle in the legal arena. I'm going to call Jim's guy, Padget, on Monday to get some references. I have no idea what it is going to cost, but I'm going to assume it won't be cheap. I have plenty of money saved to get things going, but if things get lengthy I'm afraid of the possibility of running out. I may need to move home and start doing my chores again for an allowance," Bryan said, grinning at his dad.

"If that's your round about way of asking if we'll be there as a financial backstop, then I guess I'd have to say yes. I was hoping that we were done paying for you when you finished college. You never know what life's going to throw you though. Luckily we're in a good position now to help you if need be."

"Anything I'd need would be a loan though. No handouts."

"Well that's admirable, Bryan. From a fairness standpoint though, we'd probably front you some money regardless.'

"Why's that?"

"Your mother decided to spend a few bucks to see if she could do what your brother-in-law, Dave, couldn't do – get your sister pregnant."

"I figured that would happen sooner or later."

"Erika was actually ok with the idea. She's also at the point where she wants to stack the odds in her favor if she can. We'll just keep our fingers crossed and hope for the best. That's some pretty heavy talk so far for a Saturday morning. I think it's time we go play golf and have some fun."

"Sounds good to me," replied Bryan, standing up.

"Try not to think too much about the coin, think about playing golf today."

"Easier said than done," said Bryan, shaking his head. "I'm really just trying to understand Jim's decision and be sure that I'm doing what he would have wanted. I want to prove that he made the right choice when he gave me the coin."

"Of course he made the right choice, he picked my son," Bryan's father said as he put his arm around Bryan's shoulder and gave him a hug.

"Thanks, Dad."

Bryan always enjoyed his rounds with his father. His dad had never pressured Bryan to play the game as a kid; only encouraged and coached him when he thought his son needed it. Jeff Minton had never been concerned about his son being the best golfer on the course, but he did want Bryan to be the happiest one.

His dad wasn't a flashy player, but he was extremely consistent – fairways and greens all day long. Having played Oak Run for so many years, the elder Minton knew the course like the back of his hand. The general course knowledge was helpful, but even Bryan had an adequate familiarity with that. Where his dad held a significant advantage was his knowledge of the greens. He had seen every pin location, knew every rise and ridge, and could sense which way the grain was flowing. If Bryan were to ever need a caddie for a tournament at Oak Run he wouldn't have to look far. Besides being good at reading the greens, Jeff Minton could also read his son. He knew that Bryan was distracted, but he did his best throughout the round to draw his son's mind to the course and the game. Several times during the round Jeff found himself smiling when he would realize how many things could be worse for his son than wondering whether or not you might become a millionaire.

The two Mintons had a close match, but in the end the steady approach won and father beat son. The sting of the loss for Bryan was not that great since there was no money on the line, just a little bit of pride.

9

B ryan had made up his mind that he was going to fight Nancy and was eager to get started. Not only was deciding to fight part of the mentality of the new Bryan, but so was his resolve to stick with his decision. The old Bryan would still be second guessing his path, the new Bryan was going full steam ahead and not looking back.

Bryan took Padget's business card with him to work and called the firm as soon as he got to his desk at Chambers. Unfortunately, Padget had not arrived yet and Bryan was forced to wait patiently for a few hours until he got a return call. When the phone finally rang he lunged for the receiver.

"Chambers, this is Bryan."

"Good morning, Bryan. It's Charles Padget returning your call. Have you made up your mind?"

"Yes, I'm calling to get some names from you; I intend to keep *my* coin."

"Good for you, Bryan. I was kind of hoping that's why you were calling. Do you have a pen and paper handy?"

"Sure do."

Padget gave Bryan several names and a website to review their credentials. "I'll let you look over things for yourself, but I'd give the advantage to Owen Draper. In terms of what you probably need in this situation he just stands out as the best fit. He has a good amount of trial experience over the years and also has a strong background in estate and probate work. Owen has an excellent courtroom presence and will garner more respect from judges than an attorney like Boyle."

"Well, thanks I appreciate it. I'm going to start working on it right now."

"Do you want to call Nancy or do I get that pleasure?" asked Padget.

"Oh, I better leave that up to you. She'll just start screaming at me again if I call."

"Alright, I'll call Mitch instead, but I was kind of looking forward to giving Nancy the news directly. Like you, I don't expect her to take it very well. I was hoping to get a good laugh from her meltdown."

"I thought you were supposed to remain impartial?" Bryan noted.

"Yeah, but I also have to tell the truth. Anyway, good luck, Bryan. I'm sure this will be interesting."

"Thanks again."

Bryan hung up and immediately went online to review the attorneys. He had already developed a level of trust with Padget and agreed with his recommendation on Draper. Bryan called the firm's office and was able to get an initial meeting set up for late Friday morning.

***

After lying about having a dentist appointment, Bryan headed to Draper's law office. He felt a brief pang of guilt for falsifying his reason, but it only lasted a moment and then it was gone.

Draper's firm was located on the edge of downtown in a relatively new office complex. Bryan found them on the directory in the lobby and took the elevator to the third floor. At the end of the hall he found a set of frosted glass double doors etched with the names Herman, Draper, & Killington. It sounded pretty respectable to Bryan and he was glad he'd be dealing with one of the names. Bryan went through the doors and approached the receptionist.

"Good morning. I'm Bryan Minton. I have an 11:00 appointment with Mr. Draper."

"Hi, Mr. Minton. If you'll have a seat I'll let him know you are here."

"Thanks."

Bryan sat down and took in the surroundings. The office was decorated with modern furniture and accessories. He shuffled through magazines on the center table and picked up one of the automotive titles. He didn't get much past the first few pages of future models before Owen Draper appeared in the anteroom.

"Good morning, Bryan?"

"That's me. You must be Mr. Draper."

"Just Owen. Come on back."

"Thanks."

Bryan followed Draper down the hallway to a small conference room.

"Can I get you anything to drink?" Draper offered, showing Bryan into the room.

"No, I'm good right now."

Draper closed the door and sat down across from Bryan, placing his legal pad on the table in front of him. Bryan guessed that Draper was a bit older than himself, probably in his late thirties. He looked pretty much as Bryan expected with well groomed, straight hair parted to the side. His suit and shirt were crisp and new looking and his tie was perfectly knotted and centered on his collar. He wore a gold wedding band with diamonds. Bryan assumed his attractive wife cruised around town in a big soccer mom SUV or at least a nice minivan. They probably had the statistically required two and a half kids, and even the half of a kid was good looking.

Bryan once again recounted his story of how he met Garris and how he came into possession of the coin to Draper. Bryan rambled on for about twenty minutes, adding in several insignificant golf stories along the way, while Draper took notes and nodded approvingly.

"That's pretty much how I ended up here," finished Bryan.

"Wow. It sounds like you've had an interesting couple of months. I have a lot of questions, but I'll stick to the legal aspects first. It sounds like they're going to have some strong angles to pursue, but we can work on how to counter each one."

"You guys aren't really building my confidence in my case. Padget seemed to have an underwhelming prognosis as well."

"We're just being honest and realistic with you. I know from your standpoint this should be a slam dunk, but when you take a legal view of all of those unique circumstances you just mentioned to me it becomes more of a half court shot. If you'd known him for years and he'd changed his documents well before he died then we'd be looking at a much different scenario. Unfortunately for you too many times when things like this happen it's because someone has manipulated the dying party. I certainly don't think you are lying to me, but the judge isn't going to make a decision based on whether or not he thinks you're an honest guy. As for the validity of Jim's documents, sure they could be perfectly valid, but any document can be contested if someone wants to take up the fight. Here in Florida you see a lot of older people who change their wishes near the end and many of them are under undue influence. If the changes benefit family members inequitably or there's a third party involved, such as you, the judges give very little latitude. There have been too many abuses so they will always lean toward using the prior documents, which I'm assuming have your name nowhere in them.

You also see it all the time in the headlines with celebrity prenuptials and estate documents. Documents that were perfectly legal, signed by competent parties, with adequate legal representation get tossed right out the window when enough money or ego is on the line. They do, however, at least give some basis for the negotiations. The same applies here. You've at least got your foot in the door. I think it might be a different situation if Nancy had made a more reasonable offer, like perhaps splitting it fifty-fifty. It doesn't sound like she has any desire to be equitable though. Her view is that she knew her dad her whole life and you knew him for just the tail end of it, therefore, you should be entitled to a much smaller percentage. She could be motivated as much by that thought process as by greed."

"I know. What I keep coming back to though is the fact that Jim was so adamant about giving it to me."

"I understand and will do my best to help you. At this point I just have the surface view. When I get more into the details that's where I hope to find some better positions to fight from."

"Alright, so what's next?"

"First off I need to do my homework. I'll be requesting copies of all of the pertinent documents to review. I want to make sure there aren't any glaring problems or potential landmines. As long as things look fine then we'll confirm that they still want to go forward. When they realize that you are prepared to fight they might back down and decide to make a better offer. We can address that when the time comes. If they're still intent on contesting at that point, then we'll have an initial hearing scheduled. The judge will review the facts and determine if they have a valid complaint. He will take testimony from both of the parties to get both sides of the matter. He'll then go over administrative issues such as the location and possession of the coin during the proceeding. I also wouldn't be surprised if he suggests that you and Nancy make one last effort to settle. Most importantly though, he will give us a preliminary indication of how he expects to rule. Depending on how things go he'll then set a follow up date for both parties to make their last appeals. At that point he'll likely make his final determination. His ruling could be appealed, but unless he makes some egregious error in judgment his verdict is unlikely to be overturned."

"That's actually better than I expected. I was afraid it was going to be some long drawn out process. I'd rather get it settled and move on either way."

"I think I've got my marching orders and I want you to know that I'm going to work hard to win for you. I don't know Boyle very well, but I've met him at different events and he seems pretty cocky. I'd definitely get some enjoyment from beating him. So do you have any other questions or concerns?"

"I do have one thing. What kind of ballpark do you think we are talking in terms of fees?"

"I'll get you a copy of our fee schedule on the way out. It'll be an hourly rate, plus any extraordinary expenses. I can't give you an exact number, but if things go as planned I would expect something in the three to five thousand dollar range."

"Okay," said Bryan, swallowing hard and hoping that things did go as planned.

Bryan left the office feeling good about his choice. Draper appeared quite competent and the uniqueness of Bryan's case seemed to stimulate his interest. The course of Bryan's future was very much in Draper's hands; hopefully he would find a way to validate Jim's final documents and keep the coin in Bryan's possession.

****

The next several weeks were difficult for Bryan to bear. It was killing him to have the coin, but not know whether or not he'd be keeping it. He remained busy at work, which served to provide some distraction. However, he often found himself daydreaming about the coin and replaying his conversations with Garris in his head. Frequently when asleep at night his mind gravitated toward the Double Eagle. He had a dream with pirates standing over chests that were overflowing with gold coins. They laughed insidiously as Bryan tried to grab their doubloons, but couldn't seem to get close enough.

Another evening he dreamed that he was walking down a street in New York City. It was a wintry scene with holiday decorations and passersby bundled up in their coats, carrying their full bags and packages. He stopped in front of a retail display window and pressed his face to the glass. The store workers were busy assembling a collection of gold toys under a gold Christmas tree. There were stockings topped out with gold candies and golden fruit. A gold model train circled laps around the floor. It was a happy dream until he noticed a pair of Grinch-like feet dangling in the fireplace. He started banging on the glass, but the workers didn't hear him. They smiled at their finished creation and left happily, not aware of the danger lurking up the chimney.

The other difficulty that he faced was keeping his secret under wraps. As the days went on the urge to tell other friends about it grew stronger and stronger. It was especially tough when someone was giving him some gossip or inside scoop. He felt like he needed to reciprocate, and his tale would surely top anything he was being told. That little voice in the back of his head helped him hold onto his tongue though. There was just too much that could happen if he told the wrong person. Word would spread and he'd have a whole litany of issues that he didn't need right now. Moreover, if he didn't end up winning he'd probably need his job more than ever. For now, silence was golden too.

Finally he got the call he'd been waiting for. Draper's office called and let Bryan know that the hearing had been scheduled for the following week. They also scheduled a pre-hearing meeting with Owen so that they could review all of the information and prep Bryan for the courtroom.

When Bryan went to his meeting with Owen he was disappointed to find that Draper's view of Bryan's case hadn't brightened significantly. In reviewing the timeline of Jim's documents he'd learned that Garris had finalized the changes to include Bryan just a few weeks before he died. That was also the first time that Garris had made a specific mention of the coin in his documents. Owen had decided that their best option was to focus heavily on the depth of their golf relationship during the past several months. He asked Bryan to go through his calendar and note the number of rounds they'd played and the number of hours they'd spent together. The other major hurdle in Bryan's situation was the value of the coin. Draper had examined lots of other cases and had difficulty finding anything that could serve as a precedent. Even disregarding the fact that this was a late change, such a sizeable bequest was also quite an anomaly. Had the coin been worth fifty thousand or even one hundred thousand dollars it would be a more reasonable bequest. But ten million? That was off the charts. Of course, had the coin been worth that much less Nancy probably wouldn't even be bringing this action. Draper was considering the angle that Garris had set aside funds for potential tax consequences, but even that appeared to be a trap as it was just more money that would be taken away from the daughters. Despite all this Bryan was doing his best to remain positive and keep his head up.

***

When Bryan's day in court finally came he went ahead and took a vacation day from work. They had been scheduled for 9:30 and regardless of what happened Bryan had no intention of going back to work. Maybe if things went well he wouldn't have to ever go back.

Bryan arrived at the courthouse early. He was expecting a lengthy line at the security checkpoint, similar to what he'd recently experienced at the airport. Today, however, he found several deputies leisurely checking in whoever arrived. He made his way to the second floor and took a seat outside of the courtroom where they'd be meeting. To his dismay the first people that showed up were Nancy and Mitch Boyle. Nancy offered just a glare, while Boyle managed to at least say hello. Luckily it was only a few minutes until Padget arrived. He sat between Bryan and the others and tried to ease the evident tension. Bryan was starting to get a little nervous when he checked his watch at 9:20 and Draper had still not arrived. He finally turned up at 9:25 and said hello to everyone before taking a seat next to Bryan.

"How are you doing, Bryan?"

"Not bad. I was getting a little concerned though."

"Oh, sorry. I got here a while ago but ran into some people downstairs. I wasn't going to let you down, Bryan. I'm here for you," he said, patting Bryan on the shoulder.

At 9:30 on the dot a clerk emerged from the courtroom and ushered them inside. As they entered, Bryan looked around and noted that Lisa hadn't arrived. He was honestly a little disappointed, but figured that it would be just as good not to have the distraction.

Byran and Owen took their seats at a table in front of the judge. Bryan was rather surprised by the courtroom itself. The rest of the building had seemed solemn and traditional so Bryan was expecting this room to be like the courtrooms he'd always seen on TV and in movies. The layout was familiar, with the judge seated at the front faced by the two parties and the gallery. The plaintiff and defendant area here was not divided by the ubiquitous half wall with a dual swinging gate. Surprise witnesses would not be able to rise and enter with drama the way they always did in Hollywood. The furniture was very Spartan and utilitarian. It appeared that the funds they saved on furnishings were redirected toward technological enhancements. There was a full array of cameras and monitors as well as a bank of playback devices hooked to a projection system. The judge had a large laptop open in front of him and each of the lawyers had brought smaller versions for themselves. Based on what he saw, Bryan could certainly envision the time coming when even this would be done via teleconference.

Once everyone was settled, the judge looked up from his notes and began the hearing. The judge was a serious looking man in his fifties with salt and pepper hair and a gray beard. Bryan noticed that the brass nameplate sitting on the bench said Harold Stone. Stone started by going over administrative and procedural issues. He then recited the facts of the particular legal matter at hand and reviewed a timeline that had been prepared by Padget and confirmed by Boyle and Draper. Padget confirmed the information, but was clearly remaining impartial to the dispute. The judge informed Boyle that he could begin with arguments and testimony.

"Thank you, Your Honor," Boyle said, clearing his throat and putting on his game face. "At this point you are aware of the facts leading up to this hearing. It is very clear to my clients, the heirs of James Garris, that there was no valid reason for Mr. Minton to receive the Double Eagle coin in question. Yes, Mr. Garris did make modifications to his documents; however, when these changes were made he was not just sick, he was a dying man."

At this reference Nancy made several audible sniffles. Boyle paused, almost as if on cue, and patted her on the shoulder gently.

"Oh, come on," groused Bryan under his breath, "I thought we were sticking to the facts. They're leading off with the theatrics."

"I told you, Bryan. Just keep your cool and don't react. Just let them put on their little show. Attacking them won't score any points; that's just playing right into their hand. We'll get our turn and I want you to be honest, not angry," counseled Draper.

"I know. I'll bite my tongue."

Boyle continued, "He was a dying man and he made a careless mistake. No one really knows the extent of this very brief relationship that Mr. Garris had with Mr. Minton. There were several acquaintances at the club that interacted with them, but even according to Mr. Minton's timeline most of their interaction was alone. Even if they became fast friends are we to believe that anyone who was thinking straight would give away such a valuable item to the detriment of his own children? Mr. Garris had never made a single reference in his prior documents to disinherit either of his daughters. It only occurred after he met Mr. Minton. Perhaps he saw Mr. Minton as the son he never had, but why not just write him a check or buy him a car? Give him a coin that constitutes a sizeable portion of Garris's total estate? It just doesn't seem to fit with a man that had made so many reasonable decisions up until that point in his life."

Boyle spent the next twenty minutes or so going over the specifics of Jim's documents and citing a variety of other cases. Although Bryan wasn't a lawyer, it didn't appear to add much to their arguments. It seemed more like Boyle was doing it just to prove that he'd done his homework. The judge appeared to be rather bored with the discussion, but nodded occasionally to show that he was still listening.

When Boyle finished, Judge Stone shuffled though his notes again. "Thank you, Mr. Boyle. Does your client, Ms. Garris, have anything to add?" he asked, motioning to Nancy.

"Yes, Your Honor. She just has a few comments to make," Boyle said, turning the floor over to Nancy.

"Your Honor, thank you for the opportunity to discuss our situation today. The last several months have been very difficult for my sister and me. Having already lost our mother, the settlement of our father's affairs has been our responsibility. Our father did a very good job of seeing that most things were taken care of as best as could be expected, however, this misled decision has caused an undue level of turmoil. We simply don't understand how someone who just met our father could be entitled to such a valuable family heirloom. As our attorney, Mr. Boyle, pointed out, we could certainly see some type of straightforward bequest. In fact we tried to avoid taking this to court by making a very reasonable settlement offer. Despite that, Mr. Minton has shown that he doesn't care about straining our family even further by dragging this into a legal confrontation. His greed obviously outweighs any thoughts of honoring the very brief relationship he had with my dad. Your Honor, my dad may have changed his documents, but this is definitely not what he wanted. Thank you for hearing our concerns and hopefully you'll agree that my dad's prior wishes were his true ones."

"Thank you for your insights. I can understand that this has been a difficult time for you and your sister. It appears that she was unable to join us today."

"Yes, Your Honor. My sister is a single mother so between her son and her job appearing in court had to take a back seat. However, she knows that I'm doing my best to represent our joint interests."

"Thank you," said the judge with a gracious smile. After an obvious check of his watch he turned to Bryan and Draper. "Alright gentlemen, it's your turn to present arguments."

"Thank you, Your Honor," said Draper calmly. "We are now all well aware of the facts involved in this unique situation. There are a lot of other issues regarding the coin itself, such as its authenticity, which the eventual owner will have to deal with."

Judge Stone held up his hand, "That brings up a question I had regarding the coin. Would it make sense to have it authenticated first?"

"Your Honor, both parties felt that it was appropriate to settle the possession issue first. Determining the coin's authenticity will potentially be a difficult process and having an ownership conflict would cloud the situation even further."

"Fair enough, please continue."

Draper returned to his comments, "The purpose of this proceeding is to determine the validity of the final set of documents executed by Mr. Garris. Based on Mr. Padgett's filings, I don't think there is any question about the status of the documents themselves; they were properly prepared and executed. We can all also appreciate the feelings expressed by Ms. Garris. Who wouldn't feel cheated? But was she really cheated? Mr. Garris was a very wealthy man and there will be a significant amount of assets passing exclusive of the Double Eagle coin. Also, both daughters will be beneficiaries of other trusts previously established by their grandparents. Mr. Garris was undoubtedly aware of the fact that his children would be well taken care of after his passing.

Perhaps that led to his decision to exclude the coin from the rest of the family inheritance. I recently read a story about Warren Buffet, one of the world's richest men, where it mentioned that only a small fraction of his wealth would be passing to his children. Interestingly, he made a reference to the effect that he wanted his children to have enough to be able to do *something*, but not enough to be able to do *nothing*. Mr. Garris worked hard his whole life and it wouldn't be a surprise if he wanted to take care of his children but still make sure that they were productive members of society. In fact, during their final round of golf together, Mr. Garris stressed that he wanted Bryan to use the coin and its value to make his mark. He didn't want Bryan using it just to shift to a life of leisure. This was a big part of the reason why he spent the last several months of his life getting to know Mr. Minton as more than just a golf acquaintance. He was trying to find his rare possession a good home.

On top of his other wealth, Mr. Garris had this extraordinarily unique coin. A coin that he kept a well guarded secret until the very end of his life. Although Ms. Garris referred to it as a 'family heirloom', even she didn't know about it until she read the new documents. Yes, it was something that had been passed to Mr. Garris from his father, but he made a specific point to Mr. Minton in their final conversation that it was only an heirloom to Mr. Garris.

With that being said, the circumstances aren't quite as extreme as they might seem. So let's return to the issues at hand. First, why would he choose someone like Bryan to be the recipient? The initial reason was probably nothing beyond luck. Bryan and Mr. Garris had a chance meeting and played a round of golf together at Stone Ridge Golf Club earlier this year. During that round Bryan hit his second shot on the par five seventeenth hole into the cup. Making a two on a par five in golf is known as a double eagle, a shot considered rarer than even a hole-in-one. Mr. Garris later told Bryan that he got goose bumps when he saw that happen and felt that it must somehow be fate. Our guess is that, based on his health, Mr. Garris was already considering what to do with the coin at that point. Clearly Mr. Garris wasn't going to give such a coin to someone based on just a single golf shot. So what did he do? He invited Bryan back out for another round. And then another and another. Each time he was not only building a friendship with Bryan, he was interviewing the person he wanted to give his coin to. Golf is a very unique sport. Because of the time they spent together on and off the course there was plenty of opportunity for Mr. Garris to fill in the pieces of Bryan's life. He found out about Bryan's family, his friends, and his career. The other aspect of golf is the nature of the game as it relates to the rules and honor. In the setting of a golf course Garris could easily ascertain the values and principles of his playing companion.

The final question to consider is the soundness of Mr. Garris's decision. At this point we know that his body was failing, but there are no signs that there was anything wrong with his mind. Again, we point to his actions as a way of showing he knew exactly what he was doing. The development of his golfing friendship with Bryan was clearly a premeditated process. He was also well aware of his deteriorating health. Although he made the changes right before his death, it was not a snap decision. He waited until he was sure that Bryan was the right recipient. Your Honor, the relationship between Mr. Garris and Mr. Minton may have been a relatively short one, but it was a very deliberate one on Garris's behalf. Bryan, however, had no agenda beyond enjoying the game of golf with a kindred spirit. He didn't know about the coin or Garris's other wealth. He never asked for anything, nor expected anything from Garris. Because of that there was no coercion or other undue influence in the decision that Garris made. His decision was a unilateral one made entirely under his own free will. Therefore, Your Honor, the final set of documents should be deemed valid, as that is what Mr. Garris clearly wanted," Draper concluded.

"Thank you, Mr. Draper," said the judge. "I can appreciate your client's perspective, but as you know when we see last minute changes to estate plans like this more often than not there is something else that factors into the equation. Besides it being just human nature, it is our legal duty to be suspicious. I'm not a golfer so perhaps I don't understand the depth of the relationship as you describe it. I suppose this could revolve around a great shot and some good camaraderie, but I still have to be a skeptic. I don't want to sensationalize this matter, but I do need to ask you a pointed question, Mr. Minton. Was there any type of romantic relationship between you and Mr. Garris?"

"What!" exclaimed Bryan, completely stunned by the question.

"Your Honor, is that really necessary?" asked Draper, equally surprised by the direction the judge had headed.

"Understand, I'm not looking for details or dirty laundry. It's just an issue that surfaced when we were reviewing this situation. An older, single gentleman, a single young man, and a last minute change of plans..."

"That's fine, Your Honor" Bryan said, regaining his composure. "I'll be happy to look you in the eye and tell you definitively: No. Our friendship was predicated upon golf and revolved around golf. Golf is what brought us together and what led Jim to his decision. It may be hard for you and Nancy to believe, but it's as simple as that."

"Okay, I'll accept that," said Judge Stone, surprised by Bryan's forceful response. "Ms. Garris had her time to speak, now it is your turn, Mr. Minton."

"I think most of the issues have been addressed, so I'll be brief. Going into this dispute it was made clear to me that the odds were not in my favor. Nonetheless, I decided to proceed. There were two main reasons for my decision. First, despite the circumstances, Jim properly executed his documents to effect a change that he wanted. It was solely his decision and he legally did what he was supposed to do. Now, after the fact, it seems way too easy to completely discredit that based on opinion. I simply can't take that lying down. The second reason is the fact that Jim was so blatantly clear that he wanted me to have it. I didn't know anything about it and certainly didn't ask him for it. He told me it was valuable, but it stayed in my golf bag until after my meeting with Nancy and the attorneys. I didn't run down to the coin shop to grab my cash. Nancy somehow feels that I'm dishonoring her father. It's actually quite the opposite. I'm fighting because I'm trying to honor her father's wishes. She is entitled to something and she's getting plenty. I just don't know why she thinks she's entitled to everything," finished Bryan, throwing his hands up in frustration.

"Your views are also very understandable, but I'm in a bit of a difficult situation since I can only rule on the validity of the documents. I can't rewrite or reinterpret them to carve out some type of bequest for you. You were never mentioned in prior documents so if the new ones are thrown out you get nothing. Although you occasionally had fellow players with you, most of your interactions with Mr. Garris were alone. Also, the few people that were with you had no knowledge of the coin or Mr. Garris's plans. That makes it very hard for the court to be able to interpret his mind set."

"Alright, Your Honor, let me ask you this: what would it take to get you comfortable? Obviously my word is not sufficient, but is there anything that could cause you to change your mind? Otherwise it seems like this is already a foregone conclusion."

"Again, we just don't have any real first hand evidence of his intent. If he was sitting here in this courtroom I would be able to see his mannerisms and his body language. If we had transcripts of your conversations that would provide extra clarity. Just something more concrete to provide support for the decision to give you the coin. That's how I could comfortably agree that the final documents were the right ones. The fact that we don't is why we're having this discussion today."

"Okay, at least I know where I stand," Bryan responded.

"At this point I don't think I'm ready to make a final decision. This was a preliminary hearing to give all of the parties a chance to speak. I would like to schedule a follow up in a few weeks. That will give all of you added time to consider your positions and I would encourage all of you to keep the dialogue open. Mr. Minton, I understand that you currently have the coin in a safe deposit box?"

"That's correct, Your Honor."

"I expect you to leave it there and act responsibly. Don't leave town."

"I won't be going anywhere, Your Honor."

"With that we'll close this hearing. I appreciate everyone coming today and the clerk will coordinate the follow up."

Nancy and Boyle headed out immediately without any acknowledgement toward Bryan. Padgett at least offered a smile and a nod before he headed on his way.

"Well, that went a little better than expected," Draper said, turning to Bryan.

"You think so?" asked Bryan.

"Definitely. It started out according to plan, but you did a great job planting some seeds of doubt in his mind. I really sensed that he wants you to get something if possible, that's why he gave us more time and encouraged us to keep talking. Based on their departure I'm not so sure Nancy is quite as open minded. So what do you think, Bryan, do you want me to call Boyle about a settlement?"

"Not yet. We've got a few weeks so let's make them sweat a little. They'll probably be expecting us to call right away and take whatever they decide to offer now."

"Pretty bold, Bryan," said Draper grinning.

"Maybe Nancy will get nervous and decide to call us. We'll see."

"Alright. Well if you think of anything else that might help give me a call right away. I'll be in touch once we get another date set."

"Thanks, Owen, I appreciate all of your help on this."

10

B ryan was surprised to find that after the hearing he actually
felt less stressed. It was a relief to have gotten the first
hearing out of the way and Bryan felt good about the stand
that he and Draper had made. Even if he didn't end up with the
coin, at least he'd have put up a good fight. Moreover, deep down he
still had an odd feeling that he'd win, but perhaps it was just
misplaced optimism.

Two weeks had passed since the initial hearing and Bryan still
had another two weeks until the next one. He had spoken to Draper
several times, but so far there was still no communication with
Nancy or Boyle. Bryan had had a relaxing weekend playing a round
with his dad and doing little else besides. He thought he was in
pretty good shape at work so he arrived in the office on Monday
ready for their group meeting. As he entered the building and
walked across the main lobby he was startled when he heard his
name called.

"Mr. Minton?"

Bryan turned to the receptionist, Julie, surprised that she even
knew who he was, "Yes?"

"Mr. Kelly is looking for you. He wants to see you in his office
immediately. He wanted you to know as soon as you arrived."

"Oh, thanks," Bryan said, getting a sinking feeling in his gut.

He went through into the main area and headed cautiously
towards Kelly's office. Bryan's mind was racing, trying to think of
anything from the past few weeks that could have gone haywire. He
couldn't come up with anything, which made it even more
worrisome. Walking past the last few offices before Joe's he caught
several glances from the occupants that seemed to look like they
already knew what Bryan didn't. He stopped in front of Joe's door,
took a deep breath, and then tapped gently and walked in.

"Morning, Bryan, how are you doing?" Kelly asked without any
emotion.

"Okay. What's going on, Joe?" Bryan responded, sitting down
and bracing himself.

"So what's all this business about a fifteen million dollar coin?"

"What!" exclaimed Bryan, shocked as much by the question as he was by the value that his boss had just said. "How did you find out about that?"

"Well, like a lot of people, Bryan, I read the newspaper in the morning. I was surprised to say the least when I saw a story about a legal battle involving a rare coin and that one of the involved parties was none other than Bryan Minton, an employee at Chambers Data Systems," Kelly said sarcastically, motioning to the newspaper sitting on his desk.

Bryan picked up the paper and started reading as fast as he could. He couldn't believe he was reading a summary of his recent life in the newspaper. It seemned that the source of the information had been a local coin dealer. Bryan wondered how a coin dealer could have found out when the Double Eagle had been with him the whole time. Maybe it had been the judge poking around, or perhaps it was some ploy by Nancy.

"Joe, I'm sorry. I have no idea how this got out. And I can't believe that it tells where I work. This is just crazy."

"So is this all fiction or some kind of hoax?"

"Well, yes and no. I did receive the Double Eagle coin, but it hasn't been authenticated so it might not even be real. Besides that, at this point the chances are pretty slim that I'll even get to keep it. So don't worry, I'm not packing up my desk yet."

"But if it is real would it be worth fifteen million dollars?" asked Kelly, now more curious than angry.

"Again, there are a lot of big questions about this whole thing right now. Potentially I suppose it could be that high, but we've been assuming something more in the range of ten million. Leave it to the media to sensationalize in any way that they can."

"And who was this guy that gave it to you?"

"A gentleman I met playing golf a while back. Nice guy. I didn't really know him that long, but knew he had health issues. He gave me the coin just before he died. Because of the value his daughter wasn't happy about his decision so that's what has led us to court. We'll have what will likely be the final hearing in two weeks."

"Wow, that's pretty amazing. Well it sounds like you weren't the one that put this in the paper and hopefully it won't have any negative reflections on Chambers. I'm sure it will be difficult, but just try to keep your focus and not let this cause any issues in the office. It's almost time for our meeting so I'll let you go."

"Thanks, Joe. Again, I'm sorry. I had no intention of this becoming public and I definitely plan to find out how it did."

***

As soon as Bryan got back to his cubicle he was barraged by co-workers trying to find out what was going on. He simply told everyone that he couldn't talk about it. He also had full voicemail and email inboxes. He decided to ignore all of it until after the Monday meeting.

During the meeting everyone had their eyes on Bryan. Joe did his best to act like nothing was happening, but at the end he did make a pronouncement that the article in the paper was not to affect their team's performance.

Afterwards Bryan headed straight for his desk and called Draper's office.

"Bryan, I take it you saw the article?"

"Actually, I was lucky enough to have my boss see it first and ambush me with it first thing on a Monday morning. Just a great way to start off the day and the week. Do you have any ideas about where it came from?"

"I don't have the full story yet, but I've been working the phones this morning and have pieced some of it together. My first call was to Boyle and he admitted that they had been the root cause. Apparently Nancy decided to jump the gun and took some of the color photos of the Double Eagle to a local coin dealer. She had heard that he had some level of expertise in coins of that era and wanted to discuss its authenticity and potential value. My hunch is that she may have been thinking about a settlement and wanted to be a little surer about the coin itself first. The guy of course wanted some background on it so he chatted her up for a while. Somewhere along the line she let your name slip, but I'm sure she only had good things to say about you."

"Of course," said Bryan.

"The dealer then contacted a friend at the newspaper and they put together some of the details."

"Do you think she told him where I work?"

"Boyle didn't seem to think so. I've got a call into the reporter, but haven't heard back from him yet. They probably found it in an employee directory on the Internet. It's amazing how fast they can find facts on you these days. I'm surprised they didn't draw the connection to your mom being on the City Council though. That should have been an easy one for them; they must have had a deadline to meet."

"I guess the obvious question is how does this impact the case?"

"The judge may frown about it, but it probably won't make a big change either way. If we had some kind of signed settlement and Nancy blabbed that might be different. This just makes it public."

"Great. Now I'll look like a public loser when I end up with nothing," griped Bryan.

"I don't know if it will do us any good, but we could try to use it as leverage against Nancy to restart a settlement discussion. Do you want me to run it by Boyle?"

"I'm not sure. I was in a pretty good state of mind and now this has just stirred everything up again. The coin has become such a burden but this just redoubles my will to beat Nancy. I only wish we had some other angle to work or some other strategy to use."

"I'll keep thinking and you do the same. I'll let you know if I come up with anything."

"Thanks, Owen, I'll talk to you later."

"Hang in there, Bryan."

***

Bryan had plenty of work to do, but decided to call Tommy first. He could talk to everyone about it now that the secret was out, however, Tommy would provide the type of insight that Bryan's other friends couldn't.

"Hello?"

"Tommy, it's Bryan."

"I see that the horsy is out of the barn."

"Yeah, you could say that."

"I figured that you were inundated with calls already so I wasn't going to bother you this morning. So how'd they get a hold of the story?"

"I talked to Draper just now and he told me that Nancy decided to talk to the coin dealer and apparently went a little too far with the information."

"Oh, that was nice of her. I guess she's already counting her chickens."

"Really working your arsenal of farm phrases today I see."

"You know I have to be able to talk in the language of the people in my line of work. I don't head up to the ivory tower each day like you; I'm out here in trenches. Nonetheless, I still want to see you as the one who ends up happy as a pig in..."

"Well, our building is one-story, so I don't think that qualifies as a tower. And as far as what I'm 'in', what do you think? We haven't had any discussions with Nancy and the clock is ticking. I haven't really changed my mind, but do you think I should go for a little bird in hand versus two big ones in the bush? I'm just trying to use the terms of your 'people', Tommy."

"Do you think anything is still on the table at this point?"

"I'm not sure she would budge, but I get the feeling that her attorney might push her to go ahead and seal the deal especially if I agreed to the original one hundred thousand dollar figure."

"You know that I'm proud you gave it a fight to begin with so I think you should stick it out. But it's not my money to be playing with. I don't know, it's a tough call, maybe it is time to cut and run."

"I don't know if I'm being stubborn or stupid. I guess with what happened today I should just hang tight; perhaps it will force their hand or maybe Draper will come up with something else to pursue."

"Yeah, see how it shakes out. Alright, I've got to head out so I'll let you get back to your media frenzy. Call me if you need anything."

"Thanks, Tommy, see ya'."

***

Over the next several days Bryan was inundated with calls and e-mails. He quickly screened out most of them and only responded to friends and family. Even then he kept most of his replies very brief. From some of the others he did take down a few names and numbers. There were already a few who wanted to buy the coin from him if he won. He figured it wouldn't hurt to keep those around just in case. Additionally, there were a couple of calls from women expressing interest in getting to know him. He wasn't sure about the type of woman that would cold call him based just on the article, but it might be worth a few blind dates just to find out. Bryan figured that if he lost he might end up becoming a basket case so they could have a lot in common.

Unfortunately Bryan's home number was listed so he arrived back to his apartment each day to a full answering machine. On Thursday evening he was running through the calls when he came to one from a gentleman named Paul Jacobs. He said he lived on the golf course at Stone Ridge and had seen the article in the paper mentioning Bryan. He said that he had some information to share and was just trying to confirm that he was calling the correct Bryan

Minton. Jacobs left a number and indicated that he would be back in town on Saturday if Bryan wanted to meet.

***

As Bryan pulled up to the gate at Stone Ridge on Saturday morning, he had a quick flashback to the Saturday morning several months ago when he first met Garris. He reflected on the amazing chain of events that had taken place since then and remembered that it wasn't over yet. Bryan wasn't here for golf today, but he was brimming with enthusiasm. After learning of the reason for Jacobs's initial call Bryan was ecstatic that Jacobs was willing to meet with him first thing today.

Bryan followed the map that he'd printed to the Mirasol subdivision within Stone Ridge. This was a portion of the development that Bryan had not visited before. These were the newest homes in the area and it seemed that each house was trying to be bigger and more impressive than the ones that preceded it. Bryan headed toward the end of the cul-de-sac and pulled into the driveway when he found the address he was looking for. As he got out of his car, Bryan looked down the side of the house and saw the eighteenth green of the golf course where Jim had given him the Double Eagle.

Bryan rang the bell and was greeted by a cacophony of barking dogs stirring excitedly on the other side of the beveled glass doors. Bryan heard someone arrive and shepherd the dogs away before returning to greet Bryan.

"Good morning, Bryan? I'm Paul. Come on in. Sorry for all that commotion. We don't get a lot of visitors in here so the dogs like to take advantage of any opportunity they get to guard the door."

"Well thanks again for having me over this morning," Bryan said as he entered the foyer and shook hands with Jacobs.

"Oh, no problem. When I saw that story in the paper I was just amazed. I was even more surprised when I realized that the Garris involved was Mr. Garris from our club. Follow me this way over to my office," Jacobs said as they headed through the opulent home.

"So did you know Jim then?"

"No, not really. I don't play a lot of golf and we use the club more on a social basis for the family stuff. I do play in some of the events occasionally so I heard his name every now and then and knew him by sight. But we never played together and I really never knew anything about him."

"He was obviously a bit older and played with his contemporaries so that doesn't surprise me. Besides that, after his wife died he apparently did a lot less of the social activities."

"Here we are, go ahead and have a seat on the couch."

"Wow, this is quite the office," Bryan commented as he sat down on a large leather couch in the middle of the room. The office was huge and filled with computer equipment. Bryan started counting and noted eight different monitors in addition to what must have been at least a sixty inch TV.

"So how did you know Mr. Garris, Bryan?" Jacobs asked as he retrieved a massive laptop computer and set it up on the table in front of the couch.

"We met by coincidence. I was supposed to play out here with a buddy of mine and when he stood me up I ended up getting paired with Jim. During that round I sank my second shot from the fairway on number seventeen for a double eagle. That basically started our friendship and eventually was part of the reason he decided to give me the coin."

"That's pretty bizarre. Almost like it was meant to happen."

"Jim said he kind of felt the same way."

"This is a new machine, but of course it still takes longer to boot than the older ones," Jacobs said as he sighed impatiently and they both watched the laptop roll through an assortment of loading screens.

"So I'm just taking a guess here, but I've got to assume you're in some type of tech related business," Bryan inquired.

"Yes and no. I'm involved in a couple of businesses right now and I have and I.T. background. Some of this technology is necessary for my business interests and some of it is just the indulgence of my inner geek."

"It certainly looks like your inner geek has been released. It also sounds like I should be grateful that it was."

"Here we go," Jacobs said, swirling his wireless mouse on the table to find his cursor. "So as I was telling you on the phone, I was pretty upset when we got to our summer vacation home and logged on to my security network. I scrolled through the cameras and realized that the one in the back corner of the house had been turned around in the opposite direction and was facing the eighteenth green. At first I was worried that someone had intentionally moved it for malicious purposes, but all of the other cameras were in place and working just fine. I couldn't figure out how the camera could have been moved so I played my hunch and called the boys in to take a look. I just had them look at the feed and observed their reactions. They all started exchanging glances and shifting back and forth on their feet. As the two older ones started to drift away from Ricky I knew I had my culprit. They were playing baseball next to the house before we left and he hit a line drive that knocked the camera in the other direction. There wasn't much I could do so I didn't really worry about it until we got back last week.

One night after the kids went to bed I was getting things in order and just started watching some of the footage. A lot of it was boring so I just skipped through it, but there was plenty of entertaining stuff. I saw a few really good putts and a lot of really bad ones. There was some crazy body language, some nose picking, and lots of general scratching. But most importantly for you I saw a number of players that I recognized from the club," Jacobs said as he finished pulling up the footage on the computer in front of them.

Jacobs clicked play and Bryan sat with his gaze transfixed on the screen. He was quickly transported back to that Saturday morning when he played his final round with Garris. He watched in awe as the cart carrying the two of them pulled into view. Then as they got out and walked up to the green. Bryan had forgotten that he'd birdied the hole until he saw himself lining up the putt.

"There is one of those nice putts I was talking about," Jacobs complimented as the ball disappeared into the hole.

Bryan didn't respond, rather he just continued to watch the film fearful that it might somehow stop before getting to the part he was waiting for. His worries were misplaced as he soon watched them shake hands and then saw Garris hand him a dollar and the case containing the coin. Jim's manner was relaxed and he looked almost too happy for a man that was preparing to die. The camera angle was perfect and the footage was stunning. Bryan felt a wave of warmth spread across his body as he watched them finish their conversation and Jim pat him on the shoulder before walking off the green.

"So what do you think of that?" asked Jacobs, watching Bryan's expression.

"Play it again," Bryan said with a huge grin on his face. He knew his smile was equal in scale to the opposite look that Nancy would have when she had the opportunity to see this for the first time. After watching it a second time Bryan felt like he could breathe again. "I can't believe I'm watching this. I wish it had sound to go with the video, but the picture quality is awesome. When you said you had footage from your security camera I was expecting something with a grainy black and white look."

"The cost of equipment like this is a fraction of what it used to be. And since it's all digital the storage is cheap and easy. You can do it with sound, but you have to have the microphones down on the ground and isolated. If they are up with the cameras on the eaves all you get is wind noise. So judging by your reaction I take it that this will help you out."

"That would be a bit of an understatement. I don't want to get too excited yet, but this is a game changer and probably a game winner. This is exactly what the judge was looking for in terms of knowing Jim's intent. I just never thought I'd be able to provide it. I can't even begin to thank you for this."

"Hey, no problem. I'm glad I can help. I don't know anything about that daughter, but it's pretty clear that Mr. Garris wanted you to have that coin of his."

"So I'm assuming that you can e-mail this to my lawyer and me?"

"Sure, but since I knew you were involved in a legal dispute I went ahead and made you some official versions," Jacobs said as he stood up and retrieved some items from his desk. "Here are a couple of DVDs and I also saved it on a pair of USB thumb drives for you. For extra measure there is a digital time stamp encoded on everything that can verify when it occurred."

"That's great, thanks. So can I pay you anything for these?"

"Definitely not. I get that stuff in bulk so it's on the house. Also, if you need me to testify or anything feel free to ask. My schedule is pretty hectic, but I'll make it if I can."

"I appreciate it. I'll talk to my attorney first thing on Monday and see what he says. Well, I better get going and let you get back to the family. Again, I can't thank you enough for this and be sure to thank Ricky for me too," Bryan said, standing to leave.

"My pleasure, I'm glad I could help and good luck," he replied and then showed Bryan out.

When Bryan arrived home he was still smiling from what had just happened. As soon as he got in the door Bryan headed for his computer. He couldn't help himself; he had to watch it again. He played the clip over and over, slowing it down, pausing it, scrutinizing every detail. Every single second of it led Bryan to one conclusion: he was going to win.

***

Bryan e-mailed a copy of the clip to Draper over the weekend. He wanted it to be there waiting when Owen got to his office on Monday morning. Bryan was watching his phone intently, expecting it to ring as he prepared for his 9:00 meeting. At 8:50 he decided to call Draper.

"Good morning, Herman, Draper, and Killington, this is Joyce."

"Hi, Joyce. This is Bryan Minton calling, is Owen in yet this morning?"

"He just arrived and is here in the lobby talking with one of the other attorneys. Can I have him return your call?"

"Would it be okay if I hold for him? I honestly just need a minute and it's really important."

"Sure. I think they're almost done."

Bryan waited anxiously as the clock ticked towards nine. He didn't want to be late to Joe's meeting, but he also didn't want to miss Draper.

"Hello, Bryan?"

"Morning, Owen."

"Did you have a good weekend?"

"A stellar weekend. I saw a great movie."

"Oh yeah, which one?"

"An Oscar worthy performance starring Jim Garris and Bryan Minton as they play the eighteenth hole at Stone Ridge and Garris presents Minton with a gold Double Eagle coin. There's a copy of it waiting in your e-mail inbox."

"Are you kidding?"

"Nope, I got a call from a guy named Paul Jacobs who lives on number eighteen. He said he had some footage from his home security camera that showed Jim on the green. Sure enough, it was our final round together and you get a perfect view of him giving me the coin. There's no sound, but the quality is spectacular."

"So how did he know it was you?"

"Oh, that's the best part. He saw the story in the paper and knew the Garris name from the club. If Nancy hadn't screwed up he never would have found me."

"That's huge. Let me go to my office and pull it up."

"I have to run to my Monday meeting; can't quit my job yet. I just had to let you know, I've been on a high all weekend. Check it out and let me know what you think."

"Okay, we'll talk later."

***

Draper called Bryan back later in the morning to congratulate him. It was too soon to call it a sure thing, but Draper figured it was about as close as you could get. They discussed their strategy and Draper didn't see any reason to provide it to the other side before the hearing. He really wanted to surprise them and Bryan was in full agreement. In a worst case scenario, Owen thought that they might be able to claim that they needed to review the authenticity of the video. But because of the nature of the clip and the time stamp their chances of discrediting it were very slim. There was simply no way it could be a fake. Moreover, it fit perfectly with what the judge had been looking for to verify Bryan's claims.

On the day before the hearing Draper did receive a call from Mitch Boyle. Boyle was inquiring to see if there was anything to discuss before they returned to court. Draper assumed that he was just fishing or wanted to see if there was any interest in a last minute settlement. Owen let him know that he couldn't think of anything and politely wished him luck. A settlement was the last thing on their minds.

11

B ryan and Draper were the first to arrive at the courtroom. They had a difficult time concealing their smiles when Nancy appeared with Boyle. They went through the normal procedures before Judge Stone gave each side their opportunity for final comments.

Boyle led things off. "Your Honor, at this point we have little else to add to our position. We stand behind our previous arguments and feel that the last set of documents should be deemed invalid. For your reference, we did agree to keep communication with Mr. Draper and Mr. Minton open, but nothing was forthcoming during the past few weeks. I even reached out to Mr. Draper to no avail."

Owen pursed his lips and shook his head in an exaggerated fashion to show his displeasure with the last comment, as Boyle had waited until yesterday to "reach out".

"You are likely aware that subsequent to our last hearing a certain media issue arose relative to this dispute. Ms. Garris made a rather innocuous inquiry about the coin to a local coin dealer and unfortunately that individual felt it was necessary to contact the local newspaper about the story. I contacted the individual and made clear the sensitive nature of this situation and requested that he refrain from any further disclosures at this time. We're certainly sorry that this occurred, however, we don't feel that it has any direct bearing on the legal discussions at hand."

Judge Stone had obviously been awaiting their comments on the news story. "Yes, I did see that and was quite disenchanted by the whole thing. I think it was quite presumptuous of Ms. Garris to be looking into the value of the coin and it was extremely disrespectful that she allowed Mr. Minton's name to be disclosed. It was a very unnecessary lapse of judgment."

"I'm very sorry, Your Honor," Nancy said meekly as she slouched down just a bit in her chair.

Draper couldn't help himself and seized the moment. "Your Honor, we were also very concerned by that turn of events. It has placed Mr. Minton in a difficult position at work and has led to a significant disruption of his personal life. We're glad to see that Ms. Garris understands the magnitude of her error and is apologetic. Although I guess she was really apologizing to you."

"I'm sorry to everyone," Nancy added.

"Do you have anything further to add, Mr. Boyle?" asked Stone.

"No, I think that's it, Your Honor."

"Alright then, Mr. Draper, your turn."

"Your Honor, during the last hearing Mr. Minton asked you what it would take for you to decide in his favor. You indicated that you really needed something 'concrete' to determine Mr. Garris's intent. In that context, I think we brought you a truckload of concrete today, Your Honor."

Bryan took a quick sideway glance to see the stunned reactions of Boyle and Nancy as Draper noisily removed several DVDs from his briefcase. They were already on edge due to the judge's reaction to the news story and Draper's statement was even more unsettling.

"Subsequent to the publication of the story about the coin Mr. Minton was inundated with phone calls. One of those calls came from a gentleman named Paul Jacobs. Mr. Jacobs happens to live adjacent to the eighteenth green at Stone Ridge Golf Club. He called Bryan with some interesting news of his own. It seems that he had had a little malfunction with some of his security equipment and for several weeks one of his high resolution, color video cameras was pointed at the number eighteen green. Over that time period the camera captured everything that occurred on the green."

Owen stood up and handed a DVD and paperwork to Boyle. He then approached Judge Stone and provided the same. "Unfortunately, Mr. Jacobs is a very busy man and was unable to attend today. But I went out to see him and he was more than happy to sign an affidavit outlining the circumstances that created the footage we are about to watch, as well as vouching for the validity of the time stamping on the video. I've just provided you with signed copies of that document. I've also provided you both with DVDs containing the footage.

Your Honor, if it's alright with you I'd like to go ahead and show the video now so that we can all view it together."

"Please do, Mr. Draper. I'm intrigued to say the least," Stone said, motioning toward the video components.

Draper opened the DVD player and inserted a copy of the disc. The clerk helped him start up the large projector and gave him the remote control. The courtroom remained dead silent as the video began to play and everyone watched what Bryan had already seen dozens of times. Draper let it play once through in full before going back and dissecting the clip.

"As you can see, Your Honor, we are now watching the final hole of golf that Mr. Garris and Mr. Minton played together. We don't have the audio portion of their play, but I think you can agree that the high quality video speaks volumes about what occurred the day that Mr. Garris gave Mr. Minton the Double Eagle. Note the body language as they approach the green. These look like two people that have known each other for years, not just a few months. Please remember that Mr. Minton had no idea of what was going to happen. As Mr. Garris moves around the green you get numerous glimpses of his face, the face of a content and happy man. When you see Mr. Minton make his putt - by the way, nice stroke, Bryan - notice again the enthusiasm shared by Mr. Garris. Then, here at the end, we get to witness the critical point in this entire matter: Mr. Garris giving Mr. Minton the contended coin."

Draper paused the video just as Garris was placing the coin in Bryan's hand. He approached the screen and pointed to Jim's smiling face. "What do you think, Your Honor? Are you able to determine his intent from what you see here?"

"Without question," replied Stone, who had his elbows on the bench and his chin resting on his hands. He too was mesmerized by the footage. "I can't believe we are watching this." His mind was now made up but he still had to go through the formalities. "I must say that I am shocked at how this matter has changed since our last hearing. I don't know any way that I could watch that and then dismiss the final documents. Mr. Boyle, do you have any response that might convince me otherwise?"

"I'm as surprised as you are, Your Honor," Boyle said, giving Draper a look of respect for having thrown such a knock out punch.

Judge Stone continued, "And Ms. Garris, let me ask you a question. Is that your father we see in the video?"

"Yes, Your Honor, it is," she responded. She was quite choked up, but Bryan felt that this time it was actually true emotion stemming from the sight of her father rather than the realization that she'd just lost.

"Mr. Minton, do you have anything else to add?" Stone asked.

"Not really, Your Honor. Thank you for at least keeping an open mind. I'm glad I was able to prove definitively that Jim wanted me to have the Double Eagle," Bryan said, already basking in the glory of his win. In the back of his mind he knew there were still a number of hurdles to clear, but for now he wasn't going to let that bring him down.

"With that I'm going to go ahead and issue my formal ruling that the last set of estate documents were indeed valid. The court will provide each party, as well as Mr. Padgett, with documentation of my decision. As you know, Mr. Boyle, your client can appeal this ruling if you see fit. You're aware of the proper procedures, however, if you do not intend to appeal please notify the opposing party of your position. This hearing is now over."

Bryan sat comfortably in his chair while Draper gathered his items. Boyle and Nancy got up abruptly and headed out without saying anything to Bryan. On the way out, however, he heard Boyle scolding Nancy: "You have no one to blame but yourself. I still can't believe you did that."

"Congratulations," Owen said, shaking hands with Bryan. "This is one that I'll remember for my entire career."

"Thanks for all of your help, Owen. You did a great job."

"Well, this made it pretty easy today," he said, holding up the disc. "So what is your plan now?"

"Honestly, I really don't know. I think I'm going to take a few days off and go play some golf. I'm pretty worn out after all of this. I'll think about things and decided when I get back. Based on what I've read about the coin I may be in need of your services again."

"Anything I can do I'll be there to help. Alright, let's get out of here before the judge comes back and changes his mind."

***

The next day started off right for Bryan when he received a call from Draper notifying him that Nancy intended to take no further action. Emotionally Bryan was on a high, but mentally and physically he was exhausted. He'd been hoping to take a few days off and really wanted to get out of town. He had mentioned it the last time he talked to Tommy, who said he was on board for a little rest and relaxation too. Moreover, he still needed to tell Tommy about his courtroom victory.

He grabbed the phone and got Tommy right away. "Hey, Bryan. So how was the big day in court?"

"As expected, we cleaned their clocks. They had no idea what was coming. The judge was already starting to lean because of the news story, but once he saw the clip it was a done deal. They called Draper today and said they were dropping any further action.

They're getting plenty of money so she can just pay Boyle and move on. It was relatively quick so my bill won't be too bad."

"Congratulations big guy. Are you going to sell it now?"

"Not yet. I've got to figure out the best way to get it authenticated and I'm still going to have to deal with the government at some point I imagine. This was just the first step and now I need to take a breather. Are you up for that road trip we were talking about?"

"You better believe it. I was thinking about a few days up in North Carolina."

"Let's see what we can put together here."

After about twenty minutes of bouncing around the Internet and travel websites they booked a four day package and got a direct flight. Bryan hoped that a couple of days up in the mountains would recharge his batteries for what lay ahead.

***

The trip up was rather uneventful and they arrived at the Pine Meadow Resort ready to drop their luggage and hit the course. The facility had the rustic, mountain cabin look that you'd expect for the area. It featured three full championship courses and a nine hole short course. Neither Bryan nor Tommy had been there before, but it had received solid reviews online. Spending most of their time in Florida, they were accustomed to playing very flat, open courses. Here they would have to adjust to the elevation changes and forest lined fairways. By this time of year there had already been a few short cold snaps so the leaves were starting to show some color change. The resort was a few thousand feet above sea level so the elevation kept the air a little drier and the temperature a little cooler. After a long, hot and humid summer in Florida the change in atmosphere was a welcome relief to Bryan and Tommy.

The other big difference was the grass. Although Florida courses could get green in the rainy season, the grasses never got as dark and lush as those in the mountains. In Florida if a golfer sat down in the grass to wait for a green or fairway to clear they'd get up itchy. Here golfers could lie down on the grass and roll around without any such consequences. There were certainly bugs - or more appropriately in the Carolinas, critters - but nothing as bad as the ants further south. When they arrived at the clubhouse Bryan stopped and ran his fingers through a patch on the front lawn; the blades were soft and rubbery. He couldn't wait to hit iron shots off the stuff. He remembered how crisp and juicy the divots were on good shots. The club sounded like a teeth biting into a succulent piece of fruit.

Since they had arrived late morning on a Thursday, they only had an afternoon round scheduled that day. After a quick lunch they headed out to the course and got down to business. It was just the two of them and since they both needed to get acclimated to the conditions and the altitude they decided that this would be just a warm up round – no betting. The first couple of holes went alright, but they both then started to have some problems. Drifting drives led to the echoing sound of golf balls thunking off trees. A few of them caromed back toward the fairway, but as the round went on, more of them decided to get back to nature deep in the woods.

No one was pushing them so they took a break at the turn to grab a drink and regroup. Tommy brought the scorecard with him as they sat down at a table at the halfway house.

"So how bad is it?" asked Bryan.

"I'm not sure we should even keep score on the back nine if this keeps up. So far we have a two, three, four, five, six, seven, and an eight on the card. With a hole-in-one and a nine we'll hit scorecard Sudoku."

"At least we have something to shoot for."

"No, that's not a good way to look at it."

"Come on. It's just going to take a little while for us flatlanders to get used to things up here. Sure we've had some stray shots, but most of those strokes are being lost due to distance control. Between the altitude difference and the elevation changes there is a lot of acclimation to do. Now, if we still suck tomorrow I'm going to have to come up with some other reasoning."

"I guess you're our optimistic leader now."

"Hey, we're just getting started. There's a lot of golf to play the next few days so we might as well enjoy it."

"It's interesting, with everything you have going on you actually seem less concerned than I would expect of you, Minton."

"It's a see-saw ride these days, but I'm trying to stay more up than down. My perspective on life has really been changing all of a sudden."

"I would imagine so. With this coin you could be leading a whole new life soon."

"It's not so much the coin as it was Jim dying. It's been a long time since anyone I've known has died. Really no one close since my grandparents and that was a long time ago. I was much younger so I didn't think about it in the same terms. Now I've suddenly realized my own mortality. We're all going to die someday and that day is getting closer."

"You didn't know that before?" mocked Tommy. "Besides, I've been lecturing you about it for a while now."

"Yeah, but talking about it is one thing, experiencing it first hand is completely different. When I went to the funeral and realized that I was never going to play golf with Jim again it was a real wake up call. I'm thinking more and more about where I want to be and how I'm going to get there. The coin could obviously be my ticket, however, right now it seems like more of a distraction from what I should be doing. I know that I need to be patient and let things play out, but it's tough to do."

"I can understand how you feel. Jim came along and has really turned that boring corporate-monkey life of yours upside down. But I think he knew what he was doing. He wanted to challenge you first and then see that you would be rewarded."

"Maybe so. We shall see. Alright, let's get going and see what kind of damage we can do on the back side."

Their games did improve a little bit on the second nine holes. They didn't manage to get any ones, but at least they were able to avoid a nine as well.

Afterwards Bryan and Tommy spent some leisure time wandering around the resort checking out the facilities. Most of their meals were included with the package so they had dinner at the clubhouse and called it any early night. They wanted to rest up for the thirty-six holes on tomorrow's agenda.

As their games adjusted and improved on the second day, Bryan and Tommy had their competitive juices kick in and their match became more serious. In the morning round they were paired up with a couple visiting from Georgia. The two were decent golfers and moved at a good pace. They were clearly there to play their game so they didn't interact much with Bryan and Tommy who barely noticed them.

In the afternoon session, they once again had the course to themselves and they made the best of it. They were replaying the course they'd played on Thursday so they at least had a little bit of course knowledge to work with, including which trees to hit and which ones not to. Tommy was starting to get a little frustrated with his recent string of losses to Bryan and decided to up his rhetoric accordingly. In years past it might have weighed on Bryan, but his mental game was now much stronger than before. Bryan knew that with his swing and game he could birdie or par every hole on the course. The real obstacle had always been getting his mind to believe it.

Tommy played well on the front nine and shot a three over thirty-nine. But he knew he was still behind Bryan by two shots.

"You're putting up a good fight, Minton, but I know you're due for a breakdown. And when it comes I'll be ready to snuff you out."

"Well, Manson, you can keep telling yourself that all you want, but don't get your hopes too high. You're just projecting your own fears toward me. In reality, you're the one whose game is on the edge. I'm on to you. In case you hadn't noticed, despite your efforts I'm up by two. Maybe if you start rolling your putts and stop running your mouth you'll at least give me a challenge on the home stretch."

Bryan did slip a little after catching one of the unfriendly trees and carding a double bogey. However, he bounced back with a pair of birdies and was able to close out Tommy for the side and overall. As always, their banter was only good spirited and there were no hard feelings.

They played the final holes at a leisurely pace and loitered around after finishing, taking in the scenery and reflecting on the day's marathon of golf. The course ended a good distance away from the clubhouse so the area around the eighteenth green was quiet and sedate. The hole had been designed to showcase the surrounding landscape. To either side of the green the tree line had been thinned so players could see for miles out into the mountains. The sight was made even more impressive by the early fall colors and the low afternoon sun. In terms of escape and relaxation, this was hard to beat. Bryan had certainly achieved his objective of temporarily distancing himself from the issues he was facing back home. He didn't feel like he was running away from them, he just needed some time away to regroup. He was enjoying himself thoroughly and couldn't help but dream about how many times like this he could have if and when he sold the Double Eagle coin. That was still a long way away, but his win over Nancy had at least put him one big step closer.

***

155

On Saturday there was only one round on the agenda so Bryan and Tommy slept in a bit before heading out for a late morning tee time. On the first tee the starter introduced them to the twosome that they'd been paired up with. Bryan sensed right away that their tension free rounds had come to an end.

"Mr. Minton and Mr. Manson, this is Mr. White and Mr. Steffen," announced the starter.

"Hi, I'm Bryan and this is Tommy."

"Hey guys, I'm Darrell and this is Bo."

Bryan guessed that White and Steffen were probably a few years older than Tommy and him. Both were over six feet tall and looked like the kind of guys who had been good athletes in high school, but never made it any further and eventually started to let it go. They at least started the round with tucked in shirts, but their overfed midsections were noticeably straining the fabric.

During the first three holes Bryan was noting the behaviors of their playing partners. Both of them had already been on their cell phones, they both spent forever lining up every single putt, and they had ceremoniously unloaded and lit their cigars. All of these things bothered Bryan, particularly the cigar ritual. It seemed as though all of the cigar smokers he played with were following the same script: let everyone around know you're breaking out the cigars, graciously offer to share them, act stunned when they turn you down, make sure they know just how great your cigars are relative to everyone else's, and then savor the first few tokes like it's the sweetest roll of carcinogens to ever combust on the face of the earth. Tommy wasn't a fan of these things either. Bryan just hoped that one of them didn't yank the ball out of the hole with their putter and send Tommy over the edge.

Bryan and Tommy were attempting to remain cordial, but they really weren't here looking for some new buddies. This was the third course on the property and Bryan and Tommy were trying to enjoy their first round on it.

As they all walked off the third green Darrell approached Tommy and asked if they wanted to put a little money on the rest of the holes to make it more interesting. Based on everything else so far, this came as no surprise to Bryan.

"So what do you guys think?" Darrell said with a drawl. "Maybe something small like twenty bucks each man each hole?"

"Look guys, we're just out having some fun. We're not looking for any big betting action against some players we just met," Tommy replied.

"Oh, come on, that's not much. Most of the holes will end up getting split anyway. Besides, you've seen our games and we've seen yours. It looks like we match up pretty even and it looks like you guys can afford it," cajoled Darrell.

"I think Arnold Palmer once said something to the extent of: I've got plenty of my own money so I don't need any of yours and by the same measure I don't want you to have any of mine."

"How did you want to play it?" Bryan piped in to Tommy's surprise.

"Nice and simple, lowest combined team score each hole. That way nobody gets to coast."

"Alright, we're up for it as long as we're all playing by the rules. If you miss a tap in you count the stroke," Bryan announced.

"By all means," Darrell agreed before shaking hands on it.

Tommy stared at Bryan all the way back to their cart. When the other two drove away he finally spoke. "Are you nuts?"

"What? You don't want to have some fun with these bumpkins?" laughed Bryan, amused by the fact that Tommy was the worried one.

"Did you ever see *Deliverance*? It was the city boys that ended up squealing!"

"You know, you do have some pretty teeth there, Tommy."

"How do you know they weren't sandbagging us? We didn't see either of them warming up; they could be the two best bumpkins in this neck of the woods."

"Yeah, maybe, but I doubt it. If anything, they were just scouting our games out for a few holes."

"I hope you're right," said Tommy with skepticism.

"So how much cash do you have on you?" Bryan asked sheepishly.

"Plenty to cover my bet. If this goes wrong you can pay them Ned Beatty style."

The next few holes were a little tense as money was now on the line. The scoring went back and forth and by the time they reached the turn Bryan and Tommy were up, but only by one hole. Bryan was gradually coming to the conclusion that their opponents were not sandbaggers, just gamblers. Tommy, however, remained skeptical. He was continually anticipating the moment when Bo and Darrell would come over and ask to up the bet. Bryan assured him that he was only being paranoid and that he should focus on his golf game.

By the twelfth hole Tommy and Bryan had added another hole to their lead. Number twelve was a reasonably straight forward par four with the only trouble being a small creek framing the right hand side of the fairway. Bryan hit a solid drive right down the middle, which left the door open for Tommy to be a little more aggressive and try to birdie the hole. Attempting to get some extra distance, he widened his stance and made a longer, more powerful swing. Unfortunately, as soon as he hit it he cringed and leaned to the left, hoping that his body English would magically keep his drive safe. His ball caught the edge of the rough, but kicked right and disappeared over the margin of the hazard. Tommy slammed his club into his bag in frustration before heading down to see what trouble he'd found.

When they arrived at the edge to the fairway they quickly located Tommy's ball. It had crossed over the marked red hazard line and rolled partially down the bank of the creek. His lie was reasonable and it was a shot that he could still get on or near the green. Tommy took his stance and practiced a swing several times without a club in his hands to get a feel for what he should hit. After checking his yardage again he pulled his seven iron and trudged back down to his ball. Bo and Darrell were interested to see what Tommy was facing and had come across to where Bryan was standing. As Tommy prepared to hit his shot he hovered the club above the ball and took several check swings. He was careful not to ground the club in the hazard, but his practice swings did brush across the top of some longer weeds that were sticking up above the grass. Bryan noticed that Darrell kept motioning to Bo, holding his hand out and shrugging his shoulders with a look of consternation. He stayed quiet though as Tommy got ready. Finally, Tommy settled on his play and took a steep swing punctuated with a grunt. The ball emerged from an exploding clump of mud and grass and rocketed toward the green. It landed just short of the green in the front left fringe.

"That came out better than I expected," Tommy said as he emerged from the ditch.

"That was a nice shot, but are you planning to add your penalty?" asked Darrell as Tommy approached.

"For what?" responded a surprised Tommy.

"For touching the weeds in the hazard."

"Since when is that a penalty?"

"Since always. You can't touch anything in the hazard with your club."

"I can touch things. I just can't ground the club."

"I've never heard that before. I thought we were playing it straight up out here, boys."

"It's a very misunderstood rule. A lot of people interpret it in your way, but the truth is that I just can't put the sole of my club on the ground behind the ball."

Bryan wanted to diffuse the situation, but he knew Tommy was right. "Look guys, he's right about the rule. There's no reason to get bent out of shape about this so what do you want to do? Do you want him to take a stroke? Play it over?"

"I'm not taking a stroke," interrupted Tommy. "I've got a rule book in my bag."

"That's alright. Let's just play on. That was good shot he hit out of that junk," said Bo, sensing that Darrell was wrong.

"It'll only take a minute to find it," pushed Tommy.

"Tommy, let's go. I'm up."

Bryan hit his ball safely on and they headed toward the green.

"Alright, Tommy. You were right; now don't push it any further."

"Don't worry, I can let it go. I think I scared them pretty good back there with the threat of having to read something. Anything beyond the label of a beer can might be a little heavy for these guys."

"Real nice. You were the one complaining before so don't get cocky. I have no doubt that besides golf their other sporting activities involve firearms."

Tommy managed only to save a bogey and Bryan made a par. Luckily, Bo and Darrell did the same so there was no blood on that hole and they were able to move on without further conflict.

The next couple of holes bounced back and forth and Bryan actually started enjoying the company of their local competitors. Despite their bad habits, it was entertaining to watch them play and add their own brand of commentary to everything. They had a descriptive phrase for just about every type of shot and poked fun at themselves as much as others.

Tommy's game faltered a bit down the home stretch, but Bryan picked up the slack and kept them from losing their lead. When they finished on number eighteen Bryan and Tommy were up two holes. Bo and Darrell were good sports and quickly paid up what was due. They asked if Bryan and Tommy would be around for a rematch, but both of them quickly declined – no reason to push their luck.

***

Following the round Bryan and Tommy watched some football and relaxed before getting ready for their big night out. They decided that a little social activity was necessary during the trip and the only night life around seemed to be a nearby casino. The brochures promised glitz and glamour, but Bryan and Tommy set their expectations low based on the location.

Their preconceptions were confirmed upon arrival at the Rising Sun Casino and Lodge where the preferred method of transport was tour bus rather than limousine. The casino was no doubt the product of a brainstorming session seeking to spur local economic activity. The strategy was a simple one: legalize gambling, build the casino, ship in the old people. It was at the top of the playbook for many lower tier municipalities, but it was a slippery slope. Pretty soon every restaurant, bar, and gas station around was in the gambling business. At that point it became a regressive tax on the local populace, since affluent tourists weren't the ones stopping by the 7-11 for a Big Gulp and some video poker.

Bryan and Tommy made their way through the lobby area and entered the main casino. The theme of the décor seemed to be a faux frontier look with some tribal undertones. It was a rather surreal scene of flashing lights and neon dimmed only by the haze of smoke hanging in the air.

"So what do you think, Bryan? Do you want to gamble a while and then eat or hit the buffet first?" asked Tommy, surveying the room.

"I'm hungry, let's eat."

En route to the buffet they had to cross through a throng of weary looking people lined up at a glass counter filled with random items.

"What do you suppose that is? Some kind of raffle?" pondered Bryan.

"No, that's the frequent gambler loser line. These people all have cards that track how much gambling they do. Then, they come here to cash in points for something cheesy to make them feel like winners, despite having just blown their paycheck. It's pretty much like getting the Rice-A-Roni after losing on a game show."

"Mmm. Mmm. The San Francisco treat."

"I'm sure they'll have some for you over at the buffet."

Bryan and Tommy fully indulged at the restaurant, but still couldn't keep pace with many of the other hearty patrons. Although there were plenty of fruits and vegetables available, most of the choices were southern comfort foods. Bryan couldn't remember ever seeing so many different fried items.

After filling their stomachs and clogging their arteries, Bryan and Tommy finally rolled out for some gambling. Bryan was more of a watcher than a player so he followed Tommy to the poker tables and observed the action from the sidelines. He sat in on a few hands, but Tommy was far more interested in playing and settled in to stay for a while. Eventually Bryan lost interest and decided to go sight seeing and play some slot machines. As he wandered through the noisy rows of machines he was amazed at the people he saw. There were zombies who robotically placed coin after coin in the machines with one hand while simultaneously pulling the handle with the other. Some players skipped the mechanics and just pushed a button or touched a screen. Now that Bryan knew about the frequent player program he could grasp the reason behind the most bizarre behavior he witnessed: players tethering themselves to the machines. Most of them wore their tracking cards on lanyards around their necks or on little colorful extension cords clipped to their shirts. The true hardcore players had two of them and played adjacent machines at the same time. Bryan figured that these people were all looking for the big score that would take them out of the misery of their current lives. In that sense, Bryan was rooting for them because in some ways he was in the same situation.

Bryan found a video slot machine with a crazed leprechaun that seemed entertaining and saddled up on a stool. He fed the hungry machine a twenty and started playing with either fifty cents or a dollar each spin. Despite all of the other noise around him, he was instantly entranced by the soothing chime of the rolling number barrels and the subtle ding when each one came to a halt.

Bryan won sporadically and was up a few dollars. Then of course the odds took hold and his pot started to dwindle. He started to feel like he was seeing a pattern in the winning spins and increased his bets accordingly. As expected, it worked well until it didn't work. The feeling that you could outsmart the game was inescapable.

After running through his first stake, Bryan went in for another twenty dollars. Another gambling cliché hit him as his bill disappeared into the machine's belly. He thought: I know I just lost my money, but it's ok to put up some more now since I'm due for a win. It's really more of an investment at this point. Sure enough, almost on cue, Bryan's second spin landed him twenty dollars in winnings. He immediately received a little high of euphoria and kept spinning. Once again his funds ebbed and flowed, but eventually ran out. At this point Bryan didn't even think about going for his wallet. In his mind he'd been playing with house money since he was only spending his winnings from the golf course today.

Heading back to check on Tommy, Bryan took a meandering route through another part of the casino that he hadn't seen and did some more people watching. Tucked out of the way here and there were the nickel slot machines. Being such small stake machines, there were very few of them and they were intentionally in less prominent locations. Somehow, however, the older patrons had a way of finding them, as though their gray hair served as some form of nickel ante radar.

Bryan also happened to find the very inconspicuous non-smoking room. This tiny, secluded area appeared to attract spouses of serious gamblers who couldn't stand the main room or serious gamblers who were now hooked up to oxygen after spending too much time in the main room. Bryan took a few deep, clean breaths and soldiered back on his way.

Arriving back at Tommy's table, Bryan found his friend doing quite well. He was focused on the game and presiding over a stack of chips worth several hundred dollars. Tommy acknowledged Bryan's return, but then went right back into game mode. Luckily the drink girl made a quick appearance and Bryan ordered up. He decided that if he wasn't going to gamble tonight he might as well do a little drinking. He normally behaved, but every once in a while even he needed to indulge in a little vice.

"Looks like you're quickly paying for your trip, Manson," Bryan said.

"I'm playing smart and sticking to my strategy."

"I thought you said you were counting cards?"

"Don't joke about that. They take that stuff seriously and I don't want to give them any reason to ask me to leave," Tommy said, sipping his drink and scanning the table.

"I guess I'll need to drink fast to catch up to you," Bryan said, noting Tommy's empty glass.

"Yeah, I'll need another one when our waitress gets back."

"Now don't go too far and lose your edge."

"What do you mean? You think I'm getting a little too baked?"

"Not yet. Right now you're feeling confident, but if you go too much further you'll start feeling overconfident. Then you'll hit your point of diminishing returns and diminishing chips."

"Alright, you keep an eye on my reflexes," Tommy said, as he held out his hand and intentionally shook it wildly. "So how did you make out, partner?"

"Lost it all to a mad leprechaun."

"That can't be a good sign."

"Here comes your girl now."

"Here you go," she said, handing Bryan his drink and sitting down next to Tommy.

"Oh, Cara, this is Bryan."

"Hi, I saw you here earlier, but nice to formally meet you," she said, shaking hands delicately with Bryan.

"Likewise. So how do you like it here at the Rising Sun?"

"It's fun, but it has it's highs and lows. I get to meet lots of interesting people and the pay is not bad. There aren't that many great jobs in this town. The worst part is probably the shoes. My feet are always killing me so I try to sit down whenever I can."

"You certainly wear the uniform well," Bryan commented, motioning toward her skimpy, sequined cocktail dress.

"Oh thanks, you're sweet," she said bashfully.

Tommy looked over his shoulder and gave Bryan a sideways smile of approval. "So, Cara, even though he's not gambling right now, this guy over here could be the highest roller you have in the place."

"Really?" she asked with a sudden spark of excitement.

"Yeah, he's working on something in the eight figure range right now in fact."

"Really? Are you messing with me?"

"Yes, he's messing with you," interjected Bryan, his conscience trumping his libido for the moment.

"No, I'm not," retorted Tommy. "It's not a done deal, but we're talking probably a ninety-five percent chance that it happens."

Cara looked at Bryan waiting for his response.

"Okay, there is something I'm working on, but it's nowhere near ninety-five percent. Maybe fifty percent at best."

"Hey, you're in a casino. Fifty-fifty's not bad around here. So are you guys staying here at the hotel?" she asked, showing a lot more interest after Bryan's confirmation.

"No, we're playing some golf over at Pine Meadow," Bryan replied.

"You should switch over; we have much nicer rooms here."

"Well, we've only got one more night."

"That's a shame. Still maybe I can get you a casino host for the rest of the evening."

"Thanks, but we're okay. I think a host would be going a little overboard. Maybe just a guide to show me back to the nickel slots."

"Alright, but let me know if you change your mind. I'll get you another drink, honey," she said, taking Tommy's glass and heading off with a smile.

"Oh, Bryan. All of my efforts for naught," Tommy said shaking his head.

"What? I'm not going to lie to her."

"I wasn't asking you to lie, just embellish along with me a bit."

"I know. I know."

Tommy's luck at poker started to fade so eventually he moved over to the blackjack tables. He'd obviously hit his point of diminishing returns as he started to make riskier bets and ended up losing most of his prior winnings. Bryan knew when he'd reached his own limit and convinced Tommy to head over to the sports bar to watch the end of the late football coverage and sober up a bit before heading back.

Even with a good breakfast and some pain relievers, they both had nice hangovers on Sunday morning. They were just getting too old to bounce back like they did years before. Bryan and Tommy braved it out, though, and played a decent final round. It was a sedate finish to their short trip. Afterward, they packed up and caught their afternoon flight back to reality.

12

Bryan returned home exhausted. He dumped his bags and clubs and took a cursory look at his stack of mail. The number of calls that he'd been receiving had finally tapered off, but after being gone for a few days he found his machine full of messages. Most of them were quick deletes, but there were two troubling ones that caught his attention. Apparently officials from the Treasury Department had heard about the coin and wanted to speak with him. He wondered if perhaps they just wanted to help determine the authenticity of the coin. However, based on the articles he'd read he knew deep down that they probably had other intentions.

On Monday morning Bryan had planned to give them a call back, but from the moment he arrived at the office it started getting bumped further down his to do list. Being off for a few days had put him behind and his boss had whipped up some new counter-productive projects for everyone to jump right on. Despite his normal disdain for Joe's busywork, Bryan was actually glad to bury himself in some reports. Relative to dealing with the government, it seemed like the lesser of the two evils.

It was still on his mind Monday night when he wearily arrived home. As he turned the corner to the breezeway that led to his apartment he was startled by the sight of two men in suits leaning against the railing outside his door. Bryan slowed his pace as the two men straightened themselves and exchanged glances. He continued toward them waiting for them to say something. Bryan stopped about ten feet in front of them and looked from one to the other; still nothing. Bryan didn't think they were there to rob him so finally he ended the standoff.

"Can I help you guys with something?"

"Are you Bryan Minton?"

"Maybe. Who's asking?"

"I'm Agent Kraft and this is Agent Dodge, we're with the Secret Service."

"Okay then, I'm Bryan, nice to meet you," Bryan said without moving.

"We would like to speak to you about your possible possession of a Double Eagle gold coin."

"I kind of guessed that. I assume you're telling the truth, but just in case, do you have some kind of badge of something?"

"Actually, we just carry business cards, sir," said Agent Dodge, who pulled one out of his shirt pocket and handed it to Bryan along with one from Agent Kraft before stepping back into place.

Bryan looked at them briefly, knowing that anyone could print up a business card. "What about guns? You guys packing?"

"Let's just say that we could subdue you if necessary."

"Good to know. So do I have to talk to you or should I wait until my lawyer is present?"

"That's up to you, sir. We are just here to make contact and begin our investigation. We decided it best not to confront you at your office today."

"Thanks, my boss would certainly appreciate your consideration."

"We primarily need to determine your situation."

"My situation?"

"We need to know if you are going to be combative or potentially flee."

"Well, to be honest, having you two stare me down like a couple of gargoyles out here isn't really helping your cause. The only place I want to flee to at the moment is my couch. I already realized that I was going to have to talk to you at some point anyway, so we might as well get started now. You can come in as long as you agree not to Taser me," Bryan said as he groped for his keys.

"Thank you, sir," replied Dodge as they followed him inside.

"You can have a seat in there," Bryan said, motioning to his living room. "Can I get you anything? Beer, Coke, my tax returns?"

"No, we're fine, but thank you."

After Bryan set down his belongings and parked himself on the couch, he looked across at the two agents and experienced a touch of déjà vu. This was now the second time he'd been ambushed by two guys in suits wanting to talk about the coin. He hoped there wouldn't be a third occasion any time soon.

The two agents certainly looked their role. Both were probably in their mid-forties and were powerfully built – stretching most of the seams on their suits. Based on that, and their usage of "sir", Bryan assumed they were both ex-military men. Agent Luis Dodge was very stern looking with short, slicked back hair. He reminded Bryan of a football coach from the 1950's. His partner, Agent Myron Kraft, seemed a bit more amiable. He had at least flashed a big, toothy grin when Bryan had mentioned his tax returns. Kraft had a thick neck that was almost as wide as his head and looked as if it might burst if his tie and collar gave way.

"So how'd you find out about the coin? Was it the article in the paper a while back?"Bryan asked.

"Essentially yes. It came through several channels and ended up getting forwarded to our group."

Bryan smiled, realizing that he could once again give Nancy credit for this visit. "So what took you guys so long to get here?"

"Honestly, we've been busy. We get lots of leads and have to prioritize ones we think are most important. We don't have much reason to believe that your coin is real, but we still need to do a routine investigation," continued Kraft, as Dodge sat quietly and looked around Bryan's abode. "So you said you were expecting to have to talk to us, why haven't you contacted anyone in the government regarding the coin?"

"I've been kind of busy myself. As you probably know from the article, I was involved in a legal dispute regarding the transfer of the coin from Mr. Garris. I've just now prevailed in that so I can move forward with the next set of issues, which obviously involves you."

"Again, we doubt that the coin is real, but still need to be sure. I have to believe that you want to determine that as well."

"Absolutely."

"Do you know anything about the history of the particular coin, Mr. Minton?"

"Just Bryan is fine. Unfortunately I have very few details. Mr. Garris was terminally ill and he gave it to me right before he died. His daughters were pretty much in the dark about it, so any history there was in the family basically went with Jim. I know that he received it from his father. According to the one daughter, Nancy, her grandfather was an employee at the U.S. Mint during a portion of his career. That's why she seemed to believe it was authentic. That's all I ever got from her and she's probably in no mood to help me even if she knows anything else, which I doubt she does. Anyway, that's were I'm guessing it came from."

"Hmm. That's interesting to know," said Kraft. It also caught Dodge's attention as he finally tuned in to what Bryan was saying. "It provides a possible avenue for it to be real, but even more so provides credence to the idea that it's a forgery or a replica. Who better to make a fake than someone on the inside? There have been a number of cases where employees find an old die or mold and decided to make a few for old time's sake. The equipment is supposed to be destroyed, but invariably some always slips through the cracks. These coins are nearly impossible to identify as fakes based on visual examinations since they're made from the original casts. However, the metallurgists can shoot them down in no time since the original metal content is so tough to match. It's similar with paper money; the printing portion is easy compared to getting the paper fiber right."

"I hadn't thought about it that way, but it makes sense. When I found out its potential value I really had to question the authenticity as well. Nonetheless, I've still always had this gut feeling that it's the real McCoy. Maybe it's just a false sense of hope based on what it might be worth though."

"That's no surprise. Who wouldn't want to believe that they had a fortune in their hands? Speaking of which, where is the coin currently located?"

"I keep it here in my golf bag," said Bryan with a straight face.

"Really?"

"No. Not anymore at least. It was there from when Jim gave it to me to when I found out what it potentially was. After that I put it in my safe deposit box down at the bank."

"Probably a wise choice either way. It doesn't look like you have a very secure situation here," Kraft said, looking around Bryan's apartment.

"Yeah, I was thinking the same thing," piped in Dodge.

"You guys are big on the *situations* aren't you? I guess you didn't spot the snipers on the roof then? You fellas are getting a little sloppy doing this civilian work."

Kraft managed a weak smile; Dodge just stared.

Shaking his head at their lack of appreciation for his material, Bryan continued, "So that's my *situation* gentlemen. What's the next move? Are you planning to take it with you? I'm guessing that you need to have some kind of government order or something to do that."

"That's being finalized right now and we should have it in the next day or so. We needed to verify a few things first. We'll be happy to provide copies to you and your attorney before we proceed with the transfer in order to be sure everything is in order. Hopefully you'll cooperate and the process should be fairly easy. We'll accompany you, and your attorney or other representative, to the bank to obtain the item. We have a special transport case that has electronic locks and tamper proof seals. We will pick up the coin and escort it to Washington, D.C. Only officials from the U.S. Mint will have the combination to the locks and a representative from the Justice Department will witness and verify that the seals have not been tampered with. Once there, it will be housed within a secure vault that we have arranged to use at the Bureau of Engraving and Printing. The Mint's headquarters is in D.C., but they don't have a production facility there so that's why it will go to the Bureau. While there the coin will always be maintained under dual control."

"And if I don't cooperate?"

"We'll simply move forward with a seizure. We'll follow the same procedures, just without you involved," Kraft said matter-of-factly.

"That's basically what we do in situations where the involved party is already dead," Dodge added menacingly.

"I take it they'll do the verification there?"

"Yes, as I mentioned experts from the West Point Mint location will be coming down to do visual and materials analysis. The Mint's results will be verified by an outside third party expert as well. If it's a fake they'll probably micro encode it with a marker and return it to you. There will likely be some value in it for the gold or for a collector who wants a knock off. If it does turn out to be real the government will move forward with a formal seizure to finalize its repossession. In the past it would have probably been destroyed thereafter, however, since the Double Eagle has now taken such a historic place among coins any current specimens would likely be preserved and made part of the National Numismatic Collection. Eventually it would go on display at the National Museum of American History with other similar coins."

"So if it's real I'd get nothing?" Bryan asked, dreading the answer.

"Most likely yes. The judge in the seizure proceeding would determine your interest, if any. It's pretty clear that *you* didn't steal it from the Mint so there shouldn't be any charges against you. If you could substantiate some other valid ownership interest you may be able to negotiate some type of compensation payment, but that's just speculation."

"And what if I want to fight the government from seizing it?"

"Well you're certainly entitled to do so," Kraft said with a grin implying Bryan had asked a silly question, "but since we're talking about a Double Eagle here I'd say your chances are pretty slim."

When Kraft said "Double Eagle" Bryan thought about his ball rolling in on number seventeen at Stone Ridge. He grinned back at the agent and thought otherwise of Kraft's prediction. "Well, that all sounds good and well, guys. I'll give my lawyer a call tomorrow and bring him up to speed. I'll let you know if he sees any problems with all of this, but otherwise we'll just wait to hear back from you."

"Excellent. I think we're all on the same page then," Kraft said, standing to go.

"And don't worry. I don't intend to make a run for the border."

"We're not worried about that happening," replied Agent Dodge.

Bryan showed them to the door and thanked them for coming by. He went back into the living room and flopped down on his couch to reflect on the meeting. He realized that at this point he didn't have a lot of options so there was no reason to worry about it. He'd do what he could and wait to see how this next chapter unfolded.

***

First thing on Tuesday, Bryan called Draper's office and left a message. He got a call back a few minutes later and Owen sounded happy to hear from him.

"Bryan, how are you doing?"

"Alright. Unfortunately I hadn't even finished my victory lap when the government showed up and tripped me."

"That doesn't sound good."

"Yeah, there were two Secret Service agents waiting at my apartment last night. I hadn't returned their calls so they decided to stop by in person. Their objective is pretty clear: authenticate the coin and then take it if it's real. Now, on the bright side, we'll get the best experts available to examine the coin. That will at least give some closure on whether or not this darn thing is worth all the hassle."

"That is good. I want to know the truth. What else did they tell you?"

"They don't think it's real, but still need to go through the paces. They expect to have some kind of authorization finalized in the next day or so allowing them to take the coin for authentication. They'll give us copies to review, but I doubt there's much we can contest."

"Likely so, but I'd still be glad to review it as soon as it's available, you never know."

"If it's a fake I'll probably get it back as a souvenir. However, if it is real then we'll have to figure out if there's any way to fight. They weren't real optimistic on my chances, which doesn't surprise me based on what I've read about the coin."

"At that point we may need to call in some bigger guns. It's your call, but battling against the government is not my bread and butter work. I have a colleague in Tampa in mind who I think would be the perfect person to help. I can give him a call just to touch base and get him in the loop if you want."

"That's fine with me. I'm guessing their side will have more than one lawyer involved so we might as well stock up."

"As for right now, I think the prudent thing to do is work with them and follow the proper procedures. There's no need to ruffle feathers until we have to. You played it cool in the fight with Nancy; keep the same composure now."

"I'll try. The big problem is that this time the argument won't be whether or not it belonged to me, it will be whether or not in belonged to Jim and/or his father. With Jim gone now we have almost nothing to go on and I don't think Nancy or Lisa know anything, even if they did want to help."

"Still, just hang in there. Remember it looked pretty bleak the first time and then things swung in your favor."

"Thank, Owen. I appreciate it. I better get to work here, I'll keep you posted."

***

Bryan was on the phone when Agent Kraft called later in the week, but this time Bryan decided to return the call promptly. They had received their authorized paperwork and were ready to move forward. Bryan gave them Draper's contact information and they set up a meeting the following week.

On the day of their meeting they started out at Draper's office. Both Kraft and Dodge were present and the government also had an attorney join via conference call. There was a surprising amount of paperwork to review and it consumed over an hour. Draper was very careful to make sure that nothing was giving up ownership of the coin. This was only to authorize the authentication process. When they finally finished the group loaded up and caravanned over to Bryan's bank branch.

Being the middle of a weekday, the branch was relatively empty when the four of them arrived together and it drew everyone's attention. Agent Dodge, who was carrying a dark metallic case with a cable and handcuff attached, was especially conspicuous.

Bryan didn't want to draw a lot of attention so he quietly asked one of the representatives at a desk if he could access his safe deposit box. Immediately she offered the assistance of the branch manager; perhaps feeling that Bryan and his entourage were here to fill the case with bank money.

The manager appeared a moment later with a smile, "Hi, I'm Sheila Barker, the branch manager. I'll be happy to show you to your box. Our regulations require that just you enter the vault area, however."

"That's fine. I do have a favor to ask, though. These gentlemen are Agent Kraft and Agent Dodge with the Secret Service."

"Hello, ma'am," Kraft said offering her a business card.

"The other gentleman is my attorney," Bryan continued, motioning to Draper who gave her a nod. "I'll be transferring some property to them and I was wondering if we could use the conference room over there for a few minutes?"

"I think that will be ok, sir. What was your name?"

"Oh, sorry, I'm Bryan Minton. I've been a customer here for a while now."

"Are you the one with the coin?" she asked, here eyes lighting up suddenly.

"Ahh, yes, that's me."

"Oh, how exciting. I read about it in the paper. Every once in a while we see some interesting coins come through here so we were fascinated when we heard about a Double Eagle."

"It's been fascinating to say the least. Would it be okay if we go in now?"

"Oh yes, sorry."

The manager escorted Bryan into the vault. They walked past several rows of boxes; symmetrical brass squares from floor to ceiling. Bryan wondered what other secrets were hiding in this room. Most of the boxes probably held mundane items and paperwork that were only of value to the owners. Keeping them here no doubt let the owners sleep better at night. But some random box here or there likely held real treasure. Jim had probably kept the Double Eagle hidden away in solitude at his bank for years. Then finally one day he arrived and removed it.

When they located Bryan's box, Sheila fumbled through several keys before finding the right one. She inserted hers along with Bryan's and swung open the tiny door. She slid out the long metal box and handed it to Bryan before escorting him to a small room.

"Do you need to spend much time?" she asked.

"No, I just need to get the coin out."

"Okay, I'll wait right outside."

Bryan went in and quickly retrieved the Double Eagle from inside his box. He stopped for a moment and examined it closely. It was just as magnificent as he'd remembered. It was a shame that something so beautiful had spent most of its existence locked up in a box. Bryan considered that if this coin was real and he ended up losing it at least it might end up in a museum. He could always go and visit that way. Bryan envisioned the coin sitting inside a case of thick glass. In front would be a descriptive piece telling about Double Eagles and next to that would be a placard about the history of how it survived via the Garris family and Bryan Minton. After one last look he slipped it in his pocket and headed out.

"All set?" Sheila asked eagerly.

"Yep."

When they'd replaced Bryan's box and locked it up, Sheila turned to Bryan and inquired, "I know it's against our bank policy, but would it be okay if I looked at it?"

"Rather than getting you in trouble, how about this: we're going to need a witness on some paperwork so if you join us in the conference room you can have a peek there. Sound reasonable?"

"Oh yes. Thank you," she said with enthusiasm.

They walked back outside and gathered with the others in the conference room.

"All set," said Bryan, sitting down at the head of the table. He set the coin on the table and continued, "Ms. Barker here has graciously agreed to be our witness and I told her that she could see the coin." He slid the coin across the table to where she had taken a seat and watched as her eyes lit up once again. She examined it silently as Kraft sorted out his paperwork and Dodge prepared the case.

It took a few minutes to go through everything. Sheila had given the coin to Draper who hadn't seen it before and was almost as giddy as Barker. Kraft and Dodge also examined it before setting it inside the case.

"Do you want to see it one last time?" Dodge asked rather benevolently.

"No, I'm okay. I'll be seeing it again one way or another," he said with confidence.

"You sound pretty sure, but this might be it," Dodge offered one last time.

"Oh, I'm sure."

Dodge shrugged and closed the case. He snapped the latches shut and typed in several numbers on the key pad. He slid it over to Kraft who did the same. Dodge pulled a small box from his jacket and produced several adhesive metallic strips that he placed along the seams of the case carefully. He then took out a lighter and ran the flame near the stickers until they changed to darker color. Once again, the Double Eagle was locked away inside a box.

Sheila had clearly been impressed by the theatrics of the whole encounter. Agent Kraft noticed her mannerisms and decided to curb her enthusiasm.

"We certainly appreciate your help today, Ms. Barker. I hope you understand the importance of this matter and will respect Mr. Minton's privacy as a client of your banking institution. Moreover, our involvement with Mr. Minton is not to be discussed beyond the confines of this room."

"Absolutely. You can count on me," she said, glad that she was on the "inside".

"Thank you for your cooperation."

"Can I ask one question though?" she pushed.

"Sure."

"Is it real?"

"That's what we are going to determine. Although unlikely, if it is authentic we will issue a statement regarding the coin. Thank you again for your help. If you wouldn't mind, we'd like to finish up things with Mr. Minton alone. It'll just be a minute or two."

"Certainly. Take all the time you want and let me know if you need anything," she said before bouncing out.

"Alright, gentlemen, I think we're pretty much set to go. Just for your reference, our flight will head back this afternoon. We have TSA clearance so we are able to avoid the security lines. When we arrive at Reagan National we'll be met by an escort that will take us in a secure vehicle to the Bureau of Engraving. There we'll turn the coin over and, as I'd mentioned, it will be under dual control during the authentication process. They are ready and rather eager to examine it."

"See, everyone wants to take a look at it," Bryan said with a smirk.

"Indeed. Since they are already prepared it should only take a week or so to do the necessary work. We will contact you with the findings and determine the next course of action."

"Sounds like a plan to me. I'll be waiting for your call."

They gathered up everything and shook hands before departing. On the way out Bryan waved goodbye to his new friend Sheila who returned the gesture happily. He was pretty sure that she'd be spilling the beans to everyone else as soon as they walked out the door. One more thing to add to his to do list: switch to a new branch or different bank.

In the parking lot Bryan thanked Draper and then watched as Kraft and Dodge drove off in their rental car. He didn't feel particularly upset about their departure with his coin. He had resigned himself to the fact that this was part of the process and for the time being it was out of his hands – literally.

***

As time ground onward at Chambers with no news of deals involving the company the buzz had started to fade. Bryan knew a couple of people who were shining up their resumes now that they no longer saw an imminent reason to stay put. Even those that weren't looking seemed to have lost some degree of urgency to perform. Bryan was pacing himself as he compiled some data when he received a visit from Jason.

"Hey, Money Man. How's it going?"

Since everyone had found out about the coin Bryan had obtained several new nicknames at the office. Money Man, Coin Dude, and Golden Boy were some of the most used monikers. Bryan didn't mind when they were used jokingly by friends, but some people used them to be snide, which got old quick.

"Jason, come on in and make yourself comfortable on the couch."

Jason slid in and parked himself on the side of Bryan's desk.

"You getting any work done?" Jason asked.

"Well not anymore, but that's alright. I'm still trying my best, but it's pretty tough these days. I should hear from the government any day now and then I can make some decisions. No matter what happens I need to start exploring some other opportunities."

"I'm keeping my ears open, but I think I'll hang around for now unless I come across something really good. People think that it's always greener on the other side, but most of the time it's not. I've known so many people that find a new gig and brag how great it is compared to where they were. Then you talk to them about six months down the road when the honeymoon has ended and they are right back where they were. Either you have to get a lot more money to make it worthwhile or find something that you're truly going to like for a long period of time."

"You're right. So what if things change around here?" Bryan asked.

"Same thing, I'll just play it by ear. It's gotten so quiet that I doubt anything is in the works now."

"Maybe. I'm feeling a bit more contrarian though. I almost think that once it gets to the point where no one expects it that is when something will finally happen."

They talked for a bit longer before Jason decided to head on his way. Bryan got back to work, but a short time later he was interrupted by his ringing phone. He saw an odd area code on his screen and then recognized it as Kraft's phone number.

"Chambers, this is Bryan."

"Bryan, it's Kraft. I've also got attorney Sikes from the Justice Department on the line with me."

"Hello, Bryan."

"Hey guys. So what's the verdict?"

"They've checked and re-checked. It's a real 1933 Double Eagle."

"I knew it!" Bryan exclaimed feeling vindicated, despite the most likely outcome hereafter.

"You were right. So congratulations on that aspect. We wanted to call to let you know since we just got the final results. I think it would be best if we set up a conference call later in the week with you and your attorney to go over the next legal steps. Also, I wanted to give you a heads up that the Mint will be issuing a press release tomorrow about the coin. At this point they've agreed to leave your name out of it, although it won't take long to make the connection with the prior articles. The release will just indicate that it came to light via the descendent of a Mint employee and that its history is unclear. It will also say that the government plans to move forward with formal seizure now and that its ultimate disposition is still to be determined."

"Thanks for letting me know. I'll get in touch with Draper and we'll get a time set up. I'm eager to keep moving forward," said Bryan.

"Well, you know where the government stands, but best of luck, Bryan."

"Talk to you soon."

Based on the closing comment, Bryan felt like he was winning Kraft over a bit, but he would have to do a lot more than that if he wanted his coin back.

Bryan turned back to his computer and typed an email to Draper:

> Owen,
> The Eagle has landed…and it's real.
> The Mint will be issuing a press release tomorrow so everyone's going to know.
> Need to set up a conference call with them in the next few days.
> Hopefully we can have your colleague involved as well.
>
>
> -Bryan

Normally Bryan would have worried about sending a sensitive email like that from work, but since the press release was coming out it wouldn't be a secret for long.

***

It only took one day after the press release for the story to get tied back to him. It made the major local paper and then got picked up nationwide. Immediately his phone started ringing and his mailbox started to fill with all kinds of offers and requests. The release made clear that the government planned to seize the coin, which was somewhat beneficial to Bryan. People assumed that he wasn't going to end up with it and at work it was relatively peaceful since co-workers had sympathy for him. Even his boss took it easy on him when the story hit. Joe was happy that Chambers wasn't mentioned in the story this time. The local press had, however, made the connection with his mom and her position in the city government.

To escape from some of the anxiety, Bryan met up with his dad at Oak Run over the weekend. The weather this time of year was absolutely perfect for golf, and just about anything else outdoors. Weak cold fronts would come through every few days to drop the mercury. Then the next several days would be clear and mild as the air gradually warmed back up. It was this weather that brought all of the seasonal "snowbirds" back from the north as well as plenty of tourists from all around the world. Oak Run had plenty of year round members like the Mintons, but the membership definitely got a boost come fall. However, the downside was that the course was also busier and the pace of play really bogged down.

Bryan and his dad were focused on golf for the first few holes, but as things invariably slowed down they had plenty of time for conversation. Bryan had already updated his parents on the most recent events, but he was always glad to get his dad's feedback to help ease the tension.

"Have you come up with any new ideas for me, Dad?" Bryan asked.

"I've been racking my brain and so has your mother, but it seems like you're back in a tough spot. We hate to see it, especially since we were so excited for you when you won the first time. I know it's not much of a consolation, but in the long run I think you'll benefit form this whole experience no matter what. You can't say it hasn't made things more exciting for you."

"No, I can't indeed. I'm really glad to know that the coin is real. It makes me feel as though what I've done so far was at least worth the effort. It also validated my gut feeling. I always knew the chances of it being real were very slim, but as time went on I just sensed that it was. Unless he'd been misled, I didn't think Jim would have given it to me in the first place if it was a fake. Also, why would he keep it in hiding so long? He didn't need the money so he had the luxury of not having to sell it to raise cash."

"Speaking of cash, are you still doing okay?"

"Oh yeah, I'm fine for now. I think Owen has been very reasonable in his billing so far. I sense that he likes being involved with something out of the ordinary and, therefore, isn't trying to nickel and dime me. As for this other guy he is bringing in – we'll see."

"Have they come up with anything else?"

"Unfortunately not much. The precedents that are out there are not real favorable for the coin holders. At this point there's probably nothing to be gained from attacking the government so we'll likely try to work with them and angle for some sympathy. Since the coin has such massive potential value, to take it from me without any sort of remuneration wouldn't be great PR even for the government. From that aspect we're hoping to get some additional mileage from the video of Jim giving me the coin. We want to show that I was a deserving owner. I hate to demean that memory of Jim, but at the same time he was a pretty pragmatic guy and I don't think he wanted to see me wind up empty handed. I've thought about what he might recommend if he were still around and I have to believe he'd tell me to use it."

"And there's nothing else on the video to prove anything about the coin itself I guess? There's nothing else he might have said to you that day?"

"No, it was great for proving the coin was mine and where I got it from, but beyond that it's pretty much a dead end."

"Well maybe something else will come along. Just keep your head up and do what you can. You know we're here if you need anything."

"Thanks, Dad. I'm not giving up yet."

"Alright, the green's finally clear. Let's play some golf."

***

In order to work on their game plan, Bryan and Draper set up a call an hour before the official government call. They were also joined by the attorney that Owen had recommended, Daniel Lazarus, who had agreed to join Bryan's team.

"Alright, Bryan, at this stage we just want to lay the groundwork for where we will be headed with them. Unfortunately, as we've discussed they have every right to take the coin and are not required to compensate you in any way. But that doesn't mean we can't argue for it. There are two main issues that we want to highlight. First, the fact that you were a rightful recipient of the coin and in no way obtained it through illegal means. Second, we need to consider what amount to ask for as compensation," Draper began.

"I've reviewed the information that Owen provided and agree that that is how we should proceed today. Even this approach has limited legal merit, but it may be your only chance. I've reviewed several other cases involving Double Eagles and high end government antiquities and compensation payments are very rare. They don't want to set any examples for essentially paying ransoms to get property back. Also, they normally would only consider it in situations where the current holder had made an outlay to acquire the item. That's not the case here since it was given to you."

"I understand. This is what we've been talking about already. So you don't see any other routes for directly challenging them, even if it was a small possibility?"

"Unfortunately no. They've just made it abundantly clear that these coins were never legal to own and that anyone that does have one had no true ownership rights regardless of how they came into possession of it. With our lack of history and facts I don't see any way to mount a frontal assault. I think we start with what we have and try to use the time before your hearing to seek other information. So far our preliminary research on the Garris family has not turned up anything useful. I have ordered a research report from a genealogical service we use, but that will take another week or so. We are so accustomed to finding data at our fingertips, but pre-Internet and pre-computer age there's far less to work with."

"Also, I went ahead and put a call into Boyle to see if he would try to contact Nancy for us. I haven't heard anything back yet," added Draper.

"In terms of what to ask for, again we don't have a lot to go on. I did some research and don't think we could expect more than a fraction of its potential value. I would suggest we request something in the one to three percent range. Here the value of the coin is a bit of an impediment. Under other circumstances I would lean more toward the ten percent neighborhood, but since we are looking at a coin valued at ten million dollars that would yield one million. Since the government likely would not sell the coin and receive proceeds I doubt the judge would even consider it. So I think we need to look at values that are realistic in a judge's mind and still make it worth your while. I really wish I had some better advice to offer, but this is a very unique situation and the government is holding all the cards – and now the coin, too."

"None of this is a surprise to me so don't worry. Let's just go with the middle of the range and say two hundred thousand. That's basically what we talked about as a settlement with Nancy so maybe that's all I was ever going to get out of this thing. I think we're pretty well set, I'll circle back with you guys in a little while and dial in together."

The government call was quite formal and it was clear that attorney Sikes from the Justice Department was very confident in the government's case. He ran through several procedural items, including the fact that the coin would remain in the Bureau's vault until the seizure action was settled. Sikes listened to the proposal outlined by Lazarus but was skeptical of its merit. He said the purpose of the hearing would be to let Bryan make his case and that's what they would do. Nonetheless, he warned Bryan to temper his expectations in regard to any payment, let alone two hundred thousand.

They had already arranged the hearing date and scheduled it for a Friday three weeks away. Lazarus questioned the timeframe but the government intended to move quickly and had no intention of giving a longer window. It would take place in Washington D.C. so at least Bryan could make a long weekend out of it. In addition to his legal warnings, Sikes also offered a closing meteorological one. He reminded Bryan and his counsel that D.C. would be a lot colder than Florida this time of year so they should pack warm. The clock was now ticking toward what would likely be the end of Bryan's fight for the coin.

13

T he days slowly rolled off the calendar and with just over a week to go Bryan's team had made little progress. The family history was rather cloudy and the only circumstantial evidence they had was confirmation that Jim's dad had lived in Philadelphia around the time the coins had been produced. Research on the Double Eagles had also not given much hope. There were no records of any coins ever being legally issued to individuals so regardless of how the elder Garris had acquired it his Double Eagle would presumably be illegal to own. In turn, Jim would have transferred an unauthorized coin to Bryan.

Bryan was at his desk pondering his fate and trying to do some work when he received a call. He looked at the incoming number and it looked familiar, but took him a moment to recognize. When he realized it was Jim's phone number he quickly grabbed it.

"Hello? This is Bryan," Minton blurted, strangely hoping to hear Nancy's voice at the other end.

"Hi, Bryan. It's Lisa Garris."

"Oh, Lisa," Bryan replied, even more surprised. "How are you doing?"

"Not too bad. Still busy helping to settle my dad's affairs."

"Yeah, I can imagine there are lots of things to finalize. How's your son? Is he dealing with the loss alright?"

"For the most part. Sadly he didn't get a chance to know my dad that well so it's not as traumatic as it could have been. My dad and I had gone through some bumpy times the last few years."

"Jim had mentioned that to me."

"Toward the end we weren't really fighting anymore, it was kind of a slow healing period. I knew he wasn't going to be around much longer and he knew I was starting to get my life in order. Neither of us was at the point where we could just hug and say all was forgiven. But we definitely had an understanding that we wouldn't be saying final goodbyes in anger. I'm sorry. That's probably more than you wanted to know."

"No, that's okay," Bryan said, realizing Jim had made almost the exact same apology to him several months ago.

"Anyway, after what happened you probably don't even want to speak to me."

"Odd as it may seem, we've actually been trying to track down your sister recently."

"Yeah, I know. She told me. Don't expect to hear back from her. She's still bitter. Of course she's always been bitter so it's nothing out of the ordinary. We've had our share of disputes the last few months, but I don't let her get to me anymore. I also don't let her walk on me either. She came down here and thought that everything was going to go according to her plan, but she had a few wake up calls, including you."

"I'll take that as a compliment."

"She was shocked when you didn't take the settlement offer. Boyle had suggested a higher offer based on finding out if the coin was real, but she shot him down. She said, 'He'll just take the money and run, so let's not give him too much.' She was livid that night when you left my dad's house."

"I kind of figured that."

"Which, by the way, I want to say sorry about all of that. I can't believe you had to end up going to court."

"That's alright. It was pretty clear whose idea that was."

"Well, I did agree to challenge the papers. But it was only because they both convinced me that it wouldn't ever go to court and that it was the easiest way to settle the issue. Again, kudos to you for outfoxing them. I didn't think my dad would have given you the coin for any reason other than because that was what he wanted to do. I wish I could have gone to the hearings just to have seen their expressions in person."

"Oh trust me, it was worth it. I'll never forget their reactions when that video started playing in the court room."

"Even if she had won, it probably would have led to more fights about what to do with it."

"That's exactly what your dad expected," Bryan said.

"He knew his daughters' personalities well."

"So don't feel bad in any way. I don't bear any ill will towards you. And honestly, I'm not even that mad at your sister anymore."

"That's good. We aren't ever going to be best friends, but she's my sister and I still try to love her no matter what. I don't think she's greedy, although I'm sure it seemed that way. I think what happened was just part of her way of responding to the loss of our dad. He left some things to charity and she even seemed a little bent out of shape about that. And we're talking about stuff that had no value and she certainly didn't need. She just didn't want anything else to leave the family."

"I understand. At this point, however, all of those issues are pretty much moot when it comes to the Double Eagle. The government paid me a visit and decided they'd go ahead and take it home with them. They determined that it was real and now don't seem exceedingly inclined to give it back to me."

"I saw the articles in the paper about it. At first it seemed to re-ignite the fire inside of Nancy, but then when she saw that they were going to keep it she felt better."

"In hindsight we probably should have contacted the government first for the authentication and could have saved everyone some time and money. Live and learn I suppose."

"Well that's actually why I was calling you. When I read the articles they didn't appear to know anything about where the coin came from. Honestly, neither do we. My dad had kept it a secret probably for a variety of reasons. But we all know that he originally got it from my grandpa, who had several jobs with the government, including a stint at the Mint. So chances are that's how he came to possess it."

"Makes sense. That's basically what I told the Secret Service guys."

"Grandpa Rex passed away when I was pretty young, but I always remember him as a real detail oriented guy. He liked things a certain way and even after he retired he still had that bureaucratic mentality. He was a diligent investor and had records of everything he ever bought or sold. It's amazing the stuff he tracked, but I guess before computers that's what you did."

"Interesting. Tell me more," Bryan said, starting to get very excited about what Lisa might have to tell him.

"Anyway, he also kept all kinds of work related stuff: payroll, log books, timesheets, you name it. So as we've been going through my dad's belongings we found lots of stuff that he'd inherited from grandpa - boxes in the attic, boxes in the garage, boxes in a storage unit. We've looked through some of it, but it'll take a long time to go through everything. We just don't have the time or energy right now. So as my peace offering to you I wanted to see if you had any interest in looking through it. There's probably nothing important, but I felt like my dad would have wanted me to at least make the offer."

"I don't know if it'll help either, but that is exactly what we were looking for. The only hope I have now is to find some way to legitimize the origin of the coin. It may be a long shot, but at least it's a shot."

"I know Nancy would have a fit if she knew I was offering this to you, but it's my decision and I don't plan to clear it with her. She is back home now and won't be down again for a few weeks. Right now it looks like I'm going to be free most of the day on Saturday and was planning to spend it at my dad's house. I have to inventory stuff for an estate sale. Do you think you can come over then?"

"Definitely. I don't really have anything planned so I can be there any time. When should I head over?"

"I should be there by about 10:00 in the morning. I'll leave word at the gate to let them know that you'll be coming."

"Excellent. I can't thank you enough for calling."

"Don't worry about it. I'll see you Saturday."

Bryan hung up the phone and took a breath. He was suddenly looking a lot more forward to his weekend. Yet another turn in the ongoing saga of the Double Eagle. He slid over to his computer and tapped out an email to Draper:

> Owen,
> Don't worry about talking to Nancy. I just spoke to Lisa!
> Sounds like she has lots of records from her grandpa.
> She gave me an invite to go through them on Saturday.
> Not sure what I might find, but we'll see.
> I'll let you know.
>
> -Bryan.

Minton tried to get back to work, but was quickly interrupted by a response from Draper.

> Bryan,
> That's awesome. Do you want me to come along and help?
> I'll be glad to. Let me know.
>
> Owen

Bryan sat back and debated the offer for a moment. He had no idea what the task would involve so it might make sense to recruit another set of eyes to help search. Lisa had only invited Bryan, but based on the tone of their conversation he didn't suppose that she would mind if he brought some help. He then thought about the idea of spending some time alone with Lisa. This would be his first, and perhaps last, chance to talk to her one-on-one throughout this entire ordeal. He knew that it shouldn't even be a factor in his thinking right now, but it was an undeniably strong ulterior motive.

> Owen,
> Thanks for the offer, but let me scout it out and see what's there.
> I'm glad she made the offer so I don't want to push my luck.
> I'll give you an update as soon as possible.
>
> -Bryan

Maybe it was a mistake to go alone, but at this point Bryan didn't care. He had been trusting his intuition and he was going to keep following it now.

***

When Bryan pulled up to the gate at Stone Ridge on Saturday morning it seemed like he should be there for just another round of golf; however, that was not going to be the case today. The sky was a perfect pale blue and by mid morning the winter chill had melted into a comfortable crispness. As Bryan made his way past the clubhouse he saw golfers mulling about and wished that he could be joining them for a round.

Bryan drove to Jim's house and pulled into the driveway. He was glad to only see one car there this time, but noticed that it was a gleaming new BMW SUV. It still even had the temporary paper license tag on the back.

Bryan grabbed the small cooler from his back seat and headed up to the front door. He took a deep breath as he rang the doorbell, realizing he was a bit nervous. He felt like a high school kid showing up on prom night to fetch his date. Bryan heard footsteps quickly approach and then Lisa opened the door and greeted him.

"Hi, Bryan. Come on in."

"Hey, Lisa."

"What did you bring?" she asked, pointing to the cooler in his hand.

"Oh, I didn't know how long we'd be here so I just brought some sandwiches, snacks, and drinks. I brought plenty for both of us."

"That was thoughtful. Thanks."

"No problem. I just grabbed a few things at the store." This was only partially true as Bryan had spent about a half an hour in the gourmet section carefully selecting things that would score points, but not seem pretentious.

"Follow me this way and you can set it in the kitchen. If you want you can put stuff in the fridge too."

"I like your new car," he said as he followed her through the entry area and down a hall.

"Thanks. It's awesome. I just love it. It was a bit of an indulgence, but it was justified. My other car was falling apart and I really needed something with a little more room. I'm always toting lots of kids and lots of stuff."

When they entered the kitchen Bryan finally got a good look at Lisa and he realized just how hard it was going to be to focus on his task today. She was wearing faded jeans and a loose fitting T-shirt. Her hair was casually pulled back into a ponytail and she didn't appear to be wearing any makeup. Despite the total lack of primping, Bryan thought she looked gorgeous.

"So you're on your own today?" Bryan asked, wondering where her son might be.

"Yeah, doing a little kid swapping. I have a couple of girlfriends with kids in the same age range so we take turns giving each other some down time. Normally I'd like to spend my free time doing something else, but I need to finish things up so I can move on."

"When's Nancy coming back?"

"Probably not until after the holidays. She made her big show at the end for dad and then after losing to you it seems like she decided she was done. It's probably for the best though. I live closer and having one person make decisions will reduce the number of arguments."

"What do you do for a living?" Bryan asked, hoping to extend the conversation a while longer.

"I'm a lab technician now."

"Do you like it?"

"Actually I do. It's not the most glamorous job and it can be a little gross, but for the most part I enjoy doing it. I bounced around a few other things and never felt like I had a *real* job. This requires some skill, makes me think, and has some purpose at the end of the day."

"Do you think you'll stick with it then?"

"Probably for now. You know that financially I could certainly take a break," she said, pointing toward the driveway with her thumb, "but then what would I do all day?"

"You could play golf."

"I would need to learn first."

"Have you ever tried it?"

"I hit some balls, or I should say I *tried* to hit some balls a few times. I'd like to get better at it, but it just seems so tough."

"It is, trust me. But once you start to get a swing and hit a few good shots it becomes a lot more rewarding, and addictive."

"I've got some other priorities right now, so we'll see. I will say that having some money to fall back on reduces the stress at work. Knowing that you can leave any time makes it feel a lot less like you're a prisoner. And I'm sure I'll take some nicer vacations now too. I also plan to keep working to set a good example for my son. He's getting older now and understanding things so I don't want him to think his mom lounges around all day. I know some girls that do and I don't have a lot of respect for them. So what about you? What do you do over at Chambers?"

"Now you're going to lose all respect for me since I basically lounge around all day. We wear pajamas and watch talk shows in the morning and soaps in the afternoon."

"Sounds nice, maybe I could come by for a slumber party some day."

Bryan envisioned her wearing some silk pajamas and thought it would be a splendid idea. "I do different types of analysis work. We stay pretty busy, but it's not the most fulfilling way to spend time. Lately it's at least served as a good diversion from everything going on with the coin."

"I can imagine. Speaking of the infamous coin, let me show you where some of the stuff is so you can get started."

Lisa took Bryan toward the back of the house to a spare bedroom that was packed with boxes.

"Wow!" Bryan said as he saw the stacks. "You weren't kidding."

"Nope, and this is only part of it. There's more in the garage and some still in the attic."

"Really?" Bryan replied, second guessing his decision to turn down Draper's offer of assistance.

"Hey, I told you there's a lot. At some point it was probably well organized. Unfortunately, over the years it's been shuffled around and moved to different containers so now it's a mess. Most of it is just stuff, but here and there are things we actually want to keep. We talked about just shredding it, but were afraid we might lose something important. We've gone through some of these so I'll show you where to start."

As they went through the first couple of boxes together it was like opening a time capsule. Most of the papers were faded and brittle. Bryan was amazed at the amount of things that were hand typed. He could picture grandpa Garris sitting at and old typewriter pecking his way through one line before swinging the carriage back to start the next. He also found the first of countless manual spreadsheets. The lettering and numbering were truly impressive. Bryan wondered who could ever make such perfect letters and numbers and do it so consistently page after page. Some of the more extensive ones that consisted of green, lined paper strung end to end were almost artistic in quality. Bryan imagined how funny it would be to take one and put it in the middle of his next presentation at work, just to see how his boss would react. It also gave him a new found appreciation for all of the systems at work that drove him nuts.

Although Lisa had said she needed to work on other things, she didn't seem to be in any hurry to get to them. She spent the next two hours looking at things and talking with Bryan about what they'd found. She hadn't known much about her grandparents so this was helping her to at least fill in some of the pieces.

Bryan wasn't finding anything meaningful as most of the items were personal in nature. Nonetheless, he was enjoying the shared trip down memory lane. He also figured that since he was going to put in the time he might as well review everything. There was no telling where something vital could be hiding.

Eventually Bryan's stomach told him to look at his watch and he saw that it was already 12:30.

"Alright, Lisa, I'm ready for a break. You up for some lunch?"

"Definitely. It's really nice outside today. Why don't we grab your stuff and eat out on the porch?"

"Sounds like a plan."

They gathered everything up and headed outside. Lisa laid out the spread on the green PVC furniture and sampled bites of everything as she did, complimenting Bryan on his choices.

As they ate, the two of them talked about all of the interesting things they'd come across that morning. Bryan once again almost forgot what the real purpose of his search was. Eventually, however, Lisa decided to change the subject.

"So what's your story? Do you have a girlfriend?"

Bryan was caught a little off guard and paused a second to consider his answer. He didn't want to say something lame and sound like a loser. "Nothing serious at the moment. Obviously my personal life has been a little sidetracked recently. What about you?"

"Same thing, I think my personal life has been sidetracked a bit longer than yours though. My real focus has been my son and my job. There are always going to be some sacrifices, but I'm content with that for now."

"Were you ever married?"

"To Troy's dad?"

"Well, to anyone."

"Definitely no and no. We did talk about it; however, we both know full well that neither of us had any real interest in it. It wasn't that long ago, but my decision making skills have changed a lot in the last few years. Not getting married was probably the start of some better decisions."

"Is he still around at all?"

"No, he put in a little effort early on, but he couldn't handle it. He faded away quick and then moved out west so he's effectively out of the picture. Again, probably the best thing for both of us. And you? Ever married or engaged?"

"No and no as well."

"So why not? You're a good looking guy with a good job, you seem pretty smart, it seems like you should have had some opportunities."

"I agree," Bryan said immodestly, "I don't know why I haven't found a keeper."

"Do you scare them off before they get a chance?"

"Maybe so. It's such a fine line between romance and stalking these days."

"Well, my dad must have thought a lot of you. He wasn't one to do things on a lark and was usually pretty sure of his decisions. When I first found out about you and the coin I was honestly surprised, but once I learned the facts of the situation I understood things much better. My dad evaluated his options, gathered information, and then made up his own mind."

"I certainly think he anticipated some family resistance. But I wonder what his mindset was in terms of the government. I have to believe he knew there'd be an issue if the coin came to light. Perhaps he thought I'd hold onto it for a while and eventually its status would change. As time has gone on the Double Eagles have gradually moved from being contraband to be destroyed toward historic artifacts to be treasured."

"I don't know either. That may be the only rash part of his decision: the fact that he was running out of time. In his circumstances he was in no position to take on the government so he was probably looking for someone that could," she said with an approving smile.

"I'm still trying," Bryan said, motioning toward the inside of the house, "but the end of the line is quickly approaching."

"I really respect the fact that you also stood up to Nancy and wouldn't take the quick money and run. With everything else going on I sure couldn't do it. Even though Nancy was his daughter, my dad would have been proud of you as well. I wish I could help you more, but we were all pretty much in the dark about it."

"Thanks. It is an interesting mystery indeed. I've got to tell you that even if I end up losing, I'll be just as disappointed if I don't find out how your grandfather ended up with the coin. He clearly didn't find it lying in the street."

As they chatted through he rest of lunch, Bryan continued to realize the similarities between Lisa and her father. Being too much alike might have actually contributed to their conflicts over the years.

After lunch Bryan headed back to the bedroom and quickly finished the remaining boxes. He was rather disappointed that Lisa had moved on to her tasks and he had to work alone. The next stop was the garage where he was greeted by an even bigger stack of boxes. Many of these had stuff that belonged to Jim and his wife. Although Bryan was curious about that story as well, he tried not to be too nosey and focused on searching for items of the elder Garris.

As had been the case inside, Bryan found lots of interesting things but nothing of value as the hours wore on. The sun was starting to get low in the garage window when Lisa once again appeared. She was clearly tired of what she had been doing and needed a break. Bryan showed her a few items of interest that he'd set aside during his search.

Bryan was talking and looking through another box when Lisa approached him and leaned over his shoulder. "Still not finding what you're looking for?" she asked.

Bryan turned and faced her, but didn't reply.

Biting her lip and looking him straight in the eyes she continued, "Come on, Bryan. I think there's one more place you need to look back in the bedroom." She took his hand and led him out of the garage.

Bryan still didn't say a word, but in his head he heard the obnoxious, omnipresent golf fan who yells, "You da' man!"

***

When Bryan left Stone Ridge on Saturday nightfall had arrived. He didn't think his spirits could get any higher, but the sight of all the holiday lights and decorations made his huge smile even wider. Bryan hadn't found anything to help him keep the Double Eagle, but in his opinion the day had still been an unmitigated success. Besides everything else she had just given him, Lisa also gave Bryan a key to the house and the code to the alarm so he could come back on Sunday to continue his search. She clearly didn't seem to think he was a real security risk at this point.

On the drive home Bryan grabbed his cell phone and gave Tommy a call.

"Good evening, Minton."

"Evening Manson. Are you in the middle of anything?"

"No, Tina's picking up some dinner and should be here in a few minutes. What are you up to?

"Just calling to give you an update on my visit out to Stone Ridge."

"Oh, how did it go? Did you find anything?"

"Well, not yet. But along with the double eagle I can now say that I've also scored a hole-in-one out there."

"No way! You didn't!"

"Oh, I did indeed."

"You are just an animal. So let me get this straight, first you got his multi-million dollar coin and now you get his hot daughter. What's next? Are you going to move into his house and start wearing his slippers around?"

"I don't know about the slippers, but they are going to be selling the house in the next few months and I've already put in a good word for you about getting the listing."

"Gee thanks. Apparently you were *putting in* more than just good words today. So come on, tell me more."

"I'd be lying if I told you I'd gone over there with just thoughts of the coin on my mind, but apparently I wasn't the only guilty party. She was getting noticeable flirty at lunch so I figured things were at least headed in the right direction. Then she went off to do her thing and I headed out to look for stuff in the garage. Then she wanders in late in the afternoon and we start talking again. A few minutes later she comes over to me and makes her move."

"Come on, Bryan! She made the move? You should have been the one making the move. Now you've gone and ruined the story for me. In that situation if it has gotten to the point where she's making the move it means she's already given you five or six good chances to make *your* move. Were you wearing blinders and headphones?"

"There were not five or six opportunities. This was the first real time I'd ever spent with her and we were at Jim's house. Remember him? Her recently departed father. Ring any bells? I really didn't think *it* was on the list of potential options for today."

"Alright, I'll give you that. At least you didn't turn her down. In that case I would have had to come slap you."

"Once you see her you'll realize that there was no chance of that happening. The way I see it she had to be the aggressor. Even if she wanted me to make the play, it would look like I was trying to take advantage of her. That's no good, especially for my conscience. This way it was a win-win, right? Actually there was another win, but I'm not going any further into details."

"Wow. This is quite the little soap opera you've gotten wrapped up in, Minton. So what's next?"

"I don't know. I'm certainly digging her, but I have no idea what she's thinking. I haven't had a whole lot of time to analyze it. My hearing is at the end of the week so I have to be ready for it. After that I can shift gears and work on my Lisa strategy. I have to go back to Jim's house tomorrow to finish my search, but she won't be there. Besides the keys and code she made sure to give me her cell number, so I'm pretty sure she at least wants me to call her."

"Very perceptive, Grasshopper."

"Anyway, I'll give her a call to thank her for helping with the coin info and update her on my progress. I promise not to be too eager."

"That a boy!"

"Well, I'll let you get back to your nesting there. I'm heading home to clean up and get some rest. I had no idea researching would be such a physical activity."

"See ya', Bry'. I hope you have even better luck tomorrow."

***

When Bryan arrived at Jim's house on Sunday morning he felt a wave of disappointment as he pulled into an empty driveway. He'd known that Lisa wouldn't be there, but that didn't stop him from hoping. Once inside, Bryan stopped and looked around, the only sounds he heard were the refrigerator running and a clock ticking in the living room. It seemed like every time he came here his life got stranger and stranger.

Bryan needed to get to work, but he decided to take a few minutes to look around. After everything that had happened he felt like he was entitled to take a little voyeuristic journey. Many of the rooms had been sorted through and packed up, but the formal living room was still intact. There was a large built-in wall unit with a number of pictures. Bryan had noticed these when he came for the first meeting with Nancy, but didn't have an opportunity to look closely. Most of the pictures were of Jim and his wife, Kathy, and appeared to be from the latter portion of their life. There were a couple of family shots as well as a few individual pictures of Nancy, Lisa, and Troy. Looking at the different photos, Bryan could see that Nancy had many of Jim's physical traits while Lisa seemed to be a mix of her parents. It was of course a mix of all the best parts in Bryan's opinion.

Toward the end of the main shelf was a black and white picture of an older couple. The man bore some definite similarities to Jim so Bryan deduced that this must be the mystery man, Grandpa Rex. Bryan picked up the frame and looked closely at the picture. As he studied it Bryan asked in his head, "Where did you get that coin from, Rex?" Bryan paused for a moment as though the picture might answer him, but no reply was forthcoming. Bryan carefully put Rex back in his spot and moved on.

In the cabinets below were a number of family mementos as well as some photo albums. Bryan grabbed one of the large, bound books and sat down on the floor with it. The spine crackled as he opened it and started thumbing through the cellophane covered pages. It was filled with all the clichéd shots that you'd expect to find: pictures from school, family trips, and holidays. Besides the different qualities and photo papers, the pictures could be dated by the various hairstyles and fashions. The seventies and eighties were particularly easy for Bryan to spot as he lived through many of the same horrific trends.

Bryan finished with the first album and quickly scanned a few of the others. There were a few serious shots and a few impromptu ones, however, most of them were staged and reflected happy, smiling family members. There were plenty of pictures showing Nancy with a youthful grin; maybe she was happier back then or perhaps they just forced her to smile before taking the shot.

Looking through some of the other family items, Bryan reflected on the album of mental images and memories of the Garris family that he had been accumulating over the past few months. Most of his thoughts of Jim were positive and happy ones. Those of Lisa were definitely now keepers as well. Nancy's were without a doubt memorable, although smiles were hard to come by. Bryan looked again at the picture of the newest member of the cast, Rex. The jury was still out on him.

After drifting through the house for a few more minutes, Bryan headed back out to the garage and picked up where he'd left off yesterday. Unfortunately he had a tough time concentrating as his mind kept wandering back to the cause of his interruption the day before. At least it served as a good distraction since his search continued to yield no results. Bryan finished the last box around 1:00 and took a break for lunch. He had leftovers from yesterday and this time ate alone out on the patio.

Bryan's last chance was the attic over the garage that Lisa had mentioned. After lunch he went back to the garage and pulled down the retractable staircase. The flimsy wooden steps creaked loudly as he ascended toward the dark rectangle above. At the top he felt around and found a pull string that turned on an uncovered bulb in a ceramic socket. Bryan knew from experience that attics in Florida were the last place you'd ever want to go in the summer. Luckily he was doing this in the wintertime and the temperature was bearable. Nonetheless, the air was musty and completely still. He crawled back down and opened the garage door and windows, which created a slight breeze up above.

When Bryan returned to the attic and surveyed the situation he was a bit disheartened. There were plenty of boxes, but they were interspersed amongst all sorts of other random junk. Dealing with the attic's contents had been low on Lisa and Nancy's list for obvious reasons. Bryan took a deep breath and gathered his will for one final push. He started by sorting out some of the mess; this would make his task easier and probably score a few extra points with Lisa. Making his way through the first several boxes, Bryan found a number of very old items. There were newspaper clippings, magazines, and books from the early 1900's so Bryan thought he might be getting warmer. Although these things were very interesting from a historical standpoint, there still seemed to be nothing relating to Rex or the coin.

Bryan worked his way down the rafters and eventually came to two large trunks. He slid the first one down to the floor and tried to open it. There was no lock that he could see but the latch mechanism appeared to have broken. He pulled as hard as he could, but it wouldn't budge. Not to be deterred, he went down to the garage and found a screwdriver. The brass clasp fought him mightily, but finally gave way. Bryan opened the lid cautiously as though something might jump out at him. The only thing that did was the pungent smell of old clothes that had been in an attic for a long time. Based on the styles and quality of fabric Bryan could tell that these had belonged to Jim and Kathy's parents or even grandparents. Bryan poked around gently and couldn't find anything but clothes inside so he closed the lid and slid it out of the way.

He grabbed the second one and popped the top expecting to find more clothing. This one, however, had paperwork, files and folders. The first items on top were heavy paper stock sheathes that had various certificates and awards inside. Most of them were in the name of Rexton Garris. Below that he found some crusty ribbons and several property deeds that he quickly set aside. Next was a number of accordion style folders tied shut with decaying cloth strips. Bryan opened the first one and immediately felt a rush of adrenaline. There were employment records dated in the 1920's including hiring letters, reviews, and memos notifying Rex of pay raises. Bryan thought to himself, "Come on, Rexton, show me the money." The second one had more of the same, but Bryan now found items on U.S. Mint stationary. He ran through the items quickly, but carefully knowing he could do more extensive reading downstairs. The third folder went backward chronologically so he dropped it on the stack. Finally in the fourth one he found U.S. Mint items from the 1930's. He shuffled back closer to the light and removed all of the contents.

Bryan immediately knew that if there was any information about the Double Eagle it would be contained in the papers now in his hand. The first pages were Mint items from 1931. Then came several from 1932. Finally, a page dated 1933. Bryan paused for a moment realizing just how anxious he'd become, his heart pumping rapidly. When he got to the fourth page he noticed it was on higher quality paper and had a different logo and header. It was dated March 18, 1933 and the subject line listed "Special Projects". It was short and to the point and just what Bryan was looking for.

Dear Rex,

I am writing to thank you for your exemplary performance over the past several months. Your efforts have gone well above the normal call of duty. It is even more appreciated because of the difficulties being faced by our Department and our Country. Your tireless devotion and countless hours of overtime have allowed us to meet our ambitious goals. In recognition of your achievement and as payment for your services I am pleased to award you a bonus of $20. This particular award is being paid to you in the form of our new 1933 St. Gaudens Double Eagle piece. As you are well aware, this coin came from the series that just began striking this week.

Thank you again for all you have done to benefit the United States Mint.

Sincerely,
Robert J. Grant
Director of the United States Mint

Bryan leaned back against the truss he was sitting by and shook his head in disbelief. Now that he knew what Rex looked like, Bryan could envision him receiving the coin and reading the letter. He could imagine Rex smiling with pride about his accomplishments and being satisfied with the recognition of a job well done.

Bryan didn't think there could be anything better than what he'd just found, but still made a quick pass through the remainder of the items in the trunk. When he finished he gathered up his prize and the other folders and went back downstairs to the house. He set everything down in the kitchen and called Lisa.

"Hello?"

"Lisa, it's Bryan. Am I interrupting?" he asked, hearing lots of voices in the background.

"No, we're just getting ready to go into a movie. Are you at the house?"

"Yeah, I think I may have found the smoking gun in the attic."

"Really? What is it?"

"I found some papers form your grandpa's Mint days in an old trunk up there. One of them is a letter thanking him for his service and it indicates that he received a Double Eagle as compensation. I'm not sure if it will make a difference on Friday, but at least we know where the coin came from and that it was given to him, not stolen."

"That's awesome. Go get 'em, Bryan."

"I've got the letter and some other papers that I'm going to take to the attorneys and then up to the hearing in Washington, D.C. if that's okay with you?"

"Take whatever you need. It's one less thing I'll have to deal with."

"I won't be back until Sunday night, but maybe I can help you with the rest of the clean up after that."

"Oh, I'd love some more of your help," she said with a giggle. "Don't worry about that right now. Go up there and get your coin, Bryan."

"I'm going to try. I'm feeling a lot better about my chances now. I'll let you go and I'll pack up over here. Thanks again for everything, Lisa."

"Good luck, Bryan. Bye."

When Bryan got home that afternoon he spent some time reviewing and organizing the papers. Although many of the items supported the fact that Rex had been an exemplary employee, Bryan knew that it would all come down to the March 18th letter.

Bryan planned to get copies of everything to Draper and Lazarus first thing in the morning. In the meantime he sent a quick heads up to Draper:

Owen,
If you thought the video of Jim was good, wait until you see what I've got now!

-Bryan.

14

T he hearing that Bryan had been dreading now couldn't
happen soon enough. Bryan knew that the letter was an
extremely compelling piece of evidence to prove his claim and
his attorneys were equally enthused. He had dropped off copies at
Draper's office and faxed duplicates of everything to Lazarus.
Although the letter was blatantly clear about the origin of the coin,
the lawyers wanted to be sure they weren't missing something that
the government might be able to discredit. They also debated
whether or not they should provide the new information to the
Justice Department officials before the hearing. Surprising them
with it on Friday would certainly add to the drama, however, they
were concerned that the judge might not appreciate the theatrics. In
the end they decided to send Sikes just the primary letter and they
waited until Wednesday afternoon to get it to him. That way they
could say that they provided it, but Sikes would have limited time to
prepare a response.

On Thursday they had scheduled a pre-hearing review meeting
at Draper's office. This would be Bryan's first face-to-face meeting
with Lazarus. Bryan was already there talking with Draper when
the other member of his team arrived. From an appearance
standpoint, Lazarus certainly made an imposing first impression.
He was well over six feet tall and nearly broke Bryan's hand when
they shook. Bryan thought he would come in handy if they ever got
into a fight with the Secret Service guys. He was probably close to
fifty, but looked younger due to his dark hair and mustache. He, like
Draper, was impeccably groomed and dressed and fit Bryan's
stereotype of a South American drug lord.

"Well, Bryan, you've once again made our role a lot easier by
providing a stunning piece of evidence," Draper began.

"I'm just doing what I can to get my coin back."

"Now for the record I did offer to help search so if you'd let me
come along I could have possibly claimed credit for finding it,"
Draper said smiling.

"Noted, but I think it worked out just fine nonetheless," Bryan
replied, grinning for his own reasons.

"So let's go over things for tomorrow. For the most part the
structure is going to be similar to the hearing with Judge Stone. The

judge will review their seizure action and go over the procedural issues. Originally the plan was going to be that we would acknowledge the seizure and seek compensation, however, that is obviously no longer the case. Before we wanted to be nice and hope the judge was feeling charitable, but now we can go on the offensive. Daniel has been doing some background work on what the letter means relative to the Double Eagle so I'll let him go through that aspect."

"Again, Bryan, great job finding the letter. I can't tell you how excited I was when I got the copy and read it. I knew it had all of the requirements that we would need to meet. I'll talk about that in a minute. The first thing we will be doing is cut them off at the knees by requesting that their seizure action be invalidated. Their argument is that the coin is government property and they simply want it back. We're going to prove that the coin is *your* legal property. If they want to seize something that belongs to you they have to take a different route, but it won't matter because it'll be too late.

Now, back to the letter. The first thing we needed was a valid authorization of the coin itself. The Garris letter was signed by the Director of the Mint, who conveniently has the power to make coins legal tender. If it had been signed by anyone else we would have a hard time arguing that it was a valid coin. So it's a good thing that he was reporting to the right person.

The next thing is that the coin needs to be monetized. The letter indicates that Garris was receiving it in exchange for his services so again we have the perfect document to clear that hurdle.

And, as if the stars hadn't already aligned perfectly, the letter is dated March 18, 1933. In doing my research I discovered that Roosevelt's executive order to ban gold coins was not finalized until April 5th of 1933. Therefore, prior to that date the Double Eagles could technically be issued as legal coinage. It would have been a weaker argument for them, but now they can't even say that the Director was breaking the law by paying Garris with a gold Double Eagle.

The content of the letter is exactly what we needed. In fact it's so perfect that I'm waiting for you to tell me that you wrote it," Lazarus concluded, turning to Bryan.

"No sir. I can't guarantee that Grant was the one who actually wrote it, but it definitely wasn't me."

"Well that is the final issue about the letter, making sure that it did come from Grant. Putting it in the context of the other items you found certainly helps corroborate Garris being the recipient. However, the real key will be having it submitted for testing. My guess is that they will want to examine the paper and ink content. They should be able to do some dating on it to prove that you didn't just pick it up at the office supply store. Beyond that they'll have a handwriting expert review the signature and they should be able to find some other sample items from Grant to compare the typewriter strokes. Most old typewriters had their own unique 'fingerprints' that could be used to identify documents that were typed on them, such as a letter that didn't strike all the way or was shifted slightly to one side. Looking at everything we have here I have a tough time believing it is a fake.

Considering all of that I think we can confidently establish Rex as a legal owner. Now, we don't have anything about the transfer from Rex to Jim, but being father and son there's really not much to dispute. From there I think we have some pretty fresh tracks legally bringing it to you.

The last thing we will need to do is ask them to issue you a Certificate of Transfer. That's a document that will certify that you are the current legal holder of a legal Double Eagle. It's essentially your seal of approval from the government. I'm not sure what your intentions are, but if you do decide to sell the coin you are going to want and need the certificate. Also, any buyer stroking an eight figure check for the coin is certainly going to be looking for it. So that's the plan guys. Questions? Concerns? Comments?"

"I like it. I'm feeling very good about tomorrow," Bryan said with satisfaction.

"Well we still need to work out one other detail, Daniel."

"What's that?"

"Finding a good place in D.C. for a victory celebration tomorrow night."

"I like your confidence, but let's not get ahead of ourselves, Owen."

"I was just kidding. Although we should still plan to go somewhere nice and bill it to our client."

"Oh, that's a given," Lazarus said matter-of-factly.

"You guys realize I'm still sitting here, right?" interjected Bryan.

The three of them looked over some other paperwork and then chatted for a while. Eventually they wrapped it up and finished by reviewing their itineraries for the trip the next day.

***

Bryan barely slept on Thursday night, but he was so excited that he had no problem getting ready early Friday morning. They had booked an early direct flight to make sure that they would arrive mid morning, leaving enough time to check into the hotel and get lunch before the 1:00 hearing. Bryan and Owen were carpooling to the airport where they would meet Lazarus.

It was still dark when they arrived at the airport, but with holiday travel starting to pick up and security measures there was a surprising number of fellow travelers there. After finding Daniel and checking in they headed for the terminal. They had intentionally built in some extra lead time, but Bryan's anxiety level shot way up when they rounded the corner and saw the security lines stretching as far as the eye could see. There was a collective groan followed by a quick analysis to try and pick the line that might be the shortest and fastest.

Bryan was carrying the letter and other documents in his carry-on messenger bag. Along with the important stuff he had also interspersed some other random paperwork from Chambers. Bryan wasn't planning on doing any work during the trip; rather he wanted to provide some padding and camouflage for the Garris papers. Although there was nothing illegal about carrying old documents, he didn't want to draw any unnecessary attention to them. Bryan was getting closer and closer to reacquiring his coin and he didn't want anything to go wrong. He was pleased when the security officer thumbed through his things indifferently and handed it back to him at the end of the x-ray conveyor belt.

Their flight was uneventful and set to arrive on time. Bryan had been watching the weather report all week. Although it was cold, the skies were clear in the nation's capital. The last time Bryan had been to Washington, D.C. was on a trip during high school, so he was glad to have the window seat to see all of the landmarks as they circled before landing. Using the Washington Monument as his compass needle he was able to follow the Mall to locate many of the nearby structures. From up above he could see the flow of tiny people on the sidewalks, cars on the streets, and boats on the Potomac. There were plenty of signs of life, but what Bryan noticed was missing was the color green. Instead, Bryan saw grass that was a brownish-gray mat across the landscape. Just as bad were the black, spindly branches of the leafless trees. There was a lot to be said for the year-round lawns and palm trees of Florida.

After landing, they gathered up their items and made their way through the terminal to ground transportation. It seemed cool in the airport, but when they exited out the sliding glass doors the cold air greeted them with a slap in the face. They threw on their jackets and scurried into a cab. Bryan once again felt like a kid on the ride to the hotel. He had his face pressed against the window taking in all the sights as they went. There was a great variety of architecture in the homes and buildings and most of the neighborhoods were older and more mature than anything in Bryan's area. Another big difference was the abundant use of brick. Compared to Bryan's stucco jungle, it seemed to add a much more historic feel.

The team checked in and ate before making one last review to make sure they had everything. They had chosen their hotel in part due to its proximity to the courthouse where the hearing would take place. It was only a few blocks away so, despite the cold temperature, they decided to walk. The mid-day sun had warmed the air up a little bit and they were all excited about finally getting to the hearing so nobody seemed to mind. When they reached the courthouse building it was exactly what Bryan had envisioned: a massive Greek revival building fronted with thick columns and fed by a broad marble staircase. Bryan enthusiastically bounded up the steps and had to wait at the top for Draper and Lazarus to catch up. Once inside, they visited the information desk and obtained directions to their courtroom.

In the hallway Bryan was greeted warmly by Agent Kraft. "Mr. Minton, glad to see you arrived safely. Good to see you again."

"You too, Agent Kraft. Good to see you as well, Agent Dodge," Bryan said, shaking hands.

"Mr. Minton," acknowledged Dodge.

"I think you remember Owen Draper and this is Daniel Lazarus."

"Good to see you and nice to meet you," said Agent Kraft. He turned to Bryan and continued, "I hear you brought some big, new ammunition with you today?"

"I think it will be pretty convincing, but we'll wait and see what happens in there today."

"This is the first high profile case we've had in our group in a while so it has created quite a stir. It was big enough based on the fact that a Double Eagle was involved, but when it came to light the other day that you might actually have a claim on it people really got interested."

"I just keep finding new ways to take it up a notch. I'm hoping this will finally be the peak of excitement."

"Here come Sikes and his people now, we'll see you inside."

Bryan, Owen, and Daniel entered the courtroom and took their seats. This room was laid out in a much more traditional manner. The appearance was also more of what Bryan thought a courtroom should look like. The lighting was inadequate and it was filled with dark wood furniture and trim that made it seem even dimmer. The stone floors and high ceilings made every noise resonate and echo.

Sikes and his team followed and introductions were made between the two parties. A number of other individuals, including the Secret Service agents, also made their way in and took seats in the gallery area. A few moments later the judge arrived and began the hearing right on time.

Judge Donald Maclamore was an older gentleman that looked like he had been presiding over courtrooms for a very long time. He took his seat at the front and cordially welcomed both sides. He then started reviewing the background information and the Justice Department's seizure action. The judge finished by noting the new information that Bryan had discovered before allowing Sikes to begin his arguments.

Sikes started off by going over some of the history of the Double Eagle and the government's decision to eventually destroy the coins. He then talked about the handful of coins that had surfaced over the years and their ultimate fates. Finally, turning to Bryan's coin, he ran through what seemed to be their case before the Garris letter came to light. He noted that the coins were illegal for individuals to hold and that any surviving coins were still the property of the U.S. government. It quickly became clear that up until Wednesday Sikes had prepared for what seemed like a slam dunk victory. Only at the end did he address the issue of the Garris letter.

"Your Honor, with respect to this letter from the Director of the Mint, we have a number of issues to contend with. First and foremost is its validity. We are concerned about the fact that this letter of potentially very high importance surfaced at such a late point. It seems unlikely that neither Rex nor James Garris would have used it to seek official ownership of the coin before their deaths. Now after decades of being hidden away it fatefully appears just days before the government plans to seize the coin. Even if we assume Minton's story is true, it certainly could have been forged by

Rex Garris to one day lay claim to the coin. He would have had the necessary information and materials to craft such a letter. What makes this scenario of the supposed 'bonus' so unlikely is that it clearly contradicts the Mint's cashier records from 1933. As has been the case in prior actions involving Double Eagles, we have once again done an extensive review of the coin issuance records and there is not a single entry for the Double Eagle."

Judge Maclamore interjected, "I can appreciate your concerns; however, the circumstances that allow for is to be fake also allow that it could be real, probably even more so. I've seen a copy of the letter and if it's a fake it appears to be a good one. I also understand that there are a number of other documents supporting Mr. Garris's employment history with the U.S. Mint. We will discuss the letter further this afternoon, but at this point I am operating under the assumption that we are dealing with an authentic document and I suggest that you do the same. I'm not making any decisions yet, but the content of the letter significantly undermines your arguments about the legal status of the coin."

"I understand, Your Honor, but we've had so little time to prepare to address the letter that it doesn't seem appropriate to rush into it at this hearing."

"Mr. Sikes, we're talking about a one page letter, not some complex legal document. Again, I think you already know its potential impact. We are all here already and these gentlemen traveled a long way to attend so let's move forward. Do you have anything further, Mr. Sikes?"

"No, Your Honor."

"Alright then we are going to let Mr. Minton's side present their arguments. After that we'll take a short break to review the original letter and the other documents that they've brought. Mr. Lazarus, you may begin."

"Thank you, Judge Maclamore. As has already been discussed, our position for this hearing has changed drastically in the past week. The first thing we are requesting is that you deny the Justice Department's seizure request. The basis for our request is that their action indicates that the Double Eagle in question is the property of the United States government. We have full confidence, and intend to prove, that this is not the case."

Lazarus made arguments against other related details of the government's document and then spent time giving the history of how Bryan had come to know Garris and receive the coin. Before he had a chance to move on to his next items Judge Maclamore interrupted him.

"So you hit a double eagle, Mr. Minton," the judge asked.

"Ahh, yes, Your Honor," Bryan replied cautiously, not knowing the legal bearing of the question.

"Wow, that's a heck of a shot. An albatross is even rarer than an ace. I've played for a lot of years and know lots of guys with hole-in-ones, but nobody with a double eagle. Congratulations."

"Thank you, Your Honor. Now you can say you know somebody with one," Bryan responded, relieved that Maclamore was simply appreciating his feat. He also felt far better now knowing that his fate would be decided by a golfer.

"Sorry for the diversion, please continue, Mr. Lazarus."

"No problem, Your Honor. Now that you have some of the background on Mr. Minton, I want to turn to the letter and his claim to the coin. Let me first touch on a few of the points made by Mr. Sikes. In terms of the timing of the discovery of the letter, it has nothing to do with the proximity to this hearing. It was simply due to the chain of events that led us here. As I've already noted, Mr. Minton formalized his possession of the coin after winning a dispute with Mr. Garris's children. The letter was in their father's home and, therefore, Mr. Minton had no access to it until Mr. Garris's daughter, Lisa, contacted him a little over a week ago. The letter was stored away among numerous old belongings and appeared to have been there quite some time. James Garris may or may not have been aware that it existed. Unfortunately, that's something we'll never know.

As for the validity of the letter, there is nothing to show that Mr. Minton or James Garris could have or would have created a forgery. The only real possibility would be Rex Garris. However, Mr. Garris was clearly a stellar employee who had an outstanding long-term career with the Mint. We have plenty of other records and evidence to show that. Would he really be the type of person to jeopardize all of that to steal a twenty dollar coin? And what would be the point of having the letter as proof if his boss, Grant, was still around? If Garris tried to use the letter to say it was his, Grant would be the first person who could say it wasn't real. Finally, let me re-emphasize something I just said: it was a twenty dollar coin. We're sitting here today discussing a Double Eagle with tremendous potential value. Back then it was worth twenty dollars. Now, that was still a lot of money and *after* the rest were destroyed there would have obviously been additional value and significance as collectors' pieces. But would that have been enough for someone in Rex Garris's situation to swipe the coin and forge the letter? It seems very unlikely. Also, there are no signs that Mr. Garris was ever numismaticly inclined so the possibility that he would have wanted the coin as a collector seems equally remote."

Bryan was watching the reactions around the courtroom as Lazarus spoke and noticed a lot of expressions, including Judge Maclamore's, change when Daniel brought up the value issue. It was as if they were having the light bulbs above their heads pop on in an "ah-ha!" moment. Even Sikes seemed to look as though he was thinking: "Yeah, that actually makes a lot of sense."

Lazarus continued, "As for the cashier's records that Mr. Sikes mentioned, again we have to put that in the context of 1933 versus today. Even now, with computerized tracking and advanced record keeping, errors happen and things don't get accounted for. We'd all like to think our systems are perfect, but we know that they're not. In 1933 all of the tracking was done manually. At the time Grant wrote the letter there was a lot going on at the Mint and within the government. To say that this coin could have easily been lost in the shuffle is an understatement. Shortly after the letter was written, President Roosevelt issued Executive Order 6102 to ban the hording of gold, including coins. Perhaps Grant realized the coin to Garris could be impacted and intentionally decided not to log it in order to avoid taking back the bonus to Garris. Also, on April 26, 1933, just a month after giving the coin to Garris, Grant was replaced as Director of the Mint by Nellie Taylor Ross who was appointed by FDR. Clearly there are a lot reasons why this coin might not have been logged.

Another question to address is whether or not Grant would have had access to the Double Eagles and would it be reasonable to think that he would give one to an employee. The officials here today from the Mint may be in a better position to address this; however, based on our research it seems very possible. We have found a number of examples where the Director of the Mint has, for various reasons, made special coin issuances. Additionally, Grant would have been one of the few people with access to the coins themselves. There's no doubt that he could have procured one or more samples.

Now I'll turn to the letter. I think its legal importance is clear to everyone here, but I want to review the salient points from Mr. Minton's perspective. First, the letter is signed by Robert Grant, Director of the Mint. He had the capacity to authorize the issuance of the coin. Next, he indicated that Garris was receiving the coin for his services, so there was consideration made and the coin was monetized. Those two aspects establish that the coin had become legal tender and that Garris was a valid owner. The other critical piece of data is the date of the letter, March 18, 1933. The legal transfer of this Double Eagle took place more than two weeks before FDR's executive order was finalized on April 5th. Therefore, Grant was in no way breaking the law when he gave the coin to Garris. Finally, the order itself allowed individuals to own up to one hundred dollars in gold coins. This coin was already in circulation and under the threshold so the order has no bearing whatsoever on it. In turn, the government effort to recover the coin under the auspices of the order has no legal grounds.

Based on the legal merits of the letter we are asking that you deny the government's seizure request and rule that Rex Garris legally received this coin. Earlier I discussed how Mr. Minton has already legally established his acquisition of the coin from James Garris. Therefore, we are also requesting that the U.S. Mint be required to issue Mr. Minton a Certificate of Transfer that will name him as the owner of the coin and will allow him to legally transfer that title if he so chooses.

We feel that the facts and legal aspects are quite clear at this time and that you can provide your ruling subject to an adequate examination of the Grant letter. We too appreciate the concerns surrounding it, but have the utmost confidence that upon qualified examination it will be deemed authentic.

At this time we have nothing further, Your Honor, and will be happy to share the original paperwork we brought for your review."

Lazarus then provided the original items to Judge Maclamore and a full set of copies to Sikes. The judge called for a half hour break to examine the documents in his chambers.

Bryan was very relaxed and waited patiently for the judge to return. He congratulated Lazarus on a job well done and they talked about their previous trips to Washington, D.C. Meanwhile, Sikes and his team had moved to the far corner of the room to look over their copies and address possible responses.

Maclamore returned and reconvened the hearing, "Thank you for your patience, gentlemen. I have gone over the information and done some additional background research. Before I make my ruling, do you have any further comments based on the information, Mr. Sikes?"

"Your Honor, this is all very interesting, but does nothing to add to the legal foundation of the letter. What we really need is more time to evaluate the letter itself and the legal ramifications."

"Again, I think the legal ramifications are quite simple. It shows that the coin was legally issued and transferred to Mr. Garris. What I am asking for is if you have any legal rebuttal to Mr. Minton's requests. If the letter is real, can you see any way that this coin is not legally his?"

"Well, Your Honor. At this stage it's difficult to draw any real conclusions. That's why we feel it is important to provide additional time to research all the critical facts."

"Mr. Sikes," Maclamore said, clearly getting a bit impatient. "The purpose of this hearing was to evaluate and rule on your seizure request. Mr. Minton's role was to make his case for why the coin should be his and not be taken by the government. He has done that quite well."

"But, Your Honor," Sikes interrupted, seeing where the judge was heading. "I just think that we should..."

"Mr. Sikes," Maclamore said, raising his hand to stop the attorney. "Are you going to answer my question?"

Sikes shook his head and said nothing.

"So based on the facts presented to me today I am denying the government's request for seizure. Additionally, I am granting Mr. Minton's request for a Certificate of Transfer."

"Your Honor!" blurted an exasperated Sikes.

Maclamore glared, "May I finish?"

"Sorry, Your Honor," Sikes replied.

"Subject to a reasonable verification of the original letter given to Mr. Garris. We are located in a city with numerous experts who can perform the various tests and I feel it should be evaluated by both government and independent analysts. Additionally, the criteria should be mutually agreeable to both sides. I am looking for an adequate standard, but not an undue one. If there are any problems with the process please feel free to contact me and I will be happy to assist. In terms of timeframe, I think that in a high profile case such as this that the analysis should be able to be conducted within the next several weeks. Unless there is some unavoidable delay I would like to see the Certificate of Transfer issued within four to six weeks."

"I'm sorry, Your Honor, but considering the 'high profile' that really isn't much time," pleaded Sikes.

"We had all of three weeks to prepare for this hearing," Lazarus added sarcastically.

"I think the time is adequate unless something changes dramatically."

"Judge Maclamore, a Certificate of Transfer will be a binding agreement. That means that once it's issued we essentially won't be able to appeal."

"I know that Mr. Sikes. However, I'm here today to decide on the legal ownership of the coin, which I have done. If you can find something in my decision to legally contest you're certainly welcome to appeal it. If that's the case, perhaps you should stop interrupting me so that we can finish up here today and you can get back to work."

Maclamore paused, giving Sikes a chance to respond but this time none came.

"Now, as for this marvelous coin. Until we get a determination on the Garris letter I am going to ask that it stay put. It is in a secure location right now and it should not be moved for any reason until this matter is concluded. Are there any further comments from either side?"

"No, Your Honor, thank you," replied Lazarus.

"Nothing further," replied a disgruntled Sikes.

"Thank you all for attending and with that this hearing is adjourned."

As Judge Maclamore departed, Bryan stood up with a huge grin and thanked Owen and Daniel for their efforts. They both reminded him that he was really the one responsible for the victory but they were glad to help. As Sikes and the rest of the government's contingent headed out Bryan received a smile and a congratulatory wave from Agent Kraft. Bryan wanted to thank him again for getting the coin safely to Washington, D.C., but assumed that Sikes wouldn't be pleased if he saw anyone else weighing in on Bryan's side today.

***

After stopping back by the hotel to clean up and change, Bryan, Owen, and Daniel departed for their victory dinner. The mercury had dropped as the sun went down so they decided to take a cab to the steakhouse that had been recommended by the hotel concierge. Although he didn't like the temperature, Bryan had to admit that he liked the feel of the city at night; it was active and vibrant. On the drive he saw countless restaurants and stores that were filled with people. There seemed to be so many different things to do.

The restaurant had a very cosmopolitan feel. There was a hushed level of verbal white noise that never quite rose above the sound of silverware clanging on plates. Bryan had worn one of his nicer outfits yet he still felt underdressed. After ordering and getting a round of drinks their talk of course turned to the coin.

"Here's a toast to our fine client, Bryan Minton. Ninety-nine percent on his way to being the owner of a 1933 Double Eagle," offered Draper.

"Hear! Hear!" added Lazarus.

"Thank you, gentlemen. I'm still going to hedge on ninety-nine percent, but I finally feel like it's getting closer. Sikes wasn't happy about what happened today, however, I don't think he's consumed by vengeance either. I'm guessing he'll do some work to see if he can find some angle to exploit. If not, I'm sure he has lots of other cases he's working on and he'll move onto something else."

"Let's hope so. D.C. is a nice place to visit, but it's too darn cold up here," said Draper.

"I think he'll have a hard time finding anything to use. I'll be stunned if the letter is anything but the genuine article," added Lazarus.

"I think so too," admitted Bryan. "I'm especially glad that I finally found out how the coin made its way to the Garris family. Of course now I'd like to find out even more. The stuff in the attic fills in a lot of holes, but it's just information, it doesn't give you any of the color commentary surrounding things. I wonder if Rex ever thought about turning the coin back in voluntarily or if he ever looked into selling it. It's hard to guess since there's no way he could have known what it would be worth today."

"But even later in his life it would have seen some decent appreciation. Seems like there would have been some incentive to cash in on it," Lazarus said.

"By then he probably didn't need the money. I found lots of stock transactions and records. Although he probably never made a lot of money working for the government, it looks like he was a diligent investor and did well with what he made. A good part of the assets that Nancy and Lisa inherited actually came from their grandparents. The funds had been held in trusts that paid income to Jim and then distributed to his children after he died."

"Do you think Jim held onto it for the same reason?" Draper asked.

"Probably so. I know he had a successful career and he didn't live an overly ostentatious life. By the time he likely received it from his dad he wouldn't have needed to sell it."

"It would have been nice if he'd given you some kind of background on the coin when he gave it to you," Lazarus mused.

"I agree, but maybe he was being intentionally vague. He knew the baggage that might come with it and just wanted me to sort it out on my own, which is pretty much what I've been doing. When considering the value, everyone thinks it's a winning lottery ticket. But along with the good comes a lot of trouble; the coin just seems to attract it."

"Well, hopefully most of the bad stuff has rubbed off of it now. So tell us, Bryan, what are you gong to do with it? Tuck it away for a rainy day or cash in your ticket?" Draper asked. "And don't tell me you don't know."

"I knew you were going to ask that. At this point I don't see any reason to hold on to it. I don't have a sentimental attachment to it and that's the one thing Jim made clear to me: do whatever I think is best. Of course if I do sell it that opens a whole new can of worms. The easy route is to just find the highest bidder, but is it worth it to give it to some rich guy who will keep it locked away in his own collection? I guess the only sentimental aspect for me is that I'd like for other people to have a chance to see it. Owen, you know how amazing it is, you saw how people react when they get to look at it. So to answer your question, yes, I plan to sell it. How and to whom, that's yet to be decided. When the time does come I'll be coming back to see you guys again. I'm not planning to do it myself on eBay."

The trio had a great dinner together and enjoyed the rest of their short visit to Washington, D.C. The flight back to Florida was a bumpy one, but Bryan didn't particularly mind. The trip had been a success and he fully believed that in just a few more weeks he'd be able to move forward with *his* Double Eagle.

15

D ue to the pending letter evaluation, there was no press release made following the hearing. Bryan was pleased as it gave him a little bit of respite from the attention he knew would be coming soon. He had still been receiving a steady stream of inquiries about purchasing the coin so he made note of ones that seemed credible opportunities. He also started quietly looking into auction houses and coin dealers that might be able to facilitate the sale of the coin. Work was relatively slow as it was year end and lots of employees were taking the last of their vacation time.

Bryan didn't want to seem too eager, but Lisa was the first person he'd called from D.C. to give the results of the hearing. She congratulated him and told him to call her when he got back. He did as he was told and was pleased when she took him up on his offer to help out with things at Jim's house. She also told him that he was responsible for bringing lunch again since he'd done such a good job last time. He was happy to oblige.

When Bryan arrived on Saturday morning he was greeted by Lisa at the door before he even had a chance to ring the bell. He was glad to know that she had been watching for him to arrive.

"Good morning, Lisa."

"Hey, Bry'. Glad you made it. I've got lots of work today and I'm going to need some big strong muscles to help."

"In that case maybe I should call someone," Bryan deadpanned.

"Oh, I think you'll do just fine," she said, smiling as she grabbed him by the arm and gave him a kiss on the cheek before leading him inside.

Bryan was once again glad that she had taken the initiative on the greeting as he had been debating what was appropriate. After she kissed him he gave her a casual hug in return. It had been a while since he'd felt this way about a girl and he was still bustling with nervous energy.

Lisa helped Bryan put lunch away in the kitchen while looking over her agenda of things to get done.

"So what else did you do up in D.C., Bryan?"

"The normal tourist things; mainly spent some time on the Mall visiting the museums and monuments. It's been a while since I was up that way so it was neat to see things in person that you see on

TV all the time. I'm not sure I'd want to live up there, but it's a fun place to visit. Have you been up there before?"

"Same as you, years ago when I was a kid. I don't remember how old I was, but everything seemed so big. Maybe it was because I was so little."

"The buildings still seemed big to me. A lot of them just seem to dwarf you when you stand in front of them. I guess they want you to understand your place relative to the power of the government."

"So do you like art museums?"

"Depends. Most of the stuff there is very impressive. It's easy to appreciate it as art. I guess that's what I like: things you don't have to think too much about. I've been to some galleries and museums over the years and seen works that I simply can't consider art. I also went by the monetary collection at the Smithsonian. I definitely have a new found appreciation for that genre."

"Are you going to have to go back up again?"

"Hopefully not. If the Justice Department files an appeal then we'll probably have to go back. If I end up getting my certificate then I will have to decide how to move the coin. Since it's not the kind of thing you want in your pocket while walking down the streets of Washington, D.C. I'd probably have a security company handle it. In my online searching I found info on a couple of companies that move expensive items. Depending on what it is and where you need it to go the prices are pretty reasonable. More importantly, you can get huge amounts of insurance. They're used to dealing with things in the ten, twenty, thirty million dollar range."

"You could just tote it around in your golf bag again. If anyone tried to take it you could whip out a club and beat them with it."

"I think walking around with a golf bag in downtown D.C. would lead to a quick arrest these days."

"So where will you move it?"

"Those same companies have high security storage facilities so as long as I wasn't planning to keep it for an extended period of time I'd just park it with one of them."

"Makes sense. Did you see anyone famous up there?"

"No. Again, with the security issues, even second tier people probably get chauffeured around. It's hard to imagine that the President used to be able to walk down the streets there. I felt reasonably safe, but luckily I'm a nobody. I did pick up some things while I was there," Bryan said, reaching into his backpack. "Here are a couple of toys I picked up at the museum stores for Troy. I didn't have them wrapped since I figured I'd let you screen out anything that he won't like or might be too dangerous for him. I asked the clerks at the stores for things that were age appropriate."

"That's so thoughtful, Bryan. He'll love these. He's big on animals and dinosaurs right now."

Bryan smiled with satisfaction knowing he'd picked wisely. "And this is for you," he said, handing her a thin, rectangular box. "Merry Christmas."

"You didn't have to get me anything," she said, looking at the box.

"It's nothing fancy, just spreading a little holiday cheer."

"Oh, I love it! That is so pretty," she exclaimed, opening the case and finding a small, black bracelet with various colored stones.

"I'm glad you like it," Bryan said, satisfied that he'd found the right gift for her as well. He'd spent a lot of time thinking about what to get her. He wanted to get something nice, but simple. She didn't seem like the kind of person to wear fancy or gaudy accessories. He picked a bracelet since it was a nice gesture, but didn't imply too much of a commitment like a ring or necklace.

"Don't think this gets you out of doing work today."

"Absolutely not. I'm ready to go."

"Good. I've got lots of things I have to get done this weekend so don't try to distract me either," she added with a devilish grin.

She put Bryan to work moving items to the garage that were gong to be picked up by a charity. She then used his analyst's skills to look up and record estimated values for various donations. Normally on a beautiful Saturday Bryan would dread being inside rather than out playing golf, but today he didn't mind given the company. The hours flew by and once again they had lunch together outside. After lunch Lisa gave out her remaining orders and Bryan worked diligently to get done with plenty of time to spare before she had to leave. He finished around 3:00 and went to look for Lisa. Bryan found her in Jim's office, sitting hunched over on the floor and going through what looked like bank statements.

"That looks like some exciting reading," he said, standing behind her and looking over her shoulder.

"My dad tried to keep things simple, but over the years he still ended up with so many different accounts. Most of this stuff is redundant, but just like the personal items I don't want to miss anything."

"You are quite a soldier," Bryan said, kneeling down behind her. He had decided in advance that he was going to be the one on the offensive today. He began rubbing her shoulders and leaned in close to her ear, "You seem awfully tense. I hate to see that. I think you need to take a little relaxation break."

She giggled as he started to kiss her neck, "Bryan, come on. I really need to finish with these statements."

"Don't worry, I'll help you finish...later," he whispered as his hands began to wander.

"Bryan!" she barked, elbowing him and shaking him off.

Bryan fell back, leaning on the floor and looking at Lisa's back. He got a terrible sinking feeling in his stomach and wondered if he had just blown his chances. He wasn't sure if he should stay or go.

"Sorry," he said softly.

She let out a small laugh and turned around to face him.

"Bryan, if this is going to work you're going to have to learn the importance of bank statements."

"I'm sorry. I didn't realize."

As he stammered she smiled and started laughing.

"Bryan, I'm just screwing with you!" she said. She picked up two handfuls of paper and threw them at Bryan before lunging and landing on top of him. Between kisses she said, "I need to test you and make sure you're not too fragile. It's okay to be serious, but I can't take uptight."

Shaking off his stunned reaction, Bryan rolled her over aggressively and pinned her down with his body. He looked her straight in the eyes and just nodded without saying a word. In the back of his mind he started to worry a little bit about what he was getting himself into. However, about an hour later that was the last thing on his mind.

***

Bryan was lying in bed with his arm draped over Lisa. They had been that way, frozen in silence for a few minutes when Bryan decided he would be the one to talk. "So how long am I going to be able to drag out your estate settlement? I'd like to go ahead and block out my Saturdays for the next few months if possible."

"Sorry, once I get back and finish with those statements that will be it," she said, elbowing him much more gently and playfully this time.

"I'm going to take your statements outside and burn them," he said, shoving her back.

"Well, the estate sale will be in about two weeks and then after that everything left will get donated. I'm going to keep some furnishings so the house will show better for open houses. Hopefully my work over here will be done within the next month. After that I'll have to cut you loose, Minton. You could see if Mrs. Crowley next door needs some help around her house."

"Isn't she like seventy years old?"

"Yeah, she was after my dad, but she told me she prefers younger men."

"Great. Anyway, if this job is coming to an end I guess my only option is to ask you out on a real date."

"Is that what you want to do or what you feel like you should do?"

"Well I'm happy to skip the dinner and movie if you would rather just come straight to my place. But I don't mind putting in a little effort first. Either way is fine with me. I'm just trying to figure out which way the winds are blowing."

"What do you mean?"

"You certainly took me by surprise last time we were here. That was the first time we'd really spent together so I was trying to figure out what your motives were."

"You'll learn that I don't spend too much time thinking about decisions. I'm less spontaneous than I used to be, but I still trust my instincts when necessary and go for it. Why did I come out to the garage? I just felt like it. That and probably one other reason."

"And what was that?"

"With everything that had been going on I'd been without for a while. So I was feeling pretty horny that day."

"I guess I picked the right day to stop by then," Bryan said, thinking about how fortuitous the timing of his first meeting with Jim had been as well.

"And what about you, Bryan Minton? What was your motivation?"

"Well, any day is a good day for me."

"So would you have made an attempt?"

"Probably not. I wouldn't want to feel like I was taking advantage of you. However, looking for the letter wasn't my only reason for wanting to come over that day."

"You seem like you think about things quite a bit before making a decision. That's probably why you're an analyst."

"Maybe. But I have been doing a much better job going with my gut lately and it's been working well for me. From an analysis standpoint, taking the money you guys offered would have been the easy call. That little voice just told me to fight, though."

"I'm glad you did."

"So are you just interested in having some fun or looking for something more?"

"I don't know. Don't try to overanalyze it, Bryan. Let's just go with it and see what happens," she said, turning around and facing him.

"That's fine with me."

"Alright, that's enough talk. Time for action," Lisa said and then started kissing him before he could say another word.

Before leaving Bryan got Lisa to agree to go out with him in the next couple weeks as long as she could find a babysitter. He was very pleased with the way things were progressing. Driving home Bryan turned his cell phone back on and found that he had a message from his mom. It didn't sound like anything important so he decided to wait until he got home to call her back.

***

With the holidays upon them Bryan knew that his mom would be in festive overload mode. Besides events that she was involved with in an official capacity, she would normally attend several holiday parties each week. If there were conflicts she might even double up and do two in one night. Occasionally Bryan would get roped into attending one, but he did his best to dodge when possible. Bryan had talked to his parents a few days ago so he was afraid she wasn't calling just to chat. Nonetheless, he figured he better make the call and get it out to of the way.

"Hello?"

"Hey, Mom. It's Bryan."

"Hi, Dear. How are you doing?" his mom asked in a somewhat hushed voice.

"Doing fine, Mom," thinking that was a bit of an understatement based on the time he'd just spend with Lisa. "What's up?"

"Oh, nothing much. Did you play golf today?"

"No, I had some other things to take care of. I got your message so I was calling you back. Did you just want to talk or is there something else?"

"Well, I do need to ask a little favor."

219

"Where do I have to be and when? I'll go, but I'm not wearing a suit."

"No, it's not a function. Just a lunch."

"Lunch? Oh, that's even worse."

"It's not an event, Bryan. I just want you to have lunch with somebody."

"A set up? Sorry, no can do. I'm actually working on something of my own right now."

"Bryan, listen to me. It's not a set up. I just want you to have lunch with a friend of mine. You don't even have to get dressed up."

"Go on, Mom. Why do I need to have lunch with this person?"

"He's a good friend of mine who happens to be a big coin collector, too."

"This is about the coin?"

"Sort of. He's very interested in the Double Eagle and wants to talk to you about it."

"If he's a collector he probably knows more about it than I do so I think he's going to be disappointed in my limited breadth of knowledge."

"He wants to talk about your coin specifically, Bryan."

"Did you tell him I don't have it right now?"

"Yes, he knows about that. He's been following your story closely in the papers."

"So who is this guy?"

"His name is Stuart Middleton. He's a retired businessman who lives out on the Key. He's very involved in charitable activities and social functions. I'm sure you've seen his name and picture in the paper."

"Maybe. It kind of rings a bell. I try my best to ignore that kind of stuff these days."

"I'm sure you'll recognize him when you see him."

"Anyway, why should I be having lunch with him?"

"I'd really like for you just to meet him and hear what he has to say. Can you do it as a favor to me?"

"Mom, what is it he has to say? Why don't you just have him call me? I have no interest in having lunch with one of your social buddies."

"Bryan, he may be interested in buying your coin."

"Mom, you know it's not for sale yet."

"Yes, yes. He just wants to get to know you now so that when the time comes he'll have a chance."

"I'll be happy to give him a shot. But if he thinks he's going to get some special treatment, I'm sorry, he's not."

"That's not what he's looking for. Can you just meet him for a casual lunch? I'm sure he'll even pay."

"A free lunch, eh? I hear there's no such thing," Bryan said, refusing to give ground.

"Bryan, I really don't ask a lot from you. Can you please just do this for me? I've already told him that I would arrange it," she replied, her voice starting to sound distressed.

Bryan noticed the change, "Mom, what's the real story here?"

"Can you please just meet him?" Mrs. Minton asked again, even more exasperated.

"Alright, Mom, I'll talk to the guy. But why can't I just call him?"

"He wants to meet you in person."

"Fine. Either Wednesday or Thursday this week should work. Just let me know when and where."

"Thank you, Bryan. I really appreciate it."

"Bye, Mom."

When Bryan set down the phone he had a very uneasy feeling about the conversation he'd just had with his mother. Her behavior had been very atypical. And if Middleton was her friend why wasn't she going to come to lunch with them? He was listening to his intuition and it was telling that his lunch date was not going to be a good one. Regardless, Bryan had agreed to do it so he decided to just go and see what this Middleton guy had to say. If there was a bright side it was that this would give Bryan some practice for what would hopefully be coming soon. If he did end up selling the Double Eagle he would be dealing with wealthy people and he knew that meant lots of big egos and eccentricities.

***

Mrs. Minton had arranged for Bryan to meet Middleton on Wednesday at noon at a small bistro not far from Chambers. When Bryan checked in with the hostess she led him to a small table tucked away in a back corner. Already seated was an older gentleman waiting patiently with his hands clasped on the table. He stood up as Bryan approached.

"Hello, Mr. Minton?"

"Yes."

"I'm Stuart Middleton, nice to finally meet you," he said, offering his hand.

"Likewise," Bryan replied, shaking hands reluctantly and sitting down.

Bryan looked Middleton over as he sat back down across the table. He was probably in his sixties and was wearing an expensive suit. He had a full head of hair that was now mostly gray. The only thing Bryan noticed about his face was his eyes. They were very dark, almost as though his pupils had been dilated, and sat behind a pair of thin, rectangular Euro-style glasses. He had a familiar look like most people his age that Bryan saw in the society pages, but Bryan didn't recognize him in particular.

"Thank you for joining me today, Mr. Minton."

"Just Bryan."

"Alright, Bryan. It sounds like you've had an exciting year so far. As with most numismatics, I've been following your story with interest. I was stunned to find out that a Double Eagle had surfaced so close to home."

"Yes, it's been one to remember. So what can I do for you, Mr. Middleton? My mother was very insistent that I come here today despite my reluctance."

"Please, call me Stuart. So what has you mother told you about me?"

"Not much. She said that you were a successful businessman and a coin collector. So I'll just make a wild guess here, Stuart, and say that you're interested in buying the Double Eagle."

"Yes, I'm very interested in the chance to acquire a Double Eagle. But before we discuss that, has your mother told you anything else about me?"

"Nope, that's it."

"So she hasn't told you anything about our *friendship?*"

Bryan raised an eyebrow and looked more intently at Middleton, starting to realize where he was heading. "No, she hasn't. Are you going to enlighten me, Stuart?"

"We've known each other for a number of years on both a professional and personal level. On the professional side it's been a mutually beneficial relationship. She's helped me at the government level with some development projects that I've done and I've helped out with her campaign efforts. On the personal side, we often attended the same events and became close acquaintances."

"Close?" asked Bryan.

"Very close," Middleton said, nodding with a fiendish grin.

"Great. This should be a cheap lunch for you since I've already lost my appetite."

"So that's the background of what has brought us together today. I know that you haven't formally taken ownership of the coin, but it appears that you are very close."

"Did my mom tell you that?"

"Yes, she did mention it. Anyway, I thought now would be a good time to approach you to begin discussions about a possible sale. I'm sure you will have lots of offers and I wanted to be sure to make mine early."

"I haven't made any decisions about what I'm going to do yet so there's not much to discuss. If I conduct an auction I'll be sure to give my mom the details so she can let you know."

"That's actually what we need to discuss. I'd rather help you avoid having to go through with all that hassle. I think if we can come to agreeable terms it would be mutually beneficial. I can acquire an exceptional coin and you can walk away with a tremendous amount of money."

"I've already been investigating my options and don't think an auction will be a hassle. It will generate the most publicity, bring the biggest bidders, and get me the best price. Sounds like the most beneficial route for me. If you end up being the highest bidder then there's your ever popular win-win."

"You see, that's my concern. A high profile auction will indeed bring some major bidders; people who may be able to surpass my generous offer."

"Ah, now I see. You're not a heavy enough hitter to play with the big boys so you are trying to get a bargain price before the market establishes one for me."

"Currently I have funds that are locked up in projects that are in progress so my liquid funds may not be as high as other collectors."

"Would you give me an I.O.U. for the rest?"

"No. I am proposing a large, one-time upfront payment."

"Okay, Stuart, cut to the chase. What's your number?"

"At this time I'd be willing to offer you seven million dollars cash."

"Seven million? And you call that generous, Stuart? Maybe generous for you. All signs are that this coin will start at ten million and likely go well above that figure," Bryan said, containing an urge to almost laugh at Middleton's offer.

"But, Bryan, you have to also figure in the fact that my offer comes with 'additional consideration' shall we say."

"*Additional consideration*? Oh, so this is the blackmail lunch? And here I thought it was just grabbing a friendly bite together."

"Now, Bryan, that's not the direction I want to head. Seven million dollars is a tremendous amount of money for someone your age."

"Of course it's not the direction you want to head, because it's toward a place called reality. People like you and my mom live in your little fantasy world where you are the biggest fish in this little pond. You consider yourselves movers and shakers and play your little games. '*For someone your age?*' Does that imply that you are the adults? Because you act like a bunch of kids. Unbelievable. Well, this is my mom we're talking about so what else are you offering?"

Middleton's passive tone changed a bit as he was now clearly on the defensive. "Obviously first and foremost would be the fact that my relations with your mother would remain private."

Bryan coughed up a laugh, unable to control himself. "And you don't call that blackmail? Wow! What else?"

"Although payment for the coin would be one time, I would certainly continue and increase my support for you mother's political career. I think you know she has greater ambitions and I would help with funding and connections."

"Hmm," Bryan mused, feigning serious interest in Middleton's proposal. "Are you going to put this in writing for me?"

"Bryan, that's not something you put in writing. That part would be a 'gentlemen's agreement'."

"Oh, I see. I'm not sure that would meet the legal definition of 'consideration', I may need to check with my attorney."

Sensing Bryan's growing sarcasm, Middleton pressed on, "Bryan, I understand your reaction and fully expected resistance. I know this is a bit of a shock so I want you to give it some time to sink in. All I'm asking is that you keep an open mind. I think that if you weigh all the variables you will realize that this is the best option for everyone involved."

"I will think it over. However, I doubt that I'll come to that conclusion. Anything else, Stuart?"

"Well, I was hoping to find out a little more about you. Again, I'm trying to make this a friendly transaction. So maybe we can talk about some other things during lunch. I hear you are quite a golfer."

"I don't think that will be necessary. I think you already have one too many friends named Minton," he said, starting to get up to leave.

"Bryan, you don't have to leave. Please stay for lunch."

"I do need to go, but thanks for the offer. As for your other offer, I will think about it and let you know."

"Thank you for coming today and thanks for keeping an open mind. Here's my card where you can reach me," Middleton said, standing up and offering the card and his hand.

Bryan just glared at him, took the card, then turned and walked out without shaking his hand.

Despite what had just happened, Bryan was still hungry so he stopped and grabbed a sandwich. He couldn't believe the conversation he'd just had and kept replaying Middleton's words over and over in his head. He had no desire to sell the coin to someone like that, but he had to consider the implications for his mother. He wasn't worried about the financing aspects – he would soon be able to fill that void himself if need be. He was, however, concerned about the impact on his family if it became public. Apparently Draper had been wrong in D.C. when he said all the bad stuff had rubbed off the coin. Bryan had just received a fresh dose. He started weighing his options and it didn't take him long to figure out what he had to do. He pulled out his phone and called his dad.

"Bryan?"

"Dad, how's it going?"

"Good. Are you at work?"

"No, just out for a quick lunch. Are you up for a round this weekend?"

"I've got some stuff to do on Saturday and I've got a game set on Sunday morning already. I could squeeze in a few more on Sunday afternoon. Do you want to come over Sunday afternoon for nine?"

"Yeah, that should work. What time?"

"About two should be fine. I'll call over just to be sure they don't have anything scheduled."

"Sounds good. I'll see you there."

Bryan finished his lunch and started thinking about what he was going to say to his dad this weekend.

***

When Bryan arrived at Oak Run Sunday afternoon he was little disappointed by the sky. After looking forward to playing for the last few days he was hoping for perfect weather as always. Despite all the rounds he got to play in optimum conditions, or perhaps because of it, he was let down when they were sub par. The weatherman had clearly predicted that the front would move through early Sunday, but here it was mid-day and it was still in progress. There was a consistent blanket of gray clouds sliding across and dropping occasional sprinkles.

Bryan found his father in the clubhouse grill saying goodbye to his morning partners after eating lunch and settling bets. Bryan said casual hellos to his father's friends, but he wasn't feeling chatty. There was only one person he really wanted to speak to today.

After checking in for their afternoon session, Bryan's dad switched his clubs to his walking bag and they grabbed Bryan's clubs that were waiting in the rack. They hoofed around the edge of the practice green and walked right to the first tee. Normally this time of year there would be plenty of afternoon players, but the weather seemed to have kept most of them home. It looked like they would be able to play their pace without being pushed or held up. Bryan was also glad that it would just be the two of them, he had no interest in having anyone else tag along on their round.

Bryan got his equipment organized while his dad teed his ball and swung away. It was his course and he'd already been playing so he was ready to go. His ball rose smoothly and then landed gently in the right side of the fairway. Bryan marveled at his father's consistency and stepped into the tee box. He did his best to change his mindset to golf, but it was proving difficult due to the other issues weighing on him. He took a deep breath, took his stance, and sent his drive way left into the tall pines bordering the hole.

His dad turned to him with a smug look, "I thought you wanted to play *together* today. I'll see you up at the green."

He marched off as Bryan put his driver away and headed in the other direction. Jeff Minton started with an easy par, while his son had to scramble for double bogey.

On the second tee the elder Minton had the honor and easily mimicked his shot from the first hole. Bryan went next and unfortunately also managed to copy his first drive. This time, however, there were no trees to stop his ball's wayward progress and it carried way into the rough, barely staying in bounds.

"That's some thick stuff over there, but I think I spotted you pretty good. You should be able to get back to the fairway...with a sickle."

"Thanks, Dad."

"Come on, Bryan, I'll walk that way with you."

As they walked down the fairway together Jeff Minton looked over at Bryan a few times waiting for him to say something. Bryan stared ahead toward his ball and walked silently.

"So what's going on, Bryan?" Jeff finally asked.

"I'm pulling it way left. That's what's going on."

"That's the obvious problem."

"Yeah, I know. I need to talk to you about something."

"Is it something about the coin?"

"Sort of."

"I thought you were just in a holding pattern waiting to hear back about the letter."

"For the coin itself, yes. This is something kind of tangent that came out of left field."

"Well, lay it on me."

"It's kind of a tough one, Dad. I'm not sure how to deal with it."

"You know I'll help you in any way I can."

"I know, Dad."

They walked on a little further into the rough where Bryan had sent his tee shot.

"I had you going toward this little clump of overgrown grass," Jeff pointed out as they arrived in the area.

They plodded around for a moment before locating and identifying Bryan's ball. He hadn't put a sickle in his bag that morning so he used his pitching wedge to hack down on it and pop it out almost to the edge of the fairway.

"That's a good shot out of that junk."

"Thanks."

They headed across to Jeff's shot and he routinely put it on the green in regulation. Bryan was at least able to hit his third shot on and had a reasonable par putt left.

As they headed toward the green Bryan continued, "So, Dad. Do you know Stuart Middleton?"

"Sure. We've known him for a while. Your mother knows him a lot better than I do though."

Bryan thought to himself, "That's for sure!"

"So what about him?"

"I had lunch with him the other day."

"Really?"

"Yes. He's apparently a big coin collector and is interested in buying my Double Eagle."

"That doesn't sound like a problem to me."

"Well, the thing is mom was the one that set up the lunch."

"Oh, I see," his father's tone changing a bit.

"I had no interest in meeting the guy, but mom insisted so I did."

"Hmm."

"He would really like to but the coin, but wants to do it on his terms. He has certain information that he is trying to leverage against me."

"And what information is that?"

"That's the tough part," Bryan said, pausing, not wanting to say anything further. "Remember, I said that *mom* insisted that I meet with him?" Bryan added, glancing sideways at his dad.

"Oh, I see," his father replied, with less surprise than Bryan had expected. "That is a tough one."

They walked to the green without saying anything further and both two-putted for par and bogey, respectively. They continued to the next hole, a par five, and hit their drives. Jeff Minton hit the fairway like clockwork, apparently not troubled by Bryan's revelation. Bryan, feeling a little relieved after broaching the subject, hit a better drive that just rolled into the first cut of rough. On their way up to their shots they continued.

"So what's Stuart offering you?"

"He'll pay seven million dollars and provide 'additional consideration' for the coin."

"Boy, never in my life did I think I'd say seven million seems low," he said with a laugh.

"He said that's all he can swing right now and obviously wants to avoid me going to auction because he knows he'll be outbid. I have no interest in selling it to him, even less now in fact, but I have to consider mom. Her job and her social scene are her life. She's spent so long building up her little world and I'd hate to be the reason it comes crumbling down."

"It doesn't sound like you'd be the reason."

"Well, I'm the one who has to make the decision."

"Exactly. It's your decision, not Stuart's and not your mother's. You need to do what's right for you, not them."

"Isn't that being a little selfish?"

"I think it pales in comparison to their selfishness."

"I guess. You seem a lot less freaked out about this than I expected. I mean look at this drive you just hit."

"Bryan, it's actually not that big of a surprise to me."

"Really?"

"Bryan, we've been married a long time, raised two great kids, and shared a lot of wonderful memories. But things change over all that time. We still love each other, but it's different than it was. It used to be that we had to do everything together. As the years went on though she started to do more of the things that she liked to do and I did the same."

"I'm aware of that, Dad, but isn't this crossing the line just a bit."

"Again, Bryan, your perspective is a lot different. You still see it as part of the romance. When you're older it can be something completely different. I don't know what your mother's motivations are, but I highly doubt she's in love with him. In her mind it's probably just part of the game. I've certainly guessed that she's had some outside relationships so this isn't earth shaking."

"Wow, I guess I'm just naïve. So is there something I need to know about you too, Dad?"

His father laughed again, "Me? No, I won't be setting up any lunches for you any time soon. As I said, Bryan, things change. Hopefully you still have a healthy interest in that, however, mine's not what it used to be. It's just a fact of life, Bryan. I used to worry about it, but eventually you get to the point where you realize it's not worth it."

"You're really making me look forward to retirement, Dad."

"It's still a long way off for you, Son. Nonetheless, you don't want to wait too long, you're not twenty anymore."

"Well, there's some good news for you, Dad. I've started working on something recently."

"Good for you. I guess that's a good excuse for why you haven't been working on your golf game," Jeff said, pleased that he extracted a smile from his son.

They switched back to golf and finished the hole before picking the conversation back up on the way to the par three fourth.

"I know it's my decision, but I'd still like to know your opinion, Dad."

"From my standpoint I'm mostly upset about the fact that you got dragged into this. I'm a lot angrier about that than I am about Stuart Middleton. So my opinion is that you should be taken back out of the discussion."

"Just say no?"

"Yep."

"That's what I wanted to do already. I just didn't want to be to hasty in my decision. I was pretty mad after I met with Stuart so it was hard to be sure I was thinking clearly. You're sure?"

"Very sure. And don't worry about your mom; I'll take care of her."

"Alright, but I still want to talk to her. Let me tell her of my decision first."

"If that's what you want to do."

"I'll tell her and I'll definitely tell Middleton. I'm not that worried about his little threat. I'm sure it was easy for him to scare mom, but I don't find him real intimidating. I think he just threw this out there and hoped I would flinch. If I say no then what does he really have to gain by going through with it?"

"Not much."

"Exactly. So I'll call him this week and tell him to keep his seven million."

"Good for you, Bryan. Now hit your shot."

They played another hole before his dad decided to swing the conversation back to Lisa.

"So are we going to meet this new girl of yours?"

"We'll see. Things have definitely started off right. But she's very different from most of the girls I have dated before."

"Maybe that's a good thing."

"That's what I'm hoping. She's a bit younger, but she seems pretty mature. Oh, and she's got a young son."

"Really?" Jeff said, showing the first surprise that Bryan had seen all day.

"You didn't see that coming did you, Dad?"

"Definitely not. But that's okay, there's nothing wrong with that. It's just not what I expected you to say."

"Well maybe you need to be sitting down for the next piece of info."

"Uh-oh."

"She also happens to be Jim's daughter."

"Jim Garris's daughter?"

"Yeah."

"Not the nasty one I hope?"

"No, not Nancy. The other one, Lisa."

"Oh, that's good. So how long has this been going on?"

"Since right before I went to Washington, D.C. In fact it was the day before I found her grandfather's letter. Remember she was the one that called and let me look through the stuff."

"That's right. Well congratulations. I hope it works out."

"I hate to be corny, but it almost seems a bit like fate. I think I'll give it a little longer before I bring her to meet the Mintons."

"Probably a good call."

Bryan felt a lot better after getting the coin issue off his chest. He was also glad that he told his father about his new relationship with Lisa, as it seemed to raise his dad's spirits. In turn, Bryan's game quickly improved as the tension in his muscles subsided and his swing became more natural. Over the last few holes the clouds finally cleared out and the low afternoon sun helped to further clear Bryan's mind. Walking up number nine they cast long shadows as the sun slid toward the horizon. Neither of them moved too quickly as they both wanted to enjoy their final hole. Bryan's only disappointment of the day was that they didn't have time to play longer.

On the green Bryan replaced the flag after his father finished putting out and then shook hands. His father pulled Bryan in and gave him a big hug.

"I love you, Son."

"I love you too, Dad."

"Don't worry. Everything's going to work out fine."

"I know."

Bryan headed off toward the parking lot while his father walked to the clubhouse to drop off his clubs and get cleaned up. As Bryan approached the high hedge that buffered the parking lot he turned and exchanged a silent wave good-bye with his dad. All that needed to be said today had already been said.

***

Knowing it would be a while before his dad returned home; Bryan went ahead and called his mom. He wanted to finalize this matter as soon as possible.

"Mom, it's Bryan."

"Oh, hello dear. How was golf?"

"Golf was good. I'm calling you about my meeting with Stuart Middleton."

"Yes?"

"You knew my hesitation to meet with him in the first place, but I listened to what he had to say. Honestly, I didn't like it one bit. I know he put you in a difficult situation and then he tried to do the same to me. I'm just calling to let you know that I won't be accepting his offer or making a counteroffer. I was going to tell him that he wouldn't even be allowed to bid, but for your sake, Mom, I'll let him when the time comes. I'm guessing he won't be able to pull it off anyway. As for his threat, I wouldn't worry too much about it. You know him better than I do, but I think he's bluffing.

Over the past few months I've gained a much better understanding of why the Garrises never did anything with this coin. It has a way of causing family problems, but it shouldn't."

"I know, Bryan, I'm sorry. I just didn't know what to do."

"That's okay, Mom."

"Does your father know?"

"This is something for you and him to discuss."

"I agree."

"I'll call Middleton in the next day or two and let him know."

"I'm so sorry, Bryan. I shouldn't have done this."

"That's alright, Mom. It'll pass."

"I love you, Bryan."

"I love you too, Mom. Bye."

***

On Monday the first thing on his agenda after Joe's meeting was to call Middleton. He had been thinking about what to say to him and really wanted to tell him that the deal was on just to see how he would react. However, since his mother was involved he thought it best to keep spite out of the conversation. He fished the business card out of his pocket and called.

"Good morning, Middleton Group."

"Hi, my name is Bryan Minton. I'm calling for Stuart Middleton."

"Mr. Middleton is not available right now, can I take a message?"

"Is he in the office this morning?"

"Yes, but he's not taking calls right now."

"Oh, I see. Well, I think he'll take mine. I'll hang on while you go let him know. Thanks."

"Hold on, sir."

Bryan waited for a moment, rolling the card over in his fingers.

"Sir, I'll put you through now."

"Thank you."

"Bryan?"

"Stuart, how's it going?"

"Just fine. Have you considered my proposal?"

"I have indeed. The answer is a very firm: No."

"Bryan, are you sure you've thought this out thoroughly?"

"It didn't take a lot of thought, Stuart, trust me. In the spirit of being civil I have decided that if and when the time comes I will allow you to bid on the coin. However, if one word comes out about my mom your chance will be gone."

"I'm very disappointed in your decision, Bryan."

"Too bad. Take care and good luck bidding," Bryan said and then hung up.

16

After all of the excitement of the past few months, Bryan was happy to start the New Year off with relative quiet. He was glad the holidays were over and the situation with his mother seemed to have passed without further conflict. There were no updates on the letter yet as many of the people involved had been out on vacation. Nonetheless, all expectations were still that they would have an answer in the next week or two.

In the meantime, Bryan now had Lisa to help keep his mind occupied. She had been busy with her son's activities and her regular babysitter had been sick so they hadn't been able to go on a date yet. Still they kept things progressing by talking every few days on the phone and trading emails. The email had proven to be a good test. Bryan was impressed that Lisa would actually write things out and check her spelling and grammar. Bryan hated when younger associates at work filled their messages with excessive shorthand – that took just as long to translate – and didn't bother to read what they'd written to see if it even made sense. He was all for brevity and efficiency in email communication, but people were taking it too far.

The stars finally aligned and they were able to schedule a date. Bryan was looking forward to it, but was feeling a little nervous. It was the good kind of nerves, though. Like the way you feel standing in line for a roller coaster as you hear the wheels pounding and the riders screaming above. Although he didn't really need it, Bryan had gotten a haircut and bought some new clothes in preparation. Even though it wasn't their first time together, he still wanted to make a good first date impression.

Lisa lived about forty miles south, but Bryan was able to take the Interstate for much of it making it a quicker drive. He pulled into her apartment complex and found her building. They were modest units and Bryan noticed that Lisa's new car stood out in the parking lot compared to those of her neighbors.

Lisa greeted him at the door and invited him inside. Her son was sitting in the living room playing video games with the babysitter.

"Troy, can you say hi to Mr. Minton?"

"Hey," he said without looking away from the screen.

"You remember him from Grandpa Jim's house, don't you?"

The boy glanced over quickly and just nodded to appease his mother.

"And he got you those neat dinosaurs."

"Thanks," he mumbled.

"Good to see you again, Troy," Bryan said, trying to break the ice.

Troy clearly wasn't interested in chatting so Lisa moved on.

"Alright, Amber, you've got my number and Bryan's so call if you need anything. Troy, you behave, okay?"

He gave her another nod of acknowledgement and she patted him on the head gently. She grabbed her purse and then Bryan and headed out the door.

Walking out to the car she tried to reassure Bryan, "Don't worry, it's not you. Most kids aren't real big on having conversations with adults they don't know."

"That's okay. I was really here to see you tonight anyway."

"Also, he's always going to be a bit suspicious of any male friends that I bring home. And trust me; I bring home lots of different guys. It's sometimes hard to keep track."

Bryan looked at her sideways, but didn't respond.

"I'm kidding," she admitted.

Lisa navigated as Bryan drove to the restaurant she had chosen. It was a quaint little place along the inter-coastal waterway and since the weather was mild they sat outside under the flickering flames of tiki torches.

"So what do you like to eat besides my free lunches?" Bryan asked.

"I eat just about everything. I'm not a big fan of fast food, but I tolerate it since Troy and his friends like to go to those places. There aren't a lot of fancy restaurants around here, but I enjoy places like this that have decent food and a nice atmosphere."

"And you?"

"I'm pretty easy. It seems like when I go out with friends we end up at the chain places pretty frequently. It's not the best food, but it's good and it's consistent."

"You like your consistency, don't you?"

"Hey, there's nothing wrong with consistency," he said, pointing at her. "If you're going to pay good money for a meal you might as well know what you're going to get. And for the record I'm always willing to try new things and branch out."

"Alright, we'll see about that."

"Do you think you'll stay around here or move somewhere else?" Bryan asked.

"Once dad's stuff gets settled I'm going to start looking for something more up your way."

"You can't stand all this distance between us?"

"No, I was thinking more about better schools for Troy next year. But I guess there could be some other benefits of being up that way," she said suggestively.

"What kind of place are you looking for?"

"Luckily my options are pretty wide open now. I think I'd like to find a nice modest house though. I want something new enough so it will be in good shape with a pool and a yard for Troy to play in. I don't want anything too big because then you just have more stuff to clean and more things that can break. What about you, Bryan? If things work out are you going to upgrade or head somewhere else?"

"I think I'll stick around here. I love the weather and this is where my friends and dysfunctional family are."

"What's wrong with your family?"

"They're actually not too bad, but every family has their own set of issues. Someday I'll tell you about some of ours, but not tonight. I finally told my dad about you the other day. He was pretty surprised, but looking forward to meeting you one of these days."

"So are you going to move to a golf course?"

"Maybe. It would have to be like your dad's place though – close to the golf course, but not right on it."

"There you go. His place is going to be available pretty soon. I think I can get you a good deal."

"Thanks, but I think that would be just a bit too creepy," Bryan said, thinking about his recent conversation with Tommy. "Although I have to say I've had some very good luck in that place recently."

"So what about me? I'm not your typical kind of girlfriend am I?" she asked bluntly.

"I wish I could say I had a 'typical' kind, but if I did you're probably right, it would be a lot different than you. That being said, you're turning out to be a lot different than I expected."

"Why? What were you expecting?"

"I don't know. I guess I had a bit of a stereotype formed for a young, single mother. I thought you'd be serious and dour, more like your sister."

Lisa laughed, "And why is that your preconception?"

"Experience I guess. When I'm at the store and see a younger girl with a kid and no ring they never seem to be smiling. They look frazzled and angry."

"Well you're right about that. I can get pretty stressed when Troy decides to test me, especially in public. Afterwards I always realize that it's payback for the grief I dished out as a kid."

"I think you're still dishing it out," Bryan jabbed.

"Ah, you are funny. Anyway, raising a kid on your own is a challenge. I know some girls that have more that one. I can't imagine how much tougher that is. There are times when it feels like they're dragging you down and taking your life away. But then they turn around and fill it with even more joy. They can do that one little thing that makes it all worth it. Everyday he writes a new page in my life; sometimes it's drama and sometimes it's comedy. I love them all."

"I can tell. It's pretty clear that you still have plenty of life left in you. He hasn't sucked it all out."

"So what do you think about kids?"

"Well, I'd definitely like to be one again."

"Oh, wouldn't we all."

"I don't know. I don't have a lot of experience to be honest. More and more of my friends have kids now, but I only have limited interaction with them. I guess I'm not real high on their babysitter lists. Of the ones I do know it's tough to make a blanket statement. I think they're just like the big ones: there are some that you like and some that you don't."

"That's very true. I try not to be too judgmental with kids; however, there are some nasty ones. Most parents won't admit it, but we all compare other kids to our own and try to find ways that ours are superior. And there's plenty of exaggeration, too. I have a friend that is always bragging about how her daughter was using words at six months. I'm not sure what those words were, because I knew her back then and the only thing coming out that kid's mouth at six months was spit-up."

"Nice."

"That's another thing; kids can be very different at various ages. Babies are cute and all, but I don't miss the sleepless nights, the diaper changing, and toting around all that junk. It took you an hour just to get ready to go somewhere. Now we're out the door in just a few minutes. It's so much easier."

"Yes, I don't envy the parents I see staggering along under their baggage like urban Sherpas."

"It's hard to put Troy in any category yet. He's still a work in progress. But I think if you do get to know him you'll like him a lot."

"At some point when you're ready I'd like to do something together. Maybe something he'd like to do so he doesn't feel like he's being pressured to go."

"Sure, when the time is right. It's been pretty hectic lately so I don't want to overload him with anything else."

"So for now I get you all to myself," he said, looking deeply into her eyes.

They enjoyed their dinner and then followed it with a movie. Bryan savored the fact that it was all at a leisurely pace. He felt like Lisa wanted to make the most of their time together and wasn't rushing to get home to her son. They held hands when they were walking and she spent most of the movie leaning on him and holding his arm. At the end of the night he walked her to her door and kissed her goodnight. It seemed very natural as though they were both thinking the same things. Although their date lacked the raw passion and physical intimacy of their prior trysts, Bryan still left feeling the same glow of satisfaction.

***

The following week Bryan received an update on the verification process. The evaluations were nearing completion and there would be a conference call on Thursday to present the results. Sikes was probably ahead of the curve as the government experts had likely informed him of their results. Bryan was very confident that the letter would be deemed authentic, but there was still a chance that something would go awry. It had certainly become par for the course with the Double Eagle.

At noon on Thursday Bryan drove over to Draper's office to join the call. This allowed them to be together in the same room if they needed to discuss things offline and also afforded more privacy than the paper thin walls of a Chambers cubicle. Bryan arrived a few minutes early and they had a quick call with Daniel Lazarus. There wasn't much to discuss as everything was now basically hinging on the letter.

Since the meeting was being originated from Washington, D.C. all Bryan and Owen could do is sit and wait for the phone to ring as the clock in the conference room clicked past 12:00. Owen had his laptop set up and at 12:05 he got an email from Lazarus asking if they'd received their call yet. The clock ground away until 12:09 when it finally rang. Bryan and Owen both jumped and exchanged a look of relief.

"This is Owen Draper and I've got Bryan here with me."

"Hello, gentlemen, sorry we were running a few minutes late today," came Sikes's voice over the phone.

"No problem."

"We have Mr. Lazarus on the phone as well."

"Hi, guys," Daniel added.

"Let's go ahead and get moving. We are also joined today by the folks over at Lanier Analytics. I'm going to turn it over to Cliff Mays who will be presenting their findings."

"Thank you, Mr. Sikes. As you are all aware we were asked to do a comprehensive evaluation of the document referred to as the Garris letter. We did a review of the paper, ink, type strokes, and handwriting on the document.

From a visual perspective, the paper's aging and deterioration are consistent with the date of the letter. An analysis of the paper composition evaluated two elements. First, the paper fibers were manufactured with wood pulp originating from forests in the North Eastern United States. This pulp was widely used during the early 1900's, but began to decline significantly mid-century. The second factor examined was the bonding agent used on the fibers. Chemical analysis shows traces of several compounds that were used during that period, but have since been discontinued from use in paper manufacturing. We also examined the U.S. Mint seal on the paper and found the embossment to be original. The seal was applied via a screening process that embedded the colors in the paper fiber. This logo could not have been applied using modern technology such as laser printing. These factors can not prove the exact date of the paper; however, they certainly place it in a reasonable range for the indicated year.

We examined both the signature ink and the type composition and came to a similar conclusion. The pigments in the ink are characteristic of those used during the period and breakdown shows that the signature was clearly made several decades ago. Interestingly the type strokes have held up remarkably well. Typewriter ribbons during that period were actually much thicker and heavier with inking compound. Over the years the ribbons became thinner and less impregnated as manufacturing methods improved and cost cutting came into play. The older ribbons were also less consistent in the dispersion of ink so within each line, and even within each stroke, you can observe different densities. These patterns are present on the Garris letter.

Moving on to the type font on the letter. We compared the Garris letter to the other samples provided by Mr. Minton as well as several other specimens obtained form the Mint and other historical records. The typed letters on all of the samples were created by a Worthington Stylist typewriter. This model was widely used at the time and Worthington had contracts with the government so their machines were found in many different departments, including the Mint.

Now, drilling down to the specific typewriter used, under the microscope we found certain character traits for several of the letters on the Garris document. The dot on the tail of the lower case 't' has a shadow, the bottom curve of the small 's' has a consistent shallow spot, and the period is unevenly weighed toward the left side. There were several others, but these were the most noticeable and, therefore, the most likely to be detected from one sample to the next. These markers were identified on the additional samples of letters and memos from Mr. Garris. Therefore, we can declare with confidence that they were all generated on the exact same typewriter. In terms of the additional outside samples we again were able to make several exact matches with documents signed by Mr. Grant. We did find several that do not match; however, looking at the context of the documents we found that these were general correspondence items. It is very likely that these documents were generated by a typing pool and, therefore, came from different machines. Every personal correspondence we had from Mr. Grant was an identical match to the Garris letter."

As Mr. Mays was going through his information, Bryan and Owen were smiling and nodding at each other as each piece of the puzzle was put together and fit perfectly.

Mays continued, "The final and perhaps most important element of the letter is the signature of Mr. Grant. Our handwriting analysis experts reviewed several criteria. There are typically two types of signatures that we come across: those that are nearly identical every time and those that have very similar characteristics but change from one time to the next. The latter can still be confirmed, but it takes a much greater examination of the samples. Luckily, Mr. Grant's falls into the first category. The size and formation of his signature is extremely uniform in all the samples we examined. Beyond the two dimensions visible on the paper we also did a 3D analysis and the weight with which his signatures were created showed high levels of consistency. The last thing we look at when considering a possible forgery is if there are signs that the signature was traced from an original specimen. Even very light tracing will create damage to the paper fiber that can be differentiated from that made by the ink signature. There were no signs of any such damage on the Garris letter.

In summary, we have found no reason whatsoever to question the authenticity of the letter. We have prepared our full report and will be overnighting you copies today. Included is our letter of certification for the Garris document. With that do we have any questions, gentlemen?"

"None from us, that sounds pretty definitive. Thank you," said Draper, after clicking off the mute button.

"That was very comprehensive. Thank you, Mr. Mays," added attorney Sikes.

"Excellent. If it's appropriate, may I ask what the results were from the government's testing?" Mays asked, clearly curious to compare the two outcomes.

"Their results matched yours, Mr. Mays," admitted Sikes.

"Great. I expected that to be the case. If there's nothing further I'll drop off and let you gentlemen continue with your business. Let us know if we can help in any other way," Mays said before a beep sounded his departure.

"Well, it sounds like we've cleared the last hurdle, Mr. Sikes. Are you ready to allow the issuance of the Certificate of Transfer?" asked Lazarus.

There was a brief pause and then Sikes said, "We are."

Bryan and Owen jumped up and exchanged high fives.

"I will be sending a draft of the certificate to attorneys Lazarus and Draper this afternoon for their review. If the language is agreeable I would anticipate that we can generate and execute an original in the next few days," Sikes added.

"Wonderful. We will review it as soon as it arrives."

"I'll await your response. Is Mr. Minton still there?"

"Yes, I'm here," said Bryan.

"This certainly isn't the outcome I anticipated, but you can't win them all. Congratulations on you acquisition of the coin. I hope it brings you many great rewards."

"Thank you, Mr. Sikes. I really appreciate that. It's been a long road, but hopefully this was the last major bump in it."

"We can coordinate with the officials from the Bureau once you decide what you're going to do with the coin. In the meantime, we'll keep it safe. Take care."

Owen dropped the phone line and then called Lazarus.

"Hey guys, I'm not sure that could have gone any better. Congratulations, Bryan, on the big victory."

"Thanks, Daniel."

"I'll take a look at the draft as soon as it arrives and then circle back with you, Owen. It should be pretty straightforward and we'll get this thing wrapped up."

"I agree. I'll talk to you later," Owen replied. He turned to Bryan and asked, "So has it sunk in yet?"

"It's just a feeling of relief."

"I understand. So what's next? Are you going to take a break?"

"Not yet. I've already decided to sell it so I'm going full speed ahead. I'm gong to get back with the auction house people and decide how to best move the merchandise."

"Good for you. Let me know if I can help."

"Thanks, Owen."

Bryan had planned to go back to work, but when he left Draper's office he took a breath of the cool, fresh air and decided otherwise. After everything that had gone on Bryan figured he was allowed to skip out for the rest of the day. He drove home, changed clothes, and picked up his clubs before heading over to the Lakeside Links Golf Course. He was able to get right out and walked eighteen before the sun went down. It was just what he needed to regroup in preparation for the sale of the coin.

***

Over the next several days Bryan began his discussions with the major auction houses that dealt in high end coins. Often they handled large collections made up of multiple lots so they would organize an auction for a broad range of buyers. In Bryan's case it was a single, high value item that would draw a large group of interested bidders.

Bryan quickly found out that there was a tremendous level of buzz surrounding his coin. As he made inquiries he was pleased to find that upper echelon representatives were the ones returning his calls and they were eager to talk to him. He also found out that buyers had proactively been checking with the houses to see if they had obtained a listing yet. Besides Middleton, numerous other collectors were anticipating a near term sale and didn't want to miss their chance. Bryan hadn't been sure what to expect, but he had some concern that the sales process would take a while to complete. Fortunately, everyone involved seemed to be ready and waiting. All they needed was Bryan and his coin.

There was one other item they needed: the Certificate of Transfer. Bryan's attorneys had expediently reviewed the draft and turned it around to Sikes. The following week Bryan received an overnight letter package at his office. He took it back to his cubicle and carefully opened it with the pull tab. He slid the papers out and found his executed Certificate of Transfer. Now he finally felt like he was holding the winning lottery ticket.

Based on his prior research and his conversations over the past week, Bryan had made up his mind to sell his coin via the Kensington Auction Company. The auction house had the best track record for high end coin sales and had worldwide affiliates. Bryan was also impressed by Peter Stanford, who was the seller's representative that he had been dealing with at Kensington. Stanford seemed extremely knowledgeable about the coin auction market and was well versed in American gold coins such as Eagles and Double Eagles. Additionally, their commission structure was right in line with the other firms.

Bryan put down his certificate and made a call to Stanford.

"Kensington, this is Peter Stanford," came the dignified voice.

"Peter, it's Bryan Minton."

"Ah, the man of the moment. How are you doing, chap?"

"Just fine thanks. Do you have a minute?"

"For you, absolutely."

"I just received the executed Certificate of Transfer so I think I'm finally ready to go. If we can just go over a few issues I think I'd like to move forward with Kensington."

"Splendid. I'm very pleased to hear that. Now I know this has been rather sudden, are you sure you're ready?"

"I know it kind of feels like I'm rushing, but in reality this has been a long saga for me. I've had lots of time to think about it. So, yes, I'm ready."

"That's what I was hoping you would say. What else can I answer for you?"

"One thing that I mentioned that I'm still thinking about is whether or not I should have an open auction or qualify the bidders first and then let them participate. Again, I'm not that sentimental about the coin, but I do have this lingering desire to see it end up somewhere that the public could at least have a chance to view it."

"Yes, I can certainly understand your wishes, but as we talked about I think it could very well interfere with some lucrative buyers. How did you want to go about the evaluation?"

"I was thinking about having them submit something about their background or perhaps a collector's resume. Also, maybe have them put in writing why it is that they want the coin."

"Again, very noble in concept, but you have to understand that when someone pays out a sum such as this they typically don't want to have to answer for it. Now this is a Double Eagle so you do have some leverage in that even the top players might agree to go the extra mile to get it. However, in my professional opinion I honestly don't think you should put any strings on the coin. Maybe think of it this way, Bryan: get the highest amount that you can for it and then allocate a portion of those dollars for altruistic endeavors; somewhat of a Robin Hood approach. The other issue is that it will add a lot of extra time and potentially cost if you want to give it any legal teeth."

"Yeah, that makes sense. If I'm going to sell it I really need to be able to let it go. Alright."

"As I've told you, we already know a fair amount about many of our buyers and for the most part they are a very respectable lot. At this price range we do our own background check to assure that the funds are both available and from legitimate sources. I think starting the auction with a minimum price of ten million dollars will separate the men from the boys."

"And you're still confident that that figure isn't too high?"

"One hundred percent. Bryan, I could make a few calls right now and within a few minutes have a private sale for you at that price. Don't worry; you won't be pricing yourself out of the market."

"And you also still think that having the auction in two weeks is adequate?"

"No doubts. Anyone who is an eligible buyer knows it is coming and has plenty of cash available."

"Okay, I like the idea of having it sooner rather than later, I'm just concerned about possibly squeezing out some potential bidders."

"Once again I understand your concerns, however, always remember that we get paid a percentage commission of the sales price. The higher the price the more we get paid and vice versa. It's a good system in that our interest in it is directly tied to yours."

"That's true. Well, I think I'm comfortable with everything. Let's go ahead and get moving. My attorney has reviewed the copy of the offering contract that you sent and everything seemed in order. I'm going to sign my copy and fax it to you right now."

"Thank you, Bryan. I'm glad you chose Kensington and I think you will be very pleased with our services."

***

As soon as he hung up the phone, Stanford got to work. He had already laid out a game plan so that he would be ready if they were awarded the listing. First, he sent emails and made calls within his organization to put the rest of his team into action. Like so many other businesses, the auction world had embraced technology and transformed the way auctions were held. Many were still staged in a formal setting, but the pomp and circumstance was just a vestige from days gone by. Most of the true business took place via phone and computer so the organizational process was much different than it used to be. The Double Eagle was going to remain in its secure location so it wouldn't even be at the auction.

Peter then moved onto his list of top potential bidders. He had been in touch with most of these individuals already and was just confirming the upcoming auction. He wanted to be sure that they had funds available and were ready to bid. The last groups that he reached out to were feeder organizations such as major collecting clubs, high end dealers, and other auction houses. He wanted to get the word out there so they could pass it on to their members and clients. There was less likelihood that these organizations would generate a winning bidder; however, for a coin like this there was still a chance that an outlier could make a run for it. Besides spreading information, Peter was also spreading his enthusiasm. It wasn't just a sales pitch either; it was genuine. This was going to be a historic auction and Stanford was ecstatic to not just be a part of it, but to be the one running the show.

The following day Stanford grabbed the morning paper on the way to his office in New York City and was delighted to see that the Mint had put out a press release on the status of the Double Eagle. The release had been picked up and reported on by all of the major newspapers and was also getting some television news coverage. This generated more indirect advertising for Kensington than they could ever have possibly gotten by traditional means.

Over the next several days he sent Bryan a regular stream of email updates. As expected, he was seeing a tremendous level of interest. Stanford even offered Bryan the opportunity to use a Kensington condominium in New York if he came up to attend in person. It sounded like fun, but Bryan decided to stay home and watch the drama unfold from the comfort of his own living room.

***

The auction was scheduled for a Saturday afternoon at 1:00 so that day Bryan had time for a morning round with Tommy and some of his co-workers from the real estate firm. Bryan had finally accepted the fact that the coin was officially his and that he was soon going to be a very wealthy man. Bryan was excited that the auction had arrived, but he didn't really have any anxiety. The only question to be resolved was just how much the coin would go for. He was very relaxed on the course and, as had been the case for a while, easily won his match against his friend. Bryan was glad to see that his pending windfall hadn't affected their relationship yet as they exchanged their normal level of criticisms during the round. Tommy had planned to join Bryan for the afternoon festivities, but work called so he had to back out.

After lunch Bryan headed home, grabbed his computer, and settled in on the couch. The auction would be hosted on the web and Bryan would have full access to everything in real time as it proceeded. Bryan checked his email and found a number of messages from friends and family wishing him good luck. He sent a few quick responses and then found the email from Stanford that had his access information. He logged onto the Kensington site and entered his codes. The screen that came up was segmented into three different windows. One frame had a web cam showing the Kensington auction floor in New York. Most people had taken their seats, but there were still a few people mulling around the room and socializing. The next frame was the bid window, which was currently blank as the auction had not yet started. The frame along the bottom was an informational pane that had a picture and description of the Double Eagle.

Typically an auction like this would start with smaller lots and work its way up to the main attraction, however, today Bryan's coin would be in the lead-off spot. Stanford was pitching it as the marquee item and he didn't want any of the other auction items distracting bidders. There were some other nice coins being put up, but none of them were even close to the Double Eagle in terms of potential value. The sellers of these items were still happy to be in a follow-up position as there would likely be a piggy-back effect. The Double Eagle would bring out both the big dollar bidders as well as plenty of second tier spectators. This would create a large pool of interested bidders looking for a consolation item if they failed to obtain the top prize of the day.

As 1:00 approached Bryan saw Stanford on the screen buzzing around the front of the room apparently barking out orders and instructions. He took a call on his phone and then headed off to the side of the room. A well dressed man came to the front and put down a stack of items on the podium and sorted through them. After another minute or so he tapped his gavel to quiet the room.

"Welcome everyone," the auctioneer began. "Thank you for joining us here at Kensington for what promises to be an exciting and historic auction. We're going to go ahead and get things started promptly with the coin that everyone has been waiting for. Our first item, lot number one, is a 1933 St. Gaudens Gold Double Eagle twenty dollar piece. This extremely rare and amazing specimen is in uncirculated condition and carries an MS-70 grade. The coin has been verified for authenticity by the United States Mint and is offered with a Certificate of Transfer providing full free and clear ownership of the coin. This is a coin that may never again be seen for sale; truly a once in a lifetime opportunity. We will start the bidding now at ten million dollars."

Immediately the bidding window on Bryan's computer screen came to life with a flurry of numbers. Even the auctioneer seemed a bit surprised by the level of activity as bid paddles shot up around the room in New York.

"Excellent. Do we have ten million five hundred thousand?"

Another surge of bids shot across, despite the sizeable increment increase.

"Eleven million?"

No slow down. The auctioneer continued on to twelve million and then thirteen million. Bryan suddenly started thinking about even larger numbers than he'd previously imagined. Finally at fourteen million the bidders started to thin. Stanford had told Bryan that fifteen million would probably be the tipping point and he was right. As tough as it was to believe he said there were plenty of people who could afford ten million, but fifteen million started to be a stretch. At fifteen the auctioneer dropped the increments down to one hundred thousand. The auction started to slow and the tension started to rise. It was like watching a roulette wheel gradually slowing to a stop and just waiting to see where the ball finally came to a rest. The auctioneer remained patient, waiting for signs from the representatives staffing the phones as the price ticked past fifteen five. At fifteen seven the price sat and sat. Finally a bid popped up on the screen, then quickly fifteen eight and fifteen nine.

"The bid stands at sixteen million," said the auctioneer with a mix of excitement and pride. "Do we have sixteen million?"

Another pause as whispers spread across the room in New York. There was some movement by the phones and they had sixteen. Another sudden flurry and they were up to sixteen five. Bryan could really start to sense the emotions at work. The bidders knew they were getting close to a final price and despite what they may have had as a price threshold before the auction started they didn't want to lose out now for just a few hundred thousand more. Over the next few minutes they inched onward toward seventeen million.

Again there was a long wait and the auctioneer resorted to a little bit of scare tactics warning bidders that they might be missing out on their only chance at a magnificent coin. Bryan realized that he'd hit the double eagle on number seventeen at Stone Ridge and thought that it had to be a lucky number.

The auctioneer looked around, not wanting to stop yet. "Ladies and gentlemen, the window of opportunity is preparing to close."

More waiting as everyone in the crowd looked back and forth waiting for any sign of movement. Finally a hand went up at the side of the room.

"Seventeen million!" the auctioneer said with gusto. "We'll drop the increments to fifty thousand."

Several additional bids and they had seventeen two. It stayed there and the auctioneer finally showed some signs of desperation. "Will anyone consider seventeen two twenty-five?"

The auctioneer started heading into his closing terminology and then one more bid came in. It was quickly trumped at seventeen two fifty by the same bidder that had been at seventeen two. It seemed clear that this bidder intended to own the coin at any price now.

Several more tense moments passed and it became evident to everyone that the auction was over.

"Final call at seventeen million two hundred and fifty thousand dollars. Final call. No more bidders? Going once...going twice...sold! Congratulations to bidder number six twenty-five on the winning bid for the 1933 Double Eagle. Very exciting indeed. We'll take a short break and then move on to our other items."

Bryan sat back and pondered the auction. It would have been hard to be disappointed with anything over ten million dollars, but Bryan was very pleased that they had hit the high end of the range and smashed the previous record for a coin at auction. He was confident that his new record would be safe for a while. Bryan was startled from his thoughts by the phone.

"Hello?"

"Bryan, it's Peter. Congratulations."

"Thanks. Same to you for a job well done."

"So what did you think? Pretty exciting wasn't it?"

"That was great. I hope your auctioneer gets his blood pressure checked regularly. That's quite an emotional rollercoaster to have to ride on for a living."

"No worries. He's a true professional. So the winning bidder was a U.S. resident who we've dealt with before. I don't expect any difficulties with payment. We'll coordinate his payment to our escrow account in the next few days. Once it has posted I'll let you know and we'll schedule delivery of the coin. Upon confirmed receipt from the bidder we'll release your net proceeds."

"That sounds awesome, Peter. Let's hope everything moves smoothly."

"I think it will. Well I need to get back to the auction. Congratulations again and call me if you have any questions."

"Thanks, Peter. I appreciate all of your help."

A few days later Bryan got a call from Peter confirming that the payment had arrived. He also received a package of documents to effect transfer of ownership of the Double Eagle. Kensington was coordinating the movement of the coin so there wasn't much left for Bryan to do but wait. Stanford had said it would take about a week for the pickup and delivery to be scheduled and completed. As Bryan signed and sealed the paperwork he had mixed feelings. He appreciated what an incredible gift Jim had given him, but he was also very glad that he had finally removed the albatross from around his neck.

17

P rior to the auction, Bryan's efforts at Chambers had been in a steady decline. He was enjoying social time with his co-workers and just trying to keep his last few tasks moving along. Bryan was also noticing changes in the mood at the company. The giddiness and optimism that had been rampant just a few months ago had steadily faded. As the New Year set in and everyone got back to work they seemed to collectively realize that the holidays had passed and they still hadn't received the gift of a corporate windfall.

On the Monday following the auction Bryan decided he might as well go into work for what might be his last week with the company. As he entered the building he noticed what seemed like a lot of extra activity. Here and there workers were gathered in little groups and talking quietly. As Bryan approached his cubicle he was intercepted by Alex Barrett.

"Bryan, did you hear?"

"No, what?"

"Company-wide meeting this morning at 9:30. It's got to be the big announcement," Alex said with an excited voice.

"Really? Well that is good news because it means Joe's meeting is probably cancelled."

"Yeah, definitely. Everyone has to be over at the auditorium."

"This sounds like a fun way to start the week. I hope it's everything that everyone was wishing for," Bryan said, with limited enthusiasm.

Bryan went to his desk and checked his email to see if there was any other information about the big event. The only thing he had was an invite to the mandatory meeting. He didn't really see any point in getting to work now so he read the news headlines online and then checked out the sports for a while. Shortly thereafter he was interrupted by his friend Jason popping his head in.

"Wow! You're actually here today, Money."

"I needed to be here for the announcement of course," said Bryan matter-of-factly.

"You know about it already?"

"Sure. Do you want to know what's going down today?"

"Really? Heck yeah, tell me," Jason said inquisitively as he moved into Bryan's cubicle hoping to get the inside story.

"Since I had all this money coming in I had to do something with it. So I've decided to buy the company. They'll be introducing me as the new owner on stage at the meeting this morning."

"No way!"

"Way!"

"Did you really take in enough to buy Chambers? That's awesome."

"No you moron. And even if I did do you think I'd waste it on this dump? I don't think so," Bryan said chuckling.

"Oh I see. Now that you're rich you indulge yourself by messing with us poor folks. Real nice, man. So you don't know what's going to happen?"

"No idea whatsoever."

"Great."

"You seem worried. I thought this was the dream."

"It *was*. Now I don't know. It feels like things have been changing for the worse the last few months. You felt it too, right?"

"Yep. I told you it would happen when people finally stopped expecting it to happen."

"I think my job is safe. It's just the uncertainty that gets you freaked out. Well, I guess it doesn't get you freaked out."

"No, not really. My pulse is pretty steady right now."

"It's almost time. Are you ready to start heading over?"

"Sure, let's go.

***

The auditorium was already packed when Bryan and Jason arrived. They had to walk all the way up to the back to find two seats together. As Bryan walked up the steps he noted the demeanor of seated employees. There were only a few smiles and the people who were talking were doing it very quietly. He observed lots of lip biting, pencil chewing, and general fidgeting. The atmosphere was quite different from the last time he'd been here.

When they took their seats Bryan sat back and continued to look around as a bemused observer. He was by far the most relaxed person in the room.

The meeting started promptly at 9:30 with CEO, Wayne Marsh, taking the stage. The low murmur of the crowd immediately dropped to dead silence. It reminded Bryan of a classroom where the kids quickly sat up straight and shut their mouths when the stern teacher comes through the door. Marsh walked over to the podium and got right to business.

"Thank you everyone for coming this morning. I know it is out of the ordinary to have a meeting like this, but I have some exciting news to share and wanted to do it in person with all of my fine fellow employees here at Chambers. Our company has been highly successful and experienced extraordinary growth over the years due to your exceptional efforts. Because of our great people I'm very confident in our ability to continue that success in the future. However, as companies mature they often have to look beyond just organic growth and seek out other opportunities. Chambers is at an important juncture in its history. We can continue on our current path and hope that we don't get left behind or we can control our own destiny and seek a higher trajectory. Your management team decided that we needed to aim higher and over the past several months we have been reviewing a number of strategic alternatives."

As Marsh spoke Bryan looked around and noticed several people in suits near the stage that he didn't recognize. He also noticed that the company's founder, Phil Chambers, was no where to be seen.

"Today we are ready to present to you the results of our efforts and share with you our vision for the future of our great company. I am proud to announce that Chamber Data Systems has entered into a strategic alliance with Cornerstone Group International. This alliance will allow us to leverage the numerous strengths of each individual company, while harvesting the synergies of a powerful combined entity."

"Oh, that can't be good," Bryan whispered to Jason.

"Oh, man," Jason said, staring at Marsh on the stage.

"We really should have put together a quick run of the Chambers Derby just for this meeting. I've got the feeling it's going to get real deep, real quick."

"Uh huh," muttered Jason.

Marsh continued, "Our business, our industry, and our economy continue to change. We have to adapt to face that change and we have to innovate to stay ahead of it. Our new partnership will position us as the player to beat across our spectrum of businesses. Some of you may already be aware of Cornerstone while to others it may be a new name. Let me assure you that we didn't take a union like this lightly. We would only consider top tier partners and, to the credit of Chambers, Cornerstone would only do the same.

The management team and I have spent a great deal of time cross-pollinating with our peers at Cornerstone to make sure we are all on the same page as we move forward. So far we have found it to be an amazing fit. Our strategies and goals dovetail unbelievably well with their plans. At this point I'd like to take a few minutes to introduce some of their team and let them say a few words."

The lovefest continued as each of the Cornerstone managers stepped up and babbled in corporate lingo yet seemed to say absolutely nothing. It appeared that as each one acted more happy and optimistic the crowd's mood grew even more pessimistic. It was almost as though the Cornerstone people were trying too hard to impress and the audience was seeing right through it. They eventually turned it back over to Marsh. Everyone in the room was hoping that he was going to wrap it up and let them go back to their desks and ponder their fates. Unfortunately that wasn't going to be the case.

"I know this is a big announcement and I'm sure there will be lots of questions. Right now I'd like to go through a presentation we've put together that will provide some of the answers. Over the next day or two we'll be cascading additional information down through departmental managers to provide further detail. Let's get started," he said as the lights dimmed and he wielded the remote control.

"Here comes the PowerPoint presentation," warned Bryan.

"I was hoping he was just going to do shadow puppets on the screen to get a few laughs," Jason replied.

"Oh no. This is where we start to get our first taste of things like streamlining, consolidation, and efficiencies. Fear the almighty PowerPoint reaper, it spares no one."

Bryan was right and took win, place, and show as all three of the terms he mentioned appeared on the screen during the next few minutes. During the presentation Marsh's smile seemed to fade and he took on a much more serious expression. Although the slides were still dealing with topics at the macro level they definitely gave a glimpse of the ominous things to come. It was clear that jobs were going to be lost, but the employees also started to realize that things like the perks and parties would also be getting down-sized.

Marsh finished up his presentation and made a quick exit without taking any questions. The Cornerstone guys didn't stick around to shake any hands either. As Bryan and Jason made their way back down the stairs Bryan noticed a number of employees still sitting in their chairs. They seemed to be a bit shell shocked and in no hurry to get back to work. It was pretty clear that not much actual work was going to be done at Chambers the rest of the day.

Bryan already had a very limited amount of motivation; however, the meeting had still managed to leave him with even less. He started thinking about just leaving for the day, but quickly found that his co-workers needed him as their corporate therapist. Jason followed Bryan back to his cubicle and didn't want to leave. They were soon joined by other teammates who were somehow looking to Bryan for wisdom. It seemed to be in part due to his accurate view of Chambers' situation over the past few months as well as his obvious position as the person least likely to be affected by what had just happened. Bryan had done a decent job of settling the group down and lifting their spirits when they all heard the email alert from his computer. Bryan had changed the audio tone for incoming emails from Joe Kelly to differentiate them from other senders' mail. Recently he had switched it to a sample of the evil theme music from *Star Wars* so it got everyone's attention.

"Uh-oh. Let's see what Joe has for us," Bryan said light heartedly as everyone exchanged nervous glances. "Ah, our second mandatory meeting of the day. Joe seeks the presence of your company at 3:30 this afternoon. I can almost sense the excitement he must have had writing this email. Now is his time to shine."

"As bad as it was listening to Marsh it'll be even worse spouting from the demonic Joe Kelly. He's probably sharpening his pitchfork and turning up the thermostat in the conference room right now," Christie lamented.

"I can't believe we work in a one-story building. Where are we supposed to jump from?" asked Jason.

"It's a shame that I'll be checking out of this nut house shortly, it seems like things are going to get very interesting," Bryan said.

***

Bryan took a long lunch before wallowing away the first few hours of the afternoon. He had a macabre sense of anticipation about Joe's meeting. As unpleasant as the regular meetings were this one had the potential to reach new lows.

Sitting at his desk he realized how quiet it was. Normally there would be the sound of muffled voices from the general vicinity as people went about their business. Today, however, they all must have been whispering as they talked amongst each other in the wake of the announcement.

When the time finally came Bryan strode confidently down to the conference room. His co-workers all seemed to have notepads and pens ready while Bryan arrived empty handed. He flopped down in one of the chairs and rocked and spun casually as the team waited for Joe to arrive. After a few minutes he looked down the hall and saw Jason and Joe walking down the passageway together. They came into the conference room together and Joe took his spot at the head of the table, while Jason sat down next to Bryan.

"Negotiating a last minute deal with the devil?" Bryan asked.

"No, we just met on the way in. I wanted to run, but he'd already made eye contact."

"Sure...oh, Jason, rub your shirt like this," Bryan said as he dragged his sleeve across his face.

"What? Do I have some food on me?" he asked as he rubbed vigorously.

"No, it looked like you had something brown on your nose," Bryan said smiling.

"I'm not in need of any comic relief right now," Jason said, glaring at Bryan.

"Sorry, just trying to keep it light. It's about to get heavy."

Kelly finished organizing his papers and began the meeting. "Thanks everyone for coming this afternoon. Obviously some big news this morning and as you all know there will be plenty more to come. I know change like this can be unnerving, but I need all of you to remain focused. There will be a lot of speculation and hearsay going around so I know it will be tough. We are going to do our best to give you the facts and keep you posted as information becomes available. Although today was the formal announcement, there has been a lot of lead work going on already so management is ready to hit the ground running. I'm going to review the Phase One materials for our group now. Hopefully it will answer a lot of your questions. Is there anything before I get started?"

Everyone stared at the table. Then Bryan asked, "So when did you find out, Joe?"

Kelly clearly hadn't expected there to be any questions. "Umm, well for confidentiality reasons only the very top level of management at both companies was involved in the preliminary work. Now it's being implemented across all levels."

"So you didn't know until today?" Bryan asked bemused.

"Yes, Bryan. Is that important for some reason?" Kelly replied, quickly getting agitated.

"Nope, I was just curious," Bryan shrugged. Normally teammates would be trading glances during such and exchange, but today nobody even dared. For the benefit of his friends he decided not to antagonize Joe any further.

"As I was saying, this is the information that will be the groundwork for what we will be doing over the next several weeks," Joe said, as he handed out the presentation. "This is a hard copy version for you, but I will be emailing it out to everyone right after the meeting. You are going to need to keep it handy as we move through the different stages."

The papers were passed down the table and as recipients started flipping through the packet you could sense blood pressures starting to rise.

"The pages are specific to our division, but dovetail into the strategy outlined by Wayne this morning," Kelly continued.

Bryan noted how his boss referred to the CEO by his first name as though they were actually close. As had already been established, Kelly was well outside the center of power at the company.

"In terms of impact, I'm going to cut right to the chase people," Kelly said. "When you combine two similar companies like this there is certain to be personnel overlap. An evaluation of these redundancies is ongoing and the decisions will be rolled out and implemented in stages. Both companies are committed to maximizing resource reallocation wherever possible, but at the end of the day there will only be so many chairs available when the music stops. I suggest you all strive your best to make sure you are in one of them, starting right now.

There are some functions where the optimal solution set will not involve employees from either company. When available, third party alternatives are going to be examined to provide maximum cost savings for the combined entity. Outsourcing can have a negative stigma attached to it, but it is an integral part of doing business today. We're competing in a worldwide market so we have to be able to take advantage of worldwide resources."

Bryan thought about the workforce at Chambers and shuddered when he realized just how many employees could be outsourced.

Joe started working his way through the presentation. He kept asking if anyone had questions and not surprisingly there were no takers. Nobody wanted to hear one more word out of Joe's mouth than they absolutely had to. Some of the team members still seemed to be in shock and just gazed at the pretty charts and diagrams in the package before them.

Kelly had made it through most of his material when he came to something noted as a *Key Strategy for Integration Execution.* "We'll be organizing and scheduling sessions in approximately six to eight weeks to promote information exchange between peers. This will allow management to identify conflicting processes and determine surviving ones."

"Information exchange?" wondered Bryan in his head. "Ah, that's where you're expected to give away your accumulated knowledge from years of hard work to someone with less experience who will in turn use it to do your job after you get axed. A key strategy indeed."

As Bryan listened to Joe he began to wonder if this was really a merger or more of a takeover of Chambers. It seemed that the underlying message of the integration strategy was: here's your rope, here's how to make a noose, now please place it around your neck and step up on that wobbly chair.

When Joe finished he once again asked for any questions and once again was greeted with silence. Not even some of the better brownnosers bothered to raise a hand and offer Joe a soft ball question. Despite his own confident tone, it seemed that his team's response, or lack thereof, was a bit disconcerting to Kelly. He had hoped to see at least a little bit of enthusiasm about the merger, however, there was nothing but fear seated around the table.

"Well if there's nothing else I'll let you get back to work. I'll keep you posted with updates as we proceed. Thank you everyone."

The team got up and started filing out in a solemn manner. Bryan was almost to the door when he heard his name.

"Minton, could I speak to you for a minute?" Kelly called.

In the past the call would have sent pangs of anxiety to Bryan's stomach, but today he just turned and wandered back towards the head of the table.

"What'cha need, Joe?"

"I just wanted to ask you a few things," he replied, waiting for the rest of the employees to leave. "Bryan, in the context of everything that's going to be happening I need to know what your status is. With the sale of your coin are you planning to stick around or hit the road?"

"In the context of our new partnership I think it's pretty certain that I'll be opting for the road."

"I figured so much. We're going to be moving very quickly with our changes so I need to start laying out my game plan."

"Your game plan? Corporate America's merger play book only has one play in it: cut jobs. I'm sure you'll have plenty of firing to do so you can pencil me in and hopefully keep a spot for one of my teammates. I fully expect to have my money before you get the chance though."

"Fair enough. In the end it's probably for the best that everything worked out with your coin."

Bryan's nonchalant attitude suddenly took a U-turn. "What do you mean, Joe? Are you trying to stick it to me?"

"Bryan, you've done some good work here, but from a progression standpoint I'm not sure your leadership skills are quite up to pace with what will be needed in the new paradigm."

Bryan chuckled, "And yours are, Joe? Maybe my perceived shortcomings are due to the fact that I've had weak leadership? Maybe you need to look in the mirror? The fact is I never wanted your job, Joe, so that's why I never put in the effort to take it. But if I did I'm quite sure I could thrive in your new paradigm. I could have skipped out on the last few days, but I came in because I didn't want to leave my teammates hanging on the last few things I'm trying to finish up. What's interesting is that on a day like this they came and talked to me about their concerns. I'm not sure if you noticed or not, but they didn't have anything to say to you just now. The problem is people like you seem to see leadership and management as synonymous. But they're not. You may have succeeded in managing us here, Joe, but there's rarely been any type of leadership on your part. Maybe I couldn't manage your way, but I could do a lot better job of leading these guys. Unfortunately it's rare to find someone who can do both. I get the sense that Phil Chambers was one of those people and it allowed him to build this company into what it now is. It's too bad that it came to the point where someone gave him a big enough check to let it go. I guess the good news is that I'll soon be able to empathize with him."

Joe struggled for a response to Bryan's attack, "Well, I think you're mistaken in your opinion, Minton. But you're welcome to think what you want."

"And for the record, even without the coin my time here would have been short on my own accord."

Joe shrugged, "Well, good luck, Bryan."

"You too, Joe," Bryan said insincerely before walking out without shaking hands. Bryan didn't want to leave on bad terms, but he was glad that he had a final chance to put Kelly in his place. He stopped by his desk, grabbed his stuff, and went home.

***

During the next several days Bryan came and went as he pleased. He felt committed to helping his friends and co-workers at Chambers and wanted to make sure they didn't get left holding the bag on his projects. He especially didn't want any of them to look bad in Joe's eyes in light of what was happening. Luckily Bryan was able to avoid any further altercations with Joe. Kelly was so wrapped up in his plans and schemes that nobody had to see much of him.

Bryan spent some of his new found free time at the driving range, the gym, the bookstore, and the beach. He was discovering the wonderful feeling of freedom. However, he also noticed that there seemed to be a nagging undercurrent. The reality of his situation was starting to set in and there were some unexpected revelations. For the first time in his life he was actually going to be in control of every minute of the day and it was a bit scary. No one he *had* to report to, nowhere that he *had* to go, nothing he *had* to do. He obviously had no desire to stay at Chambers, but to go completely to the other end of the spectrum was going to be a tougher move than he expected.

The social aspects were also going to take some adjustment. All of his current friends were still working, although some of the Chambers gang might soon have some extra time on their hands. Nonetheless, he had already experienced a sense of loneliness. Bryan was sure he could find some new acquaintances, but he would have to expand the circle from which he'd drawn in the past and probably find some new hobbies too. Bryan could now spend more time with his dad, which would be nice. However, his dad had his own group of friends and was busy with his own things during the week. Winning the lottery is always the dream, but as Bryan had already found out over the past several months as he fought for the coin, the reality can certainly be less glamorous.

***

Although he had stopped using an alarm clock, Bryan woke up early on Friday morning and couldn't go back to sleep. Today was supposed to be delivery day and it was likely to be Bryan's last day at Chambers.

He arrived at work and sat looking anxiously at the phone. At just after nine he received the call from Peter Stanford that he'd been waiting for.

"Hello?"

"Bryan, it's Peter."

"Good morning."

"Good morning to you, sir. Are you ready to finish things up?

"Absolutely."

"I think we are set to go. Our finance manager is originating the wire as we speak. We will be sending the net proceeds of $16,042,500 per the instructions you provided for your money market account. Within the hour you should be able to contact them and confirm their receipt of funds. As we discussed, we have not done any tax withholding per you request. I know you said that you'll be working on the tax issue with your accountant. Any questions?"

"No, I'll just give them a call in a little while to make sure it arrived."

"Excellent. If you have any problems give me a call right away. I should be around most of the day."

"Thanks again, Peter. Great transaction. If I stumble across another Double Eagle I'll plan to use Kensington again."

"You're welcome, Bryan. Enjoy your new wealth. I hope it brings you nothing but happiness."

"Thanks."

"Oh, I almost forgot. I found out that the collector who bought your coin is considering keeping it on display part time. He lives in California and is working with a museum out there to have it as part of an exhibit that his available for private tours. Unfortunately for security reasons he's not yet ready to have it on public display, but at least your coin won't be spending all of it's time locked away again."

"That's great news. I'm glad to hear it."

"Take care, Bryan."

"You too, Peter."

Bryan hung up and immediately called the fund company where he'd set up a money market account. They were very happy to be receiving sixteen million dollars on his behalf and let him know that they would track the wire and let him know when it arrived.

At just before ten o'clock his representative called him to confirm that the funds had arrived from Kensignton's escrow account and had been deposited to Bryan's account. Bryan Minton was now officially a multi-millionaire.

His first task as a millionaire was to send Joe Kelly an email resigning. He'd already pre-written a resignation letter, but decided it wasn't really necessary. He simply told Joe he was leaving and his security items would be in his desk. Bryan had previously removed all of his personal items so he turned off his computer and walked away.

Bryan made a quick round of goodbyes. His departure was fully expected so he kept it short and simple. He didn't want to rub his good fortune in the faces of his co-workers who were about to go on a roller coaster ride.

As he left the building he flipped open his phone and called Lisa at work.

"Hey, Bryan. What's the news?"

"The funds just arrived and I'm walking out of Chambers right now."

"Good for you, Bry'. Congratulations."

"I have to say it really feels good. So are we set for a celebration dinner tomorrow night?"

"Yep. And Amber agreed to stay the night so we'll have some time together after dinner as well."

"I like the sound of that."

"So what's next for you, Bryan Minton?"

"I don't know."

18

Tommy Manson smiled as he drove toward the Lakeside Links Golf Club. It was a beautiful fall day and he was looking forward to his round of golf. He followed the row of orange cones that led him to the far side of the parking lot. The main portion of the lot was being redesigned and resurfaced. Tommy parked and popped his trunk. He was surprised that by the time he got to the back of his car an attendant was already loading his clubs onto a cart.

"Good morning, sir. Are you playing in the event this afternoon?" asked the polite young man.

"Yes. My name is Tommy Manson. I'm playing with Bryan Minton."

"Oh, with Mr. Minton. Excellent. I'll drive you up to the clubhouse."

"Thanks."

As they drove up they passed a shiny, new gray pick-up truck with the license plate: DBL EGL. Tommy smiled, glad to see that Bryan was here already.

In front of the clubhouse were several banners. The first one welcomed golfers and proclaimed that Lakeside Links was now operating under new management. The next one asked for golfers to bear with them as the club completed its renovations and upgrades. The final one announced today's charity golf tournament.

Tommy stopped for a moment and gazed around. Everywhere he looked he saw workers toiling away on improvements. The place was buzzing with activity. Tommy went inside and walked over to the counter in the pro shop.

"Hi, I'm Tommy Manson. I'm playing in the tournament today."

"Welcome. We aren't starting registration until noon, but please feel free to use our practice facilities in the meantime."

"Actually, I'm having lunch with Bryan Minton first. Do you know if he's around?"

"Sure, he should be upstairs. You head through those doors, up the steps, take a right, go to the end of the hall and you should find him."

"Thanks."

On the way up Tommy encountered even more construction. The hallway was filled with the sound of banging hammers and the potent smell of fresh paint. The crunching sound of plastic sheeting under his feet announced his arrival as he walked to the end of the hall. He poked his head inside the door and knocked.

"Bryan?"

"Tommy, my man. Good to see you," Bryan said, getting up from his desk and walking over to shake Tommy's hand. "Have a seat."

"I like what you've done with the place. It seems to be coming along nicely."

"Thanks. We've got a pretty aggressive agenda, but so far we're staying on schedule. We want to get most of the big stuff done before season gets here and business picks up."

Tommy stood back up and walked over to the large, plate glass windows surrounding Bryan's desk. "That's quite a view you've got here."

"Oh, I love it," Bryan said, joining his friend at the window. "Sure beats the industrial carpet walls of my old cubicle and it affords me a nice view of my kingdom. I chose this corner since I'll get a great view of the sunrise and sunset for most of the year. It was stunning to watch the sun come up over the front nine this morning. Everything was glistening with dew; the shadows of the trees were stretching across the fairways; and all of the colors were coming to life. Simply awesome."

"You're here for sunrises and sunsets? I figured you'd be sleeping in."

"What can I say, Tommy. When you love what you do you don't really worry about the time clock."

"Hmm," Tommy grunted, not sure if he should believe what his friend was telling him.

"Let me give you the bird's eye tour of what's going on out here," Bryan said, as he stretched out a large set of color prints across the top of the credenza next to the window. "The good news was that most of the greens were still in pretty good shape. They just needed a little love. We're making a few modifications next month, but nothing major. Our plan is to eventually redo them in three to five years. So that let us focus on the fairways and tee boxes.

Here are the changes to the front nine. You can see how we're going to reshape and lengthen number three, number four, number five and number seven. The start and finish on that side were already pretty good, but now we'll have a much stronger middle too. If you look past the corner of those trees there you can see the view down four and five," Bryan directed, as he pointed toward the course.

"We'll pick up somewhere around three hundred yards on that nine. Plus we still have plenty of room if we need to stretch again sometime in the future.

On the back nine we're updating ten, fifteen, seventeen and eighteen. It was kind of the opposite over there where we needed to improve the start and finish. In terms of distance, about the same level of gain, but maybe closer to three hundred and fifty yards. We expect that once all of the tee boxes are set and measured the tips will have gone from just over 6,500 yards up to 7,150 yards. But we're not doing it just for the sake of adding yardage. I think the changes we're undertaking will make it more fun to play by giving a lot more options on a few of the holes.

The rest of the work is odds and ends like cart path repair and irrigation upgrades. You'll get to see it all first hand this afternoon and I'll point out the details."

"I'm looking forward to it," Tommy said, marveling at Bryan's enthusiasm. "Is the course pretty playable?"

"Oh, yeah. We're able to stage it so that you only get interference on one or two holes at a time; a minor inconvenience to get a much better result in a few months."

"What about the name? Are you going to indulge your ego and call it something else like Minton Links?"

"No, not yet at least. I think most people already have a good enough impression of Lakeside Links that we don't need to purge it. You know I always liked the course. It just needed some investment to bring it back up to par. So are you hungry?"

"Definitely."

"Alright, let's go downstairs and we'll get some lunch."

As they walked to the restaurant Bryan continued to dote on his new baby. He described the remodeling underway and introduced Tommy to some of the staff.

"Tommy, this is Al Redner. He's been here longer than anyone," Bryan said, as they encountered the gentleman Tommy had spoken to earlier.

"We met informally already. Tommy Manson, nice to meet you again," Tommy said, shaking hands. "So is this guy really coming into work before the sun comes up?"

"He sure is. So far he's really been putting in the hours," Redner replied.

"And he's a pretty tough boss, eh?"

"We've only worked together a short time, but so far he's the best we've ever had around here. Of course the other guys all set the bar pretty low for him," he said, smiling at Bryan.

"Thanks, Al. Everything looking okay for this afternoon?"

"We're all set."

"Good deal, we'll see you in a bit," Bryan said, turning and continuing on his way with Tommy in tow.

After they turned the corner Bryan asked, "Tommy, you were nice to my staff, right?"

"Have I ever not been?" asked Tommy innocently.

"You know that just because you're here with the owner doesn't mean you get to play without your ticket."

"Are you kidding me? I need to have my ticket?"

"No ticky, no washy! We've got to have our rules and policies. This is a place of business."

"I thought you were trying to improve this place."

"There's a suggestion box up front. If you come up with a better idea fill out a card."

They crossed through a small lobby area and went into the restaurant. Bryan said hellos to everyone and introduced Tommy to several other golfers who were there eating before taking a seat at a table by the window. They were quickly approached by a smiling waitress.

"Hi, Bryan. How are you doing today?" she asked.

"Doing great, Mary. And you?"

"Just fine."

"Good. Mary, this is my friend, Tommy."

"Hi," Tommy said, nodding and smiling back at her.

"Usual drink for you, Bryan?" Mary said.

"Yep."

"And how 'bout for you, Tommy?" she asked.

"What's the 'usual'?" Tommy inquired.

"An Arnold Palmer. Half lemonade, half iced tea."

"Sounds good. I'll have the same," Tommy decided.

"I'll be right back," she said, turning to go.

"Thanks, Mary."

"You seem pretty popular with everyone here, Bryan," Tommy noted.

"So far I think I'm doing a decent job. I'm sure there will be some bumps in the road, but it's really not rocket science. Treat people nicely and treat them fairly and they'll do a good job for you. Contrary to the belief of many lousy managers you can manage effectively without having to crack the whip. I'd love for my old pal, Joe Kelly, from over at Chambers to stop by for a visit. Right before I left we had a scrape about what represented talent in a manager. He didn't feel that I had any, but so far I've proven him to be quite wrong. Plus, his self view was apparently slightly misplaced."

"What do you mean?"

"Well after I left they started the whole 're-engineering' process. They convinced Joe to fire off a number of people, which he did happily. However, he then ran a much smaller team. In turn, the group got merged together with two others and now you had three managers for the surviving team. At that point Joe didn't make the cut and got axed."

"Ouch."

"Yeah, it couldn't happen to nicer guy. He didn't have any personal acquaintances at the office so nobody knows what happened to him."

"What about the rest of your friends?"

"A couple of them are still over there grinding it out. A few got the boot, but all of them have been able to find new jobs. The little life the company did have has now been sucked out of it. They've cut out all of the extras around the office and they even killed the summer picnic. I can't imagine how miserable I'd be if I were still there now," Bryan said, wincing at the thought.

"Executives seem to forget how far a few well placed dollars can go towards morale. Occasional flowers and gift cards get so much more out of the office staff for me compared to the other brokers who don't do anything. Happy employees are productive employees," Tommy said.

"I know it. I'm amazed at how positive the reactions are when I do even little things around here. The people that were running it kept cutting back on everything. Sure you want to be smart about expenses, but eventually it will get to the point where it hurts your business. If the employees aren't happy they won't be as nice to the golfers and the golfers won't come back. Word has already spread about the new regime here at Lakeside. I've had a lot of golfers come up and tell me how happy they are with the changes. A number of them have said they used to play here all the time but then stopped coming. Look around," Bryan said, motioning to the number of full tables at the restaurant. "A few months ago this place was empty. Nobody wanted to hang around after a morning round or get here early before an afternoon round. Last month the food and beverage revenues were more than double what they did in the same month last year. And that's even with all of the work going on. It's the same with the course. Over time it's going to get worn out so you have to spend some money to keep it in shape. They let it go too far and golfers responded by playing elsewhere. Now players are telling me they like it already and can't wait to come back and play it when it's done. In turn, that inspires me to make it even better."

"Even I'm looking forward to it! Enough shop talk. So how's Lisa?"

"Doing great. We all need to go out again soon. It's been too long."

"I know. It's tough when we're all so busy. You certainly did well for yourself with her. I have to admit that I'm impressed. Normally that's the kind of girl you would have considered out of your league."

"Yeah, you're right. But like I keep telling you, Manson: it's all about the attitude. I think standing up to her sister and never wavering is part of why I got a shot and then when I had the chance I was just myself and that closed the deal."

"That's good, Minton. Don't let her get away."

"I'm not planning on it. Things are going great and neither of us wants to force it to move any faster. Troy has really warmed up to me and we even hang out sometimes without Lisa. I got a set of junior clubs for him and he loves hitting balls. He's a good kid, but he needed a good male role model. When we took those trips this summer and it was just the three of us he started to come out of his shell. You can sense that he wanted someone like a big brother. And Tina?"

"I think we've finally finished the test drive and now we're both ready to sign the contract."

"Really?"

"Yeah, we've been doing some ring shopping and talking about wedding plans. I have to come up with a memorable way to formally pop the question. It's tough since we're already pretty much there."

"Congratulations, man. I think she's a great choice. Now when you start thinking about the wedding reception I want you to be sure to consider us here at Lakeside. I'll put together a good deal for you."

"Listen to you selling, Minton. That's my job."

"It's mine too, now."

"So are you pretty much running the show yourself or is your partner adding his input?"

"Our relationship is working fine. He's involved in some of the course related moves, but beyond that he's basically a silent partner. We go out for nine holes together every week or two and discuss things. I'm glad my dad introduced me to him. I could have paid for the whole thing myself, but it would have taken a big chunk of my proceeds. This way I've diversified my risk a bit. We're still working on the tax implications of the coin sale so I'm still not sure how much I'll really end up netting. Even in the worst case scenario I'll be fine."

"It sounds like you're enjoying things, but you really didn't want to take some time and just live off the money?"

"I did that, remember? It was fun, but it was honestly hard finding stuff to do all day. I quickly felt like I needed to do something. I felt like I needed to take a chance and that's what I did with this place. I think Jim would have approved of my choice as well," Bryan said, smiling and thinking fondly of Garris.

"He changed your life forever. I wonder what would have happened if I had actually shown up that day?"

Bryan nodded, "I know. I've thought about that a number of times. I doubt we'd be sitting here having this conversation right now. So I guess thanks for standing me up, Tommy."

"No problem."

"I feel like I owe Jim a lot, but I also know that he wouldn't have expected anything. I've made a couple of charitable donations in his name and longer term I may do something else to honor his legacy. I also had a memorial plaque made and put it by the tee out here on number seventeen. I thought that would be fitting tribute."

Bryan and Tommy enjoyed their lunch together before heading out to warm up and get ready for the tournament. Bryan continued to serve as tour guide and made introductions to other people at the course, including the two players in their group. It was a perfect day for golf and they were all excited about playing.

At the first tee they waited patiently for the fairway to clear and chatted with the starter. As part of his upgrade program, Bryan had decided to improve the atmosphere for tournaments at Lakeside as well. He had a leaderboard installed, provided the staff with new protocols to treat the players better, and made sure they had a caller on the first tee introducing the players. Even though this was a small event it still provided the feel of a larger, more formal tournament. Bryan could tell that the players enjoyed it and it was another one of those things that would make his new venture a success.

Bryan let the rest of his group hit and then stepped up and teed his ball.

As he did, the announcer said in a loud, dignified voice, "And next up on the tee, Lakeside's very own, Bryan Minton."

The End

About the author

ate Volino lives with his wonderful family in Osprey, Florida. This is his first novel. He enjoys playing golf, watching golf, and reading about golf. He also enjoys golf.